Francis I. Rickard

The Mineral and other Resources of the Argentine Republic

La Plata - in 1869. Published by special authority of the national government

Francis I. Rickard

The Mineral and other Resources of the Argentine Republic
La Plata - in 1869. Published by special authority of the national government.

ISBN/EAN: 9783337378516

Printed in Europe, USA, Canada, Australia, Japan

Cover: Foto ©Andreas Hilbeck / pixelio.de

More available books at **www.hansebooks.com**

THE

MINERAL AND OTHER RESOURCES

OF THE

ARGENTINE REPUBLIC

(LA PLATA)

IN 1869.

PUBLISHED BY SPECIAL AUTHORITY OF THE
NATIONAL GOVERNMENT.

BY

MAJOR F. IGNACIO RICKARD,

FELLOW OF THE GEOLOGICAL SOCIETY; FELLOW OF THE ROYAL GEOGRAPHICAL SOCIETY
COR. MEM. OF THE ANTHROPOLOGICAL SOCIETY; ASSOC. INST. CIVIL ENGINEERS, &c. &c. ;
GOVERNMENT INSPECTOR-GENERAL OF MINES OF THE ARGENTINE REPUBLIC.

LONDON:
LONGMANS, GREEN, AND CO.

1870.

LONDON:
DUNLOP AND CO., PRINTERS,
King's-Head Court, Shoe Lane,
E.C.

PREFACE.

PREVIOUS to 1865, when the Argentine Republic first appeared as a borrower for a small sum in our market, the very existence of such a country was almost ignored in Great Britain. Five short years have wrought a wonderful change. Its Bonds, issued then at $72\frac{1}{2}$, are to-day quoted at $92\frac{1}{2}$, and likely to reach 95 before the end of the year. This is the most eloquent proof I can give of the growing importance and settled political state of that vast Republic. If its credit abroad is good, so is its prosperity and internal wealth increasing daily at home. Ten years ago there were not 50 miles of railway in the country; now there are nearly 500 miles completed and working, whilst nearly 800 more are in course of construction or projected.

Ten years ago we had not a single mile of telegraph in the country; to-day the electric wire may be met on the wild pampa, the barren desert, or climbing the giant Andes and girding the Atlantic to the Pacific. A submarine cable connects Monte Video with Buenos Ayres. The capital of Brazil will soon be in instantaneous communication with us overland, by a route not less than 1,000 miles; and within a year we may expect to be in telegraphic communication with Europe *viâ* the Pacific, Panama, and New York.

A National Exhibition of the products of the country, and to which will be admitted a few objects from Europe, will be held at Cordoba in October next. A well appointed Observatory will be also concluded by that time at the same place, and an able astronomer has been engaged by the National Government to make observations in the midst of that "sea of land," where no intervening mountains exist to interfere with his labours, and where important discoveries are expected to be made.

All these advanced and enlightened movements will tend to show how rapid has been our progress, and how important will be our future career. With a fast increasing immigration, an arduous and long protracted war just concluded, peace and tranquillity reigning throughout the country, and a liberal and progressive Government, established on a firm constitutional basis, lead by an able President and Prime Minister, I am justified in expressing my sincere conviction that the Argentine Republic is destined to become the first in commercial wealth and influence of all the South American Republics.

I have come forward to lend my insignificant aid in making known a few of her vast resources, and I trust the following pages may serve to instruct those eager for information, whilst they will not tire the general reader.

I do not pretend for a moment to any literary merit in its production, well knowing that it has none, but simply to convey, in plain concise language, such information as I possess regarding a country comparatively unknown, and consequently unappreciated in Europe.

My very limited stay in England has not allowed me to devote that time and attention to the preparation and correction of the present work for the press that I could have wished, and this must be my excuse for any errors that may be noted, more especially in the latter pages of the book.

Consulate General of the Argentine Republic,
London, April, 1870.

CONTENTS.

CONTENTS.

BUENOS AYRES, *June* 19th, 1869.

To HIS EXCELLENCY THE MINISTER OF THE INTERIOR,
    DR. DALMACIO VELEZ SARSFIELD.

YOUR EXCELLENCY,

Under date of 19th November last I received your instructions to proceed on a tour of inspection through the mineral districts of the Republic, and present a detailed report thereon to the National Government. The principal points contained in those instructions were as follows :—

" 1. To visit the mines of La Carolina in San Luis ; those of Uspallata and Paramillo in Mendoza ; Tontal, Castaño, Huachi, Gualilan, and La Huerta in San Juan ; Famatina in La Rioja ; the mineral districts of Belen (Capillitas), and the copper, gold, and silver mines in Catamarca ; and the galena and other mines in Cordoba.

" 2. To report on the different classes of ores extracted, and on those not yet of commercial value which may be utilized later on ; on mineral substances useful in the arts, and which may be considered as auxiliaries in the smelting or treatment of ores ; on mines in active operation, with the results obtained and number of workmen employed ; on metallurgical establishments, companies, capital, machinery used, systems in practice, and the obstacles and drawbacks with which they have to contend ; on coal or carboniferous deposits—their quality, extent, and commercial value ; on roads and means of communication, and how the same may be developed and improved."

To all these points I have devoted my most serious attention, and now present to your Excellency a detailed account of my mission.

The mineral regions of the Republic are of vast extent ; the means of communication and transport slow, and in the worst possible condition.   The time at my disposal was extremely short for the accomplishment of the great task I had to perform, and this in the height of summer and in regions at once hot, barren, _and sterile_, the difficulties with which I had to contend were, therefore, neither few nor unimportant.   Nevertheless, I do not believe there is a single known mine in the provinces visited which I have not inspected, and the length of my report will prove to your Excellency with what minuteness I have collected the data submitted to your consideration.

I have had to encounter many obstacles, and to work incessantly in order to obtain the statistics which accompany my report, for the miners rarely keep books or accounts ; the majority pay very little attention to preserving a record of expenses and returns, and few could give me any information on this subject.

Few in the Republic could have believed that 2,687 persons are employed in our nascent mining industry, or at the rate of $17\frac{9}{10}$ for every 1,000 inhabitants in the country.   In California—a country which dedicates its attention almost entirely to mining—52,000 persons are exclusively employed in its mines, or at the rate of $66\frac{2}{3}$ for every thousand inhabitants.   Nineteen years ago there were not 1,500 persons so engaged.

The 2,687 persons employed in our mining industry have, doubtless, families more or less numerous dependent upon them for support. It is not an exaggerated calculation to state these at an average of say three to one, or 8,061 ; and, further, if we include those who are _indirectly_ dependent, as being occupied in providing fuel and articles of necessity for their maintenance, at the rate of two to one, we have then a total of 32,244 persons materially interested in our mining prosperity, or $21\frac{1}{2}$ for every 1000 inhabitants of the country.   But it must be borne in mind that nearly two-thirds of the entire population of the country—say, 1,250,000—inhabit Buenos Ayres and other riverine provinces almost exclusively dedicated to grazing and agriculture ; hence we must take the proportion of those engaged in mining pursuits in relation only to the number of the inhabitants of the Andine or mineral provinces ; and in this case it would represent $53\frac{3}{4}$ for every 1,000.

Our poor miners, contending against a thousand difficulties and drawbacks, and, above all, with the want of means of communication and transport, have invested £290,000 in mining operations, and in the year 1868 produced 3,654 ounces of gold, 418,273 ounces of silver, and 751½ tons of copper, the value of which, excluding 1,086½ tons of lead, amounts to about £133,000. The proportion of this gross return to the capital invested is 45·60 per cent.

These figures with regard to our mineral productions, probably fall short of the actual truth, as we have no reliable data as to what is taken away by *pirquineros* (erratic miners) and others, who steal the precious metals and carry them clandestinely out of the country. I am anxious to avoid any exaggeration in estimating the mining produce of the Republic, and have, I believe, gone rather under than over the mark in this respect.

The majority of the systems for reduction of the ores are defective and costly, and more particularly those for the reduction of argentiferous lead and for amalgamation. In the former the loss of precious metal (as also the lead) cannot be less than 25 per cent. of the total quantity of silver present in the ores. Up to the present time lead has had little or no commercial value in San Juan, and a total loss of 50 per cent. is there incurred. In Cordoba the loss is not less, but the remaining lead is utilized for the manufacture of shot.

All this shows the necessity of many reforms, which science, experience, and time can alone introduce. Schools and instruction are needed to avoid the errors which spring from inexperience and ignorance. We want foreign immigration, composed of men of intelligence and practically acquainted with mining and metallurgy. Thus the material capital will be furnished and pecuniary capital will soon follow.

Without further deviation from the subject of this report, I will simply state that during the 208 days which I have been in commission I have ridden 4,320 miles, the greater part over rough and barren country, and through rugged passes of the Cordillera of the Andes.

In conclusion, I have much pleasure to inform your Excellency that the Provincial Governments have readily afforded me every co-operation, and have done everything in their power to assist me in effectually carrying out the objects of my mission.

Trusting your Excellency will lay the present communication, with the accompanying report, before his Excellency, the President of the Republic,

I have the honour to remain, your Excellency's

Most obedient Servant,

F. IGNACIO RICKARD, F.G.S., A.I.C.E., &c.

INTRODUCTORY REMARKS.

In presenting to the English reading public a translation of my Official Report on the Mineral and other Resources of the Argentine Republic, I am only influenced by the desire to make known, in however superficial and imperfect a manner, the great fields there existing for the judicious employment of capital, energy, and intelligence, which alone are required to develop and make it productive.

For the first time since the Argentine Republic declared its independence, has the Constitutional Government been able to lay before the Congress a succint and authentic report upon the mining industry, struggling as it is gradually to raise itself into notice, and having to contend against all the preconceived prejudices of an unbelieving, because an uninitiated, public in the capital and lower provinces.

But President Sarmiento, whose practical experience in Chili, Peru, and the United States, in connection with mining matters, fully fits him for the task, resolved, on ascending the Presidential chair, to make an effort to bring prominently before the country the importance of its mineral wealth. With rapidly increasing population and railway communication, the risks and difficulties which formerly surrounded initiatory undertakings of this class are now rapidly disappearing. His great object is to occupy the attention of the masses,—hordes of wandering gauchos—whose calling and modes of life hitherto tended to induce a spirit of revolt against order or governmental restraint, and hence at every opportunity joining in riotous and revolutionary outbreaks, simply because they have not had a fixed and certain means of livelihood. Now of all the occupations likely to attract such a volatile and unsettled race as the Hispano-American, I know of none so enticing and exciting as mining, with its attendant industries.

This has been recently proved in the most unquestionable manner. I have known some of the most famous gauchos and freebooters, who were for years justly dreaded alike by Government and individuals, who are now industriously occupied in working silver mines in Rioja, attracting by their example their former companions in arms, and behaving in the most exemplary manner. Since mining has been fostered by the Government in the Argentine States, during President Sarmiento's administration, not a single outbreak has occurred, and peace seems now to be established on a sure and lasting basis.

The acquisition of mining property in that country is one of the most simple and inexpensive procedures possible to desire. The discoverer is entitled to all mineral veins he may find in the mountains, without regard to the owner of the soil, who exercises *no right* to the mineral deposits contained beneath the surface—save and except when he is the discoverer. This law, however, does not apply to coal, salt, sulphur, or quarries—all of which belong exclusively to the owner of the soil. But in the case of mineral veins, the discoverer, or his representative, by purchase or otherwise, must comply with certain rules and restrictions in order to secure his or their title. That is to say, he must work the claim (which consists of from 200 yards long by 100 wide to 200 yards square according to the underlie) constantly, or at least without allowing 90 consecutive days to elapse at any period, and with at least four miners; otherwise he exposes the property to be denounced by another (any one—the first who knows of its forfeiture), who will be entitled to it on the same terms as his predecessor, and must comply with similar obligations.

The Government are prepared to treat in the most liberal spirit all enterprises having for their object the development of the mineral resources or manufacturing industries in the republic, and I am authorized by his Excellency, the President, to assure all intending investors who may go there with this object, that every assistance and facility will be afforded them in the realization of their projects.

Boundless tracts of the most fertile land, unpeopled and neglected, exist in every state of the Republic, requiring only population and energy, with a moderate outlay, to make productive fields for profit and form the basis of a fortune and home for hundreds of thousands of our overburdened rural population. Blessed with, perhaps, the finest climate in the world—where, from the extent of territory, larger than Europe (excepting Russia), any temperature may be selected to live in,—the Argentine Republic is destined to become, at no distant day, the great rival of the United States as a field for immigration; and once populated, in even a less degree than that country, its great internal wealth and resources -agricultural as well as mineral—must make it stride far ahead of it, and become at once the Great Republic of the South.

In no country in the world is the construction of railways so facile and inexpensive. Our great pampas, or level plains, stretching away for a thousand miles east and west, present no obstacle to the laying down of permanent way, almost without earthworks. We possess iron and coal in large and as yet unknown quantities, which, later on, will be developed and supply us with that *sine quà non* for a nation's prosperity and civilization.

Already the locomotive is penetrating slowly but surely into the vast pampa, and every mile of rails laid down is equivalent to a large instalment of capital to develop our great resources.

The Central Argentine Railway has now arrived at Cordoba, one of the most important mining districts in the Republic, and surveys and explorations are actually being made by a corps of Government Engineers for its prolongation to the rich and fertile gardens of Tucuman, where sugar, rice, tobacco, and cotton, sufficient to supply Great Britain, might be produced with facility and success. On its way there this important line will open up to lucrative development the great auriferous copper mines of Catamarca, where, at the present moment, and notwithstanding the enormous expense of land carriage over 800 miles of country on pack mules, the operations in bar copper holding gold leave a reasonable profit to Mr. Lafone, the spirited owner of the mines. Last year his net profit amounted to £12,000.

This line will also tend to develop the resources of the rich and important province of Santiago del Estero, so long isolated from the centres of commerce. We find growing there, in the wildest luxuriance and abundance, as an indigenous plant, the *indigofera tinctoria*, producing a first-class indigo, whose value has been determined by competent judges in Europe. There we also find in abundance the cochineal of commerce, but neglected, save by the peasantry in dying their rough fabrics.

The eastern extension of this great trunk line, now being carried out, in the direction of San Luis, Mendoza, and San Juan, will open up a vast field in agricultural, pastoral, vinicultural, and mineral wealth.

The rich silver-lead mines of San Juan and Mendoza will then become objects of earnest competition, and their produce, instead of going across the Andes to Chili, will flow down to its natural outlet, the River Plate, and swell the value of our exports by some millions of dollars. The rich gold fields at Gualilan, in the province of San Juan, now being worked by the Anglo-Argentine Company with exclusively British capital and enterprise, are second to none yet discovered in South America, and will rival the famous Don Pedro North del Rey, in Brazil, which has paid 100 per cent. for some years past, and still continues. The able chairman of this latter, Mr. Henry Haymen, is also at the head of our Anglo-Argentine enterprise.

The San Luis gold fields are no less important in extent and quality, and I trust to see within the next year such an amount of capital and intelligence brought to bear upon them as will produce brilliant results and positive returns.

Mendoza and San Juan can produce wine enough to supply the whole of the lower Riverine Provinces, and if proper care were exercised in its manufacture and subsequent treatment, it would be of a class superior to the majority of wines imported to Buenos Ayres from Europe. I give, in its proper place, approximate statistics of the actual produce, which is much more than there is consumption for on the spot, and this might be increased to an unlimited extent had we a cheap and expeditious means of transport.

The provinces of Cordoba and Santa Fé as agricultural districts offer many inducements to the overburdened tenant farmer and small occupier in Great Britain, where the introduction of high class machinery for cultivating the soil has now made their calling most precarious and comparatively profitless. For they cannot compete with steam on the one hand, nor on the other afford to purchase expensive fertilizers to renovate the already exhausted soil, which their ancestors tilled for centuries. In the new world the reverse is the case. There we find virgin ground so rich as almost to require impoverishing before it will yield *quality* in preference to quantity, in cereal and other crops, which in Europe must be humoured and coaxed to mature at all.

Flax will grow in such abundance on our plains, and of such long fibre, that manufacturers will eagerly compete to secure it on presentation in European markets, and the day is not far distant when the Argentine Republic may stand foremost in the ranks as an exporter of this important staple.

The Central Argentine Railway Company possess some 900,000 acres of first-class land, which is now being rapidly populated by eager colonists, who, within the next ten years, will form a large and important community in themselves. Towns and villages will rapidly spring up at intervals along the iron track, and what is to-day a wilderness will soon become a luxuriant garden, peopled with bright faces and studded with happy homes.

In the province of Santa Fé, and accessable by large navigable rivers (the Paraná and its tributaries), recent valuable concessions of land have been acquired by one of the first commercial firms in Great Britain. Persuaded of the great future opening up in that territory, the house of Messrs. J. Thomson, T. Bonar & Co., have resolved to people a tract of 166,000 acres of valuable land along the rivers, and will offer freehold farms there for such a trifling sum, and with such guarantees to the colonists, as cannot fail to attract a first-class British population.

Owing to a scarcity of labour the Argentine Republic has hitherto been an importer of flour, but from all appearances it is soon likely to exceed in production the internal consumption, and within a few years will begin to rank as a large wheat exporting country—superseding Chili and California in this respect, from its more favourable geographical position, and proximity to Europe and Brazil.

The system I have adopted in laying before my readers the information contained in the following pages is simply a translation of the original text, written by myself in Spanish, and published by order of the National Government at Buenos Ayres. I give the different provinces in their order as they were visited by me during my late tour of inspection, and being obliged to omit some of the provinces of the Republic, as they do not bear upon my principal subject—mining.

The Republic consists of 14 independent provinces, I only describe 8, and the general description of some in their physical and commercial aspects only, I have found so exact and faithful in the new standard work on the Argentine Confederation, written by the late Dr. Martin de Moussy, that I cannot do better than follow his text, translating it from the French. Unfortunately comparatively few copies of this valuable book (3 vols.) are now in circulation, as nearly the whole edition was destroyed by a fire which not long ago occurred at the Government House in Buenos Ayres, and which also resulted in the loss of a great part of the public archives.

Having come to Europe on a mission from the President of the Republic, I am obliged, amid a host of other things, to pass this work rapidly through the press, as my time is so very short before returning. I must therefore beg for indulgence from my readers, and pray they will not look upon it as a literary production, but simply as a plain statement of dry facts, and an irregular compilation of diversified matter, having only for its object the publication of data from the most reliable sources never heretofore given to the British public.

PROVINCE OF SAN LUIS.

GENERAL PHYSICAL ASPECT, DESCRIPTION OF SOIL, CLIMATE, &c.

THE province of San Luis is situated between 32° and 34° 30′ south lat., and 67° and 68° 30′ west long., and covers about 2,000 square leagues. On the north it joins the provinces of Rioja and Cordoba, where the *salinas* or salt marshes of the River of Concaran mark its limits; to the north-west its confines with San Juan are marked by the lagoons of Guanacacho and the prolongation of the Sierra of las Quijadas; to the west with that of Mendoza, by the Rio Desaguadero; to the south it enters the pampas, stretching away to the Indian territory; on the east it joins the province of Cordoba at the Sierra de la Estanzuela, a spur of the great Cordovese chain.

To the north-east the general aspect is mountainous, presenting a series of lovely valleys stretching away to the Sierra of Cordoba. The first is that of the "Cañada," to the north, which extends between the points of the Sierra de Santa Barbara (connected with that of San Luis), and the buttress of Chaquinchuna, south border of the plateau of Pocho and of Nono; the other, the magnificent valley of Concaran, which is between the two principal ranges. There are also some isolated mountains towards the south. The remainder of the province is flat; the plain to the west of the mountains is wooded, but to the south has fine pasture lands, which, by a series of undulations, mingle with the pampas.

There is only one important river in this province, the Rio Quinto, which takes its rise in " La Corolina," and flows through the heart of the Sierra, where there is a series of roaring cascades; diverging to the east, then to the south-east, it makes a vast semicircle and is lost in the pampas at 34° lat., and forming the "bañados" or lagoons of the *Juncal*, thus named from the aquatic plants which grow there. This river now forms the Indian frontier on the south, guarded by various new forts, established by Colonel Mansilla, under President Sarmiento.

The other rivers of the province are the Rio de Coulara, which waters the valley of the Concaran; the stream of San Luis, which furnishes the water necessary for irrigation and domestic use of the town; and the streams Nogoli, San Francisco, and Quinés, which are exhausted by the inhabitants. The lake Bebedero, situate to the south-west, is probably the remains of a vast interior sea which supplies the actual basin of the Salinas. This lake furnishes salt for all the neighbouring provinces, and supplies some very good fish ; after heavy rains and freshets it receives a branch of the Desaguadero, and forms some bañados, or pools, towards its southern extremity. There has been a remarkable fall in its waters during the last 20 years. The large increase of population may gradually affect the quantity of water so necessary for the preservation of future generations. The province of San Luis wants water, although it receives a good supply of rain, and cultivation is possible without irrigation, but the success of sowing is never certain without it.

The Sierra of San Luis occupies all the north-east o. the province. Its western boundary is the highest. "La Punta" as far as San Francisco, " Pancanta," and the " Monigote," elevate their naked summits to an altitude of from 1,500 to 2,000 métres. The Tomalasta at 2,200 métres is the highest of the system. The range sinks in gentle declivities towards the east, and terminates towards the north by several links, of which the principal encloses the valley of Santa Barbara, and which forms the thoroughfare to the northern provinces.

Near Tomalasta and Sololosta are evidences of original volcanic action, but no crater is found, and the chain is grassy upon its ridges and upon its plateau; it has also some in its valleys. Although principally of gneiss and mica schist, we find some limestone and numerous quartzose veins, holding gold, copper, lead and antimony. To the south the Punta de San Luis, or rather of Los Venados, which was its first name, terminates the range. Some isolated groups exist further south, such as Lince, Tala, Cholanta, and Varela, in the neighbourhood of the lake Bebedero. To the west are other granite ridges, running from north to south, the Alto Pencoso giving rise to the secondary chains of Las Palomas, Gigante and Las Quijadas, which border the Rio Desaguadero and the lagoons of Guanacacho, and are lost in the salines of Rioja.

The plateau at the base of the hills of San Luis is covered with a thick bed of granitic sand, very rich in mica, of a peculiar lustre. At two leagues from the foot of the mountains the soil is purely argillaceous and often saline, especially in the district known as the Cañada de la Travesia, and which appears to be the dry bed of an enormous sea, that, coming from the north, would discharge its waters into Lake Bebedero.

The wells which have been sunk in these lands often give salt water, but on approachng the mountains the water is always sweet, and here are situate the principal estancias or grazing farms. Water is found at a depth varying from 8 to 30 metres. The argillaceous earth is light and very fertile. In the south-east of the province the earth is more vigorous and less salt. The borders of the Rio Quinto and the adjacent plains have a soil suitable either for cultivation or pastures, and sweet water is found near the surface.

Earthquakes are sometimes felt in the province of San Luis. In 1849 one occurred so severe as to injure some houses which were not of very solid construction; but generally this phenomenon is light, and the inhabitants do not regard it with fear. The heart of the mountains shows evidences of volcanic action, for Tomalasta, Sololosta, and Intiguasi are trachytic, as are the peaks of the Yerba Buena, Agua del Tala, la Cienega, &c., in the Sierra of Cordoba.

The central range of high mountains in the midst of vast plains attracts the clouds which come from various parts of the horizon, and rain falls in all seasons, but principally in summer. A remarkable phenomenon is the formation of storms upon the Alto Pencoso; the clouds seem balancing between the Sierra de San Luis and the Andes, are forced to unite, and are condensed upon this ridge, which is only 200 metres higher than the neighbouring plain, and of an altitude of 6,000 above the level of the sea; whenever it rains at

San Luis, it is generally from the west, and upon this point, where the clouds gather, whence they advance towards the interior plain and the sierra. The prevailing winds are from the north.

The winter is extremely mild, and only a little frost falls, except in the mountains where the temperature is regulated by the altitude. The heat in summer is intense, although the air is often refreshed by storms and rain. It freezes sometimes near the mountain, but never over a great extent of land. The autumn and winter are magnificent; the purity of the sky and the calmness of the atmosphere are not to be surpassed. In short, the climate is delicious and salubrious, intermittent fevers are unknown, but rheumatism is prevalent, and is accompanied with a remarkable debility in the muscular system. Goitre is sometimes seen in the department of San Francisco. The pneumonia of the Andes shows itself now and then as an epidemic, but is not so severe as in the north.

The natural vegetation is not remarkable, and is only found in the well watered districts, such as the valley of Concaran and the borders of Rio Quinto. The alternations of long dryness and short but heavy rains make the arborescent vegetation wretched; this is limited to jarillas, breas, chañar, piquillins, &c., and these are peculiar to the interior plain. The only tree which acquires any magnitude is the white quebracho, and it sometimes attains eight metres. Towards the south, on the plains of Rio Quinto, grows the " calden," a species of caroubeir, to the height of twelve to fifteen metres, and is a fine and beautiful tree. The palm of Cordoba is found near the town of San Francisco, at an altitude of 800 metres. The southern plains produce only herbaceous plants; some gorges in a south-westerly direction possess true trees; among them the "tala" is predominant, which, with the algarrobo, calden, and the white quebracho, furnish all the timber necessary for the province.

All the vegetables imported from Europe succeed admirably; the poplar is as vigorous as at Mendoza (of which later on), the orange, pomegranate, fig, peach, and vine are excellent, and there has been recently introduced the almond, pear, apple, and apricot, which are perfectly acclimatized. It is the same with vegetables; all succeed, if the inhabitants would only take the trouble to cultivate them.

Wheat yields very abundantly, also lucerne, but maize is everywhere most extensively cultivated, and its yield is profuse. Although it rains plentifully in the vicinity of the Sierra and of Alto Pencoso, yet irrigation is generally practised where practicable, but agriculture may possibly succeed without it. The inhabitants know that by irrigation they can *insure* the success of their cultures, and very wisely employ it wherever there is water, not only by the aid of canals derived from the streams, but also from wells. San Luis cultivates only for its requirements; still agriculture is making progress, for the soil and climate are favourable,

I would call special attention to the viniculture which is easy there, and would give good results, if only for internal consumption.

The inhabitants occupy themselves principally with, and bestow their greatest care upon their flocks; if the plain is dry and wooded in the north and unfit for pastoral purposes, those to the south offer an unlimited field for breeding and rearing cattle; there are also excellent lands for this purpose in the Sierra. On the other hand, the provinces of Mendoza and San Juan are essentially agricultural, and breed few black cattle; they therefore buy those bred in San Luis, fatten them on lucerne, and send them in favourable seasons to Chili, where they realize large profits.

Besides its important commerce in cattle, San Luis exports some wool, dry hides, goat skins, and ostrich feathers. Two tanneries in the capital produce a fair amount of kid and goat skins and imitation morocco.

The productions of agriculture are insufficient for local consumption, for they are obliged to draw supplies from Mendoza and San Juan, such as flour, wines, and dried fruits.

They manufacture a light blue woollen cloth for pantaloons and ponchos, for the use of the peasantry; this industry was peculiar to women, but it is being rapidly discontinued in consequence of the importation of a better article from England.

The principal route is the great road to Chili, of which Rosario and Mendoza form the two extremities in the Argentine territory. San Luis is situated 80 leagues from Mendoza, and 160 from Rosario, but these may be reduced by making more direct roads. It is 90 leagues from San Juan in passing to the north of the lagoons, 180 to Rioja by Quinés and Los Llanos, 90 to Cordoba by Quinés, San Pedro de los Sauces and Nono, and 100 by the Morro and Rio Cuarto: this latter route is available for carriages, whilst the others can only be made available by mule. The Sierra is everywhere accessible by rude paths, but only on mules or horses. It is, however, absolutely necessary to improve the road from the capital to Cañada Honda, and open another from this point to San José del Morro if this rich district is to be developed; its approachs are very difficult, and it occupies much time to reach the mines.

The routes to the south are across a pampa covered with long grass, and the only improvement to be made is to sink wells throughout their course and produce water for travellers. The routes from the north of the Province are all accessible to carriages, and there are some farms where the traveller may rest. The valley of Concaran has few roads practicable for carriages, but the country is magnificent.

The Province of San Luis is divided into eight departments, and these are subdivided into districts. The departments are :—The Capital and its districts to the south and south-west ; Saladillo and San José del Morro, to the east ; to the north-east, Renca ; Santa Barbara and La Lomita, to the north ; San Francisco and Nogoli, to the west. San Luis is situate in 33° 17' of south lat., 67° 47' west long. (Paris), 766 metres above sea level. The capital of the province is a little town, founded in 1597 by Don Martin de Loyola, Governor of Chili, and situate at the south point of the Sierra, called " La Punta," or the ancient name " Punta de los Venados " (point of deer), hence the name of " Puntanos," given to the inhabitants of this province. This town is only remarkable for its very picturesque situation, and having a fine extensive prospect over the basin, or a semi-circle whose arc may be 20 leagues, which extends from Lince to the lake Bebedero and the chain of the Gigante, passing all the little isolated links scattered on the plain. The peak of the Punta, which slopes to the town three kilometres distant, is at an altitude of 1,400 metres, from whose summit, which is easily accessible, one may obtain a view of the whole province. The town of San Luis is built on a declivity which, although it appears almost level, its inclination towards the south-west is certainly very manifest. Lake Bebedero being situated only eight leagues distant, the difference of altitude is not less than 400 metres. The stream of Los Chorillos furnishes water for its plantations of poplars, willows, orange trees, vines, peach trees, &c.

The capital does not possess any public buildings of importance. Its only church is very inferior in architecture, and only within the past few years have they commenced building substantial houses. The position of the town is, however, very advantageous, inasmuch as it is on the great high road of transit from Chili and Mendoza, and sooner or later railway communication between Buenos Ayres and the Andine provinces must make San Luis a town of much importance.

The Department of San José del Morro joins the province of Cordoba on the east, and extends to the south of the Sierra del Morro, a promontory 2,000 metres above the sea, and slopes gradually down to the Rio Quinto on the west, and which latter forms its boundary towards the pampa. The chain of the Morro connects the main range of San Luis with that of Cordoba by the secondary chains of Rosario and the Tiporque, which, extending towards the west, unites the system of the Tomalasta, Sololosta, and Intigua. All this northern part of the department is exclusively pastoral; in some valleys of the district of Cuchato the land is cultivated to some extent. San José del Morro, proper, is a village whose altitude is 1,040 metres; the climate is vigorous, but the crops sometimes suffer from wind and frost. The new district of Fort Constitucion, or Mer-

cedes, occupies a fertile spot on the western bank of the
Rio Quinto.   This town was founded in 1856, and has
become nearly as important as the capital itself, owing
to the fertility of the surrounding districts, the abundance of water for irrigation, and consequently rich pastures, together with its timber and pure climate.

Formerly both banks of the Rio Quinto were inhabited
to the *Paso del Lechuzo*, now Fort 3 de Febrero, 15
leagues down stream to the southward from Mercedes.

There still exists the old fort, the oratory, the large
farm of Las Pulgas, and several others of less importance, but the repeated attacks of the Indians in former
times drove away the inhabitants who are now fast returning.   Fort Constitucion, or Mercedes, is now a
thriving town, and, owing to the excellent measures for
securing the frontier against Indians, will not be again
abandoned.   New estancias have been formed, and a
large extent of land placed under cultivation; even in
case of a serious attack by the Indians the population
can retire into the citadel with walls *en pisé*, where they
might effectually resist any attack however formidable.
The savages of the south have made this town the centre
of their commercial and exchange operations with the
Christians, and this traffic is now a source of considerable
profit to the province.

Within the past year President Sarmiento has successfully driven back the formidable tribes of Indians
who formerly overran the country, and gained to the
Republic a vast extent of territory, stretching away to
the lagoons and marshes which mark the extreme
southern limit of the Rio Quinto.   New forts have been
established, and military colonies formed, wherein the
soldier may become a proprietor after a certain term of

service on the frontier, and secure for his family in his old age a sufficient competence.

To the energy and skill of Colonel Lucia Mansilla is due the realization of this important scheme of the President, and future generations of happy settlers will remember with gratitude their gallant, kind protector and benefactor.

MINERAL RESOURCES, &c.

The mining industry in this province may be described, so to speak, as being at once in its infancy and old age. Some gold mines are so irregularly worked and destroyed that they not only leave no profit upon the actual working, but are positively dangerous to the lives of those who are obliged to labour in them. On the other hand, there are many new veins, not only of gold, but also of silver, copper, and lead ores, which are still either in superficial workings or abandoned from the want of capital and perseverance on the part of their former owners. There is no special law in the province respecting mining, and the general dispositions of the Mexican " Ordenanza " of mines are generally followed; nor is this industry subject to any duty or fiscal impost whatever.

The mining districts of San Luis are situate to the north of the capital, and the most remote are about forty leagues distant from the latter.

The first mine, nearest the capital, which I found in work, is that of " Birorca," about nine leagues to the north, and at an altitude of 3,873 feet above the sea level, on the eastern slope of the Sierra of San Luis. It was formerly worked for copper, and abandoned up to the year 1865, when a German, Mr. David Levingston, opened it anew, with the view of reducing the ore on the spot. For this purpose he did in fact construct a small smelting furnace, and endeavoured to reduce the ore obtained from the mine.   But as this could not be done without the requisite sulphureous ores to form a regulus, the attempt did not prove successful.   During the brief period the furnace was at work he burned about 12,800 cubic yards of wood, and with this enormous quantity of fuel he only produced 12 bars of metallic copper, the total weight of which did not exceed 20 cwt.

Convinced of the futility of his attempts to produce regulus, he endeavoured to obtain sulphureous ores (copper and iron pyrites), in order to assist his smelting operations, and he also undertook the construction of a new furnace, built of refractory materials, a species of steatite or soap stone, a natural product of the neighbouring mountains.

In this enterprise he is at present engaged, and ought shortly to have his new furnace in active operation. At the same time, he is working an old gold mine in La Carolina, yielding arsenical iron pyrites, which to some extent will answer the purpose of sulphureous ores to form regulus.   He is also working a vein of auriferous copper, recently discovered in the department of Santa Barbara, about thirty leagues from his furnace. The ore, a bi-sulphide, which this vein yields on the surface, holds some 50 per cent. of copper,—with an ounce and six-tenths of fine gold per ton; but at further depth this class of metal disappears, and the vein degenerates into red oxide, with silicate of copper and iron ; and at a depth of 11 fathoms in the vertical shaft it again degenerates into an almost pure oxide of iron, holding only $5\frac{1}{2}$ per cent. of copper and three-tenths of an ounce of gold per ton.

This small proportion of gold is the more remarkable and strange, from the circumstance that in some pieces of ore the native gold is found in little specks and thin lamina; but on taking a general sample from a large heap of ore, and assaying it, it becomes manifest that the gold is not disseminated in the mass, but only exists as isolated specks in some stones. Besides this degeneration in the quality of the ore, the shaft is choked with carbonic acid gas, which prevents miners from working in the lower levels; as this would be fatal to life, unless ventilation be provided it will be impossible to follow up the workings.

I pointed out the means of removing this evil, and perhaps at this date the inconvenience has been overcome. Other works have been commenced further to the north on the same vein, in order to effect communication with the shaft, and so afford the necessary ventilation.

Up to the date of my visit to this mine, called " La Angelita," the ferruginous ore had been carefully put aside on the supposition that it was copper, the red oxide of the latter being so very similar to that of iron that the difference can only be distinguished by the aid of practical experience or scientific knowledge. I fear that this vein, which promised so much at the surface, will eventually become worthless, degenerating into auriferous quartz holding very little gold. Nor has the " Birorca " mine, above mentioned, in its actual condition, any commercial value, since the ore which it produced—about 100 tons—yielded only 8 per cent. of copper on the average, and consequently Mr. Levingston abandoned it at my instance and advice.

Having seen all these drawbacks, I am unable to express a favourable opinion of this enterprise, although there is every desirable facility for the cheap smelting or reduction of the ore, *i.e.*, fuel, refractory material, means of transport, and provisions in abundance; but, without the principal *sine quâ non*—the ore itself—no good or profitable result is possible. Nevertheless, according to statements made to me by old miners in that district, there are many veins of copper, prolific in yield and of good ley in the adjacent Sierra, but which remain unworked from the want of capital and enterprise. I was shown many stones, rich in copper and silver—the latter semi-bar silver—which I was assured had been found in the immediate vicinity, but, despite repeated efforts and requests on my part, I could never succeed in prevailing upon them to take me to see the veins.

There is extreme apathy among the wealthy inhabitants of the province in reference to mining industry, and nearly all of them regard it with contempt and incredulity.

Mr. Levingston's furnace is situated about two leagues to the east of the " Birorca" mine, in the centre of a populated district, possessing plenty of wood, principally algaroba and a resinous species of lignum vitæ (retamo), which is strong and burns well. A considerable stream of water passes near the furnace, irrigating the lands and enclosed farms, the chief of these being El Trapiche, formerly the site of an establishment for the amalgamation of gold ores from La Carolina. This site is now occupied by a mill, which serves to grind the cereals of the neighbouring people, who produce grain regularly and in abundance, as the whole of the slope of the Sierra, from San Luis up to La Carolina, a distance of twenty leagues, is well populated and fairly cultivated. The farmers utilize the numerous rivulets and streams which descend by the ravines to irrigate the lands under wheat, maize, potatoes, &c. Much land still remains, which might be cultivated with beneficial results, but the scarcity of labour, as also no doubt of capital, is the principal cause of its non-cultivation.

The Rio Quinto—here called the Rio Grande—passes at a short distance from El Trapiche, following its course between high banks towards the south-east, and is a somewhat wide and rapid stream. It has its source at La Carolina, and its sandy bed exhibits for many leagues further down striking indications of gold.

The road up to the smelting works of Levingston is suitable for carriage traffic, but, beyond that point, towards the mines of La Carolina, many deviations would be necessary, following the course of the valleys, and it would entail an outlay of £3,000 to £4,000 to render it properly transitable. Still, carts, laden with machinery, as I have been assured, have recently passed even as far as La Carolina itself.

The men employed in the mine of Birorca, at the time of my visit, were four in number. The capital invested in it, I was told, was from £1,300 to £1,600.

The following workmen were employed at the smelting furnace : A manager, a book-keeper, two foreman smelters, a blacksmith, a carpenter, and six labourers. In addition, there were 23 muleteers, with 120 mules, 47 wood-cutters, and two carters. The daily consumption of fuel in working the furnace was 96 cubic yards, the cost of which is about $\frac{3}{4}$d per cubic yard. Mr. Levingston, up to that time, had invested between furnaces and mines about £5,000, but I was not able to obtain exact information on this head.

The construction of the furnace is expensive in consequence of the mode of preparing the refractory material, the want of economy in this department being most striking. The first reveberatory furnace built there was constructed of English bricks, but now he is using soap-stone, which is obtained, as I have already stated, from the Sierra of San Luis, at a place called Pancanta, eight leagues to the west-north-west. Two men quarry eighty mule loads per month. Each load consists of two masses of stone, from each of which about 25 ordinary sized bricks are cut, and the cost of freight is about 3s. 4d. per load. Immediately they reach the furnace, they are cut with hand-saws, forming bricks of nine inches by four and a half by two and a half, and each man can cut ten per day. In this way labour is wasted, and much time and money would be economised if the stones were cut and faced in large pieces at the quarry and, used thus in the construction of the furnace, would serve the same object, and avoid the expense of sawing, which is important, while completing the work in half the time.

I will now pass on to describe the districts of La Carolina, celebrated and renowned for ages for their great auriferous wealth.

LA CAÑADA HONDA.

Following almost the same route northward from the capital, and passing through El Trapiche and Levingston's works, the Sierra is penetrated by tortuous roads, ascending and descending numerous ridges, and frequently crossing streams of limpid water, and reaching Cañada Honda, distant about 10½ leagues from the furnace and 20 from the city of San Luis. Here, at the height of 4,126 feet above the sea level, the first gold placer washings are to be found. The temperature is cold in winter, but agreeable and healthy in the summer. The Cañada (a valley) runs north-west to south-east. It is over a league in length, by 175 yards in average breadth, and enclosed on three sides by lofty mountains, opening towards the south-east, whence issue the waters of a stream which rises at the north-western extremity.

At the entrance of the Cañada are situated the placer washings of Don Pepe Gonzalez Otero, an active Chilian miner, recently established there, and working in association with Don Antonio del Canto, the owner of copper smelting works in Chili, and in the Paramillo of Mendoza.

Formerly the placer miners of Cañada Honda were unable to work at any great depth, from the invasion of water, which sprung very copiously precisely at the part most productive in gold,—a depth of eight to ten yards. In consequence of this obstacle, the previous workers had been forced to abandon their labours at the very moment the fruits of their toil appeared within their eager reach; but one of them, Don Mauricio Morales, a Chilian, who had resided there for sixteen years, succeeded at length in partially overcoming the difficulty. He sought a lower level at the foot of the Cañada, and from that point excavated a canal, pushing his way through the rocks until he effected communication with the auriferous deposits situated higher up. He covered over this canal with flags, leaving a conduit beneath, by means of which the workings in the auriferous beds above are to a great extent drained of their water.

This canal has always to be carried forward to the foot of the placer washings, which are thus kept workable ; but I am afraid that rocks will be met with higher up the Cañada, whose removal, in order to let the water pass, may entail considerable labour and expense.

During my visit two placer washings were being carried on; one by Gonzalez Otero, and the other by Morales. The system of extracting gold is extremely simple. It consists of " Long Toms" with riffles, fifty feet in length, fifteen inches wide, and eight inches in depth. The "Long Toms" are fixed at an angle of ten degrees, and the current is therefore strong and rapid. The *modus operandi* is as follows :—

The auriferous bed lies at 24 to 30 feet from the surface, and the superincumbent strata are :—

1. Alluvium, about 4 feet in thickness, but varying to 6 and 8 feet;

2. Beds of yellow marl, mixed with alluvium, from 8 to 12 feet;

3. A bed of black sandy clay, 4 to 5 feet;

4. Yellow auriferous sand, with particles of the primary rocks, which form the surrounding mountains, 3 feet;

5. The primary rocks, consisting of mica-schist, gneiss, and granite, with felspar and talc.

A stream of clear water runs on the surface, and is utilised for two purposes. First, it is led by small channels in different directions, and made to pass over terraces, each lower than the other. About a yard in depth of this upper stratum is loosened and broken down by labourers into the water, by which it is carried away, and this is continued until the overlaying strata are got rid of and the auriferous deposit eventually reached.

A single labourer can, in the course of a day, remove about 320 cubic yards, and he is paid at the rate of £2 10s. per month, without maintenance. Secondly, when water is abundant, another canal carries it to the " Long Tom " or sluice, placed as above described, and suspended in the air at the height of about ten feet above the auriferous bed. Two men with long-handled shovels are stationed below, and heave the yellow earth into the sluice above their heads, where it is carried over the riffles by the water with considerable force. All the gold (I was told) is caught by the riffles, from its great weight, while the earth and sand are discharged at the foot of the sluice and removed to one side with shovels by two men employed for that purpose. As the auriferous earth consists of stones of various sizes, with fine sand, &c., a strong current of water is needed to carry it through the sluice, but part of the gold is doubtless also carried away, as fine particles are seldom found in the riffles, this consisting of small nuggets and grains.

Two men, so engaged, can pass twenty-five tons of auriferous sand through the sluice in a day, and on the average extract four ounces of gold. From the approximate calculations I was enabled to make during the brief period of my stay, I do not think that the ley or yield generally exceeds four dwts. of fine gold per ton; but there are parts extremely rich, from which two men have extracted as much as a pound of gold in one day.

Señor Morales informed me that, during the six years he had worked there, on a very restricted scale from want of capital, he had extracted about 1,600 ounces of gold at a cost of about £2,166 sterling.

Taking the extension of the Cañada yet unworked at 8,700 yards in length, with an average breadth of 25 yards in the part where the gold is found; and the auriferous bed at a yard in average thickness, we have 217,500 cubic yards, which, calculating from its specific gravity (about 30 cwt. per cubic yard) would yield a total of 326,250 tons, and this, at four dwts. per ton, is equivalent to 50,976 ounces. On account of its low percentage of fine gold (0.720 milesimos), this can only be estimated at £2 14s. 2d. per ounce, and would, therefore, produce a total value of about £138,000.

The workmen employed in the Cañada Honda, in these placer washings, were 12 by Gonzalez Otero, and five by Morales; but there were about 28 more who are occasionally occupied.

Beef costs about ¾d. per lb.; flour, 20s. per cwt.; maize, 10s. per fanega (300 lbs.); potatoes, ¾d. per pound. There is absolutely no fire wood, and it has to be brought from El Trapiche, ten and a half leagues distant, or from San Francisco, on the western slope of the Sierra Alta, nine leagues off; it costs 1s. 8d. per cubic yard. The water of the stream is insignificant in the winter, and is sometimes frozen up; in the summer it is more abundant from copious rains, and large reservoirs might be formed with facility, to be utilized for placer washing at seasons when the ordinary supply would be insufficient. There is good pasturage in the neighbourhood, and potatoes, maize, &c., are also produced on the spot, but in small quantities.

In the mountains which enclose the Cañada Honda there are numerous auriferous quartz veins, superficially scratched by the old miners, but none of them are being worked, with the exception of one which Señor Gonzalez

Otero was exploring with indifferent results. The water invades the workings at a short depth, and the ores being in some cases pyriteous (arsenical iron pyrites) the gold cannot be fully nor easily extracted. These lodes were rich on the surface, according to tradition, and there is reason to believe that such was the fact, for the auriferous deposits in the Cañada below can have had no other source.

LA CAROLINA.

From the placer washings of Cañada Honda the road takes a westerly direction, passing through the chain of hills which divide La Carolina from the Cañada, at a height of 4,903 feet above the sea level. At a distance of about a league is an edge-runner or Chilian mill, recently erected by Messrs. Antonio Schmidt & Co. It is fairly constructed and arranged in conformity with the requirements of the spot. About a ton and a quarter of ore is ground in twenty-four hours, after which it is passed through a sieve with 2,500 holes to the square inch. This is not fine enough, however, to separate all the gold, which in the ore is united with iron pyrites. The ground ore is carried through the sieve by a current of water into a sluice, with riffles at the bottom, similar in construction to the "Long Tom" used by the placer washers. This is about fifty feet in length, and the tailings are discharged into a vat, whence they are re-moved at convenient intervals.

At the end of every week (according to the ley of the ore) the riffles are removed from the sluice, and nearly all the gold present is found in the first four yards from the mill. The gold is always more or less mixed with iron pyrites, and this mass is thrown back into the trough or base of the mill, with mercury to extract the gold by amalgamation.   In a few hours the gold unites with the mercury, in which state it is taken out and carefully washed in wooden dishes.   It is subsequently strained through strong canvas cloths, and afterwards distilled in an iron retort; the mercury passes off and is condensed in cold water, whilst the remaining gold i generally found of the ley of .835 milesimos, or 20.04 carats of fine gold.

The ores which were being reduced at the time of my visit were extracted from the principal lode of La Carolina, called " Piñiera," which was not then in " beneficio," or productive ore.   Nevertheless the veinstuff obtained from the greater part of the lode, though in this condition, yields 1·66 of an ounce per ton, of which nearly half an ounce is left in the tailings thrown out from the sluice.   The gold, being combined with iron pyrites, and very finely disseminated throughout the mass, the whole cannot be extracted by the system at present in practice there.   In order to successfully reduce this ore, the grinding should be carried to the highest possible perfection, and so as to pass through a sieve of at least 8,000 to 10,000 holes to the square inch; whereas, as already stated, it is not reduced by the actual mode of grinding to a greater fineness than that of 2,500 holes.

All these ores also hold an appreciable quantity of silver, varying from 14·8 to 37 ounces per ton.

At a distance of about a league north of the reducing works are many old abandoned mines, situated on the principal vein of La Carolina, which runs from north to south, and is traceable for a distance of nearly half a league, having an average width of about a yard.   This lode is very irregularly worked on the surface, and probably to its lowest depths; but these workings being choked up with *debris*, I was unable to enter or examine them. The deepest shaft on the vein is about 55 fathoms and is also choked up with earth. The workings rehabilitated by Messrs. Schmidt & Co. consisted of an adit, driven so as to cut the lode at a right angle at a good depth, and at the same time to drain the old workings, which were found in every case to be inundated. This was accomplished, and the lode was cut, in an unproductive state, a yard in width, but yielding only the percentage of gold previously stated. I was assured by the owners that the yield of gold from the pyriteous ores was from 5 to 7 ounces per ton; but not having seen this class of orestuff, nor the vein in "beneficio," I cannot personally confirm this assertion.

North of the adit of Messrs. Schmidt & Co. is an old and very important mine, which formerly belonged to a Señor Piñiero. A well driven adit, on the level of the bottom of the ravine at the foot of the mountain, was commenced, and is about 120 yards in length. The vein, in my opinion, should be cut at about 40 yards further on, and at a depth of 50 fathoms from the surface. The roof of this adit has partly fallen in, and was abandoned in consequence of the death of the owner many years ago at Buenos Ayres. I believe that this enterprise, if carried on, would yield good results. The mine in the first place would have to be drained, when a rich portion of the lode would in all probability be laid bare under certain parts, which on the surface present the appearance of having been formerly very productive. This, however, would entail the expenditure of a large sum, owing to the scarcity of labour and fuel, and other drawbacks inherent to the district.

This mine is at an elevation of 4,243 feet above the level of the sea.

At present the only mine in actual work on the vein of Piñiero is that of Messrs. Schmidt & Co., and in it only ten men were employed. The capital invested in this enterprise by these people only amounted to about £800.

Towards the north-east from the village of La Carolina is another mine, on a different lode, running from east to west, and which is about three-quarters of a yard in width. The veinstuff consists of arsenical iron pyrites, mixed with galena and blende. This mine, called " Mercedes," belongs to Mr. Levingston, and is that to which I have previously referred as being worked for sulphureous flux for his smelting operations. The vein is irregularly and badly worked. At present the ores are raised by means of a vertical shaft, about ten fathoms deep, in water, and exceedingly dangerous from the unsafe state of its walls. There were about 18 tons of ore on surface dressed, of an average ley for gold of five-sixths of an ounce per ton. Six men were employed in this mine, and the capital invested is included in the total of £5,000 expended by Mr. Levingston, as noted in a preceding page.

In addition to these fixed works on the veins, three men and about twenty women are engaged in erratic and superficial operations in various parts of the Cerro of La Carolina. These also make a living by washing the sand and earth in the ravine, and on the margin of the stream, from which they extract a fair quantity of gold. In the little village of La Carolina there are 17 houses, with 50 inhabitants, who, properly speaking, constitute the whole population. At Cerro Blanco, two leagues to the east, are a few small huts and about 20 inhabitants, occupied in washing operations, but here with indifferent success.

The gold produce of La Carolina, including that of Cañada Honda, from fixed and erratic operations, is about 160 ounces per month, the value of which may be calculated at about £500.

The geological formation of the district about La Carolina principally consists of mica-schist, with gneiss, syenite, talcose and felspathic rocks, and consequently most favourable for auriferous deposits.

In Santa Barbara, a district further to the north-east, are several veins of copper and galena, not now worked, but which might be of importance if properly explored.

On the western slope of the Sierra of San Luis, at San Francisco, there are some abandoned works on a copper vein, which, having been exhausted some years ago, was abandoned, and is now commercially worthless.

The roads in this province, whether between the capital and the mines, or from one mine to the other, are simply mule tracks. The only exception is a short cart road made by Señor Levingston between his furnace and the Birorca mine, a distance of about two and a-half leagues. The general lie of country on the plains is very suitable for the construction of cheap roads, but amongst the mountains, and to reach La Carolina and Santa Barbara, from San Luis or El Morro, it would require an expenditure of £5,000 to £6,000 to make a fairly transitable carriage road.

From a commercial point of view, I think the best route for such a road would be between San José del Morro and Cañada Honda, with a branch from the

Cerro del Rosario towards the north-east to reach Santa Barbara. It would thus place the mining districts in more immediate contact with the great centres of business, with the projected railway to Rio Cuarto, and, finally, with the Capital of the Republic itself. By this route the necessity of making bridges across the Rio Quinto and several other considerable streams would also be avoided. The distance from El Morro to the Cañada Honda is not more than twenty-four leagues.

The census taken in the Republic during the past year, 1869, gives the population of the Province of San Luis as follows: City, 3,893 ; country, 49,375; total, 53,268, of which foreigners form a very small proportion.

PROVINCE OF MENDOZA.

GENERAL PHYSICAL ASPECT, DESCRIPTION OF SOIL, CLIMATE, &c.

THE Province of Mendoza is situated to the south of that of San Juan, and between the territory of San Luis and the Andes, of which the main range separates it from Chili. It extends between 32° 20′ and 36° south lat., and 68° 30′ and 72° west long. (Paris), embracing an area of nearly 6,000 square leagues. Its limits to the west are the main chain of the Andes, dividing the Argentine Republic with Chili; to the north some little cordons crossing the Andes at Yalguaras and the lagoons of Guanacache on the plains; to the east, the Rio Desaguadero and Rio Salado, the continuation of the Latuel or Chadi Leubu; to the south, its inhabited limits do not extend beyond the Rio Diamante, but have been pushed to the other side of the Latuel, and even as far as Cerro de Payen. The Indians of Aucas and Pehuenches, who inhabit these cantons, have hitherto prevented the Mendocinos from settling there, and the southern frontier limit is yet the Fort of San Rafael, near Diamante, between 35° and 36° lat., although it is nominally at Rio Grande, or the " Colorado."

The Province of Mendoza is to the north and to the eastward a vast plain *sablo-argileuse*, saline, and in many places, similar to San Juan, covered with a stunted vegetation. Nothing can be more arid than that part between the Rivers Tunuyan and Desaguadero, but irrigation produces a fair vegetation, not, however, so strong as towards the base of the Andes. To the south of the Tunuyan the country is equally arid up to the 36°, but on approaching the Andes the climate changes; it becomes more moist, rains refresh the earth during summer, numerous streams begin to flow, and their waters fertilise the soil to a wonderful extent, producing grass and trees, but these latter of a stunted growth. The first valleys of the Andes present a variety of soil; some widely open towards the east partake of the parched character of the plains; others higher, narrower, and from the mists, rains, and snows, possess fine pastures.

The boundary line with Chili is formed by a series of gigantic snow-capped mountains, from Aconcagua (23,400 feet) in the north, to Chinal in the south, including the enormous Tupungato and numerous volcanoes, some active, some extinct. In the extreme south the spurs, or minor ranges of the central chain, are detached towards the south-east in cordons less elevated, enclosing great valleys inhabited by the Auracanian Indians, who communicate freely with those on this side by numerous passes practicable during part of the year.

The absolute necessity of water for irrigation and agricultural purposes gives to the rivers of Mendoza a peculiar importance, for, without being numerous, they are plentifully supplied with water during the greater part of the year, which, if well directed, would enlarge to a great extent the agricultural districts, especially towards the south. In the physical description of the Province of San Juan, it is shown how the lagoons of Guanacache are formed by the rivers of San Juan and of Mendoza, which flow into the lagoon of the Rosario in opposite directions. These waters then stand in a series of pools, whose level rises or falls according to the quantity of snow which melts in the Cordillera. These lagoons are designated respectively Portezuelo, Sauce, Rosario, Tres Cruces, Bebida Grande, Silverio, &c., and communicate with the adjacent ones by a sort of gorge through argillaceous earth sufficiently firm to permit of passing by a ford except in heavy floods. Their borders are flat, covered with reeds and aquatic plants, and easily overflow; hence most of the lands around them are excellent for agriculture, because of their humidity. The waters are very salt in the dry season, but much less so during the floods of the San Juan and Mendoza rivers. At a little distance from the lagoons, the wells sunk to five or six metres yield sweet water. A careful survey of these lagoons would perhaps suggest the possibility of making a navigable canal. Their water is discharged by the Rio Desaguadero, which is lost partly in the Lake Bebedero and partly in the marshes to the south of the former.

The Rio de Mendoza flows out of the chain of the Paramillo, diverges towards the north by the point of the little Sierra de Lulunta, and runs into the lagoon Rosario, which receives also the Rio de San Juan; in this manner the two rivers, the one rising at the base of Tupungato, and the other at the foot of Aconcagua, describe a vast curve, the one to the north, the other to the south, and eventually mingle their waters in the same reservoir. It furnishes water for large tracts of land irrigated in the capital and surrounding country, the declivity of the earth permitting the infiltrations to accumulate in a great swamp, called "Vermejo," whence arises, as in other provinces, a natural canal—the Tunumaya—which discharges opposite the Cochagual into the lagoon of Portezuelo. It is probable that art could make these channels navigable, and thus unite the two towns of San Juan and Mendoza by an uninterrupted water communication, but I question very much its commercial results. The canalisation of the lagoons, and that of the Desaguadero up to the lake which receives it, may be yet possible, and then the three provinces of Cuyo would be united by an interior navigation of 150 leagues. There would be some difficulties in that part which separates the lakes Bebedero and Curra-Lauquen (already combined by the continuation of the Desaguadero, and enlarged by the Diamante and the Latuel); but whence to the Colorado there is a level plain, sometimes inundated, and from thence by canal communication with the Rio Negro, in the south, navigable at all times.

Certainly, in the present state of affairs, I should not propose so great a work, which, perhaps, could not be attempted unless the population of the provinces of Cuyo was increased tenfold, but at present rest satisfied with indicating its possibility in order that its future result may be anticipated, if adopted, by public opinion, and that the particular canalisation, necessitated by irrigation, may be managed in such a manner as not to divert too much the natural course of the waters.

The rivers to the south of the Diamante are comparatively unknown, for the inhabited region of Mendoza ceases at this river; nearly all beyond is occupied by

the Indians Pehuenches and Aucas, who do not care
to give up their lands, or if they yield them by treaties,
and for some stuffs or for liquors, incessantly violate
their bargains. This part of the country is perfectly
watered by the Latuel and its tributaries, the Chacay
and Malargué, whose waters form the lagoons of Chacay
and Yancanelo; further south the numerous affluents of
the Colorado fertilise some beautiful valleys. The great
future of the province of Mendoza may be said to rest
here, whenever these lands can be secured from the
Indians and are in the possession of its inhabitants.

The great course of waters caused by the overflow
of Tunuyan and of the Bebedero, and the waters of the
Diamante, goes from north to south, crossing a flat country, which a short distance from the river is a "travesia," or desert, called Desaguadero and Nuevo-Salado.
The Latuel, under the name of Chadi-Leubu, is again
united one degree of latitude above the lake La
Amarga or Curra-Lauquen; the lagoon Fureco is connected with it. In the month of December all these
are, in part, inundated, when the melted snow has been
considerable in the Andes, and the rains abundant in
the lower valleys; for starting from 36° of latitude, and
going towards the south, the climate is modified and
rains commence in the mountains. The neighbouring
regions in the vicinity of the lake Nahuelhuapi, which
crosses the Rio Negro, is humid and well watered.

The Andes and their various chains occupy all the
western part of the Province of Mendoza. On the
other side of the Rio Diamante the lower ranges are
detached from the central chain towards the south-east
and some isolated cones rise here and there on the
Pampa. Immediately to the west of the town of Men-

doza extends the chain of the Paramillo, which commences at the river of this name, and is lost in the Province of San Juan in mingling with the western buttresses of the Tontal. Behind the Paramillo, of which the height is 3,000 metres, extends the long and broad valley of Uspallata, of a mean altitude of 1,800 metres; then comes the first buttress of the great Cordillera, upon which are the snowy summits of Iglesia, Plata, Juncal, San Francisco, the Cruz de Piedra, San Lorenzo, Los Mineros, del Planchon, &c., the volcanoes San José, of Maipú, of Tinguiririca; finally, in the midst of these giants, not quite so elevated as the Aconcagua, stands their king, the snowy cone of the Tupungato, whose immaculate pyramid of snow appears from the plains of Mendoza to stand erect in the azure of the heavens. It is visible for a distance of 150 miles in clear weather.

The valley, or rather the gorge of the Rio de Mendoza, winds from east to west across the densest part of the central chain on to the south reverse of the Aconcagua, whence rises the Rio de las Vacas, opposite to which, at the Punta, a torrent discharges from the Tupungato. High valleys extend between the furrows of the mountains which constitute the centre of this prodigious mass. In fact, in starting from Paso de los Patos, it does not present the appearance of high plateaux, but only of cordons, running from north to south, with a slight inclination to the east. To the south of the Rio de Mendoza, some of these cordons, especially that of Lulunta, stretch away into the great plains. In a region yet more southerly, other ranges, detached from the Cordillera, form the chain of Cerros Nevado and Payen. Still farther are the mountains giving birth to the sources of the Colorado, of Neuquen, of Catapuliche, and other affluents of the Rio Negro. The Sierra of Ranca Mahuida, adjacent to the Rio Colorado, between 37° and 38° lat., is a spur of the latter.

Little is known of the mountains comprised in the Indian territory. The Nevado appears to have an altitude of 4,500 metres, and forms a mass nearly isolated in the plain on the other side of the lagoons of Yancanelo. It is thought to be volcanic, from the nature of the lavas accumulated on its sides, from the smoke which often crowns it, and the detonations which are sometimes heard, and which resound as far as the Fort of San Rafael.

The chain of Payen, visited by miners at various times, is connected with the Nevado by a series of hills which enclose some beautiful valleys, at the openings of which towards the west commences the pampas, where flows the Chadi-Leubu, formed from the Latuel and the Desaguadero. It separates the waters of the Rio Malargüe from those of the Rio Grande, the principal branch of the Colorado, and the frontier line of the province, nearly under 37° lat. Payen is much less elevated than the Nevado; its sides are well watered, with many parts sufficiently fertile to produce food for those miners who may one day explore its mineral wealth.

With respect to the Andes, there exist a great number of defiles, which are passable in the favourable seasons (generally from November to May); such as those of La Cumbre, Deheza, Portillo, Cruz de Piedra, Peteroa Saso, Planchon, Cerro Florido, &c. The latter are especially frequented by the Indians, and are not very elevated.

The plain of Mendoza is very uniform. Its surface is nearly quite level, the only undulations are "medanos," or sand banks (argillaceous), extremely light, and which are drifted by the wind in all directions; some saline plants, and some thorny shrubs grow there. In many places the soil is charged with salt and sulphate of soda, which give to the waters of the Desaguadero, the Salado, the lagoons of Guanacache, Yancanelo, Fureco, and the Amarga, their brackish and unpalatable flavour. The greater part of this land, as also that of the interior Argentine plain, has been evidently covered by the sea, which has disappeared by the gradual elevation of the continent, or by a slow evaporation.

A number of marine fossils have been found in the south on this plain and on the slopes of the Andes. The salt districts are limited to a line traced by the Desaguadero, Alto Pencoso, Bebedero, its bañados, and the shallows which continue from the southern point of the lake to that of the Amarga or Curra-Lauquen.

Under this argilo-sableux soil, resembling ashes, in a number of places on nearing the mountains, is found an undefined stratum of boulders, rolled evidently from the Andes, but which centuries have covered with a thick deposit of earth. This soil is prodigiously fertile when irrigated, and the excess of saline matter becomes washed out by the constant stream of running water passing over its surface.

The ranges of the Andes are composed of all formations. The principal chain is of black porphyry, but its buttresses are of sand stone, granite, limestone, and quartz. The chain of the Paramillo, which is immediately behind Mendoza, contains marble of various colours, which is found as far as the pass of Planchon, gypsum, oolite, jaspar, rock crystal, and bituminous shales, &c. The natural pastures in the mountains are excellent for cattle.

The climate of Mendoza may be divided into two regions, that to the north of the 35°, and that to the south.

The region of the north has the same climate as the province of San Juan, *i.e.*, it scarcely ever rains; sometimes a storm breaks over it in the summer months, but this phenomenon is rare. To the south of 35°, on the contrary, the rains commence in the spring and autumn, and often even in the summer; as we approach the Cordillera the rains are more frequent. This explains the source of the numerous streams which descend from the Andes, and the lovely vegetation found in this region.

The town of Mendoza and its environs have a mean temperature of 59° Fahr., if we judge of it by its vegetation and altitude, which approaches 800 metres. It freezes a little in winter; the summer is extremely hot, the more so as there is little wind, and the storms are confined to the Cordillera.

The winter is very dry; the evaporation is less in this season, consequently water abounds in the Cienega de Vermejo, which extends to the faubourgs of the Capital. The floods or freshets in the rivers coming from the Andes take place only in the summer, towards the end of November, at which time the snows melt rapidly. Two months later the lagoons of Guanacache overflow in their turn, discharging their surplus waters by the Desaguadero. The floods cease in April and May.

The vegetation of Mendoza resembles that of San Juan, but the orange and date do not mature so well. All the fruit trees of temperate Europe grow and fructify perfectly.

The natural vegetation, as far as Rio Latuel, is confined

to stunted brushwood and herbage, often saline, of the plain of the interior,—such as retamo, chañar, the jarilla, jume, algarrobo, rabougri, &c. To the north of this (Latuel), and in the humid valleys of the Andes, the plants become more vigorous, and several of the arborescent species of Chili are seen.

The province is almost devoid of wood for construction, the trees just named being only suitable for fuel, but are sometimes used in the construction of their simple cottages (ranchos).

The poplar, introduced in 1810 by a Spaniard, Don Juan Cobos, still holds its place as the best timber in the province, and though of poor quality, has rendered immense service to the country. It grows with extraordinary rapidity, so that trees of forty years reach an enormous size. The elm grows equally well, but its cultivation has only just commenced. The walnut tree has been introduced from the Chilian Provinces, but is cultivated only for its fruit; it could be, however, propagated with advantage for timber.

The cultivation of cereals occupies the most important place in the products of the province, and nearly on a par with it is lucerne for fattening cattle for the Chilian market. Wheat yields an average of thirty-five to one. The judicious distribution of water would make the production of lucerne inexhaustible. Maize is cultivated in large quantities. All the vegetables commonly grown in Europe are cultivated with success, as also the fruit trees; but at present the inhabitants are more anxious for quantity and there is ample room for improvement in quality. The vine yields considerably, and lately the manufacture of wine is not only greatly extended, but much improved. The rearing of the mulberry tree is neglected; it was introduced in 1835 by a Spaniard, Don Juan Godoy, and promised good results, but was abandoned in consequence of an epidemic amongst the insects. The total lands under cultivation in 1860 was estimated at 150,000 acres, but the most recent statistics from reliable sources give the present extent of land under cultivation and irrigation at from 400,000 to 480,000 acres. This includes about 10,000 acres of vineyards, where more than 40 distinct classes of grapes are cultivated. These produce, on an average, about 2,400 bottles, or four Spanish pipes of wine per acre. The greater part of this wine consists of what is termed there "Carlon," or red wine, resembling very strong claret or Burgundy, and sells on the spot for 3d. per bottle, or by wholesale at 1s. per gallon. White wine, or a species of Sauterne, forms about a third part of the annual crop, but is not much consumed as a beverage, being utilized for the manufacture of brandy, or aguardiente; this latter is sold on the spot for 1s. per bottle, but by wholesale at about 3s. 6d. per gallon.

Thus, of wine alone we have, according to the foregoing statistics, a total annual produce of 24 millions of bottles, or 40,000 Spanish pipes,—and this, at 3d. per bottle, would yield a total value of £300,000. Now, when we consider that this might be increased to a very large extent, and the quality materially improved by a careful manipulation in its production and subsequent treatment, and, with the advantages of a cheap and expeditious mode of transport, we must confess that the Province of Mendoza possesses within itself the materials for a vast industry and commercial prosperity.

The actual production of wheat is very large, and at least from 12,000 to 16,000 acres are sown every year, yielding, on an average, 33 cwts. of first class flour per acre, or a total of 24,000 tons.

To manufacture this into flour there are 10 first-class mills in the province, worked by water power, capable of grinding from 5 to 10 tons of flour daily; and, in addition, there are from 40 to 50 smaller mills distributed throughout the province.

Wheat, in harvest time, costs generally from 4s. to 5s., and first flour from 8s. to 12s. the cwt. in sacks. The great cost of transport to the lower provinces precludes the possibility of exportation on any considerable scale. The cost of tilling, sowing, reaping, and thrashing an acre of wheat in Mendoza averages about £1 5s., and the produce, as already shown, is worth about £12 to £16.

It is calculated (without any fixed certainty) that about 20 per cent. of the cultivated land is sown under wheat, indian-corn, potatoes, and green crops generally, and the remainder (exclusive of vineyards) under lucerne or alfalfa.

All the fields and farms at Mendoza are secured either by mud walls or live fences, the latter consisting of closely planted rows of poplar trees, acacias, willow, tamarind, and others, but the poplar is most abundant, and is the only timber for construction and carpentery in the province.

The value of enclosed and cultivated land may be set down at nominally £6 per acre, freehold; I say nominally, because it is most difficult to find a purchaser, or realise it, owing to the great distance from the coast, or great centres of commerce, and the cost of transport on produce.

The production of honey has of late years assumed

vast dimensions. Only ten years ago *one* hive was introduced by a foreigner, and I am credibly informed that
the number now existing in the province passes 20,000.
Their procreation is very rapid and successful, and the
quantity of wax produced is very large. The honey is
mostly converted into a fine rich flavoured spirit, and
thus either consumed or exported. There are some 400
hives in one garden alone, the property of an industrious,
thriving Frenchman, Don Miguel Pougét, who has introduced and cultivated, with great success, many new
fruit trees and plants. His wines are the best in the
province, but unfortunately, the extent of his vineyard is
small. Some white wine produced by him was exhibited at
Paris, in 1867, and obtained the silver medal. The few
bottles left were purchased by Baron Rothschild at 25
francs each.

The most important feature in Mendoza, and its most
productive industry, is that of fattening up cattle in the
luxuriant clover fields, and driving them over the Andes
to supply the Chilian market, almost wholly dependent
upon the Argentine Republic for its supply of meat.

An ox or bullock, purchased in San Luis or Cordoba,
and fattened up in Mendoza, will cost on an average,
when ready for market, from £3 5s. to £3 15s., and in
this state (yielding about $2\frac{1}{2}$ cwts. of fat) sell in Chili for
from £7 to £7 10s. The number exported to Chili from
October, 1868, to May, 1869, passed 60,000 head of all
classes, oxen, bullocks, and cows; and I am informed
that the present year's exports will far exceed these
figures.

The Province of Mendoza, like that of San Juan, in
consequence of the position of its rivers and the absolute
necessity for irrigation, has its population congregated

only in select districts. The town and its environs, within a radius of four leagues in one direction and six in another, concentrates more than half the inhabitants. It has, therefore, two departments, viz., the town and its dependencies on the one part, and the country, more distant, on the other. Exception must be made for San Vicente and Lujan, which are a sort of continuation of the town. Before 1854 the province was divided into five parishes— the Capital, San Vicente, Lujan, the valley of Uco, San Martin, and the lagoons. The actual administrative division comprises 12 departments, viz., the Capital and its four sections or country departments, San Vicente, Lujan, San Martin, the lagoons, La Paz, San Carlos, and San Rafael.

The town of Mendoza and capital of the province, was destroyed by an earthquake in 1861. Its destruction was so complete that the Government hesitated to re-establish its old site, but wished to transfer it to Las Tortugas, situated three leagues south-east from its actual centre. However, the inhabitants refused to abandon the ruins of their city; they were the owners of the soil, and besides, the bricks, timber, and *debris* of all sorts, would aid them to rebuild it; and, what was of great importance, the old canals were made, and with them they enjoyed their rights to the water for irrigation. They followed instinctively the example of many towns, both in the old and new hemispheres, who have always rebuilt from the ruins, and besides a new place might also be subject to a similar calamity. Mendoza, then, is established almost on its old site, but the streets are broader and the houses lighter, being constructed prin cipally of wooden frame-work, filled in with *adobes*, or sun-dried bricks. The proceeds of the subscriptions collected in America and in Europe were first applied to relieve the pressing necessities of the population, and then for establishments of public utility, such as hospitals and schools.

The houses were built very elegantly in 1836, but were destroyed by the calamity, notwithstanding their solidity, as also the " Pasaje de Comercio," a kind of bazaar, and an active centre for transactions in cattle. Here commenced the fire which immediately followed the earthquake. The new city is principally built along the *Alameda*, a large and beautiful promenade of a kilometre long, ornamented with a quadruple row of elms and poplars, watered by a double canal of running water. The houses which formerly bordered it were destroyed, but the trees suffered little. It is now the most populous and the most lively quarter of Mendoza. The principal square is to the south-west of the Alameda, and there are built the Government offices, barracks, cathedral, and prison, forming two sides of the quadrangle.

The town is traversed by a great canal, " Sanjon," and also the canal Guaimallen, the name of the Indian prince who occupied the canton at the time of the conquest. This canal is derived from the Rio de Mendoza, not far from Lujan, and is thought to be the work of the Indians; but it appears rather a naturally detached branch of the river, and feeds a number of canals which water the town and its environs. Water is laid on to all the streets, most of which are well paved, and every facility afforded for cleanliness and comfort, if the inhabitants would only attend a little more to hygiene, and follow the oft-repeated, wise counsels of their able and learned physician, Dr. Edmund Day, M.D., an English practitioner of many years' residence amongst them. The town has five plazas or public squares.

Owing to the intense heat of the country towards the north few wild animals exist. The guanaco dwells in the mountains, and the couguar abounds on their slopes. It is, however, quite different in the south. The jaguar is found in the woody plains by the River Diamante and the Latuel; the ostrich and various species of deer are very abundant near these rivers; game of all sorts abound. The little animal called pichiciego (*chalmydophorus truncatus*) is exclusively found in the region of the lagoons; the aguará and the otter in the marshes of Vermejo, near Tunumaya, and the lagoons, and in the valleys of the southern rivers and their marshes. The streams and rivers about Mendoza have plenty of fish, but it is only in the lagoons of Guanacache that the fine trouts so much prized in the capital are found. The fishermen carry them a distance of 30 leagues to market, which is accomplished at a gallop in one night.

Mendoza is favoured by a numerous immigration from Chili, consisting of the poor hard-working agricultural classes, who, attracted by the facility for acquiring good land and its cheapness, come over and settle definitely, often realising a moderate fortune, and always making an excellent living and independence. This is mainly owing to their superior industrial and thrifty habits, energy, and hard work, accompanied by a thorough knowledge of agriculture as practised by irrigation.

Mendoza boasts of a fine college, supported by the National or Federal Government, and in which are taught mathematics, physics, chemistry, classics, and foreign languages.

MINERAL RESOURCES, &c.

Mining in this province is at present limited to a single district, that of the Paramillo de Uspallata, about 22 leagues distant W.N.W. from the city. Numerous lodes and mines exist in the southern part of the province—some of them of importance—but they are not being worked. The nearest of these is in the Cerro de Cacheuta, at a distance of about 10 leagues S.S.W. from the city. It only consists of a small lode from which a few tons of ore have been taken out, but of a character exceedingly interesting from a scientific point of view; the commercial results, however, were not very satisfactory. The ore is a remarkable combination of silver, lead, copper, iron, and cobalt. Its composition is entirely new in mineralogy, and was unknown until the year 1858, when I first saw it in Chili, directing thereto the attention of Señor Domeyko, Rector of the University of Santiago, whose analysis confirmed that of Professor D .Forbes, F.R.S., &c., and my own previously expressed opinions. This analysis was effected at the cost of much time and labour, and, according to Señor Domeyko, the composition of the mineral was as follows:—

ANALYSIS OF FIVE SPECIMENS.

	1.	2.	3.	4.	5.
Lead	43.50 %	6.80 %	37.10 %	21.25 %	59.80 %
Silver	21.00 ,,	20.85 ,,	9.80 ,,	3.73 ,,	
Copper	1.80 ,,	12.91 ,,	10.20 ,,	13.80 ,,	
Iron	2.20 ,,	3.10 ,,	1.20 ,,	3.35 ,,	0.80 ,,
Cobalt	0.70 ,,	1.26 ,,	2.80 ,,	1.97 ,,	
Selenium	30.00 ,,	22.40 ,,	30.20 ,,		23.60 ,,
Ferrugineous matrix			6.50 ,,		3.50 ,,
Carbonate of Lead...				15.20 ,,	10.90 ,,

This ore is not abundant, the lode being very narrow, and at a depth of 8 fathoms it almost entirely disappears.

Owing to the rainy season and consequent rising of the Rio de Mendoza, and the danger of crossing it, I was unable to visit this mine, or those situated further south. With this vein I was, however, previously acquainted.

Another mine—" La Salamanca "—30 leagues to the south, has lately been worked, but is now suspended. It is an important vein, yielding yellow and purple copper pyrites, and was worked by a Chilian company for some years, who abandoned it when the yield of good copper ore began to fall off (35 to 40 per cent.).

In the year 1867, Messrs. Canto and Villanueva acquired the mine, and worked it for the poor yellow pyrites, which yielded only 10 to 12 per cent. copper when well dressed, and generally only 6 to 8 per cent.; but, being in need of fluxes to form regulus in their smelting operations at the Paramillo, they were obliged to extract this ore (of which I will speak hereafter), and notwithstanding the high charge for transport to the Paramillo (150 miles) of £4 13s. per ton, these gentlemen make a profit by the transaction. The vein is extremely abundant, being upwards of six feet in width, and the ore is raised to the surface at a cost of not more than 13s. 4d. per ton.

To the south of the Fort of San Rafael are numerous mines of copper and silver, but from their present inaccessible situation among the savages of the pampa they are not worked.

Still further south, on the banks of the Rio Colorado, are the celebrated deposits of auriferous copper in the Cerro de Payen.* The Abbé Molina, in his valuable and authentic work, first volume, page 96, speaks of them in the following terms :—

* " Payen" in the Indian language means *Copper*.

"The most famous copper mine yet discovered in the kingdom of Chili (at that time the Provinces of Cuyo belonged to Chili), was that of Payen, which at present is not worked because the Puelches, who possess that district, will not permit strangers to explore or reside in their territory; but when excavations were first made, masses of pure copper were extracted of from $2\frac{1}{2}$ to 5 tons each in weight. Historians of that period record that this copper was of so excellent a colour that it appeared to be a true counterfeit of gold, since it more resembled gold than copper, while, to extract it, all that was necessary was to kindle a fire beneath the masses of stones containing this precious metal."

M. Frezier, a French writer, also refers to these mines, in the account of his travels, volume first, page 145, where he states that "he *saw*, in Concepcion in Chili, a mass of copper which weighed 40 cwts., and which had been carried thither by the Spaniards, and that while he was there it was smelted, and six cannons of small calibre were cast from it."

Having this data before us, it would be important to organize an expedition for the exploration of those districts, but this could only be carried out with a large armed force on account of the Indians. Those regions are little known, and it is impossible to rely on the existing maps and plans, as up to the present the country in question has not been explored by any competent geographer.

PARAMILLO DE USPALLATA.

In this region great and general enthusiasm now exists for mining, resulting as much from the discoveries of mineral riches that have been made in depth, as from the success which has attended the smelting operations in argentiferous copper regulus, carried out by Señor Don Antonio del Canto, in partnership with Señor Don Eustaquio Villanueva, who also work two important mines by means of adits driven from the bottom of the valleys, and cutting the lodes at great depth. The mines are named " El Rosario " and " San Rumaldo." Both are very ancient, and perhaps date from the first mineral discoveries at Uspallata, which, according to the archives preserved in Chili, is stated to have occurred in the year 1638. They were not worked, however, until 1762, more than a century later.

The old workings are nearly all useless, the lodes are broken down and gutted on the surface and to a vertical depth of 60 yards. The old miners generally were only acquainted with what is termed amongst Spaniards " warm metals " (*metales calidos*), or those easily reduced or beneficiated directly by means of mercury, forming with it an amalgam of silver, which, after straining, is pressed and heated in a cast-iron retort until the mercury is driven off, and there remains a metallic mass of almost pure silver. In nearly every mine this class of ore disappeared at a depth of 40 to 50 yards, and was replaced by " cold metal " (*metal frio*), not amalgamable; hence these workings were abandoned, the miners returning on the bridges and pillars above, removed all the " warm metals " that remained, eventually abandoning the mines altogether. Other miners followed, who worked the " cold " ores, or those reduced by smelting, until these likewise were exhausted, the veins still continuing, but in a mass of fine porphyric stone, which of course put an end to profitable working. Some, more adventurous than others, carried on the workings at a loss, and penetrating this obstinate layer, reached again the " cold " plumbiferous ores, producing a fair percentage of silver. Immediately below this second bunch of ore they came upon another stratum of the same stone, which cut off the veins as above, and being of greater thickness than the first, completely disheartened the miners; they all, without exception, abandoned the mines as exhausted, taking away the small quantity of ore that rewarded their final efforts. So things stood, until a few years since, when some adventurers again undertook to prosecute the work, following in the track of their predecessors. Selecting the same place, they cut through the unproductive stratum, and came upon the same "cold metal," but mixed with blende or sulphide of zinc, a bad combination for smelting in the description of mud furnaces used commonly by the natives.

These being disheartened, there remained hardly any miners in Mendoza of sufficient spirit to resume afresh the workings and to risk a few thousands in testing the veins at a greater depth. About the year 1865, I visited this mineral district for the first time, and the lodes appeared to me so firm, massive, and well formed, as to inspire me with great confidence in the ultimate yield, and induced me to commence operations there.

At the bottom of the lowest valley, in the vicinity of the mine " Rosario," I began driving an adit level with the double object of cutting the vein at a much lower point than had been reached before, and of draining the old workings of the water which had there accumulated for years. In consequence of political disturbances and various drawbacks, resulting from the crisis of 1866-67, in the interior, the workings were paralysed for the time.

My then partner, Señor Don Eustaquio Villanueva, resumed them at the end of 1867, in association with Señor Canto, and at 220 yards run of adit they came upon a productive section of the vein, half a yard wide, rich in argentiferous galena, or sulphide of lead, with a ley of 250 ounces silver to the ton. This ore was found at a vertical depth from the surface of about 170 yards. From that date up to the 31st of December, 1868, the mine has produced ore of the value of about £5,000, with a total cost, including the adit, of about £3,900, leaving a profit of £1,100. In addition to this absolute profit there are 44 pillars in virgin ore, as also the entire floor of the lower working, or gallery, 55 yards in length, the value of ore in which I have roughly estimated at £4,200; so that the profit of the mine for the short time it has been at work, may be stated at nearly £5,000. In the virgin workings 25 miners can be easily placed, and these should produce monthly at least 30 tons of first-class ore of 222 ounces, and 45 tons of second-class of 102 ounces to the ton. These ores hold also about 60 per cent. lead. The deeper workings are in water, but it is being extracted easily with a hand pump worked by two men.

In the other mine of Messrs. Canto and Villanueva,—"San Rumaldo,"—they have followed the same plan of driving levels to cut two veins which unite at 81 yards from the entrance, that of the south 106 yards in length, and that of the north 80 yards. In this mine they have not yet reached the depth at which they expect remunerative results; but they have nevertheless cut some fine dark ruby silver ore (sulpho-antimonide of silver), the first-class holding 207 ounces to the ton, and the remainder, which is abundant, 128 ounces to the ton. The expenditure in this mine has been about £860, and it has produced in ore a value of about £500.

The vein varies from half a yard to a yard in width. The adits here, as in the other mine, are well driven and so as to work with wheelbarrows in raising orestuff.

Messrs. Canto and Villanueva, in addition to the works already indicated, have erected a small reverberatory furnace for producing argentiferous copper regulus, situate a short way from the mines, and on the highroad to Chili. It stands at a height above sea level of 8,702 feet, and the temperature is therefore cold even in summer. Wood is very scarce, and rather distant from the works; it costs about £1 9s. per "cajon" or perch of 16 cubic yards, but in smelting it is mixed with bituminous schists, of which there is a large deposit in the immediate neighbourhood of the furnace. These schists are found at a few feet below the surface and cover an extensive tract. The thickness of the principal bed is about half a yard, composed of seven distinct layers. It contains 28 per cent of volatile combustible matter, consisting principally of carburetted hydrogen, and of little power as a generator of heat. Still, it is used in the proportion of 40 per cent. with wood, but is fired separately, being burned on bars in another fire place, separated by a small bridge from and at right angles to the wood grate, which is furthest from the furnace bridge. Thus the flame of the latter passes over and ignites the schists, aiding considerably in their combustion. These schists leave such a large quantity of ash and residuum that it is necessary to remove the grate bars every now and again in order to get rid of these accumulations, which would otherwise interfere with the draught, or free entrance of air to support combustion. It is therefore doubtful whether the use of these schists is beneficial or economical. In my opinion they are not so advantageous as at first sight would appear.

The smelting is effected in a furnace of the reverberatory class commonly used for copper, but of smaller size. It is 12 feet in length by 6 in width, inside measurement, with a stack 51 feet in height. About 22 quin. of crude ore forms a charge, and six charges are smelted in the 24 hours. When I was there each charge consisted of the following mixture :—

Silicates and Carbonates of Copper (refractory)	of 10 % copper	480℔.
Yellow and purple Copper Pyrites...	of 10 „	350℔
Ditto, ditto, ditto, ditto, Llampos (fine grain)	of 11 „	150℔
Silver ores, consisting of Sulphides, Arsenides, and Antimonides, with galena in small proportions	of 97 oz. to the ton	570℔
Ditto, ditto, with chlorides of silver,	of 65 „ „	650℔
Total..		2,200

This charge being run down produces in regulus about 5 cwts., with a ley for silver of about 200 ounces to the ton and 20 per cent. of copper. The loss is almost inappreciable.

This is the first fusion and the regulus thus obtained is not sufficiently high for exportation; it has therefore to be smelted over, a second time, fresh silver and copper ores (silicates and carbonates) being added. These increase the ley by yielding their metallic contents to the already formed regulus, which contains in itself sufficient excess of sulphur to render the addition of new flux unnecessary. In this condition it is sent to Chili, the silver and copper realising their respective values.

By this plan of smelting the large quantity of poor silver and copper ores which exists in the Paramillo is utilized, which otherwise would not cover the cost of its conveyance to market.

The plumbiferous ores and those of good ley for silver are not smelted, but are carefully picked, and the smalls washed in jigging machines, for direct remittance to Chili—*i.e.*, when the ley is from 300 ounces to the ton upwards.

The capital invested in this business, including mines and smelting furnaces, reaches a total of £9,000.

At the time of my visit, the quantity of ore on the surface, including 240 mule loads (about 45 tons) deposited in Uspallata for remittance to Chili, and the regulus, &c., in the smelting works, represented an approximate value of £3,800.

The employés in the mines and at the smelting establishment were as follows: Majordomos, 3; foremen, 3; smelters, 4; blacksmiths, 3; carpenters, 1; foreminers, 14; assistant do., 12; other labourers, 37; there were besides of woodmen and muleteers about 30.

In addition to the works erected by Canto and Vallanueva (whose partnership is disolved, these gentlemen now prosecuting their labours apart), there are some others of importance in mining, carried on by Messrs. Maza and Correas with a perseverance and application worthy of better results than those which have up to the present time been obtained. The former has the following mines in active operation :—

Santa Rita.—The lode runs east to west, five degrees to the south; deepest shaft 45 yards vertically; in beneficio at the bottom in sulpho-antimonide of silver with galena. In this mine the geological statification is very clearly marked, and various beds of porphyry have broken up the vein, as has been previously mentioned.

Here there are four distinct layers, each thicker than the other, and invariably cutting off the vein, which, however, on this obstacle being passed, is on each occasion found to be better at the increased depth.

Ore on surface, 12 tons, containing 450 ounces silver to the ton. The people employed were: 1 foreman, 5 fore-miners, and 4 assistant do.

Mine Tajo.—This vein is wide and important, but at the present moment it is in "*broceo*," or unproductive, and the workings are being followed in depth. The ores from this mine hold 100 ounces silver to the ton.

In Uspallata, about 7 leagues distant, Señor Maza has erected a Chilian mill, with the object of grinding and reducing the ores from his mines. It was not completed at the time of my visit, but it was hoped that it would be at work at the end of three months. Its construction had cost £330.

This gentleman has expended about £2,000 in mines and other analogous works.

Dn. Delfin Correas is working the celebrated old mine of "*Ballejos*," with the lode visible on surface for about 600 yards. Its direction is N.N.E. to S.S.W., and the vertical depth of lowest working is about 100 yards. Though the workings and means of communication within the mine are excellent, the lives of the labourers are very seriously endangered, owing to the taking away and thinning of old pillars. This mine was the first worked by the Spaniards when the district was discovered, and has produced many thousand pounds weight of silver; it is now however comparatively worth-less, being worked out in the accessible parts, and dan-gerous to the lives of the workmen owing to the falling in of the roof some years ago when several miners were buried alive.

There were fourteen persons employed on this mine.

In the eastern part of the Paramillo, and close to the highroad from Mendoza to Uspallata, there are many veins of auriferous quartz, formerly worked by the Spaniards, and even by the Indians, for we find their peculiar old grinding stones or *Marayes* strewn about, and these are essentially pre-Hispano. The workings are however now choked up and may be said to be worth-less; the veins are narrow, although some were extremely rich in former times. Some four or five old miners were working in three of these mines, but only extracting fragments of ore from old shafts and levels; these ores hold from 7 to 10 ounces of fine gold per ton, but the quantity is so insignificant that it can only afford a miserable existence to such men. There is no water nearer to these old mines than at a distance of two leagues down valley, and that so trifling that it scarcely affords sufficient for the necessary domestic use of the workmen.

Three copper mines also exist in the Paramillo, but the ley of these ores is inferior, not exceeding on the average 16 per cent. They are carbonates, oxides, and silicates, and difficult to smelt, save when mixed with the sulphureous fluxes contained in the mine Salamanca in the south. The copper deposits in Paramillo cannot be classified as veins, but as bunches, or accidental deposits, of considerable extent and importance: but they may suddenly give up at any time. They are at present being worked, but their prospects are not of a very promising character. They are named " El Manto de Cobre," " Santa Elena," and "Sud California," and in former years yielded large quantities of copper. The ores were smelted by Señor D. Felipe Correas in his furnaces at Uspallata, but he failed to obtain good results, for want of sulphureous ores, and in consequence of the heavy cost of carriage of the latter, which prevented the transport from La Salamanca.

At that time the value of copper in bar, placed in Chili, was, on the average, about £4 3s. 4d. per cwt. (at present it is only worth £2 10s.), and, with the high charges for working and transport, no profit was possible. Now it is otherwise. A cwt. of *regulus*, holding silver of the ley exported by Señor Canto, is at least worth £3 15s. to £4 3s. 4d., while, provided it be not converted into bar copper, the expenses of reduction are less than one half.

In the Paramillo water is very scarce, and the little that exists is of inferior quality. This is found close to the smelting works, issuing from a few small springs, and only by exercising the greatest economy in its use are the requirements of the people and the live stock barely supplied.

Fuel is also scarce, since wood can only be obtained at some distance from the furnace, costing about 1s. 3d. per cubic yard; but the chief difficulty consists in the want of mules, and muleteers to carry it to the furnace. This arises principally from the almost total lack of pasture for the animals in the mountains, while, from the elevation and arid nature of the district, the muleteers do not wish, nor indeed can they very long endure a sojourn there with their animals. Were there a carriage road it would be very easy to obviate this difficulty, as large quantities of lucerne are annually lost in the province (on the plains), and which, if collected and pressed dry, would be an important branch of industry for the agriculturist, and a signal benefit to the mining interests of Mendoza.

North of the Ballejos mine, I found various thin beds of a highly bituminous coal, covering a considerable superficial extent. The thickest is only eight inches, and is found at a depth of four feet from the surface. A shaft had been sunk on this deposit to a depth of 24 feet, but, finding no more coal, the attempt was abandoned. In my opinion the exploration ought to be continued until the primary rocks, which form the base of the Paramillo range adjoining, are reached. The geological formation observable on the surface is secondary, with patches of tertiary here and there, but the ground is so broken up and disturbed by volcanic action, that it is impossible, with certainty, to fix its true age. Nevertheless, I am of opinion that bituminous coal, of good quality, will be found to exist in Uspallata valley, sloping down about seven miles to the westward.

I have analysed several of the samples, taken by myself from the beds already alluded to, and obtained the following results:

Specific gravity, 1·1375; colour, black; lustre, resplendent as polished jet; smooth, hard, brittle; fracture concoidal; opaque. Composition:

Hygroscopic moisture	0.84	per cent.
Volatile combustible matter	54.80	,,
Fixed carbon	40.36	,,
Ash	4.00	,,
	100.00	

Coke, 44·46 per cent., of which 4 per cent is ash.

Distilled in a closed retort, at a comparatively low temperature, it produces a hydro-carbon oil, containing a fair proportion of paraffin, the total products representing 36 per cent. of crude oil, and 48 per cent. of carbonaceous residue.

This coal is not so abundant in the Paramillo as the bituminous schists, which I have already mentioned as being used for fuel, in conjunction with wood, at Canto's furnace, but it is of sufficient importance to warrant a more searching exploration, with the object of determining the extent and quality of the deposits. As the analysis shows, its composition is valuable, equally for the production of gas and kerosene oil, as well as fuel in furnaces for the smelting and reduction of ores.

The bituminous schists of Mendoza, together with the liquid petroleum springs existing to the south of the city, must one day prove invaluable sources of material wealth, on account of their great commercial value.

The most important deposit of petroleum is situated at 70 leagues from Mendoza, on the road leading to the " Planchon " pass for Chili. Señor Pando (a Chilian) had experiments made on their quality and extent some years ago, and the result, as regards the quantity and quality of the oil extracted, could hardly be more satisfactory, the only difficulty being to decolorise the oil; but this, in my opinion, resulted from bad reagents and the want of proper apparatus for its purification.

The crude petroleum yields 40 per cent. of pure kerosene oil; it is found flowing lazily over the surface, discharged through subterranean apertures or sources, and when the atmospheric temperature rises in the summer, it causes the fluid to run for a great distance, when gradually cooling, it forms a hard and compact mass, without changing the important ingredients of its composition. At ten leagues from Mendoza is another deposit, not so extensive or important, but from its proximity to the city, perhaps may be of much value at some future period.

I believe that, on boring to some considerable depth, a valuable deposit of liquid petroleum will be found in the province, and it is surely worth while to try the experiment, and if possible ascertain its extent and importance. In Mendoza, however, there are neither capitalists nor enterprise sufficient to carry out an exploration of this description, and, unless the National Government assume the initiative in promoting such survey, it will never be undertaken by private persons. There exists in the country too much apathy and indifference towards this discription of enterprise, the more so in this part of the Republic, so devoid of an expeditious and cheap means of transport for its products.

The same may be said with reference to the bituminous schists of the Paramillo, whose yield of keroscne would be important, and, from its great abundance, the oil might be extracted with profitable results if only an economic means of conveyance could be provided.

At two leagues from the city, in the lower spurs of the Paramillo, towards the west, is a somewhat important bed of the same bituminous schists, but it is not worked.

In the Paramillo and other parts of the province firstclass fire clays, for brickmaking and construction of furnaces, pottery, &c., are found, covering a large extent of country, and extending northwards to the province of San Juan; indeed, I may safely assert that it reaches as far as the frontiers of La Rioja, nearly 300 miles distant.

These clays, and the formations which accompany them, having reference to their fossils and classification, furnish decisive indications of the presence of carboniferous deposits throughout the entire district. In the proper place I will allude to them, and state what I observed during my explorations.

On the road across the Cordillera to Chili (*viâ* Uspallata and La Cumbre), at a place known by the name of " Puente del Inca " (Bridge of the Inca), also in the province of Mendoza, are several thermal springs, whose medicinal properties are notorious and generally admitted; but, besides these, they contain a considerable quantity of boracic acid, or the base with which to form borax, an article of great consumption and utility. In Tuscany, in Italy, the evaporation of waters containing boracic acid, in combination with soda, is a valuable and productive industry, and one of the chief sources of revenue for the Government.

This and other industries in the province of Mendoza are capable of rapid development; but one great inconvenience is severely felt—the want of fire-wood—which every day is becoming scarcer, more distant from the city, and consequently dearer. For these reasons it is of cardinal importance to utilize the carboniferous deposits. The cost of provisions in the province is low; flour, from 5s. to 10s. per cwt.; maize, 5s. to 6s. 8d.; beef, 2s. 6d. to 3s. 6d. per arroba of 25 lbs.; potatoes, 10s. per cwt. Wine and raisins, as already stated, are most abundant and cheap, the latter 1d. per lb.

The roads from the city to the mines in the south

are good, and, at a very slight cost, might be rendered available for carriage traffic; but those leading to the mining district of the Paramillo are extremely rough, steep, narrow, and in every sense bad and almost dangerous. The route through "Villavicencio" is shorter, and, being the highway to Chili, over which all the transandine commerce passes, one might have expected it to be in fair condition, but, in point of fact, it is the very worst. I would therefore call the serious attention of the Government to this road, not merely as necessary for the conveyance of mining produce, but of great commercial and public utility, as being the national highway to the frontier and Chili. It is precisely that section of it extending between the city and the mines of Paramillo which is exceptionally bad, the road being better and more easy for traffic even in the highest parts of the Cordillera. The gully of " Villavicencio " is very narrow, and the ascent very steep and high. In the winter, when it freezes and ice forms on the stream running through the gorge, it is almost impossible to pass over it, and is so narrow that there is no space to avoid doing so by sidings; a steep declivity is encountered at the top, most difficult of ascent, whilst the prejudicial effects of the " Puna," (or rarefaction of the atmosphere so severely felt at high altitudes), inconvenience the traveller, and tend to inutilize the mules and horses. I do not consider that it would be either easy or really useful to make a carriage road, or even a good mule track by this route, as, the gully being so narrow it would soon be destroyed by violent torrents of water which flow through it at certain seasons of the year; but there is another route, a little more to the north, by which a carriage road might be constructed at a very small cost, the results and commercial value of which would be incalculable. With a carriage road to Uspallata, the cost of which, I believe, would not exceed £2,000 sterling, the painful passage across the Cordillera would be rendered comparatively light, and the distance to be traversed on mule back shortened by two or three days. In addition, the merchandise and produce of the country could be transported with greater facility and at less cost, while the numerous mines and coal deposits might be worked with success.

The route which I would propose is by the actual road on the plain as far as Los Cerillos, seven leagues from the city to the north; thence by Las Higueras, five leagues to the north, deviating towards the west, in a course more or less W.N.W. to El Carrizal; the whole of which is over almost level ground, presenting no greater difficulty than the removal of shrubs and stones. From Carrizal the route would then pass through the gorge of Las Cuevas to an elevated point reached by a very gradual ascent, afterwards traversing the Arroyo de las Cuevas, and coming out upon the road from San Juan to Uspallata, at a height about equal to that of the Paramillo mines, and higher, in point of sea level, than the former. In the gullies of Las Cuevas and Carrizal alone would works of any importance be required to render this route perfectly available for carriage traffic, and even these might be reduced to a little blasting away of rock so as to widen two or three points which are rather narrow. Once above the Paramillo de las Cuevas, the road is easy and level, presenting no inconvenience up to Uspallata and the mines.

This road would also serve in part for the traffic of San Juan, and for that of the mines of Tontal and

"Castaño," which are at present isolated from the plains for want of a carriage road. There is little work to do in making a road from Las Cuevas of Mendoza to "Calingasta" and "Castaño," as the ground is comparatively level and easily traversed.

Census, 1869 : Population, City, 8,124 ; Country, 57,332; total, 65,456.

PROVINCE OF SAN JUAN.

GENERAL PHYSICAL ASPECT, DESCRIPTION OF SOIL, CLIMATE, &c.

THE province of San Juan is situated partly upon the eastern slope of the Andes, and partly in the great plain which lies at their base, between 30° and 32° 20′ south lat., 68° 40′ and 72° west long. (Paris.) Its limits to the west are Chili by the crest of the great Andes; to the north and north-east, Rioja by the extremity of the Sierras de Guandacol, and the travesia de los Llanos; to the east with San Luis by the Sierra of Las Quijadas and the lagoons of Guanacache. These lagoons, and a line drawn due west in passing by the Ramblon, form its limits with Mendoza on the south. Its superficial area is about 3,300 square leagues.

This province represents a great arid plain, often saline towards the base of the Andes, which mountains are divided longitudinally by extensive valleys; those to the north of the capital wide and almost without water; those to the south narrower and fairly watered. The river of San Juan descends from the principal range, and describes a great curve, first from south to north, then from north to south, flowing past the town, and eventually forming lagoons in the low saline plains. The numerous canals derived from it for the purpose of irrigation have considerably weakened its flow and formed marshes along its course. The mountains of this province are almost as arid as the plain, and it is only at intervals that pasture and stunted trees are found: where irrigation is possible, the natural and artificial vegetation is luxuriant.

The province possesses only one good river, the Rio de los Patos (or San Juan lower down), thus named from the district where it rises, in the central Cordillera, and where it is fed by the eternal snows of Aconcagua and other elevated peaks around the valley of Los Patos. Its direction is from south to north, across a long valley formed by the mass of the Andes to the west, and to the east by the Sierras of Yalguaras; then, due northward, until meeting with the Castaño river (flowing south), when it turns to the west, flowing through the valley of Pismanta and by the little chain of Villicun; it then describes a curve through the valley of Zonda, passing near the town of San Juan, where it turns south-eastwards through Caucete and along the base of the Sierra Pié de Palo, after passing which it flows almost due south and falls into the lagoons of Portezuelo, the third, in commencing by the west of the series of Guanacache. Its total length is nearly 100 leagues, its breadth is very variable, according to locality; it is considerable in leaving the valley, and is reduced near Caucete, but at its mouth is not less than 80 metres During the floods or freshets, which commence in November and continue all the summer, it is navigable for small boats from Pié de Palo to the agoons. It overflows its banks if the snows of the Cordillera have been considerable and there have been some violent storms. In December, 1833, the capital was threatened with entire destruction, and about half a square league of excellent cultivated land to the west of the town was completely washed away, leaving only a bed of stones which formed the substratum of the soil. In order to confine it to its bed, and to secure the suburbs of the town against destruction, a substantial wall of solid masonry was built, under the administration of General Benavides. It is at this place that a number of canals, for irrigating the vineyards and supplying the capital and the department of Pozitos, are taken out. These waters are sometimes so abundant that the canals overflow, and, being neglected, the subterranean infiltrations form a vast marsh (Cienega) filled with aquatic plants, rendering it almost impassable. This marsh assumes at its southern extremity the form of a natural canal—the Cochagual—flowing into the first of the lagoons of Guanacache. The construction of a navigable canal from San Juan to Mendoza would have the advantage, not only of those attending on navigation, but also to supply water for irrigating 50 leagues of country, now almost entirely desert for want of proper management of the surplus waters of the two provinces.

The Rio de San Juan offers immense advantages for irrigation. At Murallon the altitude is 800 metres; at the lagoons of Guanacache, in a straight line of 15 leagues, it is not more than 600 metres, being a total declivity equal to 200 metres, which the windings of the river render less sensible. The level lands on the two banks, especially the left, would permit the formation of an indefinite number of canals, which could be conducted at will over a deep soil, better than that nearer the mountains, which is now so fertile. The waters, loaded with fertilising silt from the valleys of the Andes, would deposit a rich compost upon the country, and rapidly improve the most sterile soils.

At a short distance from the town the stream of Zonda irrigates the valley of this name and a part of the lands of the Marquezado. The valley of Jachal is watered by the river of this name, formed by the streams Salado and Carnerito, rising from the plateau of the Andes at the foot of the Nevados de Potro and Bonéte; the Rio Vermejo de Vinchina unites with them on leaving the valleys, and all those streams of water, exhausted by numerous infiltrations and minor streams, are lost under the name of Rio de Tafin, or Sanjon, on the plains to the east of the chain of the Pié de Palo; in rainy seasons and after freshets they sometimes assume some magnitude.

All the other water courses of the province are merely torrents and streams from the mountains, entirely absorbed by the necessities of agriculture. The number is unhappily small, for in leaving Aconcagua, and towards the north, the chain of the Andes is pre-eminently dry.

Nearly all the orographic system of San Juan belongs to the Andes, and presents, from west to east, one series of longitudinal chains, inclining a little to the southeast. The great mass commences to enlarge into plateaux under the parallel of Jachal; lower it is narrower, and the width does not exceed two leagues. The Sierra of the Yalguaras runs parallel to the principal chain, from which it is separated by the valley of Rio de los

Patos; Tontal, so rich in silver minerals, forms the eastern buttress; the chain of Zonda, still farther to the east, borders the plain. The river of San Juan separates these three chains from those of the north. The most westerly encloses some large valleys, in parts arid, as those of Pismanta and of Jachal; whilst their little buttresses circumscribe narrow and habitable regions, such as Mogna and Valle Fertil.

The triangular chain of the Pié de Palo is the most easterly of all. The little Sierra of Guayaguas is connected with that of Las Quijadas and belongs to the system of San Luis. There is no volcano in action in the mountains of San Juan, and these are generally arid and desolate, rich only in mineral wealth. They gradually rise in height from the plain to the mass of the Andes, where they attain an average altitude of 4,500 metres. Aconcagua and a few others are snow capped; the mountains to the east of San Juan river are only accidentally, or during winter, covered with snow.

In consequence of its physical conformation, the province of San Juan may be divided into three regions—viz., the mountainous cordon of the Andes, the valleys, and, lastly, the plain. The Sierras of San Juan consist principally of porphyry in the central chain; sandstone, clay-slate, limestone, and gneiss in the eastern. The valleys of the Andes are formed by an immense deposit of boulders, covered by a crust of vegetable earth more or less thick; in some of the largest valleys the boulders are bare, such as the Pismanta and Jachal. Farther off from the mountains the soil is a sandy clay, very often saline, with some chlorides, carbonates, and sulphates of soda, rendering the vegetation scarce and stunted

The plain of San Juan is everywhere a desert (travesia), but no sooner is a small stream of water brought to it than the aspect changes like magic, and the soil, formerly dry and saline, becomes exuberant with rich vegetation, and yields a hundredfold; but it drains and dries up so quickly that it is necessary to irrigate constantly in order to secure good crops.

Those lands which are not carefully drained become spoiled, probably in consequence of the salt absorbed, which renders them useless and marshy (cienegas). This drawback could, without doubt, be remedied by draining and by reservoirs.

Earthquakes are very rare in San Juan; more so than in the other provinces of the Andes.

The climate is eminently dry; it rains very rarely in the mountains and scarcely ever on the plains. The temperature in the summer, December to March, is ardent; from direct observations in 1857 we have 30° Cent. for the last fortnight in January. The autumn and winter are magnificent; it freezes a little, but only in the morning. The winds from the north and south are violent; the former, called " Zonda," is horribly hot, the " Sirocco " of the country; both raise frightful whirlwinds of a saline dust, which oblige the inhabitants to shut themselves in their houses during their continuance; happily they are not frequent. Storms break over the mountains, but rarely on the plains, and only during summer.

The salubrity of the province may be said to be perfect; there is no peculiar malady. The goitre, so frequent at Mendoza, is not seen here. The only epidemics known here are the eruptive fevers and the pneumonia of the Andes.

The natural vegetation, in consequence of the dryness, is mean and stunted. It is only near the streams, and in the quebradas (gullies) that true trees are grown, such as the espinillo, quebracho, chañar, algarrobo, and especially jarillos, retamos, &c. On the plains are the same species, but blighted, as if burned, as much by the heat of the sun as by the salt of the soil. The jumé and other saline plants are abundant, and contain a large percentage of sulphate of soda. On the contrary, all plants or trees cultivated and irrigated grow to perfection. The fruit and forest trees of Europe succeed well. The poplar is as extensive as at Mendoza, although its development is less complete. It is the only tree in the province which yields wood for construction, but the quality is bad; it is therefore essential to add other useful forest trees, growing slower, it is true, but more valuable in time to come.

Agriculture is carried on at San Juan on a large scale, owing to an extensive system of irrigation. Cereals are of the first importance; wheat yields beautifully, especially in the first years. Fields lately cleared gave 150 to one, but this production does not continue, and falls to an average of 25 and 30 to one; this, however, is a good return. Maize is yet more prolific. All vegetables prosper, as also do the date, orange, fig, pear, apple, and almond, and ornamental shrubs. The vine gives considerable productions, as much for the preparation of *pasas* or raisins, as for the manufacture of wine and brandy. The white wines are of good quality, but not equal to those of Rioja or Mendoza. The brandy, which is obtained by distillation, is excellent. The cultivation of the lucerne is very extensive; the natural pastures being rare, there is an absolute necessity of replacing them by artificial ones. Generally, of all the provinces of the interior, those of San Juan and its neighbour Mendoza are most advanced in agriculture, which may even there be greatly extended, because there is abundance of water, chiefly on the plains extending towards the lagoons of Guanacache.

The animals, wild and domestic, are the same as in the adjacent provinces. The "aguara," or red wolf, is common in the great "cienega," or morass of Los Carrillos. The guanaco is seen, not only on the mountains, but on the plains. The river of Los Patos abounds with fish, among them trout of excellent quality. The lagoons of Guanacache have fish of various species, which thrive well in the briny waters.

The inhabitants do not much occupy themselves with breeding cattle, except in some estancias of the moutains. It is, in fact, more profitable to fatten the animals purchased in the province of San Luis, in the vast enclosures of cultivated lucerne, which could well nourish thirty thousand annually.

Bullocks, horses, mules, &c., are fed with care in these enclosures; the more necessary since the transit of the Andes requires a considerable number of beasts of burden The goat and sheep are only fed on the meagre natural pastures of the mountains. Merino sheep have long since been introduced, and some farmers have flocks remarkable for their large size and the fineness and abun dance of their wool. The fattening of cattle in the " potreros" (fields where the lucerne is reproductive under the influence of heat and a well-directed irrigation) is done very rapidly ; from two to three months generally suffice. The animals are then sent from the environs of the capital to the valleys of Chili, about 12 to 14 days' journey, where they are sold at very remunerative prices.

The commercial resources of the province are good, but agriculture forms the principal wealth. It furnishes food for local consumption, which is considerable, and also for export; large quantities of flour, wines, brandy, and dried fruits are sent to the neighbouring provinces, and raisins are sent as far as the coast and to Chili. Soap is manufactured by aid of the ashes of the jumé (a crude carbonate of soda) so abundant in the saline districts.

The great drawback to the country is the want of good hard wood for the joiner and carpenter. They are obliged to import them from the coast or from Tucuman on the backs of mules at an exorbitant price.

About 1848, following the example of Mendoza, the silk worm was introduced, but the epidemic which killed them at that place produced the same disaster at San Juan, and there has been no attempt to revive this industry which is admirably suited to the climate, and which had given good results.

San Juan, like Rioja, forms an oasis in the midst of a desert of dust and salt; but the water from its rivers has enlarged its boundaries, and provides nourishment for a considerable population. The capital communicates with all the departments by mule paths. Its principal routes are those to the west, which, crossing the Andes, connect it with Chili.

The pass of Los Patos is entered either by the valleys of Zonda or Acequion, or crossing the chains of the Tontal and of the Yalguaras. Uspallata and La Cumbre pass is the best, but a little longer. Valparaiso is reached by either of the two routes in eight or ten days. There is frequent intercourse with Copiapo by the valleys of Pismanta, San Guillermo, Pastos Largos, and the passes of Come-Caballo and Pircas

Negras.   Another route leads to Coquimbo and Huasco. The route from the city of San Juan to Mendoza, 40 leagues, is transitable for carriages, and a diligence runs every week; it is perfectly level, but very fatiguing, because of a travesia, or desert, of 20 leagues, without water or forage from the post-station of Guanacache to that of Jocoli.   This inconvenience could be overcome by digging two or three wells and the establishment of two post-houses not far from the Tunumaya.

There is one direct route of 90 leagues as far as San Luis, which passes along the river and the lagoons. The water available upon this route is a little brackish, but the animals do not appear to dislike it. The waggons can always follow it, but more frequently the journey is made on mule back.   The route from Rioja, by Valle Fertil, is only practicable for mules, and through a travesia of 37 leagues.   It is less difficult by way of the Sierra Pié de Palo and the point of that of Valle Fertil, or La Huerta; by this route, now open to carriages, Rioja may be reached in four days.   To Cordova there is a direct route by the desert, in touching Caucete, Guayaguas, the southern points of the Sierra Los Llanos, San Pedro de los Sauces, and the Cordoves Sierra, a distance of 120 leagues, but now a carriage track is being opened which will place Cordova in connection with San Juan, by coach, in five days. This will of course be the high road to Rosario and Buenos Ayres.

The province of San Juan is divided into seven departments, which are sub-divided into districts.   The province has two great centres of population, viz., the Capital and Jachal—all the other districts have very few inhabitants.

The department of the capital is divided into two, the capital proper and its suburbs. To the south of the capital is the department of Los Pozitos; to the west, that of Caucete; to the north-west, that of Albardon; north-east, that of Angaco; north, those of Jachal and of Valle Fertil.

The department of the Capital is comprised within the great curve which is formed by the Rio de San Juan, and is consequently very extensive from east to west. To the south it is bounded by that of Pozitos.

The city of San Juan was founded in 1561 upon the river of this name, at a place called " Pueblo Viejo," or old village, which was abandoned, and the new town formed farther east, because of the inundations which menaced it. It is bounded by four main streets, 20 metres wide, planted with poplars, forming an avenue and enclosing an oblong 1,900 yards from west to east, and 1,300 from north to south. In all there are 117 blocks, or " manzanas." The ordinary streets are 13 metres broad, and are now paved, and have foot-paths and wooden bridges over the numerous canals which traverse them, and which give water to the houses and gardens.

The principal square or plaza is now a most charming resort for the townsfolk, being planted with double rows of acacias and other trees, and under whose grateful shade are placed neat iron sofas. All this was done by ex-Governor, now President Sarmiento, who found this part of his native town in the most repulsive and filthy condition on his triumphal entrée in 1861. It had long been a series of holes, which formed receptacles for all the offal and sweepings of the town, but Señor Sarmiento forbid these practices, and had them filled up with earth and nicely levelled, and trees planted. On the western side stands the Cathedral, an unimposing edifice of brick and lime, stuccoed over, having two towers or belfries, and three large doorways. Opposite to it stands the new Government house, a neatly constructed edifice adjoining the prison. In it are the Legislative Chamber, the Law Courts, and Executive Offices. A few private houses of no importance complete the square.

The church of Santo Domingo is small and adjoins a ruined convent. The church of La Merced, commenced by Quiroga, is not yet finished. The Augustine convent is not an edifice of any pretensions, and is in a semi-ruinous condition. Nearly all the edifices are of "adobes," or sun-dried bricks; the walls are extremely thick. The roofs are made with small beams of poplar and algarrobo, covered with canes, and plastered over with mud; some have "azoteas" or flat roofs. The modern houses are pretty and tastefully laid out.

The Government is now engaged in restoring the ruined churches, in finishing those recently commenced, in building a municipal house and barracks, and repairing the schools. When all these improvements are completed the appearance of the town will be greatly changed.

One of the old unfinished churches was converted by ex-Governor Sarmiento into a fine school house, and is now finished. It is a fine edifice, two storeys, and has perhaps the largest saloon of any school in South America, furnished with all the most modern school appurtenances imported from the United States. It most justly and deservedly retains the name of its founder, and is known by "Escuela Sarmiento" all over the Republic.

There are a number of foreign settlers and skilful

workmen sufficient for works of any immediate necessity. All immigrants of the working classes are sure of constant employment, for they are wanted throughout the province; the town has made remarkable progress under its new administration during the last few years.

The suburbs of the capital are very considerable, and are divided into four sections or parishes. The one to the north, Concepcion, includes Pueblo Viejo, or the old town, and Las Chimbas. In the faubourg of Concepcion, wheat, maize, lucerne, vine, &c., are cultivated. Each proprietor has generally his house in the principal street, or in his fields, carefully surrounded with walls *en pisé*.

The second section or parish, situated to the west, is that of Los Desamparados. The street along which the population centres is nearly two leagues long, and leads to the Marquezado; here, upon the river, is the " Murallon," 300 metres long and of solid construction, which henceforth will preserve this faubourg from inundations; the cultivation is agricultural. At Marquezado are numerous kilns for lime and brick. Black marble, with white veins, abound in the neighbouring hills of Zonda. This canton leads to the valley of Zonda, on the other side of the Sierra, watered by a charming stream of clear water, which is a favourite bathing place for the families of the town during summer; the waters of this stream are muddy after freshets. The valley of Zonda is at an altitude of 1,000 metres and produces excellent fruits.

The eastern section, or parish, is Santa Lucia, and is composed of one street two leagues long, and some distant cantons, such as Las Chacaritas, Rincon-Cercado, &c., where there are canals for irrigation, and where the inhabitants are employed in raising cereals and lucerne.

The south section, or parish, La Trinidad, borders Los Pozitos; it is not so extended as the preceding, and includes principally country houses and gardens. Irrigation everywhere produces a magnificent vegetation.

The town of San Juan is situated in 31° 30′ south lat., and 69° 40′ west long. (Paris), according to De Laberge, and at an altitude of 704 metres.

The department of Los Pozitos is to the south of the capital; the south section is the most populous and best cultivated, for which it is admirably adapted, and there are large farms and estates surrounded with poplars and enclosed walls. The valley of Accquion, between the Sierra of Zonda and that of the Paramillo, belongs to this department, and here are the cultivated lands of Durasno, Barros, Acequion, Pedernal, and Quebrada de Montaño. The route to Uspallata passes through here. To the south-west, along the Sierra of Zonda, upon the route to Mendoza, are the districts of Carpinteria, Cañada Honda, and Guanacache; the first was abandoned for want of water, the two others produce wheat and vines. Near Los Cerrillos, in the district of Cochagual, there are only cattle farms, which are watered by the great Cienega, or marsh, formed by the infiltrations from irrigation on the high lands. The department of Albardon stands to the north-north-west of the capital on the other side of the river. It embraces the foot of the Sierra of Villicun, the valley of Ullun, that of the distant Calingasta, and a part of the Rio de San Juan. The village of Albardon is situated near the river, and possesses some fine cultivated farms. About a league from the town, upon the western slopes of the little Cerro de Villicun, sulphurated mineral waters are found, which are most successful in chronic rheumatism and skin diseases. Baths should be established, as now everyone brings his own tent, or lodges in the wretched hovels of the neighbourhood. The valley of Ullun is badly watered and has but little pastures. All the region to the north of the river is parched and dry, but in the valleys there is vegetation. The lovely valley of Calingasta is included in this department; it is situated upon a little river, which comes from the Andes and flows into the Rio de San Juan. Its altitude is about 5,000 feet, and it is rich in fruit and cereals. Agriculture is followed also at Los Tapiecitos, Barrial, and Pachaco.

The department of Angaco, or San Salvador, is situated to the north-east of the capital, on the other side of the river, between the Sierras of Villicun and of Pié de Palo. Here the facility of irrigation has permitted an extended cultivation as far as Punta del Monte, by a canal of six leagues long. The village of San Isidro is the most populous of the department. Angaco has only one church. This department was created in 1825, under the enlightened administration of Dr. Carril, then Governor of the province, who made the necessary canals for irrigation. These two cantons, besides agriculture, breed cattle. The lands are a little saline, and dry rapidly if the water is not often renewed. The route from Valle Fertil and from Rioja passes through them, and, on leaving Punta del Monte, up to 12 leagues from Valle Fertil, it is a travesia, or desert, of 37 leagues.

The department of Caucete is situated on the eastern side of the river, at the base of Pié de Palo, and stretches out to the lagoons of Guanacache and to the confines of Rioja and San Luis; although of enormous extent, it was formerly little cultivated, for want of water. Before 1825, this canton was a complete desert. Under the administration of Carril, a company was formed to acquire from the State a vast extent of land at a very low price, on condition of putting it in a state of cultivation; then the work of colonization commenced, but was retarded by the civil wars, and it was not till the end of 1858 that it acquired a true development. The land was divided into squares of 10 cuadras (40 acres). On one side a principal canal was opened of 4 metres broad and two deep, and then divided into a number of secondary canals, sufficient to irrigate 6,000 hectares of good land, which was cleared and levelled. Now the town of Caucete, or Villa Independencia, is situated in the midst of these fertile lands, and possesses a church, a municipal house, a school, and begins to prosper. The first concessionaires of the land have become rich proprietors and live bounteously on the products of their vines, their wheat, and the felling of the poplar, at present the only forest tree of the district.

The route from San Juan to San Luis passes here. In the little Sierra of Guayaguas there are some farms, but all these places are encompassed with desert.

The department of Jachal lies to the north of the capital, in a large valley, a great part of which is arid towards the south; but its upper portion is well watered. In the mountains, which encompass it, there are a number of little valleys, well peopled and fairly cultivated. The river of Jachal is formed by the streams from the plateaux of the Cordillera, and has given a great impulse to agriculture, irrigating large tracts of land in the department.

The town, or Villa de Jachal, has a church, school, and

large gardens. In the environs were formerly several crushing mills for the gold and silver ores, which were collected in the various mines of the department, principally from the Cerros of Gualilan, to the south of the town, where a rich auriferous quartz is found. Jachal maintains active commercial relations with the ports of Coquimbo and of Huasco, in Chili, and to where they send cattle, fattened in its vast " potreros," and receive in exchange European merchandise. Its commerce with the capital is of less importance, although only 50 leagues distant, because of the bad roads. In fact, from Rio de San Juan to within 12 leagues of the chief station, or post-house, it is a desert known as the " Travesia de Jachal," and where beasts of burden suffer much from heat and want of water.

This department is subdivided into seven districts— the town of Jachal; that of Gualilan to the south; to the north, La Pampa, where the mines of Picado and Guachi are situated; Guaco to the north-east, with well cultivated fields, vineyards, and cattle; to the west, Rodéo and Iglesia, in the valley of Pismanta, also well cultivated. The valley of Pismanta is parallel to that of Jachal, and along the Cordillera it is arid in all the lower part, but in the upper it is well watered, where the population is increasing. Here is also found sulphurated mineral waters and deposits of native sulphur and of salt. To the east, the district of Mogua is the most populous after Jachal; there is a church, a pretty valley watered by the Rio Moquina, and several flour mills, moved by water, but agriculture forms the most important feature in the district.

The department of Valle Fertil, or the fertile valley, to the north-east of the capital, opens upon the great desert of the northern Salines. Although there is water sufficient for agriculture on a large scale, yet the inhabitants principally occupy themselves with the breeding of cattle, and make butter and cheese, which they send to San Juan. The town of Valle Fertil is upon the route to Rioja, about half-way from San Juan, but, like Jachal, there is an inconvenient travesia of 37 leagues to reach it. These two routes, which can scarcely be avoided, could be rendered practicable, if wells were sunk and post-houses established, and thus travellers would be spared the inconvenience of a long and dangerous distance, especially if not well mounted. The town of Valle Fertil is fairly populated, has a good church, two schools, and a benevolent society, and is making true progress. A better distribution of the water would greatly increase agriculture. On the hills and in the valleys of the department are bred large numbers of cattle, and numerous estancias are scattered at the foot of the eastern course of the Sierra upon the confines of the *llanos* of Rioja. The springs of fresh water are very scarce, and the possession of them occasions frequent quarrels among the inhabitants.

MINERAL RESOURCES, &c.

This province, so richly endowed by nature with mineral wealth, possesses a metalliferous zone of forty leagues in length by as many in breadth, or say, an area of 14,400 square miles. I do not assert that the whole of this region is traversed by metallic veins, but in the greater part it is so, and the extent and richness of its deposits are still unknown. Mining in San Juan, as almost everywhere throughout the whole Republic, is yet in its infancy, and its true principles very little understood.

Its importance can only be demonstrated after years of scientific exploration by competent and energetic men. Unfortunately, up to the present it has been impossible to carry out a work of so useful and civilizing a nature; but a few years of peace and tranquillity, which will guarantee life and property, and secure to the industrious and well disposed the fruits of his exertion, will stimulate the rapid development of this and many other industries of vital importance for the Republic.

MINERAL DISTRICT OF TONTAL.

After my visit to the Paramillo of Mendoza, I followed the great northern Andine route along the slopes of the Tontal, until I reached the mines of the district situated near the western summit of this range, and which, further to the south forms the Paramillo. The mines are about 30 leagues distant by road, and 18 in a direct line, W.S.W. of the city of San Juan.

The road from the mines of Mendoza to those of Tontal (35 leagues) is good and comparatively level, passing through several open valleys, and with a trifling expenditure might be converted into a good carriage road, at least as far as the smelting works of " Hilario," located in the valley of Calingasta, at the foot of the Cordillera of Tontal, and on the edge of the Rio de los Patos.

The first mineral deposit of Tontal was discovered by a Chilian in 1860; but, owing to political disturbances, it was almost abandoned, until the year 1862, when the actual President of the Republic assumed the government of his native province, and had the district thoroughly explored by the author, who was engaged in Chili for that purpose.

These investigations resulted in ascertaining that this mineral district was one of great promise, and would, if well worked, yield profitable returns to investors. A limited company was formed in San Juan with the object of constructing furnaces and erecting machinery for the amalgamation of the ores. The capital was £24,000, and although too small to carry out any very extensive works, was, however, sufficient to purchase machinery and plant in England, and engage the necessary workmen to erect it and carry out operations on a moderate scale.

After encountering many difficulties in the transport and erection of the machinery in a country without roads, and with people little or not at all accustomed to this kind of work, the original company was unable to follow up the undertaking, and other arrangements became necessary. I offered to purchase all the shares at par, and to work the mines on my own account, with the ulterior view of forming a strong combination in England for developing the property.

The shareholders accepted my proposal and transferred all the property of the company to me. The erection of the machinery was proceeded with, at Hilario, being the spot selected, as preferable from the abundance of water, wood, and other articles of primary necessity in its neighbourhood.

At the end of 1865 the establishment was finished and commenced operations, but meanwhile the Tontal mines were being constantly worked with satisfactory and profitable results. In addition, the mining district of Castaño was discovered, about 18 leagues to the north, rich in plumbiferous ores, a most important ingredient or flux for the reduction of the "dry" and refractory ores of Tontal. Hundreds of miners were employed in these two districts, and at one period more than 100 mines were in active operation at the same time.

While the reduction establishment was being completed, ore was being accumulated on a small scale, and in the ten months during which the smelting and amalgamation operations were carried on at Hilario, 1,404¾ tons of ore passed through the furnaces, holding 94,562·40 ounces of silver, the value of which extracted would be about £24,000 sterling.

The whole of this ore was raised from the Tontal and Castaño mines, and I merely quote these figures in order to afford some idea of their prolific character. Large quantities were besides exported to Chili and to other works in the province.

Towards the end of 1866 operations were suspended at Hilario, owing to the revolution and impossibility of securing sufficient transport accommodation between the mines and the works. Hundreds of tons of selected ore lay at the mines which there were no means of conveying to the smelting works. The furnaces were capable of reducing upwards of ten tons a day, while the deliveries of ore did not exceed three tons. European employés and workmen, taken there at great cost, and under contract for certain periods to receive fixed wages, had to be paid; and it is easy to conceive, therefore, that, in the absence of a sufficient quantity of ore to keep the furnaces constantly at work the produce was not in proportion to the cost, and consequently did not admit of the enterprise being carried on.

In vain were high freights offered—almost double the ordinary ones—but no inducement would attract the muleteers and withdraw them from their accustomed haunts on the plains. The industry and business were new in the country, and little understood by the nomadic and erratic denizens of the pampa.

Nevertheless these obstacles might have been overcome by the construction of good roads and use of carts, but unfortunately they were not the only difficulties against which we had at that time to contend

The spring of 1866 saw the flame of civil war and revolution violently kindled in the provinces of Cuyo; and this fatal barrier to the progress of civilization and industry, appearing at so critical a moment, almost destroyed the nascent mining industry in San Juan.

The mines were abandoned by their owners, who fled across the Andes to save their lives and the little property that still remained to them. The labourers and miners left their irksome tasks in the mountains, eagerly flying to swell the ranks of the rebels, and take up arms against the Republic; committing the vilest excesses, and perhaps accumulating in one day, by heartless plunder, more than they could realise in a life dedicated to honest toil. The few muleteers who remained sought refuge in the mountains, concealing their animals to save them from the general confiscation decreed by the Vandalic hordes of the pampas. Under such a combination of disastrous circumstances it was impossible for a new industry to subsist in the province, and Hilario had therefore to succumb and suspend its operations.

The mines in work at Tontal did not at the time of my visit exceed five in all, as, from the want of a ready and accessible market for the realisation of the ores, operations in the district are not sufficiently remunerative to induce the investment of capital in mining enterprises.

The mine *Señor* was one of the first discovered in Tontal, and has always yielded good ores, the general sample holding not less than 160 ounces of silver to the ton, while the first-class, forming a large proportion, holds 400 ounces to the ton.

The composition of these ores is principally sulpho-arsenides and antimonides. We also find argentiferous sulphates and carbonates of lead, and a small quantity of chloride of silver, or "warm metals," but so mixed with "cold," or plumbiferous ores, that it does not pay to reduce them by amalgamation, being obliged to resort to smelting, mixing them with galenas. The mne has been much and badly worked, as the lode is irregularly broken up and destroyed at various parts. The deepest working is about 25 fathoms vertically, and the blende, or bed of sulphide of zinc, which makes its appearance throughout the whole of this mining district at about the same depth, has already been reached. This bed is unproductive, and must be cut through in order to reach productive ore, which undoubedtly exists below it. There are still, however, workings on different parts of the lode from which very good ore is obtained, and, judging by the quantity of ore at sight, the mine would seem to be of considerable value.

The following ores were on the surface, dressed :— About 15 cwts. first-class, holding 320 ounces per ton; about 30 cwts. of second class, holding 264 ounces per per ton; and about 512 cwts. of inferior ore and sweepings, holding about 136 ounces per ton. Their value, placed at smelting works, would be about £500.

There were nine miners employed on this mine.

The mine *Señorita* is very abundant in its yield of ore, and was in good condition. As yet the blende has not been touched, the vertical depth of the mine being only 35 yards. The lode is well formed and thick, and in the year 1868 produced 70 tons of ore, the average ley of the ore for silver was about 192 ounces per ton. The following ores were on surface, dressed :— About 15 cwts. first-class, holding 400 ounces to the ton; 80 cwts. second-class, holding 264 ounces per ton; 64 cwts. of course inferior holding 160 ounces per ton; and 500 cwts. of fine sweepings from floorways holding 144 ounces per ton. Their value, delivered at smelting furnace, would be about £390. Six persons were employed at this mine, which, like the preceding, belongs to Messrs. Vicente, Oros, and Co.

The mine *Dilirio* is in "broceo," or unproductive workings. It was formerly very rich a little lower down, yielding ore with a high percentage of silver. The continuation of the same lode was also very rich at the mine *Lucrecia*, whence a considerable quantity of ore was exported to Chili in the year 1864, holding 2,136 ounces per ton. The working of the *Dilirio* mine, which is at a lower level than the *Lucrecia*, is being carried on with the object of passing the blende. Only two labourers and a foreman were occupied. The mine belongs to Don Octavio Videla.

The mine *Colon* belongs to Don Aniceto Gimenez, an energetic man, who has worked his mine without intermission for five years and with satisfactory results. He has invested about £450 in this work, and employs eight miners. The upper portion of the mine is pretty well exhausted, but the depth to which the lowest level is carried is very small indeed, being like all the other mines of the district. At present the workings are being carried on by means of a shaft inclined at an angle of 45 degrees, and the lode is visible and well defined to a width of four feet, with specks of galena intermixed with blende, marl, and quartz. This may be called broceo, but it is hopeful, as the lodes show indications of passing very soon through the usual bed of blende found all over the district.

The quality of the ore extracted exceeds the most sanguine hopes, since it yields about 160 ounces per ton, and small particles of ruby silver ore make their appearance, an important indication, favouring the general opinion that good results and first-class ore will be obtained lower down, once the bed of blende is passed.

The *Carmen Alto* mine may be described as the principal mine in the district of Tontal, having, since its first discovery, produced ores of great value. It is a lode about two feet in width, containing ores of the two classes, "cold" and "warm," holding an average ley for silver of not less than 200 to 216 ounces per ton. The vein is visible for upwards of 300 yards in good ore; the greater part has been taken from the surface. At 35 yards depth the bed or zone of blende has been touched, and the workings pushed on through it for a distance of 30 yards, the lode still continuing firm and broader, already presenting a width of three to four feet. The body of the lode consisted of grey marl, with galena disseminated throughout, while the blende had almost entirely disappeared. The most important feature was the presence of small specks of *rosicler*, or ruby silver, well crystallized, and this alone is sufficient stimulus to carry on the workings.

Several samples, containing these specks, insignificant as they appeared, yielded 456 ounces per ton, but the average yield of the mass of the lode was not over 56 to 80 ounces.

This mine is, I consider, of great importance, and a vein of such form and width is well worth the trouble and expense of being followed to a greater depth. The bridges or pillars, of which there are many, are invariably good and rich, and, if stoped out, will produce a large quantity of ores, holding an average of 216 ounces of silver to the ton.

Thirty-two persons were employed in this mine, which is the property of Messrs. Ambrosio, Caicedo and Co. I could obtain no reliable data as to the capital invested, but believe it cannot be under £3,500.

These were the only mines which I found in work at the time of my visit. There are at least 100 more lying idle for the want of an accessible market, but once operations at Hilario are resumed, it is to be hoped their owners will be stimulated to work with perseverance and activity. The geological formation of the Tontal range is mostly clay-slate, with mica schist. The mines are at an elevation of 11,000 feet above sea level.

This mining district is well supplied with water and firewood in the vicinity. Provisions cost: Beef, 2d. per lb.; flour, 2½d. per. lb.; maize, 1d. per lb. Freight to or from the city to the mines is 6s. 8d. to 8s. 4d. per mule load of 380 lbs.; to the establishment at Hilario from mines, 13s. 4d. to 20s. per ton; to La Huerta, £5 per ton; to Castaño, 30s. per ton. There is little pasture in the mines. The miners are paid £2 per month, with maintenance, which latter is equal to about 25s. According to the hardness of the rock, the cost per yard, forward in adits, is 6s. 8d. to 16s. 8d., being 1½ yards in breadth and 2½ in height. The labourers receive from £1 5s. to £1 10s. per month, with maintenance.

Blasting powder, manufactured in Chili, costs, placed in the mines, about £2 per cwt.; safety fuse, about 7d. per coil; iron for jumpers and crowbars, £2 per cwt.; steel for jumpers, 10d. per pound.

AMALGAMATION WORKS "SOROCAYENSE."

From the mines of Tontal a wide and level gully, or quebrada, leads down westward to the important valley of " Barrial " and " Calingasta," which is watered by the Rio de los Patos, already described. From the mouth or opening of this quebrada, the amalgamation establishment of Sorocayense is situated about a league distant to the north, at an elevation of 5,694 feet above the sea level. Its rather unique name is derived from a small town or mining district in Bolivia, whence the system of amalgamation practised there has been introduced. The works consist of a reverberatory or roasting furnace, built of " adobes," or sun-dried bricks, a Chilian mill with two well-mounted edge-runners, a sieve to bolt the finely ground ores, and a rectangular trough, about 12 feet long by 4 wide, and 4 in depth, in which a transverse cylinder moves horizontally, by means of a shaft and crank geared on to the water wheel, 18 feet in diameter and 3 feet breast. This wheel drives all the other machinery as well.

The system of reduction is properly by amalgamation, but the crude ores are previously subjected to calcination with common salt, in order to chlorinise the silver. But this object is not so satisfactorily attained as could be desired, from the varied composition of the ores, and owing to the absence of sulphides in the furnace, with which to effect the necessary decomposition of the argentiferous compounds.

In the first place, the crude ore is ground in the Chilian mill until fine enough to pass through a sieve with 3,600 holes to the square inch. It is then calcined in a reverberatory furnace at a very low heat, and kept constantly stirred for the space of five to eight hours, salt being added from time to time until it reaches a proportion of five per cent.

After eight hours the charge is drawn, and is conveyed hot to the rectangular trough, where a certain proportion of water is added to make the mass into a thin paste; mercury is then added in small quantities from time to time, until about 75 lbs. to 80 lbs. are mixed with the ore. The mass is stirred backwards and forwards by the action of the revolving cylinder for many hours, according to the class of ore. When the "*azoguero*," or foreman in charge, considers the amalgamation complete, he adds more water for washing off the tailings, allowing a small jet to enter and an equal quantity to be discharged through small' holes at various heights in the trough, until nearly the whole of the mass has been thus removed; the remaining amalgam now contains that portion of the silver which was amalgamable in the ore. This amalgam (which is called "*pella*") is then strained and squeezed in a cone-shaped bag of strong canvas. The greater part of the mercury is here separated, leaving a residue in the bag, which, however, still contains about six parts of mercury for every one of silver. Finally, this amalgam is fired in iron retorts, the evaporated mercury being carried through tubes, whose extremities are introduced into cold water, where it condenses, and is collected for future use. The remaining silver in the retorts is white, porous, and almost pure, in which state it is sold, or is melted in iron or plumbago crucibles, and cast into moulds forming ingots. Its fineness is generally represented by .850 to .900 milesimos, not being so pure as the silver produced by cupellation from lead ores.

The capital invested in this establishment is not over

£2,500, and it is now in the possession of Messrs. Riera and Custo, who have rented it for two years. As the system is rude and ill suited to the class of ores found in the district, the produce is insignificant and the profit less.

Only eight tons of ore are reduced in the month and not 70 per cent. of the silver is obtained. During the year only 350 marcs of silver (equal to 7.4 oz. troy per marc) were produced, the realized value of which in San Juan amounted to about £650.

Eight men were employed on these works.

SMELTING AND AMALGAMATION WORKS AT HILARIO.

Three leagues further north, in the same valley, are the smelting and amalgamation works of Hilario, founded in 1863, and finished in the year 1866. It is distant about 33 leagues westwards of San Juan, and 48 leagues north-north-west of Mendoza, in latitude 31° 50′ south, and 69° 56′ longitude west of Greenwich. It is situated at an elevation of 5,624 feet above the sea level, and is the largest mining and reduction establishment of its class in the Republic.

The amalgamation machinery was constructed by Messrs. John Taylor and Sons, of London, and is of first-class workmanship, consisting in part of barrels, on the Freyberg system, and partly of tinas (or vats) on the South American system. The works are capable of reducing ten tons of crude ore in twenty-four hours. The motive power for this machinery (together with the grinding mills) is a large turbine having a fall of 33 feet, the water passing through wrought-iron tubes representing a column of 2 feet 6 inches in diameter. The effective power is computed to equal 95 horse.

But the most important part of the establishment is dedicated to smelting and reduction of ores by fire, with the corresponding deposits for firewood, charcoal, fluxes, &c. The land actually covered by the works is about 12 acres, not including labourers' dwellings, shops, meat stalls, hotel, &c., which form a street outside.

The system of smelting followed at Hilario is on the whole something similar to that of the Messrs. Klappenbach and Co., at La Huerta (and to which I will refer further on), but the details are very different. It is almost identical with the new system adopted at Pontgibaud, in France, by Messrs. Taylor and Sons, of London, who have now the direction of that establishment. The ores, mixed in certain proportions, are calcined with much care in a reverberatory furnace, having two distinct compartments, one for calcination and the other for fusion, thus effecting much economy in the use of fuel. The ore, thus calcined and slagged, is smelted in Castillian blast furnaces, having three tuyéres, and of large capacity, since each furnace can smelt eight tons of ore in the twenty-four hours, consuming about 3 tons of charcoal. Six men are required to work each furnace, three by day and three by night. The fuel used in this furnace is charcoal made from retamo and algarrobo, which produce 30 per cent. on the average; in all the other furnaces wood alone is used. The blowing machinery is a circular fan, five feet in diameter, which makes 1,800 revolutions per minute. There is another in reserve in case of accident. The motive power of this is a second turbine of 25 horse power. The blast is conveyed through all parts of the establishment by means of subterranean canals so as to utilize it in the forges, refining furnaces, &c.

The products of the Castillian furnaces at Hilario are two only, namely, argentiferous lead and slags. The lead is always hard, and has to be purified and softened in iron pots, or a softening furnace, before being refined by the English method, which is simply on a cupel, or test ring, formed of bone ash, where the silver is obtained pure at a single operation. The bar silver produced by this system is seldom of inferior ley than .990, and sometimes it reaches .995. There are three reverberatory furnaces in Hilario, with one for refining, and two blast furnaces. The ore deposits are capable of containing 1,000 tons, and are divided into numbered comparments for different classes of ore.

The laboratory for analysis by the humid method is a complete department in itself, with fine assay and bullion balances.

In addition, there is a laboratory for assays by fire, with its row of miniature furnaces, capable of making 100 assays daily. In the same range of buildings are the forge, carpenters' shop, &c., with tools and implements of every description, requisite for repairing any breakage or damage done to the machinery.

There are extensive deposits for wood and charcoal, which are consumed in large quantities. It requires great care to produce the latter cheaply and of good quality. The retamo and algarroba, as already stated, give 30 per cent. of charcoal. It is made in mounds in the open air, and sometimes in closed kilns.

The manufacture of fire-bricks also forms an important part of the operations at Hilario, as the consumption in the furnaces is very considerable, and, had they to be imported from Europe or Chili, the cost would be ruinous, each brick placed in the establishment costing 1s. 8d., whereas those made on the spot, from refractory clays obtained in the neighbourhood, only cost 1d. each, and are almost as good as English bricks for lead smelting.

There are about 48 acres of good cultivated land, well enclosed, around the establishment. This is under alfalfa or lucerne, as also a farm of 240 acres, belonging to the works, situated at Calingasta, a distance of three leagues.

Whilst the establishment was at work in 1866, it produced in ten months 9,000 marcs (666,000 ounces troy) of silver and 250 tons of lead, representing a value of £23,000.

The prices of provisions are, more or less, those stated in my report on Tontal, but in the valley of Calingasta they have the great advantage of possessing good pastures in alfalfa or lucerne, and all the necessaries of life.

There is abundance of firewood, which costs from 10s. to 11s. 6d. per perch of 16 cubic yards. Wood charcoal costs 2s. per cwt., delivered in the establishment. Water is superabundant and of excellent quality; the canal for the turbines and use of the works, opened from the Rio de los Patos to Hilario, is a league long by 2 yards in breadth and $1\frac{1}{2}$ in depth.

Capital invested £60,000, in mines, smelting works, &c.

Crossing the Rio de los Patos, and proceeding northwards on the road to the mines of Castaño, at a distance of about seven leagues, is situate " Villa Corral," where the Hilario company had commenced the formation of a smelting works. About 60,000 cubic yards of wood are cut and piled up there ready for use, but the paralyzation of the affairs of the Company prevented the carrying out of the project.

REDUCTION WORKS AT CASTAÑO.

Seven leagues further north, on the Rio de Castaño, and at the entrance to the mines of that district, are the reduction works constructed by Messrs. Babié and Co., which are now stopped and almost abandoned, from want of capital and the cessation of active operations at the mines, as the owner only reduces the ores without being himself actually engaged in mining operations. It is constructed exclusively for the reduction of argentiferous lead, on the same system as practised by Messrs. Klappenbach. The works comprise two blast furnaces, 6 feet high and rectangular in shape; a reverberatory furnace, one for refining on the German system, and another of smaller size for purifying the resulting impure silver from the refining furnace. A circular fan is used to give blast to the furnaces, but is badly constructed and geared, and does not produce a current of air sufficiently strong to effect the proper reduction of the ores. The loss of the precious metal must be considerable as a consequence of the crude method of smelting.

During the year 1868, 130 tons of ore were reduced, producing 12,531 ounces of silver, whose value there would be about £3,000. Good fire bricks are made there, composed of three parts of a refractory sandstone, and, to bind it, one part of finely washed earth, formed by deposits from the turbid waters of the rivers in summer. They are made by dry pressure, and thus, in their crude state, are used in the furnaces.

About £3,900 were invested at the beginning in these works, but the amount expended in their actual construction may be calculated in about £2,250. Some days previous to my visit (in February) a torrent from the mountains at the rear came down and caused great damage, almost completely destroying the establishment. Operations were in consequence suspended, but during the previous year 22 men had been employed there.

Firewood is not abundant, and costs 13s. per perch of 16 cubic yards; charcoal 2s. per cwt.; prices of provisions are the same, more or less, as at the Tontal mines.

The labourers are paid from £1 13s. 4d. to £2 per month, with rations. There is little pasturage, but plenty of water.

MINING DISTRICT OF CASTAÑO.

This district, which is situated two leagues northwards of the reduction works just described, was discovered in the year 1863, and is of considerable extent, covering an area of at least 100 square miles, i.e., the part already known. Its. ores are principally galenas, sulphates, and carbonates of lead, holding a small proportion of silver, but very abundant, since there are lodes exceeding 9 feet in width, and visible on the surface for nearly a mile.

There are many veins of " dry " refractory ores, intermixed with galena; these hold on an average from 96 to 148 ounces of silver to the ton, and some over 190 ounces.

At present there are only three mines there, viz., the *Julieta*, the *Rosario*, and the *Dos Amigos*. The first is worked for dry ores, whose ley ranges from 58 to 74 ounces per ton; the second for pure galena, with only 30 ounces to the ton—this is used for flux for dry ores in smelting; and the third for galena and dry ores mixed, with a ley of about 103 ounces. Not more than ten persons are employed on all the workings.

The mines not in work, with the exception of the *Rosario*, belong to the Hilario establishment, and are more than 20 in number, which, from the general paralyzation of the enterprise, have been compelled to suspend operations. Their lodes are wide and productive.

1. *San Nicolas.*—Lode a yard wide, visible on the surface for a distance of 500 yards from east to west, but little worked; in argentiferous grey copper ore, rich in silver and copper; ley 206 ounces; very hard to smelt, being accompanied by compact black oxide of manganese. The lode is only driven into for 20 yards by two short adits on the vein at the bottom of the valley, which is 7,008 feet about the sea level; but the mine itself is situated low in an open ravine and easy of access for carts.

2. *San Ignacio.*—Dry ores, with galena and chlorides of silver; ley from 74 to 148 ounces per ton, very abundant; there are 36 tons of ore dressed at surface; lode two feet in width, almost vertical, and visible on the surface for nearly 1,000 yards. There are two adits and some workings of little depth.

3. *La Compañia.*—Lode a yard and a half wide, and in some parts three yards; composed of galena with sulphates and carbonates of lead; very abundant, but of poor ley for silver, holding on the average 24·2 ounces per ton. The ores from this mine are used as a flux for the reduction of dry ores from Tontal and elsewhere. About 120 tons dressed on surface. There is a spacious adit driven on the lode, and the mine is only worked superficially.

4. *Sampson.*—On the same lode, in some parts 5 yards wide, and very abundant in sulphates and carbonates; of

the same ley as those of *La Compañia*.   About 30 tons dressed on surface.

5. *La Inglaterra.*—On the *San Nicolas* lode, being very wide, consisting of pure galena, of a ley of 29·6 to 44·4 ounces silver per ton.   Though of little depth, blende has been already reached.

6. *Romeo.*—On the lode of *La Julieta*, a yard in width, consisting of ferrugineous ore; ley only 37 ounces per ton, but useful at the furnaces as a flux, owing to the quantity of oxide of iron it contains; depth five fathoms.

7. *La Francia, Copeton, Dilirio, Gran Mogul, La Pandorga, San Pedro Nolasco, &c.*—The last named mine has yielded some rich auriferous galenas, but is now abandoned.   All are more or less productive, and would yield good returns if properly worked.

In common with all the other mining districts of the Republic, Castaño may be described as yet virgin, and its hidden riches have not been explored as they ought.

On the Rio de Castaño, close to the mines, a new amalgamation establishment was being erected by Messrs. Ramon, Gay and Co., consisting of a grinding mill, with three tinas or vats for amalgamation.   There are also some dressing tables for the concentration of galenas and cold ores, to be sold in that state to the smelting works.   Being in course of construction, only five workmen were employed, and in two months from the date of my visit (February) the owners assured me the works would be in active operation.   The capital invested is about £350, and the mill will be capable of reducing about 30 cwts. of ore in 24 hours.

Water and pasture are plentiful in this district, and good roads can easily be made between the mines and the various reduction works. The mines are themselves situated at a considerable height in the mountains, but, once the ores have been brought down into the ravines, the remainder of the road is free of difficulty.

GOLD MINING DISTRICT OF GUALILAN. *

This celebrated gold mining district is far-famed and renowned for the wonderful quantity of the precious metal formerly extracted during the period of Spanish colonial rule in South America. It was discovered by a muleteer, named Juan Suarez, in the year 1751. Returning from one of his frequent visits to Chili, he lost a loaded pack mule in the neighbourhood, and, on seeking for the animal, found it resting on the spot now occupied by the *Pique* mine. To drive on the mule more conveniently, this man took up several stones, and placed them in his leathern apron, but was so struck with the great weight of one in particular, that he determined to keep it for further inspection. On his arrival at San Juan he consulted with a friend, and they discovered the stone to be impregnated with metallic gold. They immediately sought out the place at Gualilan, and soon enriched themselves before others knew of the discovery. Soon, however, this became known, and hundreds flocked to the spot, and, after a superficial search, discovered many mines, which yielded large quantities of gold, until the great drawbacks to all mining enterprises in South America—water and revolution—interrupted their prolific labours. The war of independence came on and all was abandoned.

There are three lodes, but only two were worked. These are from 6 to 60 feet in width, and occasionally, when they join and are walled by elvan courses, yield marvellous quantities of gold. Their direction is nearly north and south, and they have an underlie of 43° to the west, and are visible on the surface for a length of about 4,000 yards. The hills in which they are situated are detached from the principal chain of the Tontal range of which they are spurs, and are composed of limestone. The veins are accompanied, and at parts traversed by elvan courses, which, as I have said, improve the yield of gold where they come in contact with the lode. There are 14 mines in all (on the same veins), which were worked with great energy for many years after their discovery, until, at a depth of about 40 fathoms, more or less, they were inundated by copious springs of water, and the lower works had to be suspended.

The veinstuff extracted from the lodes is properly silver ore, holding chlorides of this metal, but with other combinations which render it extremely rich in metallic gold. There are large deposits of arsenical iron pyrites, holding a fair percentage of gold, but the former miners of the country were unable to extract the whole amount, and as it caused a considerable loss of mercury in the amalgamation process followed, the greater part was left in the mines, or thrown aside as useless. The quantity of this refuse ore is immense, and may be estimated at thousands of tons, intermingled with earth, stone, &c., but all of which holds gold in the proportion of not less than an ounce per ton.

After literally gutting the veins on the surface, and as far down as the water would permit, and leaving the workings choked up, the mines were abandoned by the original owners. Others followed, however, by whom new works were established, and a vertical shaft sunk to about 40 fathoms to drain the mines at their greatest depth.   But the means thus employed were entirely inefficient, and the mines were successively abandoned and renewed by new adventurers, who expended their limited resources and capital without securing any return for their money.

Señor Don Vicente Oros is the last who has undertaken the task, and, up to the present, contends against a thousand difficulties and drawbacks, without having succeeded in keeping the water effectually under. During a few days in which he was enabled to keep down the water level and to work at about four fathoms below it in the main shaft he extracted 12 tons of ore from an old level or gallery, the ley of which for gold was 5 ounces to the ton; but unfortunately the ropes of the lift for hoisting out the water in buckets broke, and one of the labourers was precipitated into the shaft and killed.   This and other drawbacks caused a suspension of the works, while steps were being taken for the erection of new appliances, more perfect than the former ones.   Señor Oros employed four men and a foreman, working with four horses and two large buckets, geared on to a whim, and in this way 750 gallons of water per hour were taken out; but this is of course inadequate, and cannot keep down the water so as to admit of working in the lower galleries.

One of these old mines,—*La Misnata*—not many years ago, yielded ores holding 96 ounces of gold, and 4,933 ounces of silver to the ton.

My attention had for years been directed to this district, having assayed its ores and obtained authentic information regarding its produce in olden times, but my time was too much occupied with the mines of Tontal and Castaño, and the reduction works at Hilario, to permit of my exploring it thoroughly. Within the last few months, however, I have succeeded in forming a limited company in England, with a capital of £75,000, to work these mines, and at the time of my visit, I found there an English staff of mining engineers, with several European miners, engaged upon preparatory works for developing their resources on a large scale. According to the last advices these are already far advanced, and 14 claims have been rehabilitated by a single adit, which will follow up the lodes from south to north. An appropriate site had also been selected for the erection of extensive reduction works, capable of grinding and "beneficiating" 100 tons of ore in twenty-four hours. The motive power for the whole will be a powerful steam engine, by means of which the old mines will be drained and the ore raised through a main shaft with the greatest economy.

The importance of these works, in the hands of an English company, can easily be understood; for, in the event of good returns being obtained (of which I have every confidence), they would probably extend their operations, and engage in new undertakings for the exploration and development of other gold fields of not less importance which exist in many of the provinces of the Republic.

It is for the National Government, therefore, to do all in its power towards assisting and protecting the interests of the company.

LA IGLESIA.

Fourteen leagues to the north of Gualilan is La Iglesia, a village of considerable importance for its lucerne fields and other produce. Messrs. Fonseca Brothers have erected reduction works there, based on the same system as that in practice at Castaño, but the furnaces are of better construction.

This establishment had not been more than 30 days in operation, and had produced 1,332 ounces of silver. Its object is to reduce ore extracted from the mining district of Salado, whose lodes, it is said, are a continuation of those of Castaño, although it is situate 30 leagues to the east.

The mining district of Salado was discovered in the year 1844, and about 20 leagues to the north of Iglesia, three mines are in work, or, more correctly, are temporarily suspended, since no ore was being extracted, owing (as I was told) to the want of blasting powder. The lodes are very hard and firm, and not more than a quarter of a yard in width, yielding in places orestuff holding about 493 ounces to the ton; but the average does not exceed 148 ounces. About 24 tons of ore of the latter ley was in the ore yard. Some of the stones show a considerable quantity of native silver, but these are not frequently found.

Good fire clays exist near the reduction works, and of which excellent fire bricks are made; at a little distance there is also a wide vein of oxide of iron, which serves as a flux in reducing the galenas. Firewood and water are both abundant.

The capital invested in these works does not amount to more than £1,000. Fourteen persons were employed.

GOLD MINING DISTRICT OF "GUACHI."

At twelve leagues north of the town of Jachal, in the high range of mountains to the west, is situate the celebrated mining district of Guachi. The road to this place is almost intransitable either on foot or horseback; and it was only after much labour and danger that I was able to ascend the cone-shaped mountain where the mines are, and which is 12,200 feet above the sea level. The mountain is isolated, and stands in the midst of a circular cordon of others also of great altitude and frightfully steep and rugged. It is traversed in all directions by veins of auriferous quartz, and horizontal beds holding more or less gold.

The name of this mountain is an Indian word, *Guachi*, signifying the mountain of gold; and tracing thus the origin of Gualilan, we find it also indicates the existence of the precious metal, as it means the "*Land of gold.*" The prefix *Gua* in the Huarpe tongue signifies gold, and wherever we find the name there are sure to be old gold mines or placer washings, worked by the aborigines, and, doubtless, still rich if modern appliances were brought to bear upon them.

The mines in Guachi are very old and much worked, and, according to tradition, a very large quantity of gold has been taken thence.

The principal vein runs from N.N.W. to S.S.E., and in some parts is 30 feet, and in others 60 feet in width, including an enormous centre wall of quartz and elvanite, which also contains more or less gold. The lode is visible on the surface for a length of over 100 yards, but the works are choked up in consequence of a great land-slip which took place many years since. This large vein is formed by the junction of two others—the "Risco" and the "Potro"—which in their turn are traversed by veins containing arsenical iron pyrites, almost at right angles; the lode is in beneficio at the points where these crossings take place.

From assays of orestuff taken from different parts I found the general ley did not exceed one ounce to the ton,

Thousands of tons of ore undoubtedly exist in the old subterranean workings, but the local difficulties present almost insuperable obstacles to their profitable working. In the first place, it would be impossible to get machinery to the foot of the mountain in the present state of the roads, and, in the second place, there is neither wood nor water at hand to supply the requirements of extensive operations in the mines, which are now almost entirely abandoned. I only found four men, who were employed in quarrying stones for the construction of a grinding mill, about to be erected by Don José Maria Suarez, with the intention of amalgamating the picked ores from the old mines.

At the foot of the mountain water is found in considerable abundance, but is highly charged with the sulphates of copper and iron, and consequently almost worthless for machinery, as the copper in solution would destroy all the iron work with which it might come in contact, and would soon destroy the wood as well; neither is it potable.

In the narrow and short ravine at the foot of the mountain are some placer washings of more than average richness. Here the *same* earth and gravel is washed year by year after the rains, with almost equally favourable results. This proves that the gold comes from some surface veins above, being carried down by the rains, and accumulates in the sands at the bottom of the ravine.

The geological formation of the mountain is favourable for gold, being micha-schist, gneiss, and syenite. Hornblende predominates, with crystalized felspathic rocks.

Potable water is obtained at a short distance from

the mines, but it is very limited in quantity, and not of the best description.

After the rains the poor people of the neighbourhood wash the earth in the bottom of the ravine, and sometimes find small nuggets of gold, and from this and other indications there would seem to be no doubt as to the existence of a vein or auriferous deposit on the slope of the adjacent Sierra, whence these pieces of the precious metal proceed.

Despite every effort to obtain information, I could hear of no such deposit, nor discover whence so much gold is annually derived.

I was not able to obtain any data as to the yearly production of gold by the placer washings.

CARBONIFEROUS DEPOSITS AT GUACO.

Five leagues to the north-east from the town of Jachal is a deposit or vein of coal (lignite) of considerable importance. Its width is about four feet, and is almost vertical; it is found in a yellow secondary sandstone formation, at the foot of a series of calcareous hills, isolated, and of recent formation and elevation. In these limestone rocks, I found some fossil remains of ammonites, belonging to the jurasic period, and in a very perfect state, within a few yards of the coal vein.

The following are the results of an analysis of several samples of the coal, whose specific gravity is 1·766 :—

Hygroscopic moisture	5.404	per cent.
Volatile combustible matter	27.266	,,
Fixed carbon	38·934	,,
Ash	28.396	,,
	100.000	

The ash principally consists of silicates, only one third

part being soluble in hydrochloric acid, and the solution contained iron, alumina, and lime.

This coal, I am of opinion, will be found in great abundance, and of much better quality, further out in the plains of Mogna. The vertical vein in question, discovered on the surface, was no doubt accidentally upheaved by the elevation of the calcareous mountains in the vicinity.

I will allude to this later on, when speaking of the mines of La Huerta.

At a short distance from the carboniferous deposit, and on the roadside from Jachal to Guaco, situated on the bank of a stream which passes through the limestone range already referred to, is a very important and copious thermal spring of hydro-sulphuretted water. Its temperature is about 80° Fah., and it is highly charged with hydro-sulphuric acid gas, depositing sulphur and sulphide of calcium on the neighbouring rocks. I believe this water to possess highly medicinal qualities, more especially for cutaneous diseases, and if once known and proper means of communication are provided from the centres of population, it will doubtless be appreciated and frequented by thousands of invalids.

MINING DISTRICT OF LA HUERTA.

About forty leagues westward from the capital (San Juan) are situated the mines of La Huerta, which were discovered in the years 1860-61. They are being worked with laudable perseverance and energy. The mountains in which the metallic veins are situate are high, rugged, and difficult of transit. Their geological formation consists of the primary rocks, including gneiss, syenite, and granite, with serpentine and mica-schist.

They form the termination of the range which branches from the Cordillera of Guandacol, and not from those of Famatina, as represented in existing maps of the country. By a palpable error, which has been confirmed by the map of Dr. Martin de Moussy, La Huerta has been placed north, ten degrees to the west of San Juan, whereas it is actually west ten degrees north of that town. During my tour of inspection through the mining districts, I have had the opportunity of correcting this and many other similar errors, which I will rectify in a new and general map of the Republic I have now in preparation, and which will be presented to the National Government.

The mines which are most actively in work in the district of La Huerta are as follows·—

That of *Santo Domingo*, in the ravine, or quebrada of the same name, is the oldest and most important in the district, employing the largest number of hands, 25 in all, together with 30 mules and two muleteers. There were eight workings in "*beneficio*," and ten in "*broceo*," which were not yielding productive ore; the deepest is about 70 fathoms from the surface. The main adit is pushed into the mountain for a distance of 275 yards eastwards, but was being worked very badly, the incline of the floor being inward instead of outward. Some yards from the internal extremity of the adit, its course was altered, in order to follow the vein, which was there turned northwards by a fault; but this was a mistake and the enterprise has been prejudiced seriously thereby. Winzes were also commenced, some working upwards and some downwards, but without either benefit or economy. The lower ones touched water at about 10 fathoms from floor of adit, which has paralysed further operations until pumping apparatus be brought to bear. It is a pity that a lode so abundant and rich as this should be thus comparatively sacrificed. Every effort should be made to effect communication with and drain the old workings from the surface of the mountain, since they are, I am told, in rich beneficio. Twenty-five fathoms have still to be driven before reaching the nearest point to effect this, and this work should be carried on before all others and without intermission. The deepest workings below the main adit, now in water, are in good beneficio, and it is certainly worth the trouble and expense to erect proper pumping machinery to remove this obstacle, but this should be directed by competent men, of which there is a sad lack in the mine. There were no scientific instruments in the mine, with the exception of a small pocket compass, about an inch in diameter, intended more as an ornamental pendant for a watch chain than for use in works of such importance and magnitude. The capital invested in the mine is about £21,000, and a single "alcance" or bunch of rich ore, extracted in July of last year, realised about £2,000. Surely a mine of this class should have a competent engineer to direct the necessary works, and the owners would then very soon secure those profitable returns which they have hitherto looked for in vain.

The actual produce is about 15 tons of ore per month, holding not less than 518 ounces of silver per ton in pure galena. About 30 tons of this class were on the surface, and more than 300 tons of inferior ore had been accumulated, holding from 111 to 148 ounces, which might be utilized if properly dressed and concentrated. The existing machinery there is not, however, sufficient for this purpose. There are two cast-iron edge runners, well suited for grinding the ores, and with these, and the round buddle, or percussion tables and jigging machines, a fair profit might be made out of this poor veinstuff. The ores extracted from the upper workings (not yet in communication with the adit) are galenas, with sulphides and antimonides of silver, while specks and thin lamina of native silver are occasionally observed. Two pieces of ore were recently taken out (and which will be sent to the Cordoba exhibition), weighing respectively 375 lbs. and 175 lbs., holding 970 ounces of silver to the ton.

The monthly cost or disbursements for work in the mine are about £110.

The reduction works belonging to the owners of this mine are not in operation and may be considered as almost abandoned, the furnaces being in such a dilapidated condition as to be useless for the treatment of ore without complete renovation. There are about 150 tons of slag on the ground, containing 25 per cent. of lead, with 17·26 ounces of silver to the ton. The site is good, but there is no probability of the re-establishment of the works so long as Messrs. Klappenbach reduce and purchase the ores extracted from the mine,—an arrangement advantageous for both parties.

The *Providencia* and *Petorca* mines are situated in the ravine of El Señor, and though not very productive, are worked to a profit owing to the high ley of their ores. This, on the average, is 1233·33 ounces of silver to the ton. Four men are employed.

The *San Antonio* mine is situated in the ravine of "Los Tres Amigos," and is fairly productive in good ore, composed of galena, with some chlorides of silver. The average ley is 616·66 ounces to the ton.

The *Bella Isaura* mine is the property of Messrs. Yanzi and Co., and is located in the ravine Argentina. It is exceedingly prolific of ore, being upon the junction of several lodes, which at some parts reach a width of eight yards. It is very inadequately worked, only three men and a foreman being employed. Nevertheless these are sufficient to extract from six to nine tons of ore in the month, consisting of galena, with carbonates and sulphates of lead, holding on the average from 47 to 54 ounces of silver to the ton. About 120 tons were dressed on the surface, containing about 44 ounces to the ton.

The *Mercedes* mine belongs to the San Juan Mining and Reduction Company, and is situated in the ravine of San Pedro. The vein is visible for over 3,000 feet, and the whole is in beneficio; its width is a yard and a half, but the ore, in pure galena, does not exceed six inches, holding about 207 ounces of silver to the ton. Formerly it was not worked very energetically, only some three men having been employed, who raised from three to six tons per month. At the date of my visit, however, operations at this mine were carried on upon a much more important scale, the following persons being employed, viz.: 1 manager, 1 foreman, 1 blacksmith, 10 miners, 10 labourers, and 1 cook. There were also seven mules. The water for domestic use is from a well sunk in the ravine and is brackish. A capital of about £1,000 has been appropriated for the completion of an adit, under the superintendence of Mr. J. C. Rogers, an intelligent North-American, who has had much experience as a miner in Mexico.

In this same ravine are some fine lodes of hematite iron ore, from two to three metres in width, in which pieces of silver ore have been found of the ley of 1,233 to 1,480 ounces to the ton. These lodes are visible on the surface for about a league.

The mine *Dolores* is located in the ravine of Los Poronguitos; it is a very good lode, consisting of pure galena with sulphides of silver, and the average ley of the ore is 202 ounces to the ton. Two miners were employed in making a survey.

The *Muy Escasa* mine is located in the ravine of El Quebrachito. Four men were employed; and from three to six tons of ore were raised monthly, consisting generally of sulphides and chlorides of silver, with a ley of 183 ounces to the ton.

The *Carlota* mine is in the same ravine as the preceding; the class of ore is similar, and three miners were employed.

The *Reyes, Baltazar*, and *Oriente* mines are situated in the ravine of Baltazar; very few workmen were employed, just sufficient in fact to keep them open. The three mines are upon the same lode, the ores from which hold about 98 ounces of silver to the ton. The vein is laid bare to a depth of 25 to 30 fathoms, and is of a very promising character. On several occasions stones have been found with particles of native silver. These mines have been most irregularly worked and destroyed on the surface by the *pirquineros*, or erratic miners.

The *Blanca, La Paz*, and *Marsellesa* mines are located in the ravines of Rosarito and Baltazar. They abound in galenas, with a ley of about 74 to 86 ounces of silver to the ton. Very few men were employed, and do little more than keep the mines open.

The *Rosarito* mine is in the ravine of the same name. It produces from 15 to 18 tons of ore per month, principally galena, sulphides, and chlorides, with some native silver. The average ley is 160 ounces to the ton. About nine tons were on the surface. Twenty-three men were employed. There is an adit from surface in communication with a shaft inclined at an angle of 40 degrees. This mine has produced some specimens of ore very similar to that extracted from the best mines of Chañarcillo (Chili). The works at the time of my visit were in full activity. In the lowest levels the lode had narrowed almost to nothing, and the surrounding rock was so hard as to make progress very slow indeed.

The *Celestina* and *Paraná* mines are on the same vein; eight miners and two labourers are employed, and the ores are very similar to those extracted from the preceding mine. There were 21 tons of ore on the surface, holding about 197 ounces of silver to the ton.

The above are the principal mines, but there are numerous others of less importance, but which show the extension of the veins, their direction, and the quality of their ores. It is calculated that there are 120 *pirquineros*, or erratic miners, in Los Marayes, and 100 more about La Huerta and Santo Domingo.

COPPER ORES.

I have received several specimens of these from veins existing in this district. Upon assaying, I have found them to contain from 25 to 65 per cent. of copper. In some, native copper was observable, but up to the present the lodes have not been discovered, or explored, the stones assayed having been only detatched masses found in the ravines. This branch of mining industry, when more facile means of transport are provided, will give great impulse to the prosperity of the province.

In the Cerro Morado, further to the west, the old auriferous quartz veins are all degenerated and firm in copper ores of good ley, which are certain to be utilized later on.

There are many fine lodes of galena in the district as yet unworked, because their ley is not high, but which later on are also sure to be utilized; therefore no doubt as to the duration of the mines and analogous industries in La Huerta need be entertained.

COAL DEPOSITS.

The coal extracted near the Marayes is of good quality, and the deposits, as far as I could judge, are of considerable extent, covering a surface of many leagues. Explorations have not been carried to a depth of more than ten feet, owing to the influx of water and the want of proper appliances for expelling it and sinking a deeper shaft. Still, judging by what is actually visible, it is not difficult to infer how very important these deposits, at present useless as a source of wealth, will, with the lapse of time, eventually become.

I have said useless for the present, because few in the country are competent to form an exact idea of their real value and importance. Previous Governments have either neglected or not had the desire or the power to assist explorers in this field of national wealth, nor bestow upon it the attention it deserved. The Paraguayan war, and other obstacles, have, moreover, interfered with the action of the Government in fields of enterprise for whose development peace and tranquillity are necessary. Ever since the year 1862, I have not ceased to direct the attention of the National Government to this branch of industry, which might if properly fostered make the Argentine Republic become the England of South America.

This is no idle illusion nor dream of the sanguine miner, but a conclusion based on my own experience, and in harmony with the results obtained in other South American countries. I am acquainted with the almost super-human efforts of Mr. Wheelwright, our great pioneer of progress in railways, how whilst engaged in inaugurating steam navigation on the Pacific, he sought almost in vain to make the Government and people of Chili understand that their coal deposits in Lota and Coronel were more valuable to them as a nation than the richest silver mines in Capiapo. Eventually awakened to the truth, our transandine neighbours have done everything in their power to develop those coal fields; and the result is, that hundreds of thousands of tons are now annually consumed in their smelting works, on their railways, and in their steamers, and of a quality but very little superior to that of Los Marayes in San Juan.

It has been generally taken for granted that our coal deposits in the Argentine Republic were of insignificant extent; but this is erroneous, as the result of my explorations will prove. I can confidently assert that coal exists, not only in Los Marayes and La Huerta, but certainly from Jachal to Los Llanos, and possibly as far as the city of Cordoba itself. I am well acquainted with the whole of the territory indicated; I have traversed it in various parts, and on each occasion my convictions have been confirmed. On the slope of the Cordillera, at five leagues from Jachal, as I have already stated in speaking of those regions, I discovered coal (lignite) on the surface, and (as shown by the analysis previously inserted) of a very fair quality, especially when it is considered that the specimens analysed were only from the surface.   Afterwards, I proceeded to the Sierra of La Huerta, northwards towards La Rioja, a distance of 90 miles, where I found the geological formation to be identical, thus confirming all the hopes and opinions I had long entertained on the subject.   In Los Marayes the same geological formation (sandstone and shales) is also observable, with its characteristic fossils, which are the guiding stars to geologists in explorations of this nature.

From Marayes I crossed eastwards to the Sierra of Los Llanos, a distance of 40 miles, afterwards through Chepes, Salana, Ulapes, &c., and, as I had expected, found there the same indications, the same fossils, and the same geological formation.   I have collected specimens of all these for examination at the forthcoming Cordoba Exhibition, and which will prove to those who understand it that true coal exists in the Argentine Republic.

It is, therefore, for the National Government to aid in utilizing this important discovery, and not allow it to rest in oblivion, as many others have been left for years. We have boring apparatus, and the men necessary to accomplish this great work—a work of infinite importance for the regeneration of the Republic.

The Central Argentine Railway to Cordoba will shortly be finished and opened to the public, and it is to be hoped that the line will be very soon extended to the northern provinces.   How important it would be if the Government could offer to the initiators of this grand enterprise a newly-discovered coal field alongside the iron track.   And even supposing that coal is only to be found at Chepes, in Los Llanos (where I am sure it exists), this would be a sufficient inducement to make

a branch line of railway to those now uncultivated
wastes, thereby putting an end for ever to the domination
of the guacho and the unsettled habits of the rural
population; such a course would render revolution almost impossible, and remedy those evils which, up to
the present, have so seriously retarded the progress and
development of those regions.

The consumption of this class of coal would be incredible, and a source of great profit to the Central
Argentine Railway Company. The latter is bound to
populate the immense territory conceded to it along the
whole length of its track. In many parts of this no fuel
exists even for the domestic requirements of the future
inhabitants; while the cities of Cordoba, Rosario, and
even Buenos Ayres, with their gas works, their manufactories, and their numerous steamers, would consume more
than the waggons could convey. The coal is well
adapted for those purposes, being what is called in
England "caking" or "binding" coal.

Its composition is as follows :—

Hygroscopic moisture	1.57	per cent.
Volatile combustible matter	39.80	,,
Fixed carbon	36.20	,,
Ash	22.43	,,
	100.00	

It should be stated that this specimen is almost from
the surface. I believe that coal of a better bituminous
class will be found at depth, and, at a still greater depth,
coal properly belonging to the secondary era, and perhaps antracite. The ammonites found in Jachal lead me
to conclude that such will be the case.

In addition to the sources of consumption indicated
above, there are others still more important for the

country. I have before referred to the immense lodes of oxide of iron situate in the immediate neighbourhood of Los Marayes. Almost inexhaustible quantities of this ore exist in the Cerros of La Huerta, and if, at some future time, iron smelting furnaces be erected there, it seems almost impossible to exaggerate the importance of the results which would follow.

It is out of my province to specify the advantages, or enumerate the various industries to which the development of our vast carboniferous and ferrugineous resources would give birth. But we have only to look to England, and ask to what she owes her commercial greatness, and maritime supremacy? The answer is simply,—"To her iron and her coal."

REDUCTION WORKS "EL ARGENTINO."

This establishment belongs to a limited company, formed in 1868, by Messrs. Klappenbach, of Buenos Ayres, for the working of mines and the reduction of ores in San Juan. It is situated in the quebrada, or valley of La Huerta, at a short distance from the mines, and was in course of construction from 1865 to 1868. It is now in full activity, and receives all the ores which are extracted from the mines of the district. For their reduction and treatment it has two reverberatory furnaces, five blast furnaces, and one refining furnace, capable of reducing from $2\frac{1}{2}$ to $3\frac{1}{2}$ tons of ore per diem. The following statement, showing the ores received and reduced up to the 1st of April, 1869, will furnish some idea of its importance :—

	Ore Reduced.		Ounces of Silver.
In 1865 (five months)	158,839℔	containing	21157.022
„ 1866	496,455	„	47108.474
„ 1867	636,489	„	56094.590
„ 1868	752,280	„	77144.016
„ 1869 (three months) ...	207,629	„	19196.858
Total..................	2,246,692℔	„	220700.960

The following further statement shows the product in bar silver :—

In 1865 (five months) ...	10700.4 ounces, value	£2651	0	0
„ 1866......................	35342.4	„	„	8756	0	0
„ 1867......................	45887.4	„	„	11368	10	0
„ 1868......................	63455.0	„	„	15720	16	8
„ 1869......................	15267.2	„	„	3782	3	4
Stock, April 1, 1869......	39973.86					

$$\text{210626.26} \qquad \text{£32,278} \quad 10 \quad 0$$

Add for loss by vola-
tilization .... } ... 10074.70

Total................220700.96

Seventy-nine persons were employed, at a cost of £250 per month, not including the mines and agencies of the company.

The labourers are paid from £1 13s. 4d. to £3 per month, and firewood costs from 11s. 8d. to 13s. 4d. for about $2\frac{1}{2}$ tons weight.

Flour is 16s. 8d. to 20s.; raisins, 13s. 4d. to 16s. 8d.; maize, 10s. to 13s. 4d.; and beef 20s. per cwt. The daily rations of the labourers consist of one pound of beef, one of flour, one of maize, and one of raisins.

The system of treatment and reduction of ores in practice is as follows :—

First operation,—Calcination. Each charge consists of 18 cwts., made up of 12 cwts. galena (Pb.S.) holding 60 per cent. lead and 93 ounces of silver to the ton; 6 cwts. "dry" ores, holding 15 per cent. lead and 186 ounces of silver to the ton. This operation lasts eight hours, the ore being calcined at a very low heat until the charge is desulphurised. It is then drawn from the furnace, and allowed to cool before passing through the second operation.

Second operation,—Slagging. The charge of calcined ore, 18 cwts., now converted into oxides of the metal present, with a little sulphate of lead, is thrown into an ordinary reverberatory furnace, and fired sharply for from four to six hours, until the whole mass is in a thoroughly liquid state, when it is tapped by a door at the back of the furnace; the result consists of silicates and oxides of lead, in which condition it is in readiness for the next operation.

Third operation,—Reduction. This operation is effected in vertical rectangular blast furnaces, measuring 1^m 60^c in height from the tuyére to the charging door, and 0^m 60^c broad, by 0^m 90^c in depth from breast to back, being more or less equal in size to the furnaces used in Viales, and formerly at Pontgibaud, Puy de Dôme (France). The mixture for this furnace consists of 77 per cent. of the slagged ores of the second operation, holding 50 per cent. of lead and 123 ounces of silver to the ton; oxide of iron is added in the proportion of 18 per cent., together with 5 per cent. of limestone. Of this mixture about $2\frac{1}{4}$ tons pass through a furnace in the 24 hours, producing 9 cwts. of rich lead, holding from $2\frac{1}{4}$ to $2\frac{1}{2}$ per cent. of silver. A small proportion of regulus and dross is also produced, and of course a large proportion of rich slags.

Fourth operation,—Cupellation. The German or Continental system (in contradistinction to the English system) is that used at La Huerta. The furnace is charged cold, with the lead in pigs, from the third operation, and is gradually fired, until the charge reaches a red heat. The fused mass is thus oxidised and impurities begin to rise to the surface, *i.e.*, copper, zinc, iron, antimony arsenic, sulphur, &c., which substances are drawn off by a slit cut into the bottom of the furnace, and form the *abstrich* of the Germans.

When all these impurities are removed, litharge proper, or *pure* oxide of lead, soon begins to form on the surface of the bath, and the temperature being increased to a red-white heat by means of a bellows, true cupellation commences. This operation continues, with the addition of fresh lead in pigs from the third operation, until the whole charge is worked off and oxidised, when the impure silver remains in a circular plate on the bottom of the furnace. When cool the plate is removed to be further treated.

Fifth operation,—Refining. This consists in submitting the impure silver from last operation to cupellation on a fine bone ash test, beaten into the bottom of a circular refining furnace about 3 feet in diameter. This absorbs nearly all the impurities—lead, iron, copper, &c.—with which the silver was previously contaminated. The conclusion of this operation is known by the quiescent and bright surface—like that of a mirror—presented by the liquid silver. This is then allowed to cool, when it is removed from the furnace, and is thus sent to market without further refining.

The slags produced in the third stage are returned to the furnace, either alone or with ore, as they generally hold 25 per cent. of lead and 18·2 to 23·6 ounces of silver to the ton. The lead in the slags exists almost entirely as a silicate, and is reduced with oxide of iron and crude limestone.

The *abstrich* and litharge, holding a small percentage of silver, produced at the commencement and the termination of the fourth operation, are generally passed through with slags and regulus in the third operation in the blast furnace. The litharge proper is reduced to metallic lead on the Scotch hearth; the lead thus produced holds from 3 to 4 ounces of silver to the ton.

The fuel consumed in these different operations is as follows:—In the first and second about $2\frac{1}{2}$ tons of ore are calcined and slagged in 24 hours, with two tons of wood, or say 73 per cent. of fuel. In the third $1\frac{3}{4}$ tons of slagged ore, or say $2\frac{1}{4}$ tons including fluxes, are reduced in 24 hours, with 6·75 cwts. of charcoal, or 15 per cent., and 6·75 cwts. of firewood, or other 15 per cent., making altogether 30 per cent. In the fourth $2\frac{1}{2}$ tons of wood are consumed to cupel more or less 7 tons of lead, or 33 per cent. of fuel. In the fifth 1 cwt. of firewood is consumed for every 740 ounces of silver. The duration of the blast furnaces, *i.e.*, of the parts exposed to the direct action of the fire, and which are lined with fire-bricks, is on the average 15 days. Their bottoms or hearths consist of 1 part of lime, $\frac{1}{2}$ of ground charcoal, and $2\frac{1}{2}$ of clay—all well mixed together, and tightly rammed.

The bottoms of the reverberatory or slagging furnaces last from three to six months, and are composed of 1 part of lime and 1 of clay.

Four men work each blast furnace, two during the day and two during the night; and six men in all are employed in attending the reverberatory furnaces, the shifts being taken by two at a time, who are in turn relieved by the others at intervals of eight hours.

The slags, even when smelted again and thrown aside, always hold from 15 to 18 per cent. of lead, and about three ounces of silver per ton.

The bottom of the cupelling furnace is composed of 4 parts of lime and 1 part of clay, well rammed in, little by little, and allowed to set and dry thoroughly, in order to avoid cracking and rising.

The average ley of the ores reduced in the establishment is about 238 ounces of silver to the ton, and 50 per cent. of lead. It is calculated that 12 per cent. of lead is volatilised and lost in the different operations, and 15 to 18 per cent. remains in the rejected slags; it is estimated about 3 to 6 ounces of silver per ton are thus also lost.

These details and data were furnished to me by the agent of the company, and are exact as respects the system in practice at the establishment.

The commercial results of the enterprise are, I have been assured, of a very satisfactory character, as is proved by the rapid extension of the works, both at the mines and in the reduction establishment, notwithstanding many local difficulties and drawbacks, the principal of these being the want of motive power to give sufficient blast to the furnaces, as the bellows at present in use, moved by mules, are quite inadequate, and are besides very inconstant, from the carelessness of the labourers, more especially at night.

In reference to the roads and means of communication in this province—a matter of vital consequence, not only to the mining industry, but to the general commercial prosperity of San Juan—I may state that few or no roads exist between the mining districts, nor are there any facilities for reaching the highways connecting those parts of the Republic with the lower provinces.

Everything has to be carried on muleback, at exorbitant rates of freight; but this last is not so serious a drawback as the impossibility of transporting ponderous machinery and implements to the mines and reduction establishments. From this very cause many important enterprises have already failed in San Juan, and this will continue to be the case so long as there are no carriage roads to facilitate transit.

I have had personal experience in this sense, having been compelled, in conveying machinery and tools to the reduction works at Hilario, to make a temporary road of 70 leagues, only transitable perhaps once or twice by our own carts, and this by taking an immense circuit to reach a point within a distance of 18 leagues in a direct line from the capital.

The cost of carrying the machinery from San Juan, exceeded that from England to San Juan. The large sums thus invested in road-making and freights might have been applied with great advantage to the development of mines and of districts still unexplored, and when a fixed sum alone is available for such operations, it is a serious drawback to be obliged to expend so considerable a portion in works leaving no immediate profit to the miner, and which ought to be executed by the government authorities.

It is therefore of cardinal importance to make a carriage road from San Juan to the valley of Barrial and Calingasta, which would accommodate the traffic by the road from Los Patos to Chili, and materially stimulate mining industry in Tontal and its neighbourhood.

From Barrial and Calingasta the construction of a road northwards to Castaño would be easy and inexpensive, and would accommodate the public traffic as far as Iglesia and Jachal. On the other hand, there is no difficulty in placing these points in contact with Uspallata and Mendoza, by making a road through the extensive plains of Leoncito and Yalguaras. I am informed that the National Government intends making the highway already decreed through Los Patos to the Chilian frontier; and once this is done, the chief expense will have been incurred, since the cost of the others, between Tontal, Calingasta, Castaño, Leoncito, and Uspallata, will not much exceed £6,000, the total distance being about 57 leagues,—that is, to join with the road from Mendoza to Uspallata, recommended in my report upon that province.

The roads from San Juan to the mining district of La Huerta are rather better, and at least transitable, but some repairs and alterations are needed to convert them into good carriage roads. Now that the new road from Cordoba is being made to Los Papagallos it is the more to be regretted that the remaining part between that point and San Juan should continue in so bad and wretched a condition. This road was made by the Government of the Province, to unite it with that of Rioja, but, being ill constructed, it has not produced the results expected. A bridge is required across the Rio Bermejo, as well as many deviations from its actual route, as much to avoid moving sandhills as to approach water at reasonable distances along the track. A road such as that from Rioja to Los Papagallos without water is useless.

With regard to the new road from Cordoba to Los Papagallos, I consider it my duty to offer here some practical remarks, founded upon a personal examination of its track.

From Chepes, in the Llanos, the projected road takes a direct line in a south-westerly direction to Los Papagallos, a place where only a small quantity of water, is to be found, and that of a very bad description. It passes over quicksands and through part of the salt marshes. I would respectfully submit to the National Government that this is a very undesirable direction, that it will make the road very costly, and that, after completion, it will be almost impossible to maintain it in a transitable state owing to the shifting sands. I would recommend that, from Chepes, it should deviate a little to the north to within a short distance of " Señor Queves," and thence proceed in a direct line westwards until a junction is made with the carriage highway coming from the north, *i.e.*, from Rioja to Los Papagallos. Then to follow the said highway southwards as far as Las Marayes (about four leagues), and, instead of going on to Las Papagallos, to take a south-westerly course, rounding the Sierra de las Marayes, and proceeding until the present road from San Juan is reached.

This road would have the following advantages:

1. It would avoid the shifting sands, salt marshes, and places having neither water nor pasture.

2. It would pass over firm ground, through good pasture lands, and places fairly populated and watered.

3. It would place the public traffic in more immediate contact with the mines and reduction works of La Huerta, passing through Las Marayes, possessing good water, and houses where refreshment might be had; and, above all, it would pass close to the precise spot where the coal deposit exists.

The circuit involved in adopting this route, as compared to the surveyed one, would not, I believe, on the whole exceed four leagues, and most important advantages would be gained equally by the public and Señor Rojo, the contractor.

Messrs. Klappenbach have already made about three leagues of carriage road from their establishment towards Las Marayes, and it would be very advisable to accord them a small subvention to continue it up to the latter poiut, as such a means of communication would immensely facilitate their traffic with the mines and the city of San Juan.*

* Since writing the above I am glad to say that my advice to the Government has been followed, and the alterations recommended ordered to be carried out, so that many of the disadvantages complained of exist no longer. The Provincial Government has also paid the Anglo-Argentine Company for some 28 leagues of carriage road made to their mines of San Juan. This is an instalment of a high road to the Castaño and Tontal districts.

PROVINCE OF LA RIOJA.

GENERAL PHYSICAL ASPECT, DESCRIPTION OF SOIL., CLIMATE, &c.

The province of Rioja is situated to the south of that of Catamarca, and to the north of San Juan, upon the easterly watershed of the great Cordillera of the Andes, in the mean between 28° 30′ south lat., and 67° 30′ and 71° west long. (Paris), embracing a superficies or area of 3,500 square leagues. To the west it touches Chili by the crest of the Andes; to the north it joins with Catamarca; to the east it is separated from Cordoba by a line which crosses the middle of the basin of the Salinas; to the south-east it touches San Luis, likewise by the Salinas and the series of pools which border them; to the south it joins with San Juan by the desert and by a line which intersects the Andes from south-east to north-west, between 30° and 31° lat.

The general aspect is that of an immense arid plain, extending to the foot of the Andes, and composed of sandy clay, white on the surface from salt, which abounds in the basin of the great Salinas, between the central ranges and the Cordilleras. This plain is a desert (*tra-*

vesia), almost without water, covered by mimosa of moderate height, with stunted arbustive and saline plants. In its midst to the south-east, which may be described as the dry bed of a former sea, runs an isolated mass of granitic rocks, comprising three parallel ranges of various heights. This is part of the Sierra of Los Llanos, partially wooded like the plain around its base, and which constitutes a system quite distinct, not only in orography, but also in Argentine ethnology. The various cordons of the Andes generally run from north to south; they enclose long valleys, of which the principal is that of Famatina, and at their final eastern ramifications have some streams and fertile gorges, celebrated for their rich agricultural products. Where water fails the province is a desert; wherever irrigation is possible an exuberant fertility covers the soil with a splendid vegetation. Some mountain gorges, watered by torrents, nourish some beautiful arborescent species.

One single river of some importance, but not navigable, waters a small part of the province of Rioja. This is the Vermejo, which, rising in the frozen plateaux of the Andes and among the eternal snows of the Bonéte, flows through the valley of the Jagué, enlarged by the torrents from the Valle Hermoso and those from the mountains which border the valley of Vinchina, and continuing its course towards the south, receives the surplus waters from the valley of Jachal, and is lost in the sandy plains bordering the lagoons of Guanacache, towards 32° S. lat. The volume of water which flows in this river is considerable during the summer, when storms are prevalent in the Cordillera, but is greatly reduced in winter and spring. The other watercourses in the province are unfortunately few in number, and very quickly absorbed by irrigation of the soil and for domestic use. The greater part of the mountains eastwards of Rioja, such as the chain of Velasco and the Llanos, belong to the gneiss and granitic formation; they are more prolific in springs than rivers, which, I need scarcely say, are exceedingly valuable for cattle.

All the orographic systems of Rioja, except that of the Sierra de los Llanos, belong to that of the Andes. We find first, in commencing at the west, the great plateau of the Cordillera, at a mean altitude of 4,000 metres, and its buttresses, which are also very elevated, and which constitute the Sierras del Jagué, Famatina, and, lastly, those of Velasco or of Rioja, the most easterly of all. This latter, towards the north, almost joins, by a transverse cordon, the Sierra de Famatina and the chains which are lost in the southern border, in the long travesia of Copocabana at Machigasta and the great Salinas of Belem and of Andalgalá. The Sierra de Mazan, to the north of the preceding, forms a little system in itself, which undulates into the chain of Ambato, but is partially separated from it by the gorge or ravine of La Cebila. The ramifications of the Andes, or secondary chains, are generally directed from north to south; those of Velasco, Famatina, and Jagué are bound to the mass of the Andes by a sort of transverse knot between the villages Angulos and Las Campanas, where rises the Cerro de Paiman and its dependencies.

The Sierra de la Rioja stands up as a wall, supporting an elongated plateau, of which the altitude is about 3,000 metres; that of Famatina is considerably the highest, which attains and surpasses even some of those of the Cordillera; its Nevado reaches nearly 6,200 metres, and El Espino, Bayo, &c., nearly as much; the Cerro Negro is 4,500. The valleys enclosed by these chains are of considerable altitude; those of Jagué and of Guandacol attain nearly 3,000 metres; that of Vinchina, 2,500; that of Famatina, 1,200; this last, the largest and most extensive of all, terminates by losing itself towards the south, on the plains of Los Llanos.

The Sierra of this name (Los Llanos) rises, as I have already said, as an isolated oval range, assuming a form resembling an "S" in the midst of an immense saline basin, and is of very recent elevation. It is composed of three cordons, which are designated respectively Costa Alta, Costa del Medio, and Costa Baja. Its altitude is not considerable,—about 3 to 400 metres at most. Its length is 31 leagues; its breadth 3 to 6. The surrounding plains are deserts, the soil being a dry sandy clay, and water is seldom found. Where it is possible, the natives dig wells, from which they obtain brackish water, but to which the people and animals easily become habituated.

The little valleys and ravines of the Sierra are fairly supplied with rivulets and some stunted trees. The cattle, bred in large numbers, feed there, as much on the leaves as on the coarse grass about.

The principal mass of the Cordillera is porphyric, its buttresses sandstone, limestone, clay-slate, and conglomerates, as the Famatina range; that of Velasco, with its dependencies, belong to the stratified rocks, as gneiss, quartz, mica-schist, granite, &c. That of Mazan is principally limestone. The formation of Los Llanos is of the same nature as that of Velasco.

The soil of the valleys of Rioja is composed, first, of a stratum of rounded flints and small boulders from the neighbouring mountains, and of which the depth is unknown; then a deposit more or less thick of argillaceous saline earth, as if all these valleys had formed the bottom of a great inland sea. This soil is much deeper as the valley stretches away from the foot of the mountains. On the plain, the argillaceous soil is very dry and singularly light, and rises in thick clouds of dust with the least wind, and which eventually becomes whirlwinds, assuming the shape of vast columns of considerable height. In the environs of the Sierra de Velasco and of its dependencies the soil is granitic, which retains moisture and is thus of a remarkably fertile nature when irrigated; the argillaceous and salt plains even become productive and fertile when it is possible to irrigate them. The digging of numerous wells with troughs, and the sinking of artesian wells, would do much to change the aspect of the deserts of Rioja. Few provinces are richer in gold, silver, nickel, iron, cobalt, rock crystal, marbles, steatites, &c. Salts of soda, chlorides, carbonates, nitrates, &c., are in abundance. By evaporation, in some parts, a residuum is obtained, which could be and is efficiently employed in the manufacture of gunpowder.

Earthquakes there are similar to those of the neighbouring provinces, but have never caused much destruction. That of 1849 may be cited, which was accompanied with great subterranean noise.

The climate is similar to that of Catamarca (of which later on). It scarcely ever freezes in the plain; from November to June the heat is very intense. The rains fall from December to March only. The autumn, winter, and spring are dry. The clearness of the sky is constant and bad weather is rare. In this province the winter is magnificent, from the purity of the atmosphere, the absence of wind, and the cool freshness of the air. In the valleys, however, of Guandacol and of Famatina there are short but sharp frosts. Snow sometimes covers the mountains, but does not remain long; the Nevado only retains its eternal snowy mantle, and often from its summit descend the refreshing winds so agreeable in the valleys.

The salubrity of the climate is perfect; the province has no special malady, except the goitre in some valleys, especially that of Famatina. Sometimes erruptive fevers are epidemic.

The nature of the soil restricts vegetation to arborescent mimosa on the plains, to the jumé (*lycium salsum*) on the salines, which become vigorous in the moist gorges; there the quebracho and algarrobo attain a good height. A fine acacia, called *visco*, furnishes wood for joiners' work : it is very close grained and magnificently veined, and could be exported with advantage. Among the mimosas, which grow in abundance, some species give a kind of gum similar to Arabic. As in the adjacent province of Catamarca, the vegetation depends on the moisture, natural or artificial, of the soil. The arid plains of the travesia have some immense forests, but sparse in trees, which are stunted and thorny, and to penetrate which it is necessary to wear leather garments, or shields to protect horse and rider from the thorns and prickly bushes which cover the ground. These woods are the continuation of the interminable forest, which covers the interior Argentine plain, for the whole length of the Andes, from the borders of the Rio Negro, in Patagonia, to the valley of Catamarca, for a distance of ten degrees in latitude.

Wherever irrigation is possible, the soil of Rioja is

extremely fertile, and the seasons so regular that the harvests are certain. The agricultural products are of superior quality. Throughout the Argentine Confederation there is not better wheat nor richer wine. The olive attains colossal dimensions, and yields excellent fruit; the peach, orange, and all fruit trees succeed there admirably. The cotton, cultivated only for local use, is of first quality for its length and strength of fibre. The town of Rioja is widely and justly reputed for its oranges; the valley of Famatina for its wines; also the slopes of the Arauco produce very good fruits, especially olives. The stony soil, and the little depth of the irrigated land of the valleys, seem to give agricultural productions of a rare superiority over those obtained from deeper and richer soil. The farmer of Rioja is industrious and methodical, but by no means enterprising, possessing only a certain amount of ability, which is proved by the excellence of his harvests. Unfortunately, from the scarcity of running water, agriculture is limited. This could be increased by a careful examination of the gorges of the mountains, and gathering there, in reservoirs, the waters during the rainy season; but the Riojanos do not possess the energy, activity, or capital to undertake such works.

Commerce is limited and confined to the neighbouring provinces and to Chili. Wines are sent to Catamarca, to Tucuman, and to Cordoba, and some even to the coast. It is unfortunate that these, from high freights, cannot reach the ports of the Parana, where they would advantageously replace the dry wines and foreign alcoholic imports from Europe, many of which are very inferior to those of Rioja. Cordoba takes the surplus flour, oranges, and dried fruits, the remaining produce is for local consumption.   Cattle are exported to Chili by the valleys of Copiapo and Huasco; also cheese and oranges. The most valuable article of export is the precious metals from Famatina, and in exchange they receive European manufactures.   The central point of commercial transactions is in the valley of this name, and the most populous of the country.

In consequence of the political troubles which agitated Rioja half a century ago, industrial pursuits are not very advanced, and few good workmen are found there; it is necessary to introduce improvements in the method of agriculture and increase the variety of its productions. The cochineal cactus abounds everywhere, and the insect, if carefully cultivated, would become an article of profitable export.   It would be quite possible to cultivate the mulberry tree and the silkworm, but, unfortunately, the cultivators of the soil are no innovators, and the immense difficulty attending the introduction of any new industry, although promising great advantages, is well known and justly dreaded.

The isolation of this province from the others by the salt and sandy deserts, and by the travesias which surround it, limits their principal communication with Rioja to troops of pack-mules, the rearing and maintenance of which is a source of prolific industry.   The communication with the coast is *viâ* the great Salinas, and the Sierra of Cordoba, by a route of 116 leagues, of which 60 are through a desert which has only a few scattered estancias or farm houses.   At 30 leagues from the capital this road turns the northern points of the Sierra de los Llanos, and quits the Salinas, which, at this place, are 14 leagues broad, and enters the Sierra de Cordoba by Pichana and Soto; the route through the Sierra de Cordoba is being made practicable for carriages, as already stated in speaking of San Juan. The intercourse with Santiago del Estero is rare; but communication is effected by passing the long travesias, where there is here and there a farm-house near some wells or pools of brackish water, and where hospitality never fails. The distance is 90 leagues. The communication with San Luis is by the south point of the Sierra de los Llanos, the hamlet of Las Liebres, and the quebrada of Santa Barbara; the distance by this route is 180 leagues. The roads most frequented are those of San Juan and Catamarca, which is the route followed by the national courier, carrying the mails of the west, and who rides from Mendoza to Tucuman. The route to Chili is by the valley of Vinchina, the Cordillera of Leoncito, or of the Peñon, and the Portezuelo Come-Caballo. From Famatina to Capiapo the journey may be made in six days, but generally occupies eight days. The Riojanos are excellent muleteers, and well accustomed to the Andine tracks, as well as those over the salt and arid plains. To these hardy children of the desert the longest and most difficult journeys seem a pleasure. All the routes on the plain could be made practicable for carriages if there were a sufficient number of wells, or watering places, with post-houses, established near them; the water could also be used for irrigating the land, and enclosures for lucerne could be maintained. Artesian wells in the district of the Llanos would change the entire aspect of the country and aid powerfully in its civilization. The diligence, carrying the national mails, now runs weekly from Cordoba to Rioja, *viâ* the Horqueta and Don Diego, where a branch line goes to Catamarca; hence passengers, mails, and specie may reach any of these points per coach in comparative comfort to former times when only sturdy mules were available.

The province of Rioja is now divided into seven departments,—the Capital, to the east of the Cerro de Valasco; Los Llanos, Costa-Arriba and Costa-Baja in the Sierra of this name; Costa de Arauco, to the northern point of the Sierra de Velasco, adjacent to Catamarca; Famatina, in the long valley of this name; Vinchina, between the Sierra of Famatina and the Andes; lastly, Guandacol, in the high valleys of the Andes, adjoining the province of San Juan.

The department of the capital comprises the town of Rioja (*Ciudad de Todos los Santos de la Nueva Rioja*) and its confines, which are very extended. The town of Rioja is situated in nearly 29° 20′ south lat., 69° 30′ west long. (Paris), and at an altitude of 510 metres on the plains, which commence at the foot of the Sierra de Velasco, and run into the quebrada of Sañagasta, whence rises a clear stream, which waters it and creates an oasis, full of shade and freshness, in the midst of the desert.

Founded in 1591, by Don Juan Ramirez de Velasco, Governor of Tucuman, it was primitively divided into 81 squares or blocks, viz., nine for the town, and then the necessary reserves for the convents of the Jesuits, Franciscans, Dominicans, the Fathers of Mercy, the parish churches, and those designated for cultivation.

Rioja was for a long time stationary in advancement; at the commencement of the 18th century it was no longer a village; at the beginning of the present century it assumed a degree of importance of which it has since been deprived. It is easy to see, from its public edifices and houses, &c., that it has been at one time much more prosperous than now. In fact, the place is surrounded with the remains of fine buildings, but they now need repair sadly; if the parish church, the convent of San Francisco and Santo-Domingo, the church of San Nicolas, maintained by the family of Gomez, are in good repair, the convent and church of Merced are in ruins. The mint, formerly in the college of the Jesuits, is now abandoned and closed. Although the buildings show a general decay, the vegetation is magnificent; the orange trees fill the air with fragrant perfumes; in the courts and gardens the fruit is exquisite, and fruit trees generally prosper in the granitic soil of this oasis, where irrigating canals from the river maintain a fertilising influence and freshness.

Commerce is very restricted here, and reduced almost to the export of wine and oranges to Cordoba in exchange for articles of European manufacture, imported *via* Buenos Ayres.

The future prosperity of Rioja must consist principally in the progress of agriculture and its mineral wealth, for its situation prevents it from becoming a depôt of commercial importance. It could be so only to some extent, after the opening of the railway from Rosario to Cordoba, and prolongation to Tucuman. It will be essential to maintain the present track for the muleteers on the road to Famatina, by the Sierra, in good repair, for this department is the richest and most important in the province. On the other side the communication between the provinces of Cuyo and those of the north can be made only by the town of Rioja or by Famatina, and this circumstance, when the country is better peopled, will make it a point necessary to be frequented by all the traffic from the north, south, and west.

The environs of Rioja are very fertile, where the waters of the river extend, but without this it is not productive, and unhappily this charming stream of water is not abundant enough, after having watered a square league of land, to extend further its fertilising influence. The quebrada, which leads to Sañogasta, a village of the Indians in the mountain, is well wooded, but would be more valuable if cleared and subjected to the cultivation of wheat and the vine. This gorge leads over the plateau of the Sierra de Velasco, where the only occupation possible for the inhabitants is the breeding of cattle.

The plain which surrounds the capital is covered with thinly scattered trees, and here the farmers are obliged to form reservoirs for water for their thirsty cattle. But through all the length of the Sierra there are natural springs and small streams, which supply the wants of small hamlets, as Tutcun and San Cristoval, and likewise numerous estancias, such as Ampiza, Estanque, Carrisal, Amilgancho, &c., which are the chief places of the district. The principal occupation of the inhabitants of those parts is the care of their flocks, but they cultivate, in small quantities, wheat, maize, vines, and some fruit trees.

The department of Famatina is very extensive, as it nearly touches the boundary of Catamarca to the north, and that of San Juan to the south. It is situate in the valley of this name, bounded on the west by the Sierra Nevado, and on the east by that of Velasco; the transverse range of Paiman, which unites these two chains to the north, encloses the two little valleys and villages of Los Campanas and Angulo. The first, at an altitude of 1,600 metres, is remarkable for some schistose stones, which, when struck with a hard substance, produce a sound resembling a bell. This canton is highly reputed for its agriculture, and especially for its excellent apples; it also produces very good wine. The latter is a miserable hamlet, and the land badly cultivated. These two valleys are separated from that of Famatina by the Portezuelo de la Aguadita, of which the altitude is, perhaps, 2,800 metres. At the Carrisal, lower down there is a church, then comes the extensive village of Famatina, which is not less than three leagues long, being a series of houses and fields, which finish only when the water so necessary for human existence is completely absorbed. There is also a modern church in this village, erected by the people themselves, under the direction of the curé. All this canton is populous and well cultivated, having abundant streams of water from the Nevado and other mountains to the west. It is 15 leagues from the church to the mines, following the stream westwards; the path is very bad, but could easily be improved. Between the village of Famatina and that of Chilecito (or Villa Argentina), the chief town in the department, extends a stony desert of six leagues, covered with a stunted vegetation, consisting of jarilla, retamo, &c.

The cultivation is similar to Chilecito, under the beneficial influence of irrigation. The altitude of the village is 1,100 metres. The olive, orange, and pomegranate produce well. A crowd of small and pretty hamlets enrich the environs of Chilecito; those are Sarmientos, San Nicolas, Anguinan, the ancient parish (for Chilecito is a modern creation), and Malligasta, a large village with a church and schools.

A little chain of granitic hills divides the valley of

Famatina from the Portezuelo de la Aguadita up to Nonogasta. The eastern portion is arid; nevertheless the two thriving villages of Pituil and of Tinimuqui are situate there. The scarcity of water in these eastern districts is much to be regretted, as the stratum of vegetable earth is very thick, and the soil would be exceedingly fertile, as the seasons are very regular. The same remark applies to the lower valley, which forms an immense travesia to the east, after leaving the villages of Nonogasta and Bichigasta. The former is renowned for its excellent wines, which are also produced in the latter, but in less abundance; they make here "patay," or bread from the fruit of the carob tree, of which there are an immense number around this spot and about the valley, here six leagues broad. At Bichigasta opens the valley of Guachin, which is well watered, and where also touches the route from Vinchina, *via* Sañogasta, which, crossing the chain of Famatina, leads to the valleys approaching the Andes.

Silver is exported from this district partly to Chili and partly to Cordoba. The town of Chilecito, or Villa Argentina, is superior in activity and commercial enterprise to the capital itself, being the most important depôt in the province, and the true centre of business with the interior.

Population, 1869.—City, 5,647 ; country, 43,312 ; total, 48,959.

MINERAL RESOURCES, &c.

The working of mines in this province dates from a period anterior to the independence of the Republic, a number of Spaniards having been settled in the rich territory of La Rioja for many years prior to the outbreak of the Hispano-American struggle. They did not, however, develop the mineral resources of the province as their real importance deserved. About. the year 1824, when an extraordinary rage for mining operations prevailed, works were inaugurated for the development of the mineral wealth of the Sierra de Famatina, but, unfortunately, this enthusiasm was not of long duration. The operations of a German Company, which sent its engineers and miners to Famatina, were paralysed by the political disturbances then so rife in the country, and the assassination of its agent and director, by order of the rebel chief Quirogo, formed the climax of its extinction.

The workings commenced by them, which were of considerable importance, are at present almost worthless, choked up as they are with debris and filled with water.

At a subsequent period, when the country was in the enjoyment of a short interval of tranquillity, numerous miners from Chili and Peru, as well as a few natives, carried on important works, resulting in the production of a large quantity of bar silver, but, on the recurrence of revolutions and political disturbances, these were in their turn compelled to abandon their labours.

Mining is now much neglected there, and very few mines are in active work; but of late there is a tendency to re-organise enterprises amongst the few existing capitalists, and to develope the immense mineral wealth still hidden away in the celebrated Cerros Negro and Mejicano of Famatina.

I must classify the mines of Famatina as the richest in the Republic, and its ores as holding the largest percentage of silver. The lodes, it is true, are not so wide as those found in other places, but, from their great number and extent, I am convinced that Famatina is not surpassed for abundance of ore by any other mineral district in the country. The ley of its ores and their composition are of the most promising character, and afford substantial grounds for believing that rich results will reward operations at greater depth. Nevertheless, as is the case in all human affairs, there are drawbacks and difficulties which can only be surmounted by large capital, perseverance, energy, and especially mining skill.

The roads leading to Cerro Negro, in their present state, are quite intransitable, and it was with great labour I managed to reach the mines, both from the roughness of the ground and the height at which some of them are situated,—13,000 feet above the level of the sea.

There is absolutely neither wood nor other fuel in the vicinity, and this has to be conveyed from distant ravines at considerable cost. There is plenty of pasture and water, but the cold, even during the summer, and the *puna*, or rarefaction of the atmosphere owing to the great elevation, are most serious obstacles and almost insuperable for persons not accustomed to such altitudes. The miners of those regions alone can endure the rigours of nature at these great heights, which upon them appear to have no effect whatever.

From January to March the rainfall in Famatina is very heavy, causing the miners to suspend their labours, and descend (those of the Cerro Negro) to the town. They then generally pick and classify the ores extracted during the rest of the year, and the interval of the rainy season is occupied in grinding and reducing them. The means employed for this purpose are the crude systems of " *Patio* " and " *Repaso* " (so well known in Mexico), entailing the loss of a great part of the silver, and of nearly the whole of the mercury used for its extraction. To this, and the system of beneficio in practice in Famatina, I will refer later on in its proper place.

The mining district of Famatina may be divided into two sections, that of Cerro Negro (Black Mountain), and that of Mejicana (the Mexican).

The mines of Cerro Negro are scattered about at short distances, in rugged and lofty mountains, covering about three leagues in circumference, and are only accessible by narrow defiles and overhanging precipices, more resembling guanaco or deer tracks than ordinary roads. There are some exceedingly dangerous declivities and ascents, at places presenting abysses of more than 1,000 feet in perpendicular depth. It needs a strong nerve and firm step on the part of both man and mule to pass these points either on foot or mounted. How must it be, then, with heavy loads of ore or provisions for the mines? Before operations on a commensurate scale can be inaguarated it would be necessary to spend about £2,000, to provide the district with roads transitable by pack mules, and as for carriage roads I consider their construction, except in some parts, almost impracticable.

AURIFEROUS DISTRICT.

This is situated about seven leagues from the town of Famatina (Chilecito), in the Cerro Negro, at 10,250 feet above the sea level. There is a total absence of firewood, but abundance of water and pasture. It consists of auriferous lodes, the principal not exceeding three in number, much worked out and exhausted. Their deepest workings are about 30 fathoms in vertical depth, and are full of water and debris. The lodes vary in width from half-a-yard to a yard; and almost all of them consist of arsenical iron pyrites, holding a considerable quantity of gold, which cannot, however, be extracted by the crude systems of amalgamation practised in those regions.

The black oxide of manganese and iron abounds, and I found considerable quantities laying about on all sides. A sample of these ores, taken without selection, gave a ley of six ounces of gold to the ton, a yield which would make the extraction and reduction of the ore very profitable; but, owing to the difficulties of transport, the result of any enterprise in this direction would be extremely problematical from a commercial point of view. The greater part of the veins are very narrow, and their working on a large scale would not be sufficiently if at all remunerative.

SILVER MINES OF CERRO NEGRO.

Almost without a single exception, all the celebrated silver mines are now under water or choked up with debris, and are irregularly worked and exhausted on the surface. It is impossible to enter or inspect them internally; and I could, therefore, only examine the surface and take cognizance of the remains of their former greatness and wealth. From the thousands of tons of *desmontes*, or refuse orestuff, which surround them, together with the numerous openings, adits, and shafts which are observable, it is reasonable to believe that at one time they must have been of great richness and importance. In their present state, however, they are worthless, and could only be rendered of commercial value by constructing adits or employing machinery to remove the water. The form of the hills, and their immense altitude, are favourable to draining off the water by means of adits, and which would probably cut the veins at an enormous depth, at once proving their richness and extent. But the driving of such adits would demand the expenditure of large sums of money before beneficial results could be obtained; and as neither the necessary capital nor skill exists in Famatina, there is no hope of this being carried out, unless indeed by the aid of foreign capital and energy. Nevertheless, the district is so extensive, and so extraordinarily metalliferous, that erratic miners (pirquineros), working upon the surface, which is traversed at every angle and in every possible direction by hundreds of virgin lodes, extract ore of such richness that the annual product from this source alone is not less than 59,200 ounces, representing an approximate value of about £16,000.

The only mining works which I found in the Cerro Negro were those of Señor Uladislao Gordillo, who followed up a narrow lode of very rich ore—almost semi-bar silver—but at a depth of only $5\frac{1}{2}$ fathoms it ceased to be productive and water invaded the workings. Energetic efforts were being made to remove the latter by means of leathern bags, but without effect, as the locality is unfavourable from the continuous and copious rains falling at that season of the year. Only four men were employed.

Oxide of iron is found in wonderful abundance in the Cerro Negro, and a single lode—the " San Andres "—is visible for upwards of 2,000 yards, having a width of six feet, and consisting of almost pure hematite with not less than 70 per cent. of iron. If, in the future, the industry of iron smelting should be established in this country, the deposits of Cerro Negro are destined to become of first importance and to be of the greatest interest and value.

Passing from the Cerro Negro to Mejicana, the mining district of La Caldera is reached, in which there are only two mining establishments—one belonging to Señor Don Carlos Angel and the other to Señor D. Francisco Bascuñan. The first is situated upon a lode of nine inches in width, yielding ore of an average ley of not less than 1,223 ounces to the ton. Rich masses of native silver are frequently extracted. This mine belonged to Señor Cabrera, and was sold to Señor Angel a few days previous to my visit for about £670.

Bascuñan's mine, *La Esperanza*, is on a narrow vein from two to three inches in width, but yielding very rich ore, almost semi-bar silver. From this vein, with my own hands, I broke off a piece of ore 10 inches square by two thick, holding so much native silver that the stone could hardly be broken without a chisel. The ley of a general sample does not, however, exceed 370 ounces to the ton. Nine men were employed, and the lowest workings not more than 15 fathoms in vertical depth.

MINING DISTRICT OF LA MEJICANA.

From Caldera, I proceeded to the Cerro de la Mejicana, which is at the foot of the Nevado de Famatina, whose height, according to Naranjo, is 20,680 feet above the level of the sea. The snow on its summit is perpetual, and the mines, which are situated around and upon its base, are also completely covered with snow during intervals in the winter. The highest mine is at an elevation of 16,532 feet, and has in its time been exceedingly rich, yielding large quantities of semi-bar silver. It was sold to Señor Don Rafael Fraguiero for about £4,000; but, subsequently, chiefly from want of good management and the falling in of the roof, it ceased to be productive. This mine is called *La Espina*, and was abandoned at the time of my visit.

From its greater altitude and different formation, the Cerro de la Mejicana is not, as respects water, in the same disadvantageous position as the Cerro Negro; it is dry in the lowest workings of its mines, none of which, however, are of greater vertical depth than 25 fathoms, and cannot, therefore, be described as other than superficial. The summer rains never interfere with the mines, some of which I found in active operation.

The *Rincon de la Mejicana* mine was formerly worked for gold. It was choked up with earth, but has been recently opened by Don Carlos Angel. The vein had not yet been cut in beneficio when I visited the mine.

The *Verdiona* mine, which was also renowned for its richness, is now choked up with debris, and has been abandoned for many years. I was unable to enter the galleries or workings, for when mines have been abandoned a few years in La Mejicana their entrances are filled up with snow and sand from the surface, forming a frozen mass for 10 to 12 yards down, and of such hardness that it cannot be broken without blasting. As a consequence, mines are soon choked up and their entrances completely obstructed.

There is a large quantity of ore on the surface, principally sulpho-arsenides of iron, from which I took a sample, yielding about 46 ounces of silver (with gold) per ton; there were also traces of copper, but none of nickel, which these ores were believed to contain.

The *Compañia* mine, next after the *Verdiona*, belongs

to Don Vicente Gomez, and was in active operation. There were 13 men employed, and about six tons of ore were dressed on the surface, the second class holding 209 ounces of silver and about three-quarters of an ounce of gold to the ton. The first class ore gives 1,529 ounces of silver and $1\frac{1}{2}$ ounces of gold to the ton. The vein is the same as that on which the *Verdiona* mine is situated, and, being in active work, I had the opportunity of inspecting the lowest levels and seeing the lode in depth. It varies greatly in width, from $\frac{1}{2}$ to $1\frac{1}{2}$ yards; it contains a large proportion of arsenical iron pyrites, with a poor ley for silver and gold. The lode, nevertheless, promises well at greater depth, and a marked improvement is observable in it from the surface to the lowest levels. These are not, however, over 20 fathoms in vertical depth.

There is a large quantity of poor ores on the surface, holding a fair percentage of copper and some gold, which, perhaps, might be profitably reduced in suitable furnaces, and produce copper regulus holding gold and silver, if mixed with ores having a good ley of these metals.

The *Upulungo* mine is contiguous to the *Campañia*, and belongs to Don Ricardo Valdez. This mine is said to be very rich, but its mouth being choked up with debris and snow, I was unable to explore it internally. The owner of the *Compañia* had commenced a lawsuit against Valdez for having penetrated from a lower level in his mine into the vein of the *Compañia*, where ores holding a very large percentage of silver and gold were extracted. The mine had not been worked for over a year.

The *Urquiza* mine is situated further south, and

belongs to Don Ignacio Moreno. Five men were employed; the vein is very productive, about two yards in width, consisting of semi-warm ores (chlorides with sulpho-antimonides) holding an average ley of about 98 ounces of silver to the ton.

The *Chilena* mine is situated in the Cerro del Tigre, at a short distance from the *Urquiza*, and belongs to the same proprietor. Four men were employed, working on the surface in an open cutting. The lode is productive, being two yards in width, and the ley of the ores varies from 49 to 74 ounces of silver to the ton.

There are five other veins or mines in La Mejicana, all of which are out of work and so choked up with earth as to prevent any internal exploration. Their importance is manifest from superficial appearances, and they are almost identical with those of *La Compañia*. Without exception, they have all been worked upon the surface only, and none of them carried deep enough to prove their ultimate richness. The late Don Pantaleon Garcia inagurated the only work calculated to solve the problem, *i.e.*, an adit to cut all the veins of La Mejicana on a level with the bottom of the ravine. This is a very important but ill-directed undertaking.

The mouth of the adit is below, in the ravine, at a distance of about 100 yards from the *Compañia* mine, and at a vertical depth of 80 to 90 yards from the surface of the latter. It is ten feet high by six in width, but badly constructed, the main wooden props having already broken and given way owing to the great weight of the superincumbent earth and stones. Not more than 23 yards now remain open, the total length of the adit being about 50 yards. The expenditure on this enterprise was about £8,500, subscribed by an association, but the work done does not represent a higher sum than £2,500.

I do not consider the direction of this adit to be the true or best one for cutting all the veins of La Mejicana, but at the length of 100 yards, inwards, its course might be altered, taking two angles, one to the left and another to the right, by which means many gold and silver veins would be cut; for, at a short distance lower down in the ravine, are found old gold mines of good ley when formerly worked. These are now choked with earth and water, but the principal lodes go into and bury themselves in La Mejicana, and it is therefore very probable that they would be cut by the adit.

About five leagues lower down in the ravine are some old placer washings, but they are now without commercial value, unless worked on a large scale, as is done in California, that is to say, washing 300 tons a day.

The cost of firewood in this district is £1 9s. per ton (20 cwt.); beef, $1\frac{1}{2}$d. per lb.; maize, 10s. to 16s. 8d. per fanega (300 lb.); dry figs, $\frac{1}{2}$d. per lb; nuts, $\frac{1}{2}$d. per lb.; and the freight charge on provisions from the town to the mines 3s. 4d. per mule load of 380 lbs.

REDUCTION ESTABLISHMENTS.

In Famatina there are at present three amalgamation works in full activity, and two in preparation with two others stopped; for copper smelting, one; for lead, one.

The first establishment nearest the town is *La Compañia*, and belongs to Messrs. Carlos Angel and Francisco Alvarez. It is situated about one mile from the village of Famatina, to the W.N.W., on the road to the Cerro Negro. The ores are amalgamated by the new system of Kronske, recently introduced from Copiapo (Chili) by a young Chilian associate of the proprietors. It consists of four large barrels, capable of reducing nine tons of ore in 24 hours, and a vat for washing; the motive power for the whole being a vertical overshot water-wheel 12 feet in diameter and 5 feet breast. The system is simple and efficacious. The process of reduction only lasts from four to six hours, and the ley of silver and gold held by the ore is almost entirely extracted.

The great advantage of this system is the reduction by it of " cold " ores, or those whose ley previously could only be extracted by means of smelting. As the details of the process were communicated to me under reserve, I am precluded from entering into particulars, and limit myself to stating that, with the use of mercury, sulphuric acid, sulphate of copper, salt, zinc, lead, and metallic copper, assisted by steam, the ley of the ore is extracted; that is to say, when the operation is well managed and the class of ore is properly determined by analysis. When, however, these essential particulars are disregarded the results are of a very negative character.

In such cases, the mercury flours, and being thus decomposed is altogether lost. At the beginning many impediments were encountered at " *La Compañia* " from this cause, as the young Chilian, before referred to, who had charge of the machinery, did not possess the necessary knowledge for the analyzation of ores, and was ignorant of the treatment to which the different classes should be subjected.

As the machinery had been erected a very short time previous to my visit, only a few tons of tailings had been beneficiated. These are found in large quantities on

the spot, which had formerly been the site of an old reduction works on the South American system, or the
direct amalgamation of " warm " ores. These tailings,
(which are at least 1,800 tons) hold about 35 ounces of
silver to the ton. In the experiments tried upon a few
tons, about 518 ounces of fine silver had been extracted,
and, judging by these results, this enterprise should prove
most lucrative. The tailings only cost about 10s. per
ton. The scarcity of labour, and especially of skilled
workmen, renders it very difficult to carry out metallurgical operations requiring such delicacy and precision
in their manipulation.

Firewood abounds in the vicinity, and costs 6s. 8d.
per perch of 16 cubic yards. Water and pasture are
abundant. The freight of the ore from mines to the
establishment is about 23s. per ton.

The capital invested up to the date of my visit was
about £2,000, but £1,000 more would be required to
complete the establishment, and place it in a position to
work with profit.

The *Durazno* establishment, belonging to Don Uladislao Gordillo, is situated about three leagues further
westward, on the same stream as the "Compañia," and
on the road to the Cerro Negro. This is the oldest reducing works in Famatina, but operations there were
almost suspended at the time of my visit, as only a little
ore, extracted by the owner from his mines, was being
treated. It consists of a well-mounted Chilian mill or
edge-runner of granite, and two barrels, the latter almost
totally unserviceable. In these, attempts were being
made to extract silver by using sulphate of copper in
solution, similar to the Compañia, but without effect.
The site is admirably adapted for works on a large

scale as it possesses sufficient water for machinery equal to 50-horse power; abundance of firewood and pasture also exists.

There are about 1,500 tons of old tailings lying here, and the remains of the old *patio*, or Mexican system of amalgamation, are plainly discernable. This system was used in former years, by the first miners, but is now almost becoming obsolete. From the mines the carriage of ores to this place is 17s. per ton, and the distance from Cerro Negro is about seven leagues, or a day's journey for loaded pack mules.

Two other establishments exist on the same stream, called respectively the *Candelaria*, where a Chilian mill forms the only machinery erected, and the *San Rafael*; both are in a state of complete dilapidation, and almost abandoned as respects metalurgical operations.

A Frenchman, however, was about to erect some new machinery at *San Rafael*.

About six leagues north from the village of Chilecito, are situated the following works:

The *Corrales* belonging to Don José Barros Casales, located close by the road descending from *La Mejicana*, on an abundant stream of water, and distant seven leagues from the mines. Its machinery consists of four barrels, each capable of holding 3 cwts. of ore, and one Chilian mill, all driven by two water-wheels. There were about 390 tons of tailings lying about in heaps, holding about 24 ounces of silver to the ton. Some ores were being treated, but as they contained a large proportion of sulpho-antimonide of silver, the results were not satisfactory. The mercury was floured, sickened, and consequently lost. I was assured that the loss of this reagent was equal to 700 per cent, or for every 740 ounces of silver extracted, about 5,180 ounces of mercury were lost.

Four men were employed, and the system in practice was the old one of treating the ore by simple amalgamation, without calcination or the use of reagents. A German, Mr. Theodore Schröder, had rented the works, in partnership with a countryman of his recently from Copiapo, Mr. Charles Silverbach, a practical man, apparently well acquainted with the new Kronske system of amalgamation. I believe their efforts will prove successful and profitable results be obtained. Barros Casales had invested about £1,150 in the construction of the works.

The *Escaleras* reducing establishment is on the same road, a league lower down the stream; it belongs to Messrs. Soage Hermanos, and is at present rented to Don Ignacio Moreno, and consists of a Chilian grinding mill and four barrels, each capable of working off 3 cwts. of ore at a charge.

The system in practice here differs from those followed in the other establishments, inasmuch as the " cold " ores are calcined with salt in a reverberatory furnace, thus chlorinising a great part of the silver, and converting it into a state fitted for amalgamation without the loss of so large a quantity of mercury; in these works the loss does not exceed 100 per cent. But even this serious disadvantage could be obviated by mixing the ores with iron or copper pyrites, and calcining them carefully on the Freyberg system. I explained this to Señor Moreno, who, more intelligent than his neighbours, proposed making experiments, and it is to be hoped his efforts in this direction will prove successful. The works of this gentleman are the best arranged and managed of any in

Famatina. In the year 1868, he extracted about 3,700 ounces of silver, and from January to March, 1869, he had obtained 740 ounces. It is about three leagues distant from the Villa de Famatina. Eight men are employed, and the capital invested is about £1,166, including mines and reduction works. About 13½ tons of ore were in the ore yard, dressed, holding 100 ounces, and about 150 tons of tailings, holding 30 ounces to the ton.

The great loss of mercury sustained in the reduction works in Famatina, is the chief cause of their non-success. This article costs there about 6s. 8d. per lb., and if we take into account the quantity of silver produced annually, and the proportion which is wasted or irretrievably lost, together with the average loss of 400 per cent. of mercury, it will be seen that the total is a very serious and important figure to their debit.

I have been enabled to ascertain, from data collected amongst the traders who purchase bar-silver from " pirquineros " and reduction works in the district, that the annual quantity is not less than 59,200 ounces. Taking the loss on this at 40 per cent. and 400 per cent. of mercury, the total would represent 23,680 ounces of silver, whose value there would be about £6,500, and 16,000 lbs., or a further £5,400, in mercury, all of which is sacrificed to ignorance and carelessness.

COPPER SMELTING WORKS OF VALDEZ & ALVARADO.

These are located in the village of Famatina, and consist of a reverberatory furnace for smelting argentiferous copper ores and forming regulus. The furnace is 14 feet long by 7 wide, inside measurement, and its stack is 14 feet in height. It is badly constructed of refractory silicious sandstone, not at all suitable for copper furnaces.

The works had only been three months in operation, and had produced 100 tons of regulus with 10.30 per cent. of copper, 0.62 per cent. of silver, and 0.003 per cent. of gold. These figures show that the reduction process had not been properly directed, and that the percentage of copper is too low to leave a profit on the exportation of the regulus. A remittance sent to Europe, I was informed by Señor Alvarado, only realized £21 per ton, a price totally inadequate to cover even the cost of carriage, &c. The ores are exceedingly ferrugineous, and highly charged with sulphur, arsenic, and antimony. The greater part of these substances ought to be removed by repeated calcination, and the oxidised residuum, smelted with the addition of silica (sand or quartz), to get rid of the excess of iron present, forming a silicate thereof, and producing copper regulus of a high ley, and with a much larger percentage of silver and gold.

Instead of doing this, oxide of iron, in the proportion of 25 per cent., is *added* to the charge, which of course combines with the sulphur, arsenic, and antimony already existing in excess in the ores, and forming a ferrugineous regulus of the latter, thereby reduces the ley for copper and the precious metals.

The following ores were in stock, viz., 75 tons of tailings, holding 24 ounces to the ton; 60 tons, holding 60 ounces of silver to the ton; about 48 tons of regulus, holding 25 ounces of silver to the ton, with a trace of gold.

Owing to litigation amongst the partners, the works were paralysed at the time of my visit.

REDUCTION OF ARGENTIFEROUS LEAD ORES.

The works of Lancel Marozovski and Co., constructed for the reduction of plumbiferous ores, are located seven leagues to the south of the town of Famatina. They consist of a reverberatory furnace, a blast furnace and one for refining, identical with those of La Huerta, in San Juan. Unfortunately this enterprise was unsuccessful for want of proper ores, *i.e.*, galena, or sulphates or carbonates of lead, and in consequence failure ensued before reduction operations had properly commenced. They are now stopped and abandoned. Their cost was £2,300. Firewood and water are abundant. Firebricks of a very refractory and superior description had been manufactured of clay found in the neighbourhood.

The greater part of the silver extracted in Famatina owes its origin to the pirquineros—poor erratic miners—who go to the Sierra with their saddle-bags full of provisions, and, so long as these last, work upon the surface of the numerous virgin veins and others already discovered. When they have filled their bags with ores of a high ley—at times semi-bar silver—they immediately descend to their *ranchos*, or mud dwellings, where, assisted by their wives and children, they grind those fragments of ore between two stones after the fashion of the Indians. The ore is then calcined in earthen pots with salt, and, when in fit state for amalgamation, is removed, to be thrown upon the "*patio*," or circular enclosure on the floor, paved with flat stones. Water and sulphate of copper (*magistral*) being added, the mass is trodden under foot and mixed and stirred incessantly for several days, in contact with mercury, until the "beneficio" is known to be complete and the silver is all taken up in the amalgam. The mass is then washed in large iron pots, and the particles of mercury collected carefully and strained through a canvas cloth. The silver amalgam remains, and the mercury which passes through the cloth serves for subsequent use. The *pella*, or amalgam, is afterwards burned in the fire, until the silver remains pure and white, in which process almost the whole of the mercury is lost, the proportion being as six to one.

About 80 pirquineros were engaged in these primitive operations, and between them and the reduction works already referred to about 59,200 ounces of silver are produced annually, the value of which may be estimated at £16,000.

The celebrated nickel mine—*La Solitaria*—discovered by the brothers Erdmann (Germans), in the year 1845, is situated in the district of Binchina, and in the ravine of Jagué.

These gentlemen came from Copiapó, where they had metallurgical and mining establishments, but had only been working the nickel lode for a few months when they were called upon to appear before the then Governor of Rioja, who informed them that he had received instructions and commands from the tyrant Rosas, prohibiting foreigners working mines in the country, and peremptorily ordered them to leave the Republic within a specified time.

Messrs. Erdmann had therefore no other course open to them but to sell the mine, which they did for £1,000, and went back to Chili. Learning some years afterwards (when Rosas no longer governed) that the mine was abandoned, they returned to find it full of water and the lode gutted on the surface. Nevertheless, with considerable perseverance and energy, they succeeded in removing the water sufficiently to reach the lower levels, but there the vein was found less than a foot in width, and, from the quantity of water still present and coming into the mine, the enterprise could not be profitably followed up. The mine was consequently abandoned by them a second time, and is now full of water.

During the few months this mine was worked by Messrs. Erdmann, (in the beginning) they extracted ores to the value of £8,000. The ore is an arsenide, holding 36 per cent. of nickel, which is increased to 60 per cent. by calcination. Notwithstanding careful search having been made in all directions for new beneficio on the surface of the lode, no indications of ore have been discovered. The lode on the surface, and to a depth of 15 fathoms, was a yard in width, in pure ore, but it is now regarded as having been a bunch confined to one spot, since they have not been able to find more in any other direction. It was generally believed that the Famatina ores of the Cerro Mejicana contained nickel in large quantities, but not even traces have been found in the numerous samples examined, whether by myself, or Señor Schickendantz, the metallurgical chemist of Mr. Lafone's establishment in Pilciao. I am not surprised that such a belief should be prevalent amongst the miners, since it is easy to be misled and deceived by the cupriferous arsenides of iron of Famatina. This illusion, however, is speedily dispelled when the ore is submitted to the test of re-agents in the laboratory.

With respect to carboniferous deposits in this province, I refer the reader to my remarks on this subject in reporting on the Province San Juan, reiterating my firm conviction that vast coal fields exist both in Los Llanos and the Valley of Binchina. Possessing, as we do, such immense deposits of iron ore, in addition to these extensive carboniferous beds, we may reasonably entertain hopes that, with the lapse of time and the continuance of peace, these two powerful elements of civilization and progress will at length be utilized, to the great aggrandisement and advantage of the Republic.

As already stated, the roads in the mineral district of Famatina are almost intransitable, and a heavy expenditure would be necessary to render them convenient and safe. About £1,500 would be required to make the road from Chilecito to Cerro Negro practicable for loaded mules, avoiding the beds of the rivers and torrents, which are rough and stony, to traverse the slopes of the Sierra. Roads could be made on both sides, but at some places it would be necessary to blast through rock, and many deviations and curves would be necessary. The distance from the town of Chilecito to the works of Durazno is three leagues, and a carriage road could easily be made; but from the latter point to the gold mines of Santo Domingo, about four leagues, it would be comparatively impracticable to do more than construct a path for loaded mules.

From Famatina to the Sierra of La Mejicana no great difficulties are presented, but it would nevertheless involve an outlay of about £5,000 to make roads available for carriage traffic. A path for loaded mules, however, could be formed at a cost of £2,000, the distance by Escaleras being ten leagues more or less. There is another and more direct route, by traversing an elevated ridge in front of Carrisal, and descending by Las Cuevas to form a junction with the Escaleras road through the ravine. The cost would be the same, but the distance would be three leagues less.

It would be desirable to make a track for loaded mules between the mineral district of Cerro Negro and that of La Mejicana; but the road between those points will always be very steep, rugged, and exceedingly difficult of transit. In parts it rises to a height of 14,000 feet, and falls again to 10,000 feet; this being of repeated occurrence, in crossing the various intervening ranges. The cost of a road thus would be about £1,000, and the distance three leagues.

Besides in the mineral districts, the necessity of roads is very much felt to unite Famatina with the province of San Juan, starting from Jachal, and passing by Guaco, Paso de Lamar, and Los Burros, more particularly including that from Miranda and the ravine to Sañogasta. The actual road between the places last mentioned is in so dangerous a state, and the traffic over it so great, that, in the interests of the public, its repair and reconstruction should be at once undertaken. The total distance between Jachal and Famatina does not pass 40 leagues, and an excellent road could be made for about £33 per league.

Another important road would be one from Famatina to connect with that from Cordoba and San Juan. This road would be comparatively level, there being no hills nor obstacles of any kind, with the exception of clearing off the wood, and avoiding a few moving sandhills. It would have to follow the actual road from Famatina to Rioja, as far as the Sierra of Velasco, continuing along the slope of the latter up to the southern extremity, where it should double the point and join the road from Rioja to Papagallos. At this junction there is no water, which would have to be provided by the construction of a reservoir. Thence it should proceed E.S.E. to reach the road between Soto and the reservoir of Los Tellos, on the Llanos. The contractor for the construction of the road from Rioja to Papagallos, Don Pedro Gordillo, offers to make this road, of sixteen yards in width, stubbing out the tree roots to a yard in depth, and with 13 necessary reservoirs for water, together with post huts, for the sum of £6,250.

The agricultural and vinicultural productions of Famatina are of considerable importance. The estimated population of the department is 8,000 inhabitants, and these produce annually 500 tons of flour, worth £10 per ton; 9000 fanegas of maize, worth 10s. per fanega (300 lbs.). The grape grown at Famatina is of a very superior class, producing not less than 1,200,000 bottles of wine yearly, which sells there at 1s. 8d. per bottle; but there is not consumption for the whole, and, as at Mendoza, a great portion is manufactured into aguardiente, or brandy. This produce alone, it will be seen, represents a large sum (£25,000), which, added to the flour and maize, make a total value of nearly £32,000.

The valley of Nonogasta is exceedingly fertile and well populated, with extensive vineyards and orchards, lucerne, and a few tobacco plantations.

Water and firewood are abundant, and every facility (save labourers), exists for the rapid development of mining industry in the department. The climate is very temperate in summer, and not rigorous in the winter. Famatina was formerly the scene of frequent political revolutions, but it will be seen by this report that the chief *Caudillos*, or leaders in these fratricidal struggles

—Don Carlos Angel and Don Francisco Alvarez—have devoted themselves to mining and reduction establishments, gathering around them the most notorious gauchos, whom, by their example, they have converted into peaceable and well-conducted members of society, laborious and industrious in habits, and who have now no thought of abandoning their tranquil and civilizing labours for the din of battle and precarious existence of the pampa.

PROVINCE OF CATAMARCA.

GENERAL PHYSICAL ASPECT, DESCRIPTION OF SOIL, CLIMATE, &c.

The Province of Catamarca is situated to the south of that of Salta, to the west of Tucuman and Santiago del Estero, and to the north of Rioja. The boundary by Chili is the westerly summit of the plateau of the Andes. It is thus between 26° 20′ and 28° 30′ south lat., and 68° to 71° longitude west (Paris), and covers a superficial area of about 3,800 square leagues. Its limits to the north, and with the province of Salta, are a line traversing the heights of the Nevados of Calchaqui, the Sierra Medanosa, that of Chango Real, opening to the north of the valley Laguna Blanca, touching Paso de San Francisco, where it meets to the north-west the frontier of Bolivia, and on the west that of Chili. To the south it is separated from the province of Rioja by another line, which, parting from the Chilian frontier to Cerro Pulido, traverses the plateau of the Andes by Laguna Brava, descends the Estanzuela, the range of Machaco, the southern border of the valleys of the Tamberia and of Cienega Redonda; then following the crest of the mountains of Tinogasta, passes by the undulations of Cerrillos, the great travesia of Los Colorados, of Alpasinche, and of Machigasta, up to the gorge of Chumbicha, and continuing towards E.S.E. until it touches the great basin of the Salinas, near 29° 40' lat. and 67° long.

To the north-east its frontier with Tucuman is marked by the Bañado of the Abra de Santa Maria, the summit of the Sierra of the lower range of the Aconquija and Rio de Guacra, or San Francisco. Finally, to the east, it joins Santiago del Estero by a line marked by estancias, and running at the eastern base of the Ancaste range, in more or less longitude 67°, or up to the Rio Albigasta.

These lines of demarcation are those which are generally recognised, but frequently questions arise as to their accuracy on the part of the authorities of the provinces of Tucuman and Santiago del Estero, who assert that Catamarca holds unlawfully a portion of their territory, and that its limits are not quite those assigned to it by the Royal decree of 16th August, 1679, and the survey ordered by the municipality of Catamarca on the 11th February, 1684. On the other hand, the people of Catamarca claim that the occupation of the Canton of Colalao by Tucuman is unjust; also the occupation by Santiago del Estero of a part of the mountain range of Ancaste. The only arbiter in questions of limits in the provinces is the Supreme Congress, and the question is now being discussed with the view to a final settlement.

The province of Catamarca presents a varied and picturesque aspect. The northern part is covered by mountains, which enclose narrow gorges and some extensive valleys, amongst the latter the Campo de los Pozuelos, at the western base of the Aconquija range. Nearing the Cordillera, the valleys are extensive and comparatively level; towards the south-east a great plain, called the Salinas de Belem and Andalgalá, unites with the great basin of this name, which separates the Andine system from the central range of the plains. The great valley of the capital, situated between the Sierras of Ambato and Ancaste, joins with the latter. The mountain ranges which elevate their peaks in this province gradually merge into this great plain. Their summits, although very dry, are covered with a rich vegetation, and the numerous streams which descend from them, charged with silt and various salts, fertilize prodigiously the soil around their base.

In consequence of their sterility, the plains are very sparsely inhabited, the population being concentrated in the interior valleys and along the base of the Sierra del Alto and Ancaste.

This province does not possess any river of importance, its supply of water being confined to numerous small streams and mountain torrents, the whole of which is absorbed by irrigation and domestic use. The principal watercourse is that of Santa Maria, then comes Paclin and Piedra Blanca, which form the Rio del Valle and water the valley of the capital. The torrents of the Cordillera are inconsiderable. Only one lake exists in the province, that of Laguna Blanca, situated in a high valley of the Cordillera; in continuation is found the Laguna Colorada, which cannot be classified as a lake. Both, however, are salt. They are bordered by extensive valleys of a sandy clay nature, and the few inhabitants now existing there assert that in former times the district was thickly populated.

The orographic system of Catamarca is rather complicated. It consists of two grand sections, one depending on the Cordillera of the Andes and the other on the range of Aconquija. The two sections are united by the transverse range of Atajo. From Aconquija, towards the S.S.E., stretch away the long chains of the Alto and Ancaste; the latter, which is only a prolongation of the Alto, is lost on the great plain towards the Salinas. From the same range of Aconquija, but a little little more to the west, extends the lofty Sierra of Ambato, terminating to the south in the hills of Mazan and Punta Negra, which connect it through the Cerrillos with the Sierra of Velasco or Rioja. Between the two chains of Ambato and Alto is that of the Gracian, which rises near the capital, and continues northwards, uniting with the Clavillo de Aconquija. The Sierra del Atajo rises from the latter, and runs to the east, serving as a southern boundary to the great plain of Los Pozuelos joining the mass of the Chango Real and other elevated ranges, which enclose the valleys of Laguna Blanca and Fiambala. Following towards the south, it separates into two ranges, forming the Sierra de Belem, which terminates by the points called Cerros Negro and Colorado, in the great travesia of Copocabana at Machigasta. The mass of the Andes extends from the south to the north, with its high lateral valleys, and the subsidiary chains of the Machaco and Casadero de Fiambala.

The great diversity in altitude of the different parts of this province produces great variation in the nature of the soil and productions. The Aconquija range consists of gneiss, granite, serpentine, quartz, &c., as also the chains of Alto and Ancaste. The Atajo and Ambato ranges are of the same character, but also contain limestone and sandstone of various ages. The Sierra of Belem consists of gneiss in the centre, and of sandstone towards the extreme south. Gneiss is found in the hills of Tinogasta and Copocabana, and sandstone in the eastern buttress of the great mass of the Andes, at the Sierras of Chango Real and Medanosa, which on the north bound the valleys of the Laguna Blanca and the great plain of Los Pozuelos. Towards the Punta de Balastro traces of volcanic action are visible. All the mountainous region is rich in metallic deposits—gold, silver, copper, nickel, iron, and lead. Several mines are at work, especially in the Sierra del Atajo, and with profitable results. Of these I will speak in their proper place.

Some valleys are entirely sandy, such as Laguna Blanca, the great plains Los Pozuelos, vast circular plains between the chains of Quilmez, Aconquija, and Atajo, at a mean altitude of 2,500 metres, incessantly swept by the wind, which, when it blows from the north or north-west, raises a whirlwind of fine silicious sand from the Sierra Medanosa. The immense basin of the Salinas of Belem and Andalgalá is sandy clay, and contains in many places, especially towards the centre, numerous efflorescences. All those plains are arid, as rain seldom falls, but on their borders, towards the mountains, small rivulets are utilized and produce a luxuriant vegetation. The eastern slopes of the Sierras of Alto and Ancaste have a rich vegetable earth, and yield some trees and abundant pasture.

The climate varies in accordance with altitude and locality, being pre-eminently dry in the region of the Andes, and becomes humid in the valleys at the base of the Aconquija, towards the south-east. At an elevation of 1,000 metres frost is rare; above this elevation it freezes in winter. The summit of the principal range of Aconquija is covered with perpetual snow. The Sierras of Ambato and Atajo retain it only for a short time; those of the Alto, Ancaste, and Belem almost never. The line of perpetual snow commences at 4,500 metres in the Cordillera of Catamarca; the snowy peaks of Potro and Bonéte are situate in this province. The lower valleys, *i.e.*, those below 1,000 metres, are extremely hot in summer; the desert about the Salinas of Belem and Andalgalá is scorching, but happily, in the vicinity of the mountains, refreshing breezes descend and cool the atmosphere. The winds are sometimes very strong, especially those from the north to the south, and create fearful whirlwinds of dust. The rainy season is in the summer, from December to March. Rain is rare in the neighbourhood of the Cordillera, the clouds passing over, which are attracted by the range of Aconquija farther to the east, and consequently rain falls copiously on its slopes and the plains at its base.

The salubrity of the province is perfect. There are no peculiar maladies and no other epidemics than those common to the provinces of the Andes. Mild intermittent fevers are sometimes prevalent in the humid valleys of Piedra Blanca and Paclin. The goitre prevails in some of the valleys, especially that of the capital.

Vegetation is meagre and stunted in the region of the Andes, being limited to cacti, to the various mimosas, such as algarrobo, the visco, the chañar, the brea, the jarilla, &c. In the humid valleys vegetation is similar to that of Tucuman—the wild walnut, cedar, laurel, pacará, &c., grow well, but do not attain the same magnitude as in that province. Grass is abundant on the plateau and slopes of the Alto and Ancaste. Where there is a little moisture the natural vegetation is vigorous and almost tropical, but this humidity is rare and its absence is the cause of the sterility of the plains and the stunted growth of their vegetation,

Agriculture, where practised in the province, with the aid of irrigation and on the rich deep vegetable soil, is prolific in the extreme. The fruit trees and herbaceous plants prosper admirably. The orange, fig, vine, peach, olive, and, in fact, all the trees of central Europe mature and produce abundantly. The wines made in the department of Andalgalá are justly esteemed for their excellence. Tobacco and cotton of a superior quality are cultivated, as also the sugar cane near the capital. All these productions are consumed in the province. Wheat and maize yield a large return. Lucerne is cultivated on an extended scale, principally in the western districts, with the object of fattening cattle for export to Chili.

The wild and domestic animals of the province are of the same species as those of Cordoba and Santiago del Estero, which I will describe later on. The vicuña and the guanaco abound in the mountains to the northwest, which are also frequented by the couguar and condor. The conformation of the province, with its high mountains and vast arid plains, is unfavourable to the existence of many wild animals. Cattle are numerous and multiply rapidly in the departments of the east, where grass is plentiful and of excellent quality. Alto and Ancaste furnish horned cattle for all the province. The animals for export by the Cordillera are fattened in the lucerne fields at Tinogasta and Copocabana before being driven across the Andes. Asses and mules are bred in the neighbourhood of Laguna Blanca. Sheep and goats are met with everywhere. The indigenous race of sheep are naturally good, and little at present is done for its improvement. The breeding of the vicuña and alpaca might become very lucrative in this province.

The isolated position of Catamarca makes its export trade very insignificant. Cotton is little cultivated, owing to the expense of transport, and tobacco is only produced in small quantities for Chili. The cultivation of this plant might be advantageously extended, since that of Tucuman, 60 leagues more distant, is sold profitably in the market of Copiapo. Among the other products dry figs are exported, which are very good, and the *aji*, or red pepper, which is of superior quality. In addition, the wines and brandies produced in Andalgalá find a ready market in Tucuman and Cordoba, forming an important item. Bullocks, sheep, goats, and mules are exported to Chili. The commerce with Bolivia is limited to the exportation of mules. As to local industry, it is fairly advanced and resembles that of Tucuman. Some woollen stuffs, such as cloth for ponchos, horse covers, and very tasteful foot rugs are manufactured by the women in the department of the capital. In Andalgalá hides are tanned and embroidery is largely produced. The women are very active and industrious, and manufacture nearly all the preceding, and, in addition, have acquired their well-earned celebrity for the excellence and beauty of the woven fabrics produced from the wool of the vicuña at Belem. An ordinary scarf for a lady fetches readily in Buenos Ayres from £20 to £30, and would no doubt be highly appreciated in Europe if once introduced. The most important product for export, and most valuable industry in the province, is the raising of copper from the mines of the Sierra de Atajo, which has produced much enthusiasm among all classes, and tends to develope a spirit of union and activity hitherto unknown.

Owing to the peculiar position of the mountain ranges, interior communication in the province is only effected on horseback. The capital is connected with Rioja, a distance of 49 leagues, by carriage road, and also with Cordoba, a distance of 118 leagues to the south-east. The last route traverses the Salinas for 28 leagues without water, being the most difficult part of the whole journey. Weekly mail communication by coach is now established, and by this means intercommunication with Tucuman and Santiago del Estero *viâ* Cordoba is effected; but direct communication with those two towns is provided by mule tracks through the valley of Paclin, crossing the range of Ancaste by the pass of Totoral. The distance to both cities is almost equal, or about 65 leagues. Salta and Jujuy may be reached by the route of Andalgalá and Santa Maria, but the distance is the same by way of Tucuman, namely, 155 leagues. From Belem to Andalgalá or Poman the distance is 30 leagues over the Salinas. The route from the capital to Belem, traverses the southern extremity of the Sierra de Ambato by the gorge of La Concepcion; passing Poman, it traverses the desert—about in all 60 leagues. By this route one can go direct to Tinogasta (70 leagues), and to the Andes, by the desert at the point of Los Colorados and Capocabana. The road from Chili passes by Tinogasta, Anillaco, La Troya, La Tamberia, Machaco, Cordillera of the Estanzuela, and Barrancas Blancas. The distance is 133 leagues from Tinogasta to Copiapo. The route from Belem to the former is 22 leagues, passing by the *cuesta*, or zig-zag track of Zapata, which could be easily improved.

The province of Catamarca is divided into eight departments, which are subdivided into sections and districts. The first is that of the capital, including the town proper and its suburbs, forming two sections, the one to the south called " Capallan," the other to the west called " Valle Viejo." Then comes the department of Piedra Blanca to the north of the capital, between the two great eastern spurs of the Clavillo de Aconquija, Ambato, and Gracian; those of Alto and Ancaste, in the chain of this name; that of Andalgalá, at the base of the great Aconquija, to which is attached the section of Poman, on the western slope of the Sierra de Ambato; that of Santa Maria to the north of Atajo; that of Belem, in the Sierra of the same name, and in the north-west of the province; lastly, Tinogasta, to the west, comprised in the great Andes.

The department of the capital is situate in the centre of the province, comprising the broad valley, enclosed by the chains of Ambato on the west, and Ancaste on the east. This is the most populous department in the province.

The capital of the province,—San Fernando de Catamarca—is situate on a plain which slopes gently from the foot of the Sierra de Ambato. It was at first established a league lower down, upon the Rio del Valle, but was afterwards removed to its present site, to avoid the inundations caused by heavy freshets in the summer. It is a pretty little town, well built and watered by the stream Tala, which also supplies the houses. The gardens are full of fine fruit trees, the orange predominating. The plaza, or principal square, is about four acres in extent, through which pass several small streams of water. The centre is adorned by an obelisk, or column, built in brick, with a railing round its base. The only public buildings are the cathedral, and the Government house, of modern construction, ornamental and well designed. They join each other and form the western angle of the square. Another recent work of great importance and utility is a large reservoir, situate west of the plaza, 100 metres square and 3 metres deep. The embankments are well planted with trees, which afford a grateful shade to the townsfolk, who promenade there during the summer. The water contained in this reservoir is derived from the Tala and serves to irrigate the town and suburbs, and rendering productive 250 acres of excellent land, previously uncultivated from scarcity of water. The sale of this land has covered the expense of constructing the reservoir.

The town of Catamarca has recently been greatly improved by the erection of a considerable number of new houses and the restoration of old ones; the principal streets only are paved. The houses are generally built of "adobes," and roofed with corrugated tiles. The modern houses have flat roofs as at Buenos Ayres.

Besides the church of Matriz, or cathedral already alluded to, there is another—San Francisco—the orphan asylum and the college. The convent of San Francisco is contemporary with the foundation of the city, and is in a good state of preservation. The other two religious edifices possess nothing worthy of special remark. The orphan asylum is supported by revenue derived from its lands. The national college, now established there, under the jurisdiction of the Minister of Public Instruction at Buenos Ayres, is one of the most complete and best ordered institutions of its class in the country. Previous to its incorporation under the National Government it possessed valuable and extensive landed and house property, which had been bequeathed from time to time by charitable individuals, but all these have been handed over in trust to the educational department of the Government, to provide for the payment of European and other professors, and to support its alumni. Mathematics, classics, ancient and modern history, languages, physics, &c., are taught.

Catamarca is situated in 28° 12′ south lat., 68° 45′ west long. (Paris), at an altitude of 530 metres above sea level. The climate is hot, the sky clear about ten months in the year; it rains in the summer only.

The department of Piedra Blanca is situated north of the preceding, and in a long valley, which stretches from south to north, its northern extremity touching the Nevado of Aconquija. At its southern extremity it is divided into three canons, or elongated gorges; these are Piedra Blanca, Pucarilla, and Paclin. The canon of Piedra Blanca is situated between the Sierra de Gracian and the northern part of the range Ambato; it is well watered by the Rio del Valle, and produces the sugar cane, tobacco, cotton, and every species of fruit trees in abundance. It is the richest and most beautiful, as well as the most populous valley in the whole province; it is seven leagues long and two broad; the land is well cultivated and studded with houses and farms. There are six villages, centres of population with churches—San Antonio, Callecita, Rosario, Collagasta, Pomancillo, and La Puerta.

The canon of Pucarilla is similar to that of Piedra Blanca, but more elevated; cultivation of wheat, maize, wine, tobacco, and fruit trees of all kinds are industriously carried on. In the highest part and on the northern extremity towards Singuil, cattle and sheep are bred and fattened in large quantities. It is divided into three districts—Rinconda, Bolson, and Singuil. Through the latter estancia passes the road from Catamarca to Andalgalá, which is very bad and rough by way of the gorge of La Chilca, but this is avoided by taking a circuitous route a little to the southward, and passing by the Carapunco and the hamlet of Billavil.

The canon Paclin, commencing at Portezuelo, is humid and woody; its river waters, in addition to this valley, the districts of Portezuelo, of Santa Cruz, and of Guaycamas, which belong to the department of the capital. The route from Catamarca to Tucuman passes through it, but branches off at Merced to ascend the zig-zag track over the Totoral and gain the eastern slopes of the Ancaste range. The cultivation is principally of the cereals, tobacco, and the rearing of cattle.

The department of the Alto occupies all the Sierra of this name to the frontier of Tucuman and Santiago del Estero; it is not very elevated, and is everywhere covered with excellent pastures and lovely forests on its easterly slopes. Cereals are little cultivated, the principal occupation being the rearing of cattle—bullocks, horses, sheep, goats, and especially mules. Agriculture is followed to some extent in the little open valleys upon its eastern base. There are also some tanneries where large quantities of rough leather for saddlery and harness are produced.

This department is divided into two: the mountain,

with three districts, including the parish and hamlets of Alto, Guayamba, and Balismano, having its church; the plain, into three districts—village of Manantiales, with its church, and the estancias of Obanta and Las Cañas, situated on the borders of a small crystaline stream whose waters are consumed entirely by irrigation.

The department of Ancaste resembles the preceding one, having the same cultures, the same products, and occupations. It is situated to the south-east of the most easterly branch of the Aconquija range, and has one part in the Sierra and the other on the plain. In the mountain there are three districts,—Ancaste parish, Icaña, and Motegasta, with their respective churches. On the plain there are five, the village of San Francisco, estancias of Chorro and Ramblon, Rosario, with its church, and the hamlet of Anjule.

The department of the Fuerte de Andalgalá, so named after an ancient Spanish fort placed in the midst of the country of the Andalgalás Indians, one of the bravest of the Calchaquies tribes. It is situate at the southern base of the Nevado de Aconquija, and whence, to the eastward, rises the Ambato range; it is on the border of the vast saline desert, and embraces the valleys Atajo to the north, and Poman to the S.S.E. The town of Andalgalá is now of some importance, having during the last ten years singularly increased, in consequence of the great activity and progress made in the explorations of the mines of Atajo and Capillitas; it is the most important centre of population in the province, next after the capital itself. Commerce is being well developed owing to the large importation of mining materials and merchandize. Agriculture is advancing rapidly, and considerable quantities of wines, brandy, dry figs, &c.,

are exported. The position of Andalgalá is most picturesque and pre-eminently healthy, being situate at the foot of the enormous mass of the Clavillo de Aconquija, whose summits (over 19,000 feet) are crowned with perpetual snow. The numerous descending streams and rivulets from this range fertilise its virgin soil, which consists principally of decomposed felspathic rocks most favourable for the cultivation of fruit trees and of the vine, whose produce is there very superior. A large tannery has been recently established with successful results. The locust, which appears occasionally, is its only scourge.

The great desert of the Salinas extends to the south and south-east, and covers a space of 400 square leagues. The slope of this vast basin is towards the south-east, and is surrounded on all sides by broken ranges of mountains, of which the principal opening is at Quebradillas, in the province of Rioja, where the average altitude is reduced to 350 metres. Here passes the Arroyo Saladillo, which appears to be the only discharge from the southern part of the basin after freshets or rains.

The department of Andalgalá is divided into two sections—Andalgalá and Poman. The section Andalgalá is subdivided into five districts—the town itself, which I have just described; the village Cholla, at the entrance of the quebrada of this name, and by which the road to the mines of Las Capillitas passes, crossing higher up the ridge of the Negrilla. This is a most picturesque and enchanting valley, well watered by a rapid rivulet, and presents a mass of semi-tropical vegetation in trees and flowers of the most lovely and varied description; so charming is this neighbourhood that a gentleman from Buenos Ayres, at a distance of over 1,000 miles, has purchased a little vineyard and grounds, with the view of building a house and occasionally enjoying a sojourn there. The next districts are Bisbis and Amanao to the west, in the quebradas of this name, also very picturesque. Billavil, to the east, is one of the chief places in the lovely valley of this name. It is an agricultural district and its hamlet is situated on the route to Catamarca city by way of Singuil, and to Tucuman by way of Monasterio, and the eastern base of Aconquija.

The section of Poman is situate upon the western watershed of the Sierra de Ambato, in a series of gorges formed by its buttresses. The valley in this place is divided into three districts, namely, Poman, Nuetquin, and Rincon de Mulcasca. In these districts are produced white wines of a very superior class, and agriculture, although limited, is a source of considerable profit to its inhabitants. On the estancias in the neighbourhood of the Salinas some cattle are bred and reared, which feed principally on the leaf and fruit of the algarrobo. This important indigenous tree (Hymenæa Courbaril-Jetaiba) is found in great abundance all over this and neighbouring provinces, and its fruit, of the papilionaceous species, is gathered annually by the natives, and stored with much care, forming, as it does, their principal winter stock of food. It grows sometimes to a height of 40 feet, and the diameter of its trunk, generally knotted and crooked, varies from 6 inches to 3 feet. Its branches are wide spread, more especially in the case of the largest of the species. The fruit, as already stated, forms a most important article of food, both for man and beast. The long pods are pounded in a wooden mortar, and the resulting mass passes through a sieve, in order to separate the seeds, the husk only being used for human food. The meal or flour thus produced is slightly moistened with water and pressed into circular cakes or wooden moulds, and when dried in the sun are fit for use. In this state it is called " patay " (an Indian word), and is exported into other districts of the Republic not possessing the algarrobo tree in sufficient abundance to make its produce worth collecting. The " patay " has a sweetish flavour, resembling maize flour mixed with treacle, is very nutritious, but only a small quantity can be taken at a meal. The inhabitants of the country districts of Catamarca and Rioja live almost exclusively on it, and are generally strong and healthy.

Two roads cross the desert west from Poman, the one to Belem, the other to Tinogasta. The route to the Fuerte extends along the foot of the Ambato range towards the north.

MINERAL RESOURCES, &c.

This province would undoubtedly be one of the poorest and most insignificant in the Republic were it not for its mines and reduction establishments. Its geographical position and isolation from the centres of traffic and commerce militate most powerfully against its industrial progress; but, notwithstanding this, no province in the Republic is better governed as respects the administration of its commercial affairs. Order, prosperity, and industry reign in all its departments, despite the cries of angry and disappointed political parties frustrated in designs hostile to its progress, and opposed to the development of its mineral wealth. Miners have nothing to do with politics, and ought to refuse to interest themselves in anything foreign to their legitimate occupation. They only ask to be allowed to work in peace. Their labours are more exalted and more glorious for the country and its civilization than any other, and their happy and fruitful results are the most eloquent proof of their importance.

In this province I have for the first time seen realized the projects and theories of the enlightened President of the Republic, Señor Sarmiento. He has always urged upon his fellow-citizens that, to enable the Sub-Andine provinces to emerge from their actual state of prostration, they must create within themselves the consumption necessary to support increased agricultural productions. The distance and high freight charges prevent the exportation of these, and thus the cultivator of the soil would have no inducement to continue his labours in the field if no such market or consumption existed.

The normal population is insufficient to consume even half what their fertile soil brings forth, and only by increasing the number of inhabitants and fomenting permanent industries like that of mining, can the agriculturist hope to obtain a satisfactory reward for his toil.

Catamarca possesses but one mining district of great commercial importance in active operation, viz., " Las Capillitas," situated 12 leagues north-east of the Fuerte de Andalgalá, and about 50 from the capital, in mountains branching westward from the great range of the Nevado de Aconquija, which divides the province from that of Tucuman. Its geological formation is that of the primary rocks—granite, conglomerate, gneiss, and syenite. There are other districts in the immediate vicinity possessing veins of copper and silver, but as none are being worked, they cannot at the present moment be considered as representing commercial value.

The *Restauradora* mine, belonging to Mr. Samuel F. Lafone, of Monte Video, is the richest and most important in the province. The works are well directed, and economy and science applied with highly profitable results.

The mine was purchased by Mr. Lafone for 6,000 doubloons (about £20,000), and, owing to the great abundance and good ley of its ores, it was determined to erect reduction works at Santa Maria, about 30 leagues to the north. This was a grave error, as it entailed the carrying of the ores 30 leagues northward for the purpose of reduction, and the subsequent return of the copper produced almost over the same road on its way for export at Buenos Ayres. For some years the enterprise was carried on at serious loss, purely the result of mismanagement. In the year 1860 or 1861, Mr. Lafone's son, Mr. Samuel Lafone-Quevado, accompanied by Mr. Juan Heller, as commercial manager, visited the mines with the object of reforming its management; and it was fully time that some step should be taken, as about £70,000 had already been expended, and day by day further loss was being incurred. Smelting operations at Santa Maria were at once suspended, and the large estancia of Pilciao was bought, situated 5 leagues south of Fuerte de Andalgalá, and 13 leagues south of the mines. The ores were thus carried southwards, and a saving thereby effected in the ultimate charges for freight to the coast. The management was reformed, and useless employés in the mine discharged and replaced by others of a more suitable class. New furnaces were built at

Pilciao, and an intelligent metallurgical chemist from Europe was engaged to direct the operations on scientific principles. All these alterations caused a further expenditure of upwards of £30,000, but its prudent investment promised good returns, as, in fact, it has, the enterprise being now in a solvent and profitable position. The £30,000 have been already recouped, and the owners are in the possession of a most valuable property, as well in lands and reduction works as in mines. The lode of the *Restauradora* mine is on the average seven feet in width, and the average ley for copper 18 per cent.; but the ore also contains silver in the proportion of about 27.13 per ton and one-ninth of an ounce of gold. It is the presence of the precious metals which renders the reduction of copper ores at all profitable, as this latter alone barely covers the cost of extraction from the mines, reduction, freight, and other expenses incurred previous to its sale in Europe. It is in such cases as this that the want of good and cheap means of conveyance from the interior to the coast is most severely felt, for the whole profit is absorbed in charges for transport.

At the time of my visit the mine had a considerable quantity of water in the upper levels. An adit, however, was being driven for its removal, and the miners were meanwhile stoping out all the ore existing in upper workings.

The orestuff on the surface consisted at that date (March, 1869) of 450 tons of first class ore, holding 20 per cent. of copper; and 600 tons of second class, holding only 12 per cent. of copper, but richer in its ley for gold and silver. The ores are sulpho-arsenides, with antimonides of copper and iron, or what are commonly called black, grey, and yellow sulphides, with purple or peacock copper ore. About 270 tons per month are raised and dressed for the furnaces.

The mine is worked by galleries, winzes, and shafts. An adit, with tramway and waggons, communicates with the upper workings and discharges the ores into the ore yard on the surface; but there is another adit lower down, at the foot of the mountain, on which they had been continuously at work for four years, driving night and day, to effect communication with the upper workings and drain them. It is 360 yards in length, with a tramway, but fifteen months' work was still necessary before it could reach the desired point. When this is accomplished, however, the mine will be freed from water, presenting a vertical depth of 125 fathoms in virgin ground, which can then be worked without difficulty or impediment. While this is being done, ore of a suitable class exists on surface, and will be obtained from the upper workings sufficient to keep the furnaces going at the rate of 100 tons a month for over a year.

Altogether sixty persons were employed in the mine, viz., the mine captain, Mr. James Tyrrell, who is an Englishman; 5 Cornish miners, 1 blacksmith, and 1 bookkeeper, all English; 1 provision dispenser, 2 mayor-domos, 12 fore-miners, 36 assistant miners, and 1 cook.

There are four pumps, and the ventilator in the lower adit is moved by means of a hydraulic wheel. A whim is used to raise the ore to the level of the upper adit.

The *Ortiz* mine is upon another vein of much importance, situated northward, close to that of *Restauradora*. It was little worked, being merely kept open by Mr. Lafone. The orestuff consists of red oxides of copper, with very rich silicates and carbonates; the ley is not less than 45 per cent. of copper , but it contains no silver. The lode in some parts is a yard in width.

This vein joins with another, *La Montezuma*, which is also of importance, but was not being actually worked at the time of my visit. On the same lode are other mines—*La Victoria* and *Alejandra*,—yielding ore of good ley for copper, but likewise only partially worked. As previously explained, it is unprofitable to reduce vein-stuff containing copper only, and as that of the *Restauradora* holds so much copper, with silver and gold in addition, other ores are not at present in request by the smelting masters.

The *Santa Clara* mine is situated to the west of *Restauradora*, with which it joins. It is the property of Don Marcelino Augier. This vein, which holds a good ley for silver, is of great width, and consists of sulphides of copper, with blende and galena. The mine is closed, and its lowest levels (30 fathoms) are in water, to get rid of which it would be necessary to drive an adit. There is an adit on a level with the water, which is of no use for this purpose, and another must be made at greater depth.

Higher up, on the same vein, is the *Grande* mine, belonging to Messrs. Malbran. Here the width of the vein is $1\frac{1}{2}$ yards, and the ley of the ore 35 per cent., consisting of carbonates and oxides, with sulphides of copper.

The *Catamarquena* and *Bandera Nacional* mines, also closed, are both located on the continuation of the above lode. At a few yards below the surface the ore disappears.

MESSRS. CARRANZA, MOLINA, AND CO'S MINES.

The *Rosario* mine is the oldest in the district, and is energetically worked, with galleries and shafts, and a spacious adit, at 75 fathoms vertically from the upper surface of the mountain. The miners are working 40 fathoms lower than the adit level, and at this depth a considerable quantity of water makes its appearance. Nevertheless, it is easily removed by means of hand pumps.

The lode is very variable in width, which is in parts eighteen feet, but the average does not exceed three. The ley of the ore is higher than that extracted from *La Restauradora* by Mr. Lafone, but it is less abundant. Still, from its superior ley, almost an equal quantity of copper is produced.

All the orestuff raised during the year held on the average 20 per cent. of copper, 19·16 ounces of silver, and half an ounce of gold to the ton. The vein in the lower levels was is good beneficio when I saw it, and promises to improve.

About 150 tons of undressed orestuff was on the surface, together with 9 tons dressed.

Seventy-eight persons were employed here, viz., Mr. William Glanville, mine captain, 1 timberer, 1 assistant ditto, all English; 1 clerk, 1 provision dispenser, 1 blacksmith, 20 fore-miners, 46 labourers, 4 mayordomos, 1 servant, and 1 cook.

To carry on the working of this mine effectively at least 100 men are necessary, but during my visit only the above number were actually employed, owing to the scarcity of hands in the district. As in the case of the *Restauradora*, a large sum of money was uselessly expended upon the mine in consequence of bad management at the commencement, but, under the auspices of the present engineer, the results now obtained are much more satisfactory.

The *Mejicana* mine is on a large vein, eight yards in width, of ferrugineous ore, formerly worked for gold. When I visited this mine an adit was being driven on the vein, but had not yet reached good ore. I have been since informed that good beneficio was subsequently cut.

The *Esperanza* mine belongs to the same owners. The vein is a yard in width, holding 30 per cent. of copper in carbonates, oxides, and sulphides, with a higher ley for silver and gold than the *Rosario*. A vertical shaft was driven, and a whim had recently been constructed to raise ore more economically. Good results are certain to be obtained in working this lode in depth.

The *San Salvador* belongs to Don Wellington Mercado, and is located at the foot of Rosario. The vein is half a yard in width, containing 20 per cent. of copper and 74 ounces of silver to the ton. It is much worked by an adit well driven on the vein.

The *La Argentina* is close to the *Esperanza*, and is the property of Don Marcelino Augier. The vein is in beneficio, a quarter of a yard in width, and the orestuff consists of sulphides and oxides of copper, with silicates. It holds 88·8 ounces of silver to the ton.

There are many other old copper mines in the district, which are not being worked ; as, in the first place, no profit is derived from the reduction of non-argentiferous or auriferous copper ore, and in the second place, mining operations are restricted practically to the owners of smelting works, and the latter having enough of their own are not interested in purchasing ores from others.

Ores from the *Rosario*, and other mines of Messrs. Carranza, Molina, and Co., are reduced at their works at Pipanaco, to which reference will be made later on.

COPPER REDUCTION WORKS.

There are only two smelting establishments in full operation in the province,—that of Mr. Samuel F. Lafone, at Pilciao, and that of Messrs. Carranza, Molina, and Co., at Pipanaco.

The works at Pilciao are five leagues to the south of Fuerte de Andalgalá, and 35 leagues north-west from the capital, on the western side of the Sierra of Ambato. They are situated about 15 leagues from the mines, and surrounded by immense forests of algarrobo and retamo The locality is dry and good water can only be obtained at a depth of 20 fathoms.

There are 9 reverberatory furnaces, including 1 for calcination and 2 for refining; 4 Chilian mills, and 5 stamp heads. The works are very extensive, covering more than eight acres of ground. Fire-bricks are manu-factured on the spot, composed of pure quartz, ground to the required fineness, and washed kaolin, or china clay, in the proportion of 95 of the former to 5 of the latter. Excellent bricks are thus made, being capable of resisting fire and fluxes for a long time. I was kindly permitted to study the system of reduction here in prac-tice, in its various stages of progress, under the able superintendence of Mr. Schickendantz, the metallurgical chemist of the establishment. Mr. John Heller, a Dane of many years' experience and residence in the country, is the general manager.

AURIFEROUS AND ARGENTIFEROUS COPPER SMELTING AT PILCIAO.

Description of Ores received at Works.	Common Spanish names by which the Classes are distinguished.
1. Grey copper, with yellow pyrites (in large lumps)	Despinte, bronces gris.
2. Ditto, ditto, forming the smalls or sweepings	Ditto, Llampos.
3. Copper and iron yellow and purple pyrites (in large lumps)	Bronces amarillos.
4. Ditto, ditto, in dust	Ditto, Llampos.
5. Washed smalls, or dust, containing grey, yellow, and purple copper pyrites, galena, and blende	Llampos lavados.
6. Carbonates and oxides of copper, with carbonates of lead and galena	Metal de color.
7. Iron pyrites, with poor yellow copper pyrites	Rechanque.

First operation.—Ores, 1, 3, and 7 are calcined in heaps in the open air, in large quantities at a time, ranging from 40 to 60 tons. The well calcined ore is selected and separated from the other, which is reserved for further treatment, being added in certain proportion to the next heap for calcination.

Second operation.—Smelting of the calcined ores.— The charges generally are mixed as follows: Calcined ore, 18 to 20 cwts.; crude smalls, 2 to 4 cwts.; slags from the fourth operation, 6 to 4 cwts.; slags from the second operation, 4 to 2 cwts. ; total, 30 cwts. Six charges are run down in the 24 hours, the results being regulus, holding 48 to 65 per cent. of copper; poor slags, holding $\frac{1}{2}$ per cent. of copper; and rich slags, called "cogote" (neck), which is again smelted in the second operation.

Third operation.—Calcination of the regulus. About two-thirds of the regulus produced in the last operation is ground in a Chilian mill, and roasted in a reverberatory furnace. The charge is two tons, and the calcination is completed in 24 hours.

Fourth operation.—In the 24 hours five charges are run down, consisting of the following : calcined regulus, 2 cwts. ; crude ditto, in ingots, 8 to 10 cwts. ; sand, 6 to 10 cwts. ; crude ore, from ore yard sweepings, 6 cwts. The oxides and carbonates are divided between this and the second operation, according to their class. From this there are two important products, namely, regulus, holding from 80 per cent. copper, which forms about 75 per cent. of the product, and black copper of 92 to 95 per cent., forming 25 per cent. of the product, and in which latter is concentrated nearly all the gold and greater part of the silver present in the ore; this is called " bottoms."

Fifth operation.—By this the regulus is refined, and in 30 hours, 28 to 32 bars of copper are produced, weighing from 54 to 60 cwts. The slags from this are smelted in the second operation.

Sixth operation.—The " bottoms," (or black copper) containing the gold and silver, are smelted or run down in a furnace kept apart for this in order simply to give it the required form and weight. The slags from this hold from 2 to 3 per cent. of copper, and are all re-smelted in the second operation.

The word " bottoms " is used in Pilciao, and generally throughout the whole province of Catamarca, in speaking of the metallic copper produced in the fourth operation, by a judicious mixture of the calcined with crude regulus. Only perhaps 25 per cent., as already stated, is so converted or produced by the reaction of the oxides of copper and iron on the crude sulphides under certain conditions of temperature in the furnace. Metallic copper forms a thin film on the surface of the liquid bath, and, owing to its specific gravity being greater than the substratum of regulus, it falls to the bottom of the furnace. A fresh surface is thus exposed to the action of the fire, and a further quantity of metallic copper immediately forms, which in its turn falls to the bottom in the form of rain or fine grains. This process is repeated until all the oxides of copper and iron present in the furnace have been exhausted by their reaction on the sulphides. The mixtures are carefully arranged so that the total charge shall not produce more than 25 per cent. of metallic copper. The theory of this operation is, that the falling shower of metallic copper, from its affinity for gold and silver, attracts and combines with those metals, disseminated through the mass, thereby concentrating their greatest bulk in the small quantity of bottoms produced. The presence of lead or zinc in certain proportions greatly facilitates this operation.

I will proceed to explain the object of this precaution, and the great care necessary to insure success.

It is only within the past two years that Mr. Lafone has been able to profit by the percentage of gold (and I may add the silver) present in the bar copper produced at his works. In Europe, the value of these precious metals in bar copper is only realizable by the owner when the ley for gold exceeds three ounces, and that for silver exceeds sixty ounces to the ton; and previous to the introduction of the system practised by Mr. Schikendantz of making "bottoms," the ley of the exported ordinary copper rarely passed 120 to 130 ounces silver to the ton, and gold in less proportion than the standard ley for realization. With the present system all this is altered; since, instead of the silver and gold being disseminated through the entire mass of ordinary copper produced, they are concentrated in the 25 per cent. of "bottoms" obtained in the manner already described. Thus, for example, when 100 tons are remitted to Europe, 75 will contain scarcely any gold, and rarely more than 100 ounces of silver; but the other 25 tons of "bottoms" hold 200 ounces of silver and from 10 to 12 ounces of gold to the ton. The first sells for £80 to £90, and the last for £135 to £140 per ton. The buyers deduct, against cost of extracting the silver and gold, at the rate of 60 ounces of the former and three ounces of the latter per ton, paying for the excess at the rate of 5s. per ounce of silver, and £3 10s. per ounce of gold. From these explanations it will be easy to comprehend the great importance of the "bottoms" system, and the skill and great care which must be exercised in producing them. In my opinion, however, it would be still more advantageous to simply produce copper regulus, holding silver and gold, and in this state realize it in Europe, as the returning charges upon regulus are not half those paid upon bar copper. The reason of this is very clear. All bar copper holding gold and silver has to be re-smelted with sulphides in Europe, in order to re-convert it into regulus, before either the silver or gold is extractd.

Mr. Lafone employs 555 persons in immediate connection with his extensive reduction works, and as many more are indirectly engaged in providing the workmen with provisions and other necessaries of life. There is a very considerable consumption of merchandise; and it is a notable fact that, whereas, previous to the establishment of the works in Fuerte de Andalgalá, the importations of cotton goods and general merchandise from Buenos Ayres did not exceed £3,500 annually, they now represent a value of over £35,000, or an increase of 900 per cent.

The consumption of hay and the dried fruit of the algarrobo, for the hundreds of animals employed in the works, is almost incredible; in the latter alone £580 has been expended during the present year; it is purchased from the poor peons who gather it at 5d. per arroba of 25 lbs. Flour costs £1 per cwt.; beef, about $1\frac{3}{4}$d. per pound; wood, 4s. 2d. per perch of 16 cubic yards (this is only for carriage and cutting, as the country for leagues around the works belongs to the establishment). The labourers are paid from £1 3s. 4d. to £1 6s. 8d. a month with rations. The freight on ores from the mines to the works is £1 13s. 4d. per ton.

The furnaces last about 45 days without renovation.

The following table shows the ores raised at the *Restauradora* mine during the year 1868 :—

Months.	Weight. Tons. Cwts.				Weight. Tons. Cwts. Lbs.
January	261 18	Containing, by assay, of fine copper,			48 8 28
February	182 16	,,	,,	,,	33 4 12
March	265 18	,,	,,	,,	46 12 45
April	299 10	,,	,,	,,	61 10 25
May	225 3	,,	,,	,,	47 11 23
June	198 18	,,	,,	,,	35 1 28
July	223 11	,,	,,	,,	40 16 36
August	250 12	,,	,,	,,	49 7 74
September	197 8	,,	,,	,,	39 0 19
October	146 2	,,	,,	,,	30 17 69
November	129 2	,,	,,	,,	27 19 51
December	258 12	,,	,,	,,	46 1 24

Total...2,639 10 of ore with fine copper 506 10 34

The average ley for copper, 19.2 per cent.

The following further table shows the ores reduced and quantity of copper produced in the same year at the Pilciao works :—

Months.	Weight.				Weight		
	Tons.	Cwts.	Lbs.		Tons.	Cwts.	Lbs.
January	131	12	0	} Producing copper in bar,	32	10	0
February ...	98	7	9				
March	103	9	0	,, ,,	20	0	0
April	279	13	56	,, ,,	35	0	0
May	341	17	36	,, ,,	50	2	0
June	233	2	0	,, ,,	34	8	0
July	342	3	0	,, ,,	45	0	0
August	411	2	56	,, ,,	50	0	0
September...	314	4	0	,, ,,	50	1	0
October......	440	12	56	,, ,,	50	19	0
November...	273	8	0	,, ,,	51	7	0
December...	275	19	0	,, ,,	33	16	0
Total ...	3,245	0	0	Besides about 60 tons of regulus and other products.	453	3	0

The reduction works at Pipanaco, belonging to Messrs. Carranza, Molina, and Co., are situated seven leagues north-east of Pilciao, and about twelve leagues from the Fuerte del Andalgalá, at the foot of the Ambato range. There are four reverberatory furnaces—two for smelting, one for refining, and one for calcination. They are a little larger in their interior dimensions than those of Mr. Lafone at Pilciao. Their charge is 1 ton 12 cwts., consisting of 24 cwts. of calcined ore and 8 cwts. of slags, and this is run down easily in three hours, being somewhat less hard to smelt.

It is unnecessary to enter into details with respect to the system of reduction in practice here, as it is identical with that followed at Pilciao, the metallurgical operations being also under the direction of Mr. Schickendantz. The ores are, however, of better ley, and more fusible than those of Pilciao; consequently the work of reduction is simpler, and is accomplished with less fuel. Only 64 cubic yards are used for each furnace in the 24 hours; but wood is dearer, costing

6s. 8d. per perch of 16 cubic yards. The freight or transport of ores from the mines is also heavier, being £2 16s. 6d. a ton, without sacks, but only £2 a ton when those are supplied to the muleteer. All the ore traffic from mines to works, as well here as at Pilciao, is done on muleback, but the firewood is carted with oxen.

Here fire-bricks are also manufactured out of quartz and kaolin, which is found in great abundance in the neighbouring hills. Señor Don Mardoqueo Molina was the initiator of this industry. Serious drawbacks were at first encountered in consequence of the use of unsuitable bricks and refractory stones obtained from Paiman, near Famatina, in Rioja. On the other hand, the cost of English bricks is so high, owing to the heavy freight, that, commercially speaking, their use is impossible. These, placed in Catamarca, do not cost less than 2s. each. In the reduction operations, both at Pilciao and Pipanaco, the consumption of iron is greatly economised by the adoption of wooden-headed rabbles for removing the slag and stirring up the charges. Pieces of algarrobo are substituted for iron, each 9 inches long by $4\frac{1}{2}$ in diameter. These are bored and fitted on the long iron rabble-handles, forming its head, and last for one or two days. They have the advantage, being round, of preventing the withdrawal by the labourer of the regulus and copper in conjunction with the slag, which is frequently a source of loss in careless manipulation with iron rabbles.

The copper produced at Pipanaco holds a larger percentage of gold than that of Pilciao, but there is not so much difference as regards the proportion of silver. It generally contains 16 ounces of the former and 180 of the latter to the ton. This is owing both to the higher ley of the ores, and to the presence of blende (sulphide of zinc) and lead, which aids the concentration of the precious metals in the "bottoms." Ores from the *Rosario* have frequently a high ley for gold, and sometimes with native gold visible in specks on the surface. In many instances those ores hold 70 per cent. of copper and 5 ounces of gold to the ton; but when a quantity of this percentage is obtained they are remitted direct to Europe without reduction, and, of course, leave a large profit.

Pipanaco has a great advantage over Pilciao—that of possessing running water—a small stream, which descends from the neighbouring Sierra; with this alfalfa enclosures are irrigated, and a considerable quantity of pasture and vegetables grown. Its position is also advantageous from being on the slope of the hill, thus presenting an easy declivity, which is availed of to facilitate the charging of the furnaces. This is effected by means of a tramway, which runs from east to west through the works, carrying the calcined and crude ore direct to the furnace hopper, where it is dropped in without labour or difficulty, and of course effects a considerable saving.

Though further from the mines than the Pilciao, charges for transport of copper from Pipanaco to the coast are less onerous, the latter being further to the south; but this, I conclude, is hardly equivalent to the difference in freight upon the ores, which are greater in weight and quantity.

The works of Messrs. Carranza and Molina have suffered serious drawbacks in consequence of political convulsions and the arbitrary action of the authorities in past years. The whole of their work people, engaged

at the mines and at their reduction establishment, have
even been seized and compelled to serve in war contin-
gents, notwithstanding the fact that the miner, by his
profession and according to the still existing law (Or-
dinanzas of Mexico), is entirely exempt from military
service; but the Messrs. Molina, being natives of the
country, and of course having their own political views,
frequently in discord with the rulers of the province,
suffer more from these causes than foreigners should.
To these and other causes, more especially bad management and want of economy, is due a serious loss in the
carrying on of these works; but it is satisfactory to be
able to state that a favourable turn has now taken place,
and the enterprising proprietors are gradually recouping
their expenditure. In short, it has happened with
them, as with Mr. Lafone, who, after losing £70,000
and fifteen years of labour, is at present making an annual profit of nearly £13,000.

There are 311 workmen employed at Pipanaco, and
if we take into account all who are indirectly dependent
upon these mines and works in conjunction with those
of Mr. Lafone, the total number cannot be less than
2,000 souls. As the majority of these have families
more or less numerous, we may safely calculate three
for each person, from which it results that 8,000 people
live by the mines and their products, and that too in a
small department of the province.

It would be difficult to exaggerate the importance of
these works and their civilizing influences, more particularly as regards the moral effects produced, and which
are visible upon the inhabitants of the province. There
is nothing more certain than that, were they to stop, or
even temporarily to suspend their operations, the nume-

rous community dependent upon them for support would be thrown into a state of extreme destitution, or, what is worse, the greater part of those who are now maintaining themselves by honourable toil, would probably be converted into hordes of turbulent robbers and assassins.

Both the Government and the people themselves are convinced of these truths, and therefore make every effort to preserve the present happy and prosperous state of things.

In Catamarca, as in the other mining provinces, there are scarcely any carriage roads, and it is a cause of great regret that a matter of such necessity and economic importance, from a commercial point of view, should not have long since received the special attention of the authorities.

From the reduction works at Pilciao and Pipanaco there are natural carriage roads to the Fuerte de Andalgalá, but thence to the mines only mule tracks exist. The latter have been made by Messrs. Lafone, Carranza, and Molina, for their own use, and at a cost of £2,500 These it would be most desirable to widen (that of Mr. Lafone being preferable), and the expense of doing so would not exceed £2,000. Passing the mines, this road descends, skirting the mountains of Las Capillitas, to the Pampa de los Pozuelos, which presents no impediment to following northwards on the western side of Aconquija up to Santa Maria and the frontier of Tucuman.

This would then become the public high road, and most important in facilitating traffic from the south to Salta, Jujuy, and Bolivia; especially from Mendoza, San Juan, and Famatina.

At present no road exists between the city of Cata-marca and the Fort of Andalgalá, even for loaded mules, without making an immense detour to the south. The traffic between those points is very considerable, and ought to be at once accommodated with a good carriage road, which might pass by Singuil, following through the ravine, or quebrada, up stream to reach the pampa of Pucará, afterwards taking the easiest descent to the foot of the Nevado de Aconquija in order to arrive at the Fort of Andalgalá. The distance would be about 40 leagues, and the cost not less than £200 per league.

It is a matter of pressing necessity to render the road between Catamarca and Tucuman available for carriage traffic. The present mule traffic is very great, and the commercial results of such a road must be of incalculable importance. Some years ago it was proposed to accomplish this work, and the necessary surveys and plans were prepared with that object.

After passing through a rich and populous valley it would cross the Ancaste range by the Totoral, which offers no serious difficulty. According to the estimates presented when the surveys were made, the cost of a carriage road from Catamarca by way of Totoral to Tucuman would be £5,300; but, having examined the route and the several points indicated, I am of opinion that it would entail an expenditure of at least £7,500 to £8,500. As for the continuation from the foot of the Totoral pass in Tucuman to the capital of this province it is only necessary to render the actual road more direct by cutting a road through the forests. Numerous rivers (sixteen in all) flow from the Aconquija mountains to the Rio Dulce, and over these it would be impracti-cable, or rather useless, to construct bridges. For in the rainy season the beds of these rivers are swept by violent torrents, carrying down uprooted trees of gigantic size, which, with the accumulation of dense tropical vegetation, form floating islands. These would soon obstruct any bridge which might be erected, and even should this be sufficiently strong to resist the weight and force of the floating masses of trees and vegetation, the result in a few minutes would be the overflow of the banks and inundation of the whole of the surrounding country. The banks of these rivers are mostly low, and certainly not high enough to permit the construction of bridges which would allow the free passage beneath of huge trunks and trees, with their roots and branches projecting many feet out of the water.

These difficulties are almost insuperable, and I fear that it will prove impracticable to carry out the prolongation of the Central Argentine Railway to Tucuman by this route, which is one of two indicated by Señor Moneta, the chief National Engineer, and recommended by its well populated districts and large sugar and tobacco plantations.

The other route examined by Señor Moneta seems to be the most feasible, though not so commercially important as the one first mentioned. It is farther to the eastward, and crosses the Rio Dulce, once to the south, running parallel to its course north up to within a short distance of the city of Tucuman, when it again crosses this river. This route obviates the necessity of crossing so many small streams and rapid rivers, all of which empty themselves into the Dulce at different points to the north from the crossing recommended by Moneta in his second route.

This is, however, a matter for study and careful exploration, which I am glad to say is now being effectually carried out under the able superintendence of Señor Moneta, assisted by a corps of Government engineers. Within a few months we will have the surveys completed, and I trust soon after to see the commencement of this all-important extension of the Central Argentine Railway to the north.

PROVINCE OF TUCUMAN.

GENERAL PHYSICAL ASPECT, DESCRIPTION OF SOIL, CLIMATE, &c.

THE province of Tucuman is situated between 26° and 28° south lat., and 67° and 68° 30′ west long. (Paris); this gives it an extent of 1,200 geographical leagues, equal to about 1,500 Argentine square leagues. It is bounded on the north by the rivers Tala and Urueña, which separate it from Salta; to the east by a line nearly parallel to 67° long., which passes through the great plain to the east of Aconquija, the estancias of Vitiaca, Palomar, Bagual, &c., and also over the Rio Dulce west of the village of Rio Hondo; to the south, the Rio de San Francisco separates it from Catamarca and from Santiago; on the west, by the great Aconquija, a range of mountains whose summit is over 19,000 feet above sea level and is perpetually covered with snow. This line penetrates the valley of Santa Maria by the opening of Tafi, and there forms a plateau of six leagues long and four in breadth, which includes the district of Colalao. The territory of Tucuman is bordered by those of Salta, Santiago del Estero, and Catamarca.

The general aspect of the province is very varied, owing to its vast plains, its mountains, the numerous rivers and streams which run through it, and its luxuriant vegetation. It may nevertheless be divided into two principal regions—that of the plains, which commence at the foot of the mountains of Aconquija, and extend eastward to the limits of Santiago; that of the mountains formed by all the dependencies of the same chain to the limits of Salta and of Catamarca. That portion of the plain around the base of Aconquija is traversed by numerous rivers, and embellished by magnificent forests interspersed with grassy prairies. It is here that the population is most dense and agriculture is in the ascendant. The other portion to the west of Rio Sali, which, lower down, becomes the Rio Dulce, comprises very rich pasture land, equal to the best in Santa Fé or Entre Rios. The breeding of cattle here supercedes agriculture. This splendid *tapis de verdure* is studded here and there with clumps of fine timber trees, resembling our best European park lands, and divided into numerous populated estancias. This part is perfectly level, has no rivers, and only a few lagoons. Water is found at little depth by digging wells. There is always a dry season during one part of the year, although otherwise the province is abundantly supplied by rain.

The mountainous region lies to the north and west of the province. To the north, the mountains are not of great altitude, but form a net work of little chains which cross one another curiously, circumscribing lovely valleys. To the west lies the grand Sierra of Aconquija already alluded to. A number of parallel chains, which are considerably lower, extend parallel to this principal range, and enclose elevated valleys, where the rain, dew, and small streams of water from the melted snow, notwithstanding their altitude, produce a vigorous vegetation, very different from that of the other Andine regions so desolated by drought.

The province of Tucuman, although the smallest in the Republic, is most striking from the abundance of water, the splendour of the vegetation, the variety of its soil, and, in short, the great beauty of the country. Nothing can be more picturesque than the gorges of the Aconquija, with their foamy torrents and their forests of immense cedar trees; nothing more enchanting than the plains which lie at the foot of this giant mountain, and which are irrigated by an infinite number of rivers and streams. Indeed this province is the best watered of any in the Argentine Republic, possessing, as it does, the great advantage of having the sources of its rivers at such an altitude as admits of an unlimited distribution of their waters over the plains, being furnished from the high parts of the Aconquija, to the south of San Francisco; to the east of the Sali there are no rivers, but canals for irrigation might easily be taken there. The great mass of water which comes from the mountains by numerous streams, uniting, form one central course, the Sali, which lower down becomes the Rio Dulce, passing by Santiago del Estero, and finally loses itself in the lagoons of Los Porongos (Cordoba).

This watercourse takes its rise at the extremity north of the Cumbres de Calchaqui, by the branches Riarte and Chamorros, joins itself to the Rio Tala, which forms the boundary line with the province of Salta, then receives the torrents of Acequiones, Alduralde, and Vipos, at the mouth of which it is known under the name of the Rio Sali. Near the capital it is joined by the rivers Tapia and Saladillo; further down it receives the rivers Famailla, Monteros, Rio Seco del Conventillo, Medinas or Gastona, Rio Chico, Matasambe, and Marapa; this last terminates the series of westerly confluents of the Rio Dulce. The Rio San Francisco, which forms the southern limit with Santiago, is lost in the plain further south. On the north-east the Rio Sali receives only three rivulets, viz., Calera, Potrillo. and Loro, which come from the little Sierras Medina and Yorami. The Zapallar and the Urueña, whose course is eastward, are lost in the plain, and rarely reach the rivulet Los Horcones, which is itself absorbed by the sands before touching the Juramento river.

In their upper part these rivulets receive a number of small streams, which are used generally for irrigation; none are navigable, and several are dry during part of the year. With the rains of spring and summer they swell and flow in violent torrents, which makes the Sali dangerous to ford. From the mouth of the Marapa river, the Sali takes the name of Rio Hondo, and afterwards, lower down, that of Rio Dulce, whose ultimate course has been described.

Gneiss and mica-schist constitute the principal geological formation of the mountainous districts, but in some parts there are traces of volcanic action. In the little ranges to the east of Rio Sali there is sandstone and some limestone. This part suffers much from drought, and the vegetation is not so good as on the high western ranges, where the rocks are covered by a rich vegetable earth.

In the plain, the altitude of which varies from 300 to 400 metres, the mould is deep and rich. Instead of the sandy clay soil of the saline districts of the west, the earth here is black and fertile as in Entre Rios and Corrientes; the subsoil is reddish, a little marly, but loose; at a short distance from the mountain scarcely a stone is to be found on the surface. In the dry season the water in the rivers is crystaline, and flows over a bed of fine white sand, whilst in the rainy season it is thick and turbid. The soil of Tucuman is everywhere fertile, and irrigation is not so absolutely necessary for cultivation as in the other Andine provinces.

In the Sierra of Aconquija there are doubtless mineral deposits, containing gold, silver, copper, lead, and iron, together with rock crystal, marbles, limestone, and sandstone, but owing to the dense vegetation and thickness of surface soil, exploration is difficult.

Earthquakes are rarely felt, and the few shocks that have occurred have not been of sufficient violence to cause devastation, and therefore no particular precaution is necessary in the construction of public edifices and houses.

The climate of the province varies according to the altitude of the two regions just mentioned. It is much more humid in the mountainous regions than in the other chains of the Andes. This is owing, no doubt, to the absence of plateaux, and especially to the situation of Aconquija, which is on the borders of the great plain of the pampas. The year is divided into two seasons,—the rainy, which commences at the end of October and continues to March, and the dry, which lasts the remainder of the year; nevertheless there are other periods of rain in the latter season, and abundant dews fall, which stimulate vegetation.

The period of the greatest rain is the hot season, and is nearly always stormy. In the morning the sky is clear and the heat intense; two or three hours after the sun reaches the meridian, storms come on, and rain falls in torrents for about two hours; then the heavens are again clear until the next day. In the mountains the rains are more frequent and more abundant than on the plain; they commence earlier in the season and finish later. Frost is rare and of very short duration, even at an altitude of 450 metres, at which the town of Tucuman is situate, and of which the mean temperature is 21° Cent. It is fresh in the months of July and August, and extremely hot from November to May. Above 800 metres the climate changes suddenly, and as much as 3° frost is felt. The winds in general are not very strong, nor so frequent as in the lower provinces; during the bad, rainy weather, the wind changes from gusts to hurricanes.

The chain of Aconquija presents a remarkable phenomenon, dividing, as it does, the dry regions of the Andes from the more humid climate of the pampas. To the west of this chain it rains during the summer only, and then but rarely. To the east the rains are copious, especially during the hot period.

The climate, although hot eight months of the year, is neither unhealthy nor debilitating; the only malady peculiar to the country is intermittent fever, but, by a better system of drainage, this might, in a great measure, be obviated. The great rains, which fall during summer, cause the overflow of rivers, rivulets, and lagoons, which evaporate towards the end of the autumn, and being highly charged with decomposed vegetable matter, fill the atmosphere with malaria. The intermittent fevers are, however, not violent and of short duration, and might, to a great extent, be avoided by observing regular habits and abstaining from fruit. Diseases of the skin and pulmonary phthisis are met with more frequently than in the adjoining provinces. The pleuropneumonia of the Andes makes its appearance during winter. Notwithstanding all this the country is very healthy; this is proved by the considerable difference which is noted in the returns of births and deaths, being in the proportion of 2 to 1. During a period of 25 years, the register of baptisms in the department of the capital, which is the most populous, was stated at 27,399, whilst the mortality was only 13,641.

We have already alluded to the magnificent vegetation of Tucuman. It is quite tropical on the plains and upon the eastern watershed of the mountains to the altitude of 1,000 metres; higher up—above 2,000 metres—it resembles that of Central Europe.

In the lower districts the heat, combined with humidity, tends to develop, to a prodigious extent, the trees, some of which attain enormous proportions. Laurels at La Fronterita have been known to measure eight metres in circumference, and at the foot of the Sierra cedars (red and white), quebrachos, walnut, lapachos, pacarás, &c., reach a gigantic size and furnish magnificent timber for joiners, cabinet work, and building purposes. Parisitic plants of all sizes cover the old trees of the forests. Among the herbaceous plants there is an infinite number of those which are useful or agreeable for their fruits, flowers, and their medicinal or aromatic properties. In short, this province unites in itself every species of vegetation which we find disseminated over the other parts of the Argentine territory. Agriculture is well developed. After the production of wheat, maize, and rice, for which there is local consumption, they cultivate primitively, in the same soil, the sugar cane and tobacco which form the chief commercial sources of prosperity in the province. The sugar cane was first introduced from Peru, by the Abbé Colombrés, and cultivated in the year 1824, and has since been extensively increased, providing for the consumption, not only of this, but of the neighbouring provinces. Tobacco is now cultivated on a large scale, and forms the principal export to Chili, which country is almost exclusively supplied from this source. The humidity of the summer facilitates the production of maize and rice,—the latter of superior quality. Wheat produces fairly in the mountainous districts at an altitude of 800 metres, but on the plains the heat and humidity of the climate frequently engender blight and destroy the whole crop. This cause also prevents the successful cultivation of the vine near the capital, which, however, does not apply to the mountains. All European vegetables grow well, especially the potato and cabbage, which are exquisite. The plain possesses nearly all the fruit trees of hot climates, the orange, cherimollier, guava, fig, pomegranates, the pistachio nut, &c. As the province of Tucuman partakes of all climates, so all the productions of the world could be easily cultivated. To ordinary agriculture might easily be added the extensive cultivation of cotton and indigo, which latter grows there as an indigenous plant, as also does the cactus, on which the cochineal insect is found in abundance.

Independently of the animals peculiar to the lower provinces, Tucuman possesses the tapir, pecari, the vampire, which torments the cattle at night, the couguar, the scourge of goats and sheep in the mountains, and the jaguar, which is now rare; the boa is seen only in the forests and is comparatively harmless. The condor, eagles, and large birds of prey dwell in the Sierra of Aconquija; likewise the guanaco and vicuña.

Bovine cattle abound, and of a larger and better class than those found in the lower provinces, owing to the superior quality of the pasture and abundance of good water. It is principally from this province that the markets of Chili and Bolivia are supplied, the former by way of Mendoza and San Juan, where, as already stated, the cattle are fattened up on lucerne, and driven over the Andes.

Horses and mules, although found in fair abundance, are principally introduced from Mendoza and San Juan, and this branch of industry is frequently very profitable.

The growth of commerce, and consequently of transit, has raised the price of beasts of burden very considerably, and encourages the breeders in all the Andine provinces. This, however, acts injuriously on the breeding of goats and sheep; the latter produce fine wool, independently of their use as an article of food.

Tucuman is about the most industrious of all the interior provinces of the Argentine Republic. Its distance from the coast obliges it to give special attention to the mechanical arts, and the preparation of wood for building and cabinet work, which is exported to the neighbouring provinces, especially to those of Cuyo; also to the construction of carts, the manufacture of stuffs, and the tanning of hides.

At the present moment the production of tobacco and manufacture of sugar command the principal attention of the inhabitants. Of the latter, there are now 25 large plantations and manufactories, each producing $6\frac{1}{2}$ to

75 tons of sugar, and 50 to 400 barrels (600 to 4,800 gallons) of rum, without enumerating smaller establishments. The total annual production may be estimated at one million of kilogs. of sugar (985 tons); and 7,000 hectolitres (154,000 gallons) of caña or rum. Part is consumed in the province; the remainder is exported to Santiago del Estero, to Catamarca, and to Rioja.

At one of the sugar plantations, the property of Don Wenceslao Posse, I was permitted to make some notes on the produce of his estates and its annual value.

The estate consists of 2,500 acres of splendidly wooded and open pasture land, situate about 10 miles to the south of the city, and 240 acres of this was planted with sugar cane. Some of the plants had been 18 years in the ground and still produced fairly; but it is not considered advantageous to pass the fifteenth year.

It is calculated that an acre will cost about £1 10s. to plant the first year, and will of course only require ordinary care and treatment to keep productive during successive ones. Señor Posse began 24 years ago with a capital of £500; his estate cost then only £75, and this, together with the works, are now worth at least £10,000, according to the local valuation, whilst the annual income derived from it would represent about £5,000.

The annual expenses on the sugar plantation amount to about £2,500, including the boiling down of syrup and production of rum. The produce obtained is as follows:—125 tons (Spanish) sugar, at £40, realizable on the spot, £5,000; 1,600 barrels of rum, sold there at £2 per barrel, £3,200; total produce, £8,200. Deduct cost, £2,500, and 20 per cent. for extras, £500, making £3,000; which leaves a net total of £5,200.

The gathering in of the cane begins usually in June and lasts up to the end of August. It is transported from the fields on bullock carts and delivered at the mill, where it is cleaned of the leaves and passed through a powerful pair of rolls, worked by an overshot water wheel. The syrup is received in a trough beneath, and pumped into vats or deposits, whence it is drawn off by pipes into the boilers, or evaporating pans, and boiled down. The fuel used is wood, but, owing to a very old and now obsolete method of setting the pans, a great waste of caloric takes place, and makes this operation very costly and slow. Formerly the resulting mass of sugar was whitened or decolorised by being placed in earthenware jars of a conical shape, having a hole perforated in the bottom, on which was placed a thin layer of straw. These were filled up to within a few inches of the top, and the remaining space filled up with mud, when the jars were allowed to stand and the treacle to drain off by the perforation in the bottom. This continued for sometimes 60 and 80 days, when the layer of mud was removed and the sugar found to be quite dry and white, the mud having absorbed that portion of the treacle and colouring matter which did not drain off. This system required a very large amount of house accomodation and apparatus, as well as considerable capital to enable the sugar maker to wait for the completion of the process and realize his profits.

Now it is different, as Señor Posse has introduced the well-known centrifugal decolorising machine as used in the West Indies. This is driven by a small steam engine, and performs in a few minutes what on the old principle required months to effect. I believe that only two or three of these machines are as yet in use in the country, and the sugar growers who have them not are obliged to follow the old system just described.

A little rice and some oranges are exported to Cordoba. Tucuman furnishes carts for nearly all the transit of the interior of the Republic; and yet, at the present time, it sends on mule-back the wood for building, joinery, and cabinet work to the provinces of San Juan and Mendoza. They also manufacture furniture for the use of the country. Dry and tanned skins are sent to the coast; as they are of good quality, thanks to the superiority of the bark (quebracho colorado) employed in tanning, they make fair competition with the importations from Europe at Rosario and Buenos Ayres. It is estimated that 60,000 hides per annum are thus prepared. The inhabitants of the mountains excel in the manufacture of cheese, called "Tafi," from the principal estancia where it is made. These cheeses resemble the Roquefort and are of superior quality.

All this commerce enables the province of Tucuman to be large importers of foreign produce, which arrives there by caravans of carts from the coast, or by troops of mules from Chili by the passes of the Cordillera. By the latter route the cost is excessive and the carts are preferred.

Tucuman is evidently making rapid progress. A number of foreigners are settled there, especially Frenchmen and Italians, who have powerfully contributed to the commercial and industrial activity of the country. About 12 years ago the spirit of enterprise, generally so rare and dull in the interior provinces, began to de-develop itself and has produced excellent results. This is principally owing to the introduction of saw mills, worked by water power in the Sierra; iron mills or rolls for the sugar cane; and a large number of agricultural implements. Thus the population manifestly increases in number and advances in civilization.

The province of Tucuman is divided into nine departments, which in their turn are subdivided into six town districts and thirty-nine country districts. These are the Capital, Famailla, Monteros, Rio Chico Chicligasta, Graneros,—all near the eastern base of the Sierra de Aconquija; Leales, on the plain to the east of the Rio Sali; Troncas, in the mountains to the north of the province; Burru-Yacú, in the little Sierras and plains to the north-east. The town of Tucuman is situated in 26° 52′ lat. south and long. 68° 20′ west (Paris), according to Captain Page, U.S. Navy, and at 430 metres above sea level according to De Moussy. It is built on a very level plain, upon the left bank of the Rio Sali, from which it is a mile distant. The ground upon which it is built rises from seven to eight metres above the plain where the Sali flows, and consequently is not subject to its inundations. To the west of the city there are gentle undulations, which gradually mingle with the first spurs of the buttresses of the Aconquija range. The town was originally founded in 1565 by Don Diego de Villaroel, a companion of Pizarro in his conquest of Peru. He gave it the name of San Miguel de Tucuman, and it was situate twelve leagues farther south than the present town and in closer proximity to the river. Twenty years subsequently an inundation destroyed it, when it was abandoned, and the present town was built in a locality less exposed. In its actual position it overlooks the great plains to the west, and the declivity of the land towards the river permits easy drainage of the rain water, and that employed for irrigation, which is derived from the streams in the Sierra during the dry season.

The streets are very long, tolerably wide, and at

right angles. The town consists of 118 squares or blocks of houses, each with 138 metres frontage; this admits of large courtyards and gardens, where the orange tree predominates. The old buildings are generally only of one storey high, with flat and tiled roofs; the numerous modern houses, however, are often of two storeys high, and with terrace roofs as at Buenos Ayres, the system of architecture being perfectly appropriate to the climate, which, as already stated, is so very hot during eight months of the year. The materials consist of excellent brick and lime mortar. Gypsum is abundant, and in the neighbourhood marbles and freestone of excellent quality can be procured. The carpentry is furnished from the magnificent timber of the country. The town is well built, and presents an appearance of gaiety and luxury which is scarcely expected in such a remote interior district.

The most remarkable public edifices are the parish church *Matriz* and the Cabildo. The Matriz is a beautiful modern edifice, ornamented with two square towers 38 metres high, and a dome whose interior is painted in fresco by a French artist. A Doric colonnade forms the portico. The only fault seems to be the width of the lateral naves. The plan and execution are the work of a French architect, M. Pierre Echeverri, an old settler in Tucuman, who also restored, or rather reconstructed, the church of the convent of the Franciscans, which is likewise very beautiful. The decoration of the interior of the Matriz corresponds with the exterior and is in excellent taste. The subscriptions of the faithful, the assistance of the Provincial Government, the application of the tithes which then existed, the activity of the clergy, and the union of all, finally raised this remarkable edifice, under the administration of General Don Celedonio Gutierrez, and the Governors who succeeded him have applied the same zeal to finish and embellish it. The Cabildo, which occupies the west side of the plaza, or principal square, is a heavy edifice of the first Spaniards, ornamented with a high clock tower, and at one time served as a barracks for soldiers. It is now the Provincial Government House, and the Chamber of Deputies meet there. The principal plaza of Tucuman is ornamented with a high column, built in brick and plastered, surmounted by a statue of liberty. This square has been recently planted with orange trees, and provided with marble benches for public accomodation; it is situated in the middle of the town and forms an agreeable promenade. The number of shops which surround it also makes it a very animated and popular centre of resort. Neither the church of the Dominicans, nor the convent or Beatoni de Jesus, nor La Merced present anything worthy of remark.

Two monuments, although in themselves very simple, recall noble souvenirs, not only for the town of Tucuman, but for the whole of the Argentine Republic; the one is a column which is raised near the town, at a spot called La Ciudadela, where, on the 24th of September, 1812, the patriot army, conducted by General Belgrano, gained a complete victory over General Tristan who commanded the Spanish forces; the other, the identical house, including the hall, where, on 9th July, 1816, the first National Congress proclaimed the independence of the country. The plain of Ciudadela is situate southwest of the town, and has been often the theatre of numerous combats during the civil wars.

A social club, composed of the young gallants of the

town, gives a monthly ball to the *élite* of society. These
assemblies are very gay and popular, and there the ami-
able and graceful Tucumanas vic with each other in music
and dancing; indeed I was surprised to find such really
good musicians amongst the young girls—some of whom,
under the tuition of Italian masters, excel in execution.

The outskirts of the capital are well peopled and cultivated; it is here where the principal sugar plantations
and the tanneries are situate. They are divided into
seven districts, viz., Las Aguirres, Chacras del Norte,
comprising the country houses and farms to the north
of the town; Cebil Redondo, to the west, where the
great sugar refinery of Don Felix Frias is situated; to
the south, Yerba Buena; lastly, Chacras on the south-
east, north-east, and north-west. All these districts
are well cultivated and enclosed by ditches and hedges
of the *cactus opuntia.*

From what we have seen of the richness and importance
of this province, it would seem to present one of the
most enchanting places for immigration in South
America.

The extent of land which might be brought under
cultivation by a proper distribution of the surplus
waters, now partially inundating the country, is almost
unlimited. Sugar planting and tobacco growing, as we
have seen, is even now most lucrative, and when railway communication from Cordoba will have placed it
in contact with the lower provinces, and secured a ready
market for its produce, it will indeed be a rich and important territory. Land is comparatively cheap, and
may be purchased in freehold for about $3\frac{1}{2}$d. per acre,
studded with the most valuable trees and fertile in the
extreme. I need scarcely point out that once the rail-

way will have been made, and even before, these lands must increase very rapidly in value, and become eventually a most desirable investment for capital. It is true that at the present moment there is not local consumption for more than is produced in sugar and rice, and the high rates of freight preclude their profitable exportation. But the railway will of course alter all these figures, and these staples must assume their proper place very soon in the markets of Buenos Ayres and Monte Video.

Labour in Tucuman, although scarce, is very cheap, and peones or common workmen may be hired for £2 a month without food.

It would seem a most desirable arrangement to introduce here a number of coolies, to be employed in the sugar plantations, and, no doubt, later on, when men of capital and intelligence direct their attention to this "garden of the Republic," this, and many other important reforms, will take place.

As no mines or mineral veins were being worked in this province, and the existing lodes are so little known or explored, I do not give any particulars as to its mineral resources.

Population, 1869.—City, 17,438; country, 91,668; total, 109,106.

PROVINCE OF SANTIAGO DEL ESTERO.

GENERAL PHYSICAL ASPECT, DESCRIPTION OF SOIL, CLIMATE, &c.

THE Province of Santiago del Estero, to the north of Cordoba, extends between 26° and 30° south lat. and 64° 30′ and 67° west. long. (Paris), and contains 3,500 square miles, without including that part of the Gran Chaco, Tucuman, and Salta, over which it exercises the right of jurisdiction.

It is separated from the province of Cordoba by a line which corresponds nearly with the 30th parallel, and with which coincides a very remarkable division in the nature of the soil, which here ceases to be calcareous and humid, becoming granitic and dry.

To the south-west and west its limits with Catamarca and Rioja are marked by the river Albigasta, the southern prolongation of the Sierra de Ancaste, and the basin of the Salinas. In going northward by the river Albigasta, the line of division between this province and those of Tucuman and Salta passes by a number of inhabited estancias, corresponding to the 67° meridian of west long., and ends at the farm of Mojon, situated on the east side of the Rio Salado. This farm of Mojon marks the frontier on the north with Salta. To the east it borders upon the Gran Chaco and does not extend beyond the preceding river. To the south-east it touches Santa Fé by the desert, at the series of undulations known by the name of Los Altos. All the limits are very vague, and have no defined position, as they lie on a desert, and are rather those given by custom than by legal delineation. If the extent of the province is calculated by that part only which is inhabited its greatest length is from north to south, and then its breadth will be reduced to a few leagues; the territory of the Gran Chaco, inhabited only by wandering tribes of Indians, should naturally be assigned to it.

The average altitude of the province of Santiago del Estero is about 200 metres above the level of the sea, and is situated in a large plain of a sandy-clay nature, which is partly covered with primeval forests and traversed nearly through its centre by a shallow saline basin running from east to west. It is divided from north-west to south-east by two rivers, the Rio Salado or Juramento, and the Rio Dulce, which flow parallel to each other, and between which is centered the majority of the population of the province. Towards the middle is a low range of mountains of a species of granite, called Guazayan; to the south of the basin of the Salinas begin to rise by gentle undulations the mass of mountains designated in other parts of this work as the great central Argentine range.

The Rio Juramento or Salado borders the north-east of the province, and forms the frontier upon the Chaco, together with the estancias of San Miguel and Mojon. These two rivers are studded with farms, principally for breeding cattle, but when they overflow the land is prodigiously fertile and agriculture is followed. As far as Sepulturas the Juramento is engorged, compact, and deep, owing to the natural sudden declivity of the country; but from this point the country becomes so flat that the waters meander right and left, forming lagoons and shallows, and rendering navigation impossible. It is only at Navicha that one finds again the bed of the river well defined, after which it flows through the desert and to the Indian territory. From Sepulturas to Navicha there are three vast bañados or marshes, formed by the overflow of the river, namely, San Antonio, also called the lagoon of Tomacop-Hoyon, and Bracho, above the fort of this name, and those of Navicha below.

The left bank of the Salado is bordered with thorny forests so thick that it is impossible to penetrate them except by some openings known only to the natives. The right bank is more open, and produces good pasture, where numerous cattle farms are established. Near the banks are lagoons, with more or less water, according to the height of the river and the quantity of rain which falls in the province. From Navicha to the territory of Santa Fé the river is compact and deep, but nevertheless is fordable in several places. In 1860 a number of small forts were established on its banks, some on the site of the old Spanish forts, and others in new localities, chosen as much for their strategic position commanding the passes as for their fertility. From the Fort of Bracho to Monte Aguara the Salado forms the military line of frontier of the Republic upon the Chaco.

The Rio Dulce, formed by all the rivulets and torrents which descend from the great range of Aconquija, enters the province of Santiago by the village of Rio Hondo, flowing from west to east across an undulating country towards the capital, and is bordered by high protecting banks, which maintain it in its course. Passing to the east of the town of Santiago, it runs towards the south-east across a country absolutely flat; fifteen leagues lower down, at Tayuyo, there are several old beds, over which, in the course of years, the river has alternately passed. During the overflows large quantities of silt are deposited, which successively fill up these beds, and the last one which remained open was unfortunately directed towards the side of the Salinas, where it has formed a lagoon, whose waters flow sluggishly and afterwards rejoin their old bed, much lower down, forming the river Saladillo.

The Saladillo is a river of considerable size and depth, flowing through a natural fosse, which formerly received the rain waters of the basin of the Salinas and carried them to the Rio Dulce. But in 1825, when the Dulce, near Tayuyo, opened a new course towards the Salinas, its waters passed and still continue to flow entirely into the Saladillo, which it has enlarged, and whose bed it has deepened in such a manner as to make it a copious and rapid river during the rainy seasons. It is by this means that the Rio Dulce regains its old bed at Paso de San Cristoval. From this place the Dulce, now united to the Saladillo, but no longer salt and bitter, flows towards the lagoon Los Porongos.

The lands bordering the Rio Dulce towards the north are moderately wooded and fit for agriculture. Lower down they are covered alternately with pasture and thick forests, having at intervals well-cultivated farms and homesteads. The Saladillo flows through a saline sandy desert, but nevertheless, near the lagoons formed by the new course of the Rio Dulce, the cultivation of cereals is possible, and even advantageous, as the lands covered by water in the summer and autumn are fertilized and left dry in the spring.

For nearly two degrees of latitude, the two rivers Juramento and Dulce flow parallel to one another, leaving a space between them varying from 15 to 25 leagues, but which may average 20 leagues. This space is an absolute plain of sandy clay soil, covered partly with forest trees and partly with pasture, having some saline districts, in the midst of which lagoons of fresh water are found. In some places deep furrows indicate the old bed of the Rio Dulce and traces of communication between the two rivers.

The conformation of the land in the neighbourhood of the Juramento and Dulce, and in the major part of the province, is favourable to the formation of a large number of lagoons, temporary or permanent, and more or less numerous, according as the rivers have been abundant and the overflow of the two rivers more violent. These lagoons receive the name of " esteros," whence is derived that of the province Santiago del Estero (St. James of the Rivulet).

In the north of the province there exists a stream called Rio de los Horcones, whose waters only reach the Salado after very heavy rains. The different rivulets which form the main stream take their source from the eastern hills of Salta and Tucuman.

The nature of the soil of the province varies according to the locality. It is composed principally of a granitic sand in the districts bordering on the mountains of Ancaste, in Catamarca, and of the Cordovese chain, situated to the south and west of the Saladillo, as also in the district of Guazayan. It is of a sandy, clayey nature, and saline in all the lower borders of the Salinas, and generally in the region of the plains, except towards the north, where the salt disappears.

The basin of the Salinas is composed of a gritty, sandy clay, covered everywhere by efflorescent salts. The pools which are formed there by rain, when the water evaporates, leave a crust of salt on the surface. Salt is also found on the borders of the Saladillo deposited by evaporation of its waters.

Between the two rivers, Salado and Dulce, the soil is of the same nature, but of a yellow colour and very loose. Fresh water is found at a depth of from five to twenty metres. In all this region there is a thick stratum of vegetable earth, and near the river the land is entirely composed of recent alluvial. Towards the north-west the soil is firmer, more compact, and retains more moisture, gradually mingling with the fertile plains of Tucuman.

The saline substances, so abundant in the greater part of the province of Santiago, are generally chloride of sodium and sulphate of soda and magnesia, as if the earth had originally been covered by a vast deposit of salt water.

Fossils are sometimes found in this province, belonging in the major part to the tertiary period. The remains of the mammiferi, and the shells found in the strata of the banks of the Salado and Dulce, prove the correctness of this classification.

The climate of the province of Santiago del Estero is usually dry. Little rain falls, except during the hot season, that is November to March; nearly all the remainder of the year the sky is clear and bright. Frost is very rare, a fact that renders possible the cultivation of tropical plants. The summer is very hot, especially in the neighbourhood of the Salinas, where the heat rises to 42° Cent. This district is subject to scorching winds, but of short duration; the north wind especially is always intensely hot and humid, blowing sometimes for 24 hours. The mean annual temperature of the province varies from 20° to 24° Cent.

This climate is extremely salubrious. The only malady peculiar to the province is ophtalmia, but less dangerous than that of Egypt. As in Egypt, this affection is evidently owing to the intensity of the glare, and especially to the saline dust raised there by winds; this disease is most prevalent in the neighbourhood of the Salinas.

In the places where the soil is dry and light, such as near the Sierras, in the neighbourhood of the Salinas, and in the plains where the waters of the Rio Dulce become briny, the vegetation is generally meagre and limited to a thorny species of the mimosa. But near the two rivers, and in the long tract of land intersected by them, and where rain moistens the soil, all the arborescent species, such as the algarrobos, the various quebrachos, the talas, gayacs, &c., attain a great height, and might furnish all the necessary timber for building and carpentry. Notwithstanding the dryness of the climate, and the scarcity of rain during one part of the year, the forests cover at least two-thirds of the province. In these latter a cactus grows in abundance, which nourishes a cochineal insect of good quality. In the saline plain immense quantities of "jume" (lycium salsium), are found, which, as before stated, is eminently alkaline, and grows to a metre and a half in height.

There is good grass land towards the south-east, on the frontier of Santa Fé, between the lagoon Los Porongos and Rio Salado. Wheat and maize are cultivated and yield plentifully. After the periodic inundations of the Salado and Dulce, which cover the neighbouring plains with salt, wheat is sown which then yields a hundred-fold. If irrigation canals were made from the Rio Dulce a soil of incredible fertility might be produced. The sugar cane is cultivated near the capital and succeeds well. Arrow-root is also planted there and grows fairly. Vegetables are extremely rare, simply owing to the apathy of the natives, who will not produce them.

As to fruit trees, the province produces in abundance the peach, orange, fig, vine, and pomegranate; all others are neglected, although the country is suitable for almost every species of European fruit and a large number of those of the tropics; but the inhabitants are content with their natural productions.

The cultivation of cereals is considerable enough to allow of a small export trade in flour to be carried on with the provinces of Tucuman and Cordoba. The produce of the sugar cane suffices only for the consumption of the province. Tobacco is not cultivated, although the soil is most appropriate; neither is the cochineal plant or insect utilized, although in great abundance. Tobacco from Tucuman is exclusively consumed, and the inhabitants content themselves by gathering in small quantities the cochineal insects, which are dried and made up into thin cakes for use as a pigment for dyeing their rough fabrics, and for export to a very small extent to the neighbouring provinces.

The forests of Santiago abound with wild bees, whose nests are found in the crevices of the trunks of elm trees and even in the ground ; they produce an excellent honey, known as *miel de palo*, or wood honey. The inhabitants eagerly gather this natural product, and even extend their explorations for it to the forests on the eastern side of the Rio Salado ; some *mieleros* (honeyseekers), whilst so engaged in the Gran Chaco, have fallen victims to the Indians. The honey and wax collected by these people constitute an article of commerce with the coast.

The province exports both tanned and dry raw hides. Wool is of sufficiently good quality to become an article of export to some extent ; the advantages derived from this trade has induced the owners to think of improving the breed, which is small, and whose fleece is not weighty, although naturally fine.

Manufactures in the province are few, but the women are extremely dexterous in embroidery ; everywhere may be seen embroidered napkins, petticoats, and cotton laces remarkably well wrought. These pretty articles are sent to the coast and lower provinces, where they are much appreciated. They also spin and weave ponchos and coverlets, dyed with the richest colours, which the semi-Indian race, constituting the mass of the inhabitants, most ingeniously prepare from natural local sources.

The town of Santiago del Estero is the centre of commerce for the province, and is situated on the great northern route to Peru and Bolivia, by which passes the principal traffic for Tucuman and Salta. It is the only road much frequented, because the old route by way of Santa Fé and the Chaco is not yet re-opened.

Large ferry-boats have been established on the principal passages of the Rio Dulce, which facilitate the transit, but a bridge is absolutely needed over the Saladillo.

The communication between Santiago and the western provinces is simply by bridle paths which offer no other inconvenience than the want of habitations in the travesias. The road to Catamarca is good and open; that of Rioja is much less so because of the vast plain, part sandy and barren, which extends to the north and north-west of the basin of the Salinas. The roads through the district intersected by the two rivers Dulce and Salado are perfectly practicable and well peopled with estancias. Nearly all the roads are practicable for carts which are used very frequently. Some troops of mules are employed to convey produce and merchandise, but carts are generally preferred.

The mass of the population of Santiago, *i.e.*, of the working classes, is Indian, almost pure, but now civilised and docile; they still, however, retain their own language (quichua), are intelligent, industrious, and hard-working, and rather disposed to immigrate to the other provinces, where labour is better remunerated. It is thus that a great number are found in the rural departments of the province of Buenos Ayres. They make good soldiers and are excellent horsemen, as are Argentines generally. Their food is more vegetable than animal, consisting of the fruit of the algarrobo, —already described in Catamarca—and they use a fermented drink called " chicha " in considerable quantities, which is much appreciated by the lower classes.

The province of Santiago del Estero is divided into 14 departments, viz., towards the centre, the Capital; near the town to the north, the Banda; north-west upon the Rio Dulce, Jimenez and Rio Hondo; to the west, Guazayan, in the little Sierra of this name; and the south-west, Cholla; to the north upon the Rio Sallado, Copo; to the east, also upon the Rio Salado, Matara ; to the south-east upon the Rio Dulce, Robles, Silipica, Loreto, Soconcho, Salavina; to the extreme south and in the Sierra of this name, Sumampa.

The department of the Capital is composed only of the town and its outskirts. Santiago is the most ancient town in the interior of the Argentine Confederation, having been founded in 1553 by Aguirre, one of the first conquerors and colonisers of Tucuman, and has been the residence of the first bishop of the province. It is situated upon the right bank of the Rio Dulce, on alluvial soil, absolutely flat. About half a league to the south may be traced the old banks of the river. The soil about the town is very fertile, although impregnated with a quantity of sulphate of soda; this salt is injurious to the buildings in attacking and gradually destroying the foundations of the walls. They cultivate in the environs the sugar-cane, and wheat and maize, and some fruit trees, as also the orange, fig, pomegranate, vine, peaches, and some dates; few European plants are yet imported. Vegetation is vigorous, principally in those places subjected to irrigation, which is not difficult, owing to the declivity of the banks of the Rio Dulce The altitude of Santiago is 162 metres above the level of the sea; its lat. 27° 47′ and its long. west 66° 42′.

This town possesses no very remarkable edifice. The ancient church, erected in the Plaza, is in ruins, and the front only remains, which is preserved out of respect to its great antiquity; it is of fair architecture. The new parish church is small, and of the most simple form, but of solid construction and in good order. The church of the present college of Santo Domingo belonged formerly to the Jesuits; the remains of their library is deposited in one of the chambers of the convent; their books consist principally of treatises on theology. The convent of San Francisco has been rebuilt, almost entirely under the administration of Governor Ibarra. Here is shown a wonderfully preserved relic,—the cell formerly occupied by San Francisco Solano, apostle of Tucuman and Paraguay. It contains a statue of the saint, having suspended from its girdle the violin by which he attracted and captivated the attention of the Indians. The church possesses a pretty organ, manufactured in the place by a Bolivian artist, assisted by native workmen. The convent of "Beatorio" is a pious establishment, founded about 21 years ago by Doña Ana Antonia Toboada, who not only endowed it with part of her fortune, but did what she could to collect charities from the neighbouring provinces. This convent is of the highest importance to the province, as it.is the only establishment for the education of girls, the elementary schools of the department being generally only adapted for boys.

Santiago possesses no other public edifice. The Government offices are in the house formerly occupied by the Governor Ibarra, who commanded the province for nearly thirty years. The private houses are plain, commodious, and often built in adobes, or sun-dried bricks; their gardens are neglected, but the town nevertheless has not a bad appearance, aided by the arborescent vegetation which encircles it. The outskirts are well cultivated and support a dense population.

The river, upon the right bank of which Santiago is built, measures 100 metres in width, is clear, and only one metre deep during the dry season, but two or three during the floods. It flows then with violence and constantly destroys the banks. This is, however, sought to be avoided by plantations of willows and poplars in order to consolidate them and to restrain the water. This is very necessary, as in a violent flood it might leave its bed and cause great devastation in the town itself.

Santiago is now progressing somewhat faster than during the past ten years. His Excellency Don Antonio Toboada, the actual Governor, is a man of marked talent, and manifests the greatest desire to benefit his native province by liberal legislative acts and the introduction of a foreign immigration. He offers large tracts of land to be settled upon, and doubtless, when the prolongation of the Central Argentine, or other line, reaches this vast territory, most valuable tracts of now desert land will be eagerly cultivated.

From the lie of the country I would venture to prognosticate a brilliant success in agriculture by a judicious system of irrigation. There is abundance of water in the Rio Dulce, on the borders of Tucuman, and large canals might be cut with comparative facility and at moderate cost, following the natural declivity of the surface southwards. If, for example, the track of the Central Argentine Railway should pass in a straight line from Devisaderos in Cordoba to Tucuman, instead of deviating westwards to the Horqueta in Catamarca, it would embrace a new and important district which might be fertilized by a large canal from the head waters of the Dulce, cut parallel to the railway, and serving the double purpose of supplying fresh water for the locomotives as well as for domestic use and agriculture.

This is, however, a problem which only the exploration and survey now being made will determine. But if carried out, the whole of that vast territory might become, within the next twenty years, an immense indigo and sugar plantation. We find at the present moment a very large extent of country covered with the indigenous plant (*indigofera tinctoria*), and whose crudely manufactured indigo is of excellent quality.

The National Government, in its rapid march of progress, is now having the province traversed by the electric wire, and within a few months instantaneous communication with the capital will be in active operation.

One of the most striking features in passing through the province of Santiago is the almost total absence of horned cattle along the line of road. Although there are fair pasture lands and dense forests about, it is evident that the want of water is the only cause which exists to prevent the rearing and breeding of cattle in large numbers; yet, as I have before stated, nearly all the water of two fine rivers is allowed to overflow and waste itself in shallow saline basins, inutilizing the soil, and making the transit over those parts extremely difficult and dangerous.

Population, 1869:—City, 8,719; country, 124,525; total, 133,244.

PROVINCE OF CORDOBA.

GENERAL PHYSICAL ASPECT, DESCRIPTION OF SOIL, CLIMATE, &c.

THE Province of Cordoba, the most central of the Argentine Confederation, is situated between 29° 40″ and 34° south lat., and 64° and 67° 30″ west long. (Paris). It thus embraces an area of about 6,000 square leagues. Its limits to the north and south are nearly the two parallels which we have just indicated; that of the north coincides with the lagoons of Los Porongos and the borders of the Salinas; that of the south with the great pampas, abandoned to the Indians, which extend to the other side of the Rio Quinto. To the west, the line of Quebracho Herrado, of Arroyo de las Tortugas, and its prolongation towards the south, separates it from Santa Fé. To the east, the extremity of the Salinas forms its limit with the provinces of La Rioja and San Juan; the little Sierra de la Lomita, the Rio de la Cruz, and the Sierra de la Estanzuela separate it from San Luis.

The general aspect of this province is that of a vast plain, of which the declivity inclines from west to east, towards the Rio Paraná, and in the midst of which rises a high granitic mountain chain, perfectly isolated. This pile of mountains is very abrupt towards the west; it is less rugged and more undulating towards the east and south. Upon these two points the declivity terminates in rich fertile pampas, which resemble those of Santa Fé, Buenos Ayres, and the Indian territory towards the south. On the summit of this range is a plateau, at an elevation of 2,000 metres above the sea, suitable only for cattle. At 1,000 metres is another plateau, where the soil and climate are suitable for cultivation. The numerous valleys, opening at various points, are clothed with a rich vegetation. From these heights descend numerous streams and rivers, utilized in cultivation on the plains, and of these the principal unite in forming the four chief rivers of the province.

The Rio Tercero, the principal river of the province, rises from the south-western summit of the ridge, and flows through nearly the entire province, watering Villa Nueva, Frayle Muerto (Belville), and eventually falling into the Paraná ten leagues above Rosario. The other rivers are designated as follows, commencing at the north :—

The Rio Primero is formed by the union of the several rivulets watering the valleys of the range to W.N.W. of Cordoba; it descends as a rapid stream into the plain, and flows into the little valley, or narrow hollow, where is situated the capital of the province. No part is navigable, but its waters are most valuable for irrigation, which fertilises the suburbs and surrounding country. The Rio Primero flows through the valley of Cordoba, takes an E.N.E. direction, and is lost in the pampas not far from Mar Chiquita, where its waters arrive by a series of shallow marshes. Inundations, arising from the swelling of its waters during the rainy seasons, are sometimes dangerous to the town of Cordoba.

The Rio Segundo is not so important as the preceding; it is formed of two principal branches,—the one Rio de Sansacate and the other Segundo proper; these unite in debouching from the mountain range. The Segundo thus forms a river of moderate depth, about 100 metres broad, and is navigable in certain parts. When freshets come down its course is parallel to that of Rio Primero, from which it is separated by a distance of nine leagues, and, flowing in the same direction, like it, teminates in shallow marshes at a short distance from Mar Chiquita, but with which, however, it is sometimes connected. These two rivers are quite analogous in their form and the direction of their waters.

The Rio Cuarto flows towards the south-east, and is formed, like the Tercero, in the high valleys of the Cumbres de Lutis, which is the most southern plateau of the range. Large and rapid, but of little depth, it arrives at the rising town of Concepcion del Rio Cuarto, the second in importance in the province of Cordoba; then, reaching the middle of the pampas, south, its waters are lost in shallow pools, where it becomes brackish, and, reuniting, under the name of Rio Saladillo, they flow into the Rio Tercero, near the village of this name. This river, without being navigable, has a volume of water sufficiently strong for the purpose of irrigating a large tract of country.

All the other watercourses of the province of Cordoba are only rivulets from the mountains, whose waters are utilized entirely for irrigation, and which only reach a short distance into the plain. Those which flow eastward in part fall into the rivers we have just mentioned, and those on the west of the range, such as Rios de los Sauces, Soto, Pichama, Del Eje, &c., &c., are lost in the neighbourhood of the Salinas. The number of these watercourses is unfortunately very limited, but without them there would be no absolute security for agriculture, because of the dryness of the soil and seasons in this region.

The north-east of the province of Cordoba presents a very remarkable system of waters but little known until the present time. The group of lagoons in which the Rio Dulce is lost is designated Los Porongos, and there is another very large lagoon, called Mar Chiquita, or little sea.

The southern shore of this latter was explored in 1861, by the ingenuity of Laberge, who followed the traces of the Rio Primero and the Rio Segundo, which discharge their surplus waters into it. It is thought by the inhabitants that Mar Chiquita forms an immense lagoon, of which the greatest extent is from west to east, and that it unites with those of Los Porongos by another inter mediate lagoon, called Del Soldado, and by shallow canals, sometimes dry and sometimes filled with water.

What renders it difficult to gain a knowledge of these shallows is that the waters are sometimes saline and sometimes not so; the muddy borders render walking extremely difficult, owing to the acquatic plants of every species which grow about and form a sort of moving morass. All the country comprised between lat. 30° and 31° and long. 64° and 65° forms a vast basin, into which the rain water falls, and whence there is no issue except by evaporation. The Mar Chiquita has fewer islands than Los Porongos, its borders are absolutely smooth, and the waters advance or recede according to the winds, sometimes revealing uncovered a long slimy beach where salt is found and collected. There are some dwellings in the neighbourhood of the lake, and in some places sweet water is found by digging wells, while in others the earth consists of layers of saline sandy clay. The district is wooded, but almost entirely with the thorny mimosa. It is in this basin that the Rio Dulce is lost, and the swellings of this river have a great influence upon the height of the waters in the lake, which are highest in January (summer) and lowest in winter. The northern borders are slightly elevated, but to the south and south-east they are everywhere low and marshy, nearly all the neighbouring region being excessively flat; from the nature of the land the waters do not reach any considerable distance.

The soil of the eastern plain of Cordoba is similar to that of the provinces of Santa Fé and Buenos Ayres, namely, a rich vegetable earth, more or less thick, and forming a superstratum of black clay, saline in some places, but producing beautiful pastures. These plains have received the name of the " Pampa." There are trees only as we approach the mountain range, and the wood is poor and thorny, being composed principally of chañar, espinillo, or algarrobo, all belonging to the mimosa species. These woods increase in extent towards the Mar Chiquita, and mingle with those of Santa Fé. Towards the south the eye wanders over an immense grassy plain, slightly undulating. In the region of the mountains the soil is generally granitic, but there are plateaux and valleys where the earth is suitable for the production of every agricultural species. In the plain, which commences in a westerly direction, it is clayey and a little saline, being, however, very light and fertile by the aid of irrigation. All the valleys which are open to this side are wooded with trees of good height, and those species which on the eastern side are poor and stunted, such as the chañar, algarrobo, and talas, attain in this region their full development. The most elevated plateaux of the range are those which constitute its summit, and, where the rock is not absolutely bare, produce a short thick turf on which sheep thrive well.

The climate on the plain of Cordoba is similar to that of Santa Fé and Entre Rios, but the winter is always drier and more healthy than at Buenos Ayres. On approaching the mountains rains are rare in winter, but from October to March (spring and summer) they are abundant; hence the necessity of irrigation for the purposes of agriculture. The temperature is regulated according to the altitude of the place; its lowest is 16° Cent. in the capital, which is 400 metres above the level of the sea. It sometimes freezes, with snow, although rarely. In the mountain districts it freezes more intensely, but the frosts are of short duration, and the snow lies only on the top of the mountains, as the heavens are nearly always radiant with the sun. The temperature of all the plateaux, whose altitude is not greater than 1,200 metres, is generally mild, as is evident from the palm tree flourishing at this altitude. The western districts are much warmer, because of their proximity to the Salinas of the Llanos. The prevailing winds are south and north; in summer the rains are almost always accompanied by thunderstorms.

The salubrity of this climate is perfect, and the public health excellent. Indeed in no part of the Republic is the climate more suitable to invalids than at Cordoba. For affections of the chest especially it is not to be surpassed perhaps in the world, and doubtless, when communication with Europe becomes more general and less expensive, it will be resorted to by many, hitherto frequenters of Madeira and other places, not now so efficatious as was formerly supposed.

The altitude of some parts and general vast extent of the province, and nature of the soil, necessarily varies vegetation considerably. The plain produces only a species of long prairie grass, whilst, in the mountain districts, we find trees and shrubs, with good soft grass, covering a vast extent of country. In the plains, near Mar Chiquita, and in general all those north of 32° parallel, there are fine stretches of park land and true forests. These are composed principally of algarrobos, ñandubays, talas, quebrachos (red and white), chañar, &c., and in the mountains, brea, jarilla, talaquillo, palm, &c. The arborescent plants are principally of the family of mimosa, and usually thorny. These woods suffice only for local consumption.

Agriculture in Cordoba is limited to the production of wheat and maize necessary for the population, the most common vegetables, and fodder, more especially lucerne. Arborculture is neglected, although the soil and climate are suitable for almost all fruit trees. The vine, for which the soil is admirably adapted, is not cultivated. The apple tree is the only one cultivated in sufficient quantities, and might produce excellent cider if the people would only dedicate themselves to it. The variety of the soil, temperature, and situation of the province of Cordoba is admirably suited for all European plants and trees, as well as a large number of those of the tropics.

The scarcity of rain during one part of the year (winter) renders irrigation indispensable for agriculture in most southern parts of the province; for this purpose the rivulets are utilized, but the rivers Primero, Segundo, Tercero, and Cuarto would furnish water for very large tracts of land towards the east, as well as those of the mountainous district, and for the plains towards the pampas. Little attention is, however, paid to this important question, which later on must be successfully worked out, and will undoubtedly be a source of great wealth to those who initiate it.

The principal commerce is in the exportation of cattle to the Andine provinces for Chili, to Buenos Ayres, and to Santa Fé, for the slaughter house, together with the hides of those slaughtered for local consumption in the province. There is a large trade in live cattle for the numerous carts in the transport service from Tucuman to the Paraná. Mules are sent in large numbers to the neighbouring provinces and to Bolivia. Wool was also a lucrative source of exportation, principally to and from the towns of Villa Nueva and Frayle Muerto (now Belville). Goat skins are also exported in large numbers.

A little wheat only is sent to the coast; the remainder is consumed in the province, while, from the neglected culture of the vine, they are obliged to buy the wines of Rioja and San Juan, as well as the dry figs of Catamarca.

There is, however, some little animation in manufactures. Hides are tanned and imitation morocco leather produced, whilst boots and shoes for the adjacent provinces are made in fair quantities. They also manufacture coarse woollen fabrics of excellent quality, such as "jergas," or rough blankets and coverlets for beds, in brilliant colours and pretty patterns, which are very durable.

Its central position in the continent of South America

must always make Cordoba the centre of extensive commercial transit, and its capital must necessarily become the entrepôt for all the interior. The facilities of communication with the coast now established by railway and steamboat contribute greatly to its growing activity and importance, and it is fast becoming the favourite resort for Bolivian merchants, who prefer having their merchandize by way of Cordoba, to crossing the Andes and purchasing in Peru or the western ports of the Pacific.

Notwithstanding the height of the mountain range which occupies the central part of the province, the communication is everywhere easy. The first and most important route is that of the ancient road from the capital to Rosario, about 113 leagues, which is now of course obsolete, the railway being completed. That to Santa Fé, although well traced, is not much frequented. The one from Cordoba to Santiago and Tucuman, to the north, is the ancient highroad to Peru and Bolivia, and is tolerably good and level. The other road, to the south, unites with that of Rosario to Mendoza at the town of Rio Cuarto. Communication with Rioja and Catamarca are made almost uniform by carriage ways, rounding the northern point of the Sierra, and crossing the great Salinas to Horqueta and Don Diego. The mountain range, in its central part, is cut by the direct route to San Juan and Rioja, and is now an excellent cart road, with post-houses and reservoirs for water. Diligences are now established upon all these roads once a week for Tucuman, Rioja, Catamarca, Rio Cuarto, Mendoza, and San Juan, which are sufficient for the present intercourse, and can be increased whenever the exigencies of trade require it The least frequented of these roads is that of Santa Fé, all business being centred in Rosario. Of course the most important of all means of transit is the Central Argentine Railway, now opened from Rosario to Cordoba, 247 miles.

The province is divided into fourteen departments. The sections comprised in the mountain district are :— Tulumba, Rio Seco, Ischilin, the Pumilla (distinguished as Cruz del Eje), Pocho, San Javier, and Rio Cuarto.

The sections comprised in the plain are :—The Capital, Anejos (distinguished as Rio de Zeballos), Calamuchita, Rio Tercero Arriba, Rio Tercero Abajo, Rio Segundo, and Santa Rosa.

There are few large towns in the province. After the capital there are only Santa Rosa, Rio Cuarto, Villa Nueva, Frayle Muerto, Rosario de los Ranchos, Tulumba, Rio Seco, San Francisco del Chañar, and San Pedro de los Sauces. All the others are villages, or rather hamlets, with a few houses grouped around the church. The numerous estates or farms are scattered about the environs or on the approaches to the towns and valleys. Wherever there is a stream of water suitable for irrigation small farms stud its banks. The great estancias of the plain are generally near a lagoon, or an artificial reservoir, where their animals can allay their thirst.

The department of the capital is limited to the town of Cordoba, with its precincts, and is surrounded entirely by that of Los Anejos, which extends from Santo Domingo to Alta Gracia, along the mountains, sixteen leagues north to south, and ten broad.

The town of Cordoba, founded in 1573, was the ancient capital of Tucuman during the Spanish dominion. It is situated about four leagues from the mountains, at an altitude of 1,200 feet above the level of the sea, in 31°

25' south latitude. It is built in a valley, on low ground, originally formed by deposits during floods, and on the borders of the Rio Primero. The banks, whose summits form the level of the pampas, surrounding the town, are very steep, and measure about 60 feet in height. Now the Rio Primero flows altogether on the north side, where its banks are perpendicular, whilst those on the south side form a gentle declivity. This conformation of the soil places Cordoba in a sort of sandy hollow, and subjects it to inundations, not only from the river, but from torrents, for the most part of the year dry, but which increase considerably in the rainy season, and are only restrained in their force by a solid stone wall, first constructed in 1671 under the government of Peredo. On 31st January, 1863, an enormous body of water, similar to that of 1st May, 1823, half a century before, threatened the existence of the town, and produced great devastation, but by various improvements in the breakwater these disasters are no longer feared.

Cordoba is well built, and contains several substantial edifices, among them the Cabildo, constructed at the commencement of this century by the Marquis of Sobremonte; the cathedral, finished in the 17th century; and eight other churches, besides convents. The streets, marking the four cardinal points, are at right angles, and each block or manzana contains four acres. The *cuadra* (front of each block) is 150 Spanish varas long, and the houses are consequently on a grand scale. The streets are not paved (with one exception), which is, however, not of much consequence, as the decomposed granitic sand, which forms the surface, makes good roads, and each street is furnished with footways flagged with granite or marble.

The most ornamental buildings are the Cabildo, or Hôtel de Ville, in which are the Government Offices, and the cathedral, a noble edifice, well constructed, of a composite architecture, and the dome of which is most effective. The interior is ornamented with pilasters, in part overlaid with beautiful marble from the neighbouring mountains; the altars and walls are adorned by some choice pictures. After the cathedral of Buenos Ayres, that of Cordoba, with the Matriz of Tucuman and the church of Uruguay, are the finest edifices in the Argentine Confederation.

To the Marquis of Sobremonte, one of the Spanish Viceroys or Governors, Cordoba is indebted for a very picturesque promenade. This is situated about 600 yards from the principal Plaza or square, and consists of a grand quadrangular basin of water, measuring 100 metres each side, planted all round with double rows of poplars and willows, and enclosed with iron railings. There is a wide promenade between the avenues of trees, and rustic sofas are placed around at convenient distances. With the lateral streets this promenade occupies nearly six acres, and communicates on the south with the centre of the town by a long avenue; on the west, it is surrounded by lovely *quintas*, or country houses, with fruit gardens, forming a large district, divided into squares like the town, and well planted with trees along the streets, which makes it most pleasing during the sweltering heat of summer. These gardens are irrigated by small canals from the Rio Primero, and are of surpassing fertility. Here all the principal townsfolk live during summer, and pass a most agreeable existence amongst delicious fruit trees and cool rippling streams of limpid water.

After the cathedral may be mentioned the churches of the convents of La Merced, San Francisco, Santa Catalina, and Santa Teresa, which are all of modern construction, and in the best condition, owing to the superb marbles which the native mountains furnish in abundance. It would be easy and inexpensive to utilize this fine material for the formation of public edifices and private houses, but Cordoba has hitherto not been fortunate enough to possess artisans who could work it to advantage.

The church of the University, formerly that of the Jesuits, and built by them in 1671, is grand and beautiful in the interior, although now entirely neglected. Over the high altar is a fine old painting of the crucifixion, said to be from the brush of Peter Paul Reubens, and presented by him to the Jesuits. It is a magnificent building, and formerly the college of Saint Charles was attached to it. The whole of this edifice has now become the property of the National Government, and the University and Preparatory Colleges are established here. The buildings sadly required restoration, and are being gradually attended to by the Government authorities.

There is also in the town an hospital with sixty beds, which is sufficient for the wants of the population. It is annexed to the church of San Roque, and is supported by the public revenue and voluntary contributions. It is under the direction of the Sisters of Charity, who came from France some years ago. The three monasteries contain a good number of friars, but the Jesuits have been expelled for many years past. The two nunneries are limited,—that of the Catalinas to 40, that of Teresas to 24 inmates, and vacancies are filled from the postulants, who have to pay a dower of 2,000 hard dollars. These convents are well maintained, and have sufficient property to support them and for charitable purposes.

The Bishopric of Cordoba—first created in 1699—has recently been re-established. The Chapter is complete.

Cordoba at one time possessed a mint, which coined only silver of ·750 milesimos fine, but it is no longer allowed to work; the National Government only having the right to coin. The metal coined was the produce of the mines in the department of Pochi. There are two steam mills, and several *barracas* or large deposits for country produce, for which this place is a great entrepôt.

The press is fairly represented in Cordoba, and three daily newspapers, very creditably edited, retail the current events. The most important is the *Eco de Cordoba*, edited by Dr. Luis Velez, a clever young lawyer, who was formerly Minister of the province, and who is now Deputy to the National Congress. He is assisted by his brother, Don Ignacio Velez, and his cousin, Don Adolfo Mansilla, who share the editorial labours. The principles of this journal are Liberal, and it supports warmly the present national administration.

The next in importance is the *Progreso*, edited by Dr. Ramon Gil-Navarro, and represents the Conservative or Federal interests.

The third is an insignificant journal, *El Constitucional*, merely published for political ends, and supported more by private individuals than the public; its principles are Radical, and the editors are many—amongst them Dr. Nicolas Peñaloza.

In the neighbourhood of the capital is an ancient

Indian village called " El Pueblito," now consisting only of a few half-breeds. This is the last remnant of the aborigines of the valley. They do little in agriculture, and only breed a few goats and cows. Their appearance and habits are disgusting, and they form the worst element of disorder in times of political excitement.

The impulse which the completion of the Central Argentine Railway has given to commerce and agriculture in the province of Cordoba is almost incredible, and the enormous increase in the value of land and house property there is such as is only experienced in the new countries of the western world.

The numerous agricultural colonies springing up along the line of railway testify to the advantages derived by increasing the facilities of communication and intercourse with the coast and capital of the Republic. At Belville, and other places on the track, may now be seen in active operation the steam plough, with all the most advanced and modern agricultural machinery, which, in a country like this—sparse of labourers or other population—is almost a *sine qua non* for success Land, which was purchased there six years ago for £150 a square league (6,768 acres), is now worth from £300 to £500, and in the course of six years more will doubtless be worth double or treble this sum. The new Land Company, formed in London to colonize 900,000 acres of the Central Argentine Railway lands, will give such a stimulus to those districts that within ten years from this time the province will be so transformed as to be unrecognizable to the most familiar denizen of the country.

Those lands will undoubtedly fetch an average of £1

per acre, and the amount of produce which must naturally follow their development will in itself form an important source of revenue for the railway.

. To populate the lands, as contemplated by the new
company, will require about 9,000 families, which may
be taken at an average of four to each, resulting in
36,000 producers. These, as they go on prospering,
will assuredly induce their relatives and connections in
Europe to join them, and when all the company's lands
—six miles in breadth—shall have been occupied, the
adjoining ones on each side of the track must begin
gradually to be peopled; hence, once a certain nucleus
of population shall have been formed along a tract of
country six miles wide by 250 in length, it is easy to
predicate the lasting success and profitable future of
this great national undertaking.

Another great source of prosperity will be the growing of flax and utilizing of its products in the manufacture of linens, an article of great consumption all over
South America. Already a sturdy and intelligent pioneer in this branch of industry has struck the first blow,
and planted the germ of success on the pampa. To Mr.
Henly is due the merit of initiating this most valuable
culture in the Argentine Republic, and his efforts deserve
well of the country, its Government and its people. He
has taken out with him to Belville a large number of
young men, selected from the ranks of the most respec-
table agricultural classes in England, and, with such a
basis as a beginning, no fears need be entertained of his
ultimate success.

His experiments in the River Plate territories have
been already most successful in this direction, and the
flax produced on virgin soil, without manure and with

very ordinary care and tillage, has turned out superior to almost any yet produced by the best systems of culture in Europe. Its fibre is long and tough, and manufacturers will doubtless ere long eagerly seek to purchase it in preference to the European staple.

The produce in cereals this year (1870), as I have been credibly informed, will, in the province of Cordoba alone, be more than sufficient for the consumption of the riverine provinces, which have hitherto drawn their supplies from Chili and the Andine districts, of course at high prices from the distance and freights. This is a most encouraging feature in a young country and for a new agricultural district. In short, when I look back at the state of the country even five years ago, and compare it with its present condition, I am so astonished with its progress that only positive data and figures can convince me of its reality. But when I consider what the next ten years, with peace and tranquillity, and with constitutional and enlightened Governments, may do, I am confounded, and really afraid to express my honest conviction as to the enormous strides in progress, wealth, and civilization which the Argentine Republic is destined most assuredly to make.

The town of Rio Cuarto, owing to the extension of the railway from Villa Maria, will soon assume a degree of importance hitherto denied it. This line has just been contracted for by a London firm, and will be completed in 1873. The distance from Villa Maria to Rio Cuarto is only 82 miles. But this branch will secure to the trunk line of railway all the western traffic which hitherto passed on carts to Rosario direct; as the owners of produce very justly observe that, after passing some 20 or 25 days with their carts across the pampa, it is not worth their while to transfer their goods to the train at Villa Maria, which is only three or four days' extra march from Rosario. From Rio Cuarto it will be different, as the distance is greater, and the difficulties of the road between it and Villa Maria, including the crossing of two rivers, will be sufficient to induce them to make Rio Cuarto their terminus, and transfer all the goods to the railway. Land and house property has increased in value enormously about this town.

Villa Nueva is another important town, situate on the south side of the Rio Tercero, and immediately in front of the railway station at Villa Maria. This latter has grown up, as if by magic, in the midst of a wilderness, which the author remembers a few years ago as the favourite haunt of wild deer and the scene of frequent nocturnal invasions by the red man of the pampa. Now it is studded with handsome little edifices, amongst them two or three fine hotels. Business is very brisk, and all day long the yells of the noisy waggon driver, and unbearable screeching of the wooden-axled, cumbrous carretas resound through the forest, and wake up stirring echoes, which, although not melodious, proclaim the march of civilization and commerce.

Farther east, and nearer Rosario, is situated Belville —formerly Frayle Muerto,—the centre of British agricultural enterprise in the River Plate. This little village is now the property of a gentleman of energy and industrious perseverance, who, by sheer determination to succeed, *has* succeeded, in establishing a thriving colony composed of some of the first blood of our English landed gentry. To Mr. Melrose is due the introduction of the steam plough to South America, and our worthy President, Señor Sarmiento, paid him a very high compliment on his achievements when recently on a visit to the colony. It was during this visit (in February, 1870) that his Excellency wiped out the name of Frayle Muerto (Dead Friar), and in true American style, having ascertained who was the first English settler there (Mr. Bell), proclaimed to the assembled guests that thenceforth it should bear the name of Belville. Immediately on his return to the capital, the President addressed a long note to the author, detailing the experience he gathered in that memorable trip to the provinces, which will doubtless stimulate the rapid development of their agricultural resources.

I cannot do better than translate, almost literally, his Excellency's most able letter, and although it has been already published in some of the leading journals of the world's metropolis, it may prove interesting to those whose notice it may probably have escaped :—

The President of the Republic
  to Major F. Ignacio Rickard.

BUENOS AYRES, Feb. 12th, 1870.

MY ESTEEMED FRIEND,

Your letter just received contains some valuable suggestions. As you observe, the great question for this country is that of immigration, and your communication, informing me that philanthropists and capitalists propose to encourage it, reached me just two days after my return from Cordoba, Santa Fé, and Entre Rios, where I had proceeded, accompanied by all the foreign Ministers (with the exception of the English representative), in order to inspect for myself the colonies formed by Germans, Swiss, and Italians. The result of this journey will be of immense importance, and the indications in your letter tend to confirm my convictions.

What I have seen surpassed all that I could possibly have anticipated. The efforts to cultivate the land in Santa Fé and Cordoba have proved extraordinarily successful. In nineteen colonies, some of them with eight square leagues (72 square miles) under cultivation, all the families, each possessing twenty cuadras (80 acres) enjoy the greatest abundance. The President of the Municipality of Esperanza stated in his speech what, perhaps, has never been before said in any community, —" *Here, sir, we are all rich.*" And he spoke the truth. The same, and perhaps greater prosperity, exists in all the other colonies.

In Frayle Muerto, now named Belville, a number of young Englishmen have, with equal success, commenced the cultivation of the pampa, bringing into operation steam ploughs and all the most perfect mechanical appliances employed in English agriculture. Many are now rich, and propose to extend the sphere of their labours. In Cañada de Gomez, on the lands of the Central Argentine Railway, another experiment has been made by the son-in-law of Mr. Wheelwright, with the best results yet obtained, having, for instance, cultivated, sown, and reaped in ten months a square mile, the produce of which almost covered the total original outlay. Thus, 4,000 leagues of land may, in four years, be brought under cultivation, if we have colonists willing to take them at moderate prices, and with long terms for payment of the purchase money. The colonists of Santa Fé have, within the second or third year at furthest, discharged their original liabilities, which included the cost of the land and advances for provisions, implements, homesteads, and live stock. One colonist has erected a mill at a cost of £10,000 sterling, and be boasts that he had not more than five francs in his pocket when he arrived in the country. The province of Santa Fé offers, by a law of the Legislature, 1,000 leagues of land for sale at the rate of about £30 for every 80 acres, to be paid within five years. The Gran Chaco Railway possesses 190 leagues, which the proprietors are desirous to colonize as early as possible, and the province of Cordoba has all the country which has been conquered this year from the Indians between Rio Cuarto and Rio Quinto. The National Government can dispose of two leagues along the route of the railway, already contracted for, between the Rio Cuarto and Villa Maria. I need not mention to you the Chaco and Missions, for they are more distant from the populated portions of the Republic.

Therefore you need have no anxiety with reference to lands nor the favourable conditions on which they may be acquired. They are here ready for you, whether along the navigable rivers or opened up by railway communication, and sufficient for the location of 100,000 families!

The most important point, however, and to which I would call your earnest attention—is the selection of the immigrants, and our aim should be, if possible, to obtain those from the North of Europe, and Englishmen in particular. But I fear that, through the mistaken sentiments of philanthropy, the excess of population in the great cities—people little fitted for the labours of the field and frequently ill-prepared for hard work— may be sent to these countries.

I am aware that such is the state of things created in the rural districts in England by the extensive application of machinery and capital to agriculture on a large scale, that the small tenant farmers and labourers cannot find the means of subsistence. These are the people who ought to be preferred, and intelligent philanthropists should direct their efforts to provide means for their conveyance out and settlement. Within two years they would be in a position to repay all that had been advanced to them, and would have raised themselves to the position of proprietors—comparatively rich and happy.

For a distance of eighty miles the railway was laid down, as you know, upon the surface of the plains, without the necessity of raising earthworks.

The first great work here is to plough; the second to reap.

The colonies of Santa Fé were formed by giving to each family 80 acres of land, a rancho or house, a plough, a yoke of oxen, and subsistence for a year; and, in general, all has been repaid in three years at the outside. The Legislature of Santa Fé solicited from the National Government their guarantee for a million hard dollars to make advances to and secure the introduction of colonists, but the Congress refused their assent to the proposal. If associations could be organised in England to send out agricultural colonists, the land will serve as a guarantee for the advances made.

It is, therefore, important that you should make known the advantages which exist here, and which are not now so positive in the United States, where mechanics and artizans are preferred, because the American agriculturists are themselves more suitable than European labourers for farming operations in that territory.

You may, in view of these facts and data, which are unquestionable, for I have myself collected them on the spot, after having conversed with the colonists in every direction, assure those interested in emigration that in no country whatever can settlers secure superior or more tangible advantages. The impulse is given, and that part of the territory which lies between the Parana and the Rio Quinto is destined to become the arena of a dense and rapidly increasing population, to the vast profit of the country and its inhabitants.

My entire journey through those districts, though fatiguing from the heat, has been a real march of pleasure and triumph, marked by cordial expressions of kindness from people of all nations, equally with our own, the populations universally appreciating the benefits of peace, which has now taken permanent root in the country.

I may observe that the mode of settlement adopted in the English colony of Belville, Cañada de Gomez, &c., appears to me to be superior to all others; and shows me what might be done here by 4,000 or 6,000 young Englishmen, with a certain amount of capital and machinery, and possessing that intelligence which has created such enchanting homesteads in Great Britain.

The frontiers are now secure against invasion, and northwards have been carried back to the Paso del Rei; Octavian tranquillity and peace reign in the interior; and as to the credit of the Republic, you in London can judge more correctly than we can. My desire is to render these elements fruitful, and as far as possible to transform our pastoral into agricultural industry by means of an extensive system of immigration, which, as I have already said, I prefer to be English.

Hasten forward the conclusion of your work, and return as soon as possible. Inspire capitalists with confidence in the country; above all agitate the question of Agricultural Emigration, and command the support of your sincere friend,

D. F. SARMIENTO.

The sentiments expressed in the foregoing note do honour to the ruler of the Argentine nation, and ought to prove to us the vivid interest he takes in the peopling of his country by British colonists. He has passed many years amongst our half-brothers in the great Republic of the north, and is fully convinced of the great superiority of the Anglo-Saxon race.

I will conclude this sketch of the province of Cordoba by simply stating that I consider it, and the adjoining province of Santa Fé, as destined to outstrip all the others in the rapid development of their pastoral and agricultural wealth. They have enlightened and wise Governments, directed by men whose interests are bound up in the prosperity of the country, and who will not hesitate to make every personal sacrifice to ensure its success and advancement.

Population, 1869.—City, 34,476; country, 181,765; total, 216,241.

MINERAL RESOURCES, &c.

This province, from its geographical situation, proximity to the centres of commerce and population on the coast, and superior facilities for transport and communication, may be regarded as one of the most important, as respects its vast, but still undeveloped mineral wealth. From a commercial point of view, it is perhaps entitled to rank at the head of the other provinces, for, though its ores are not so rich in silver as those of Rioja, they are of greater mercantile value, owing to their abundance and the existence of easy and cheap means of transport to European markets. The mines of Cordoba are, therefore, well worthy of the serious attention of capitalists at home and abroad.

Mining operations are at present carried on to a very limited extent, and these with neither energy, enterprise, nor spirit. This is partly due to the restricted capital employed, and the want of practical knowledge on the part of the miners themselves. Besides, nearly all the mines are invaded by water at a depth of 15 fathoms, and though the quantity is comparatively inconsiderable, it is sufficiently important to defy the feeble efforts made for its suppression by the aid of leathern bags and badly constructed lifts.

The mines of Cordoba can only be efficiently drained and worked by the aid of steam engines, with good pumps. The ground and district are favourable for the transport and erection of such machinery; there is also abundance of fuel, and the completion of the new cart road from Cordoba to San Juan will render the mines easily accessible and place them in facile communication with each other.

The silver lead mining districts of the province are situate on the far side of the high Sierra to the west of the city, and at a distance by the carriage road of 40 leagues, more or less, but, by crossing the mountains in a direct line, a saving of at least ten leagues is effected. There are two districts of special importance, those of Guayco and Ojo de Agua, respectively located in the departments of Minas and Cruz del Eje.

The copper mining district is at the eastern foot of the Sierra, south of the capital, and by road is situate at a distance of 16 leagues. This road is level and good, and the district itself is in the department of Calamuchita.

MINERAL DISTRICT OF ARGENTINA OR OJO DE AGUA.

The only mine at work in this district was the *Compañia*, belonging to the Messrs. Roque Brothers. It is much worked out, gutted superficially, and exhausted to the lowest accessible levels. These are at a vertical depth of only twenty fathoms and in water. The vein runs from west to east ; 22 degrees to the north, towards which it has also an inclination or dip of 45 degrees. It is about nine inches in width, and was stated to be in beneficio in the lower levels, with argentiferous galenas, holding 177 ounces of silver to the ton; but, the water preventing personal inspection, I am unable to confirm this assertion. There is a vertical shaft sunk on the lode 45 metres in depth, which Messrs. Roque now utilize for the manufacture of lead shot.

This lode has yielded rich silver ores on the surface, principally " warm metals" (chlorides), which were then beneficiated by amalgamation; but this system has now been abandoned in the district, as nearly all the veins, on being followed in depth, are found to consist of argentiferous galenas, or sulphides of lead with silver. This mine was worked from the year 1835 to 1861, with two or three intervals of paralyzation, and the net profit to its owners is estimated to have been £5,500 to £6,500. The actual workings are limited to superficial explorations, more with the object of keeping them open and preserving legal rights of ownership than of obtaining profit; the principal beneficio being in the lower levels, a steam engine and good pumps would be necessary to drain them. Only two miners and one labourer were employed at the time of my visit.

In this department a considerable number of mines have either suspended work or are abandoned. One of these, to which special reference may be made, is called *La Argentina*, which was formerly the most famous mine of its time, and is still well worthy of attention. It belongs to Messrs. Lastra and Co., and was discovered in the year 1834. The direction of the lode is almost identical with that of the *Compañia*, and is about a yard in width. On the surface the ores are " warm" and quartzose, with an average ley for silver of 118.4 to 148 ounces to the ton. At greater depth the vein is composed of galena, mixed with " warm metals," but the walls are so loose and broken up that heavy timbering would be necessary for its safe working. There is a vertical shaft of thirty fathoms on the lode, and an eight-horse steam-engine with two pumps still exist, but not very serviceable in their present condition and after many years of abandonment. These were imported from England in the year 1838, and are consequently of antiquated construction. The engine was, nevertheless, in more serviceable condition than the pumps, and with a little repair and good pumps the water in the mine might be easily kept under. Unfortunately the political disturbances of 1840, and the despotic orders of the tyrant Rosas compelled the owners to fly the country and abandon their labours. On the return of the proprietors it was restored to working order by a French machinist, but the results were not satisfactory.

There are the remains of a reverberatory furnace, with a stack 40 feet high close to the mine. It was constructed many years ago to reduce ores with litharge and the ash of the jumé (impure carbonate of soda), but without much success.

The mine is worked for about 100 yards longitudinally, and might be re-opened advantageously.

Very wide veins of auriferous iron ore, which ought to hold a fair proportion of gold, exist in the neighbourhood; but, unfortunately, having lost the samples taken for assay, I am not in a position to state the actual ley. Nevertheless, judging by the class of ore, these veins are probably of commercial value.

There are numerous virgin lodes in this department, and many others that have been superficially worked and abandoned; but, if an impulse were given to mining industry in this part of the republic, no doubt most of these lodes would be profitably utilized.

MINERAL DISTRICT OF GUAYCO.

There are seven mines in actual work in this district :—

1. The *Buena Ventura* mine is the property of Messrs. Manuel de la Lastra and Co., and is situate in the Cerro of Casa del Tigre, at a distance of 39 leagues from the capital. The vein, which is firm and well formed, runs from south to north, and is composed of galena and blende, holding 148 ounces to the ton; it is about a yard in width. There are two workings in rich beneficio, one at 20 fathoms and the other at 35 fathoms; both are in water. There is also a vertical shaft of 18 fathoms, another of ten fathoms; two hand pumps were in use to expel the water. Many workings are in *pinta*, or first-class ore. The capital invested was about £5,800. Seventy men were employed. Only one level was being

worked, the others being neglected from want of resources.

2. The *Santiago* mine, which belongs to the same owners, is located in the Cerro Juan Chiquito, at a distance from the capital of 38 leagues. The lode is firm, half a yard in width, in argentiferous galenas, holding about 118.4 ounces of silver to the ton. Its direction is also south to north. There are four workings, two of which are in beneficio; but only one was yielding ore. A vertical shaft has been sunk to a depth of 15 fathoms. Thirty men were employed. The capital invested about £2,000. The workings are in water.

3. The *Ana Maria* mine belongs to Messrs. Adolfo Roque and Co., and is situate in the Cerro de las Vacas, at a distance of 36 leagues from the capital. This vein runs from south to north, and consists of galena and blende, holding about 254.56 ounces of silver to the ton. There are four workings in beneficio and one in brocco; the claim covers a superficial extent of 400 yards, worked to a depth of about 20 fathoms. Only one working was in actual yield, the others being neglected for want of pecuniary resources. The capital invested is not over £100, and not more than ten men were employed.

4. The *Peregrina* mine, belonging to Messrs. Gay and Illanes, is located in the Cañada de la Brea, at a a distance of 36 leagues from the capital. The direction of this vein, which is about a quarter of a yard in width, is also from south to north, and consists of galena and blende, holding 88.8 ounces of silver to the ton. There is but one working, which is in beneficio, about twelve fathoms in length and six in depth. About £300 had been invested, and only 17 men were employed.

5. The *Henriqueta* mine is the property of Don Julian Courthiade, and is situate in the Cerro San Jorge, at a distance of 39 leagues from the capital. The vein runs from south to north, and consists of galena and blende, holding 118.4 ounces of silver to the ton. One working, 25 fathoms in length, is in beneficio, but various others are in brocco. There is a vertical shaft sunk to a depth of about 22 fathoms. The lower workings are in water, and neglected on that account, the owners not possessing the necessary means for its removal. Capital invested very inconsiderable, and only twelve men were employed.

6. The *Puerto* mine belongs to the same owner as the preceding, and is located in the Cerro Aguardita de los Tunas, about 40 leagues distant from the capital. The direction of the lode is east to west, and consists of galena and blende, holding 148 ounces of silver to the ton. There were two workings, one being in beneficio and the other in brocco. Both were yielding ore. This mine had been recently discovered. Capital invested very small, and only 13 men were employed.

7. The *Niño-Dios* mine is the property of Messrs. Bustamente and Co., and situate in the Cerro La Trilla, at a distance of 30 leagues from the capital. This vein, like the preceding, runs from east to west, and consists of galena and blende, holding 118.4 ounces of silver to the ton. There are three workings, only one of which is in actual yield, the others being neglected for want of capital and means to remove the water. The workings are all in beneficio, and have vertical shafts, respectively sunk to a depth of about 27, 22, and 15 fathoms. An adit has also been driven for 250 yards. Capital invested upwards of £3,000, and 92 men were employed.

In addition to these there are about eighty mines, which have been more or less worked out, but the major part of them so choked up with earth and water as to render personal examination impossible. They are now public property, and include some lodes which might be of great importance. As in the case of the *Bella Americana* and *San Augustin*, there are a number of firm and well formed lodes, almost vertical, and varying in width from 1 to $1\frac{1}{2}$ yards, with well defined walls. Water appears in nearly all of them at a depth of 15 fathoms, which is the cause of their having been abandoned, the people being, as before stated, without adequate means for removing the water by pumps, while the mountains, from their gentle and easy declivity, are unfavourable to adit driving. All these mines are without exception worked out and almost exhausted on the surface, where chlorides of silver were abundantly found; indeed, I saw quartz stones with small pieces of this precious metal half an inch thick, holding 75 per cent. of silver.

The system of working followed in Cordoba consists principally of galleries, whose pillars are stoped out and the whole of the ore extracted.

I consider the veins to be firm, well formed, and lasting, and believe that their exploitation would prove very profitable if good and efficient machinery for removing the water and raising the ores were applied. The water taken from the mine could be utilized for washing and dressing the ores, to be sold in this state for treatment at the reduction establishments. To accomplish this, however, and to place the workings on a profitable footing, it would be necessary to invest at least about £3,400.

The geological formation is the primary, volcanic and granitic, accompanied by metamorphic rocks. Gneiss and serpentine are found in nearly all parts of the Ojo de Agua district, and the primitive schists and serpentine, with syenite, in that of Guayco.

Below I quote some figures to show the ley of the Cordoba ores as compared with those of some European countries and districts exhibited at the Paris Universal Exhibition of 1867. I take the data from a pamphlet published in France, by M. Fuchs, of the Imperial Corps of Mining Engineers, and M. Banderalli, Civil Mining Engineer.

The nations, whose ores' are compared with those of Corboba, are as follows :—

France,—ley of silver to the ton,				48.1888	ounces.
Germany	„	„	„	40.7888	„
Belgium	„	„	„	59.4000	„
Switzerland	„	„	„	13.6160	„
Italy	„	„	„	5.6240	„
Sardinia	„	„	„	10.6560	„
Spain	„	„	„	59.4000	„
Average ley		„	„	33.8920	„
Argentine Republic :—					
Province of Cordoba		„	„	103.6000	„

The actual produce of mining in the province of Cordoba is, I need hardly state, entirely out of proportion to its mineral resources, the development of which is almost at a stand-still, owing to the complete prostration of mining operations arising from the causes already indicated. When, however, from the years 1861 to 1866, the mines of the province were being worked with greater vigour and activity, highly favourable and promising results were obtained. From one mine alone—the *Santa Eufemia*—with two years' working, 34,669 ounces of silver were extracted by Don Augusto Conil, the value of which may be stated at about £9,350. Many of the mines of Messrs. Roque and Lastra were equally productive, and the annual produce of the mines in the period specified may, without exaggeration, be estimated at more or less 1,850,000 ounces of silver, or an approximate value of £50,000.

REDUCTION WORKS.

At the time of my visit only three works for the treatment of ore were in active operation, *i.e.*, the *Trapiche de Mercedes* (Taninga), the *Ojo de Agua*, and *Santa Barbara*.

The first is at a distance of 25 leagues westwards from Corboba, and is situate in the valley of Salsacaste, about 14 leagues south from Guayco. It belongs to Messrs. Manuel de la Lastra and Co., but is now rented by Don Antonio Garassini, an Italian, who was resmelting the old slags, mixed with ores, which he either purchased, or received to smelt, charging returning dues. This establishment consists of two blast furnaces, one for refining, and two reverberatory furnaces for slagging and calcining the ores.

The system followed is precisely the same as that in practice at La Huerta, San Juan, by the Messrs. Klappenbach, a description of which has been previously given. The sole difference is that here the throat of the blast furnace is not allowed to flame, which is a most important feature in economical smelting, and avoiding loss by volatilization of the lead.

In Taninga they have better blowing machines than

in La Huerta, the apparatus being what the French call the " trompe."

There is a large quantity of old slags left from former smelting operations—not less than 3,750 tons, holding about 20 per cent. of lead and 14·8 ounces of silver to the ton.   Formerly the object of reduction was solely to extract the silver from the ores, disregarding the lead, the exportation of the latter being at that time commercially unprofitable; now it is different, as the Messrs. Roque utilize it in the manufacture of shot, for which there is a large consumption.

Sixty-seven persons were employed at these reduction works, with 200 oxen, 20 carts, 60 mules, and 8 muleteers.

During the year 1868, 220 tons of ores were smelted, exclusive of the old slags, producing about 22,000 ounces of silver of an approximate value of £5,600.

The average ley of the ores received from the mines and reduced was 103·6 ounces of silver to the ton, and 50 per cent. of lead.

About 38 tons of ore are reduced per month, and the proprietor charges for smelting at the rate of £6 . per ton, delivering the resulting bar silver, but retaining the lead to the profit of the works.

Firewood is abundant, and costs 4s. per ton; charcoal about 21s, and freight on the conveyance of ores from Guayco to Taninga, 9s. 4d. per ton.   There is plenty of natural grass pasture, but little alfalfa.   A considerable stream of water runs close to the works.   There are old works close to for the amalgamation of ores on the old system, whose barrels and machinery still exist, but are now broken down and almost totally useless.

There are also a set of stamps and two jigging machines for washing the ores and ground slags.

The stock of lead in deposit consisted of 7½ tons, with 2,220 ounces of silver, and 15 tons of lead reduced from litharge for shot, containing about 13·32 ounces of silver to the ton; the precious metal is not, however, further extracted from the latter, as the cost would be too great.

The capital invested, £5,000; the houses are convenient and roomy.

The *Ojo de Agua* reduction works are situate seven leagues to the north-east from Taninga, in the direction of the mining district of Guayco. They formerly belonged to Messrs. Roque Brothers, and were established in the year 1834 by Don Leon Roque, (now sole owner) who carried them on for some time, beneficiating "warm metals" by the process of amalgamation; but argentiferous galena having appeared in almost all the veins in depth, he changed the system for smelting furnaces. At the beginning many difficulties were experienced, and these were not surmounted until Don Leon Roque visited Pontgibaud, in France, whence he introduced the system then in operation there, and which is now almost universally followed in the Argentine Republic.

This system is very imperfect, and has for this reason been abandoned at Pontgibaud; but at *Ojo de Agua* and elsewhere in the Republic the native peones are incapable of working by any other, and this prevents improvements and alterations being made.

The dimensions of the furnaces at Taninga and Santa Barbara, as well as at La Huerta, in San Juan, were taken from those of Ojo de Agua.

In fifteen years Messrs. Roque smelted large quantities of ore, realizing thereby a considerable fortune. For some years past, however, the works have been partially abandoned and fallen into a dilapidated state, owing to the repeated absence of the owner in France and the abandonment of the establishment to the native labourers.

At the time of my visit an old mayordomo was engaged in smelting slags solely with the view to extract lead for the manufacture of shot. There is only one blast furnace, one for refining, and another for calcining and slagging. The system is similar to that in practice at La Huerta, in San Juan, already described.

The motive power is an overshot water wheel, 25 feet in diameter and only fifteen inches breast; as the supply of water is very limited, the highest possible fall has to be secured. This wheel propels the fan, and another, 20 feet in diameter, further up on the stream, works three heads of stamps for preparing the ore for calcination.

The furnaces at these works were about to be repaired and others constructed upon a better system, in conformity with that now adopted at Pontgibaud, where Señor Roque had been permitted to study them, and which are more or less similar to those erected at Hilario, in San Juan.

There is a large accumulation of old slags here—about 5,000 tons—holding from 15 to 20 per cent. of lead and a small quantity of silver.

At a short distance from the reduction works is situate the shot manufactory, built over the shaft of the mine *Compañia*, which has been utilized for this purpose. About $2\frac{1}{2}$ tons of shot can be turned out daily, but of course this rate of production is not kept up continuously. This enterprise has already yielded a splendid profit, the lead converted into shot realizing about £2 per cwt.

The following were employed at the reduction works in May, 1869, namely, 1 mayordomo, 4 carpenters, 2 masons, 1 blacksmith, 42 labourers, and 20 wood cutters, charcoal burners, and muleteers, assisted by 60 peones, making a grand total of 130 persons. There were also 62 oxen, 212 mules, and 2 carts occupied about the works.

The labourers receive 13s. 4d. per month, with daily rations, consisting of 1 lb. beef and 2 cups of maize. Those employed in the mines are paid from 16s. 8d. to £1, and the fore-miners £1 13s. 4d., which is less than in any other part of the Republic.

Maize, in normal times, costs from 10s. to 13s. 4d. per fanega (300 lbs.); beef is cheap—a young ox may be bought for £2, and cows at £1 6s. 8d. to £1 13s. 4d., according to condition and weight.

There is a vineyard and a fine orchard of fruit trees at the works, as also very comfortable dwelling houses for the men.

The *Santa Barbara* reduction establishment is situate at a distance of nine leagues northwards from Ojo de Agua and two leagues from Guayco. It belongs to Don Manuel de la Lastra and Co., and was in full activity, smelting ores, mixed with bottoms from the refining furnace and old slags.

The works consist of three blast, one reverberatory and one refining furnace. The only difference between the system adopted at *Santa Barbara* and that in practice at the other establishments in the province is the calcination of the ores in "tabiques," or partially enclosed rectangular spaces, in the open air before the final calcination and slagging in the reverberatory furnace. There are two Chilian mills, or edge runners, worked by mule power, and the blast is supplied by the trompe; as already explained at Taninga, the fall of water is 36 feet, and there is abundance of it. These works are better situated than either of the others, and more adapted for an extension of business, as the abundance of water affords an important source of motive power and is otherwise of great utility. The dwelling houses and alfalfa enclosures are good, and the lands of the establishment, which are extensive, are also of superior character.

In the year 1868 eighty-four tons of ore were smelted, and produced 13,941 ounces of silver, whose value there would be about £3,700.

The total monthly disbursements were about £80. Firewood costs 2s. 8d. per ton; charcoal, £1 per ton; flour, 16s. 8d. per. cwt.; maize, 16s. 8d. per fanega (300 lbs.); beef, $1\frac{1}{4}$d. per lb.

There exists here a large quantity of old slags, about 2,500 tons. These contain 15 per cent. of lead. The stock in the ore yard comprised 36 tons of ore, holding 112·48 ounces of silver, and about 8 tons of argentiferous lead, containing about 1 per cent. of silver. There were also about 75 tons of bottoms from the refining furnace, consisting of lime and marly earth, with 29·4 to 35·52 ounces of silver to the ton.

These works were founded in the year 1832, and abandoned up to 1854, when the furnaces were renovated; since that time reduction operations have been carried on without intermission. The capital invested is about £1,300.

The following were employed at this establishment: 1 manager, 1 book-keeper, 2 mayordomos, 2 carpenters, 2 blacksmiths, 6 fore-smelters, 12 assistant smelters, 100 labourers, 3 charcoal burners, and 2 muleteers; total,

131.   There were also 40 oxen, 25 mules, and 6 carts.

The amalgamation works of *La Candelaria* were in course of construction by Don Carlos Guilmar d'Aragon, with the view to beneficiate the auriferous ores said to exist in the adjacent mountains; there are many open superficial workings on quartz veins, in some of which the native gold was visible. A few samples were submitted to me for inspection in the city, but I was unable to see or examine the veins themselves.

I was also shown samples of rock crystal and jasper, with some amethysts of good quality, which had likewise been found in these quartz veins.   Veined marbles, beautifully tinted—green, rose, &c.—exist in the same mountains, where gypsum (sulphate of lime) is also, found in fair abundance.

The calcareous or limestone formation, at a distance of five leagues westwards from the city, will be doubtless soon of the highest commercial value, as now that facilities for cheap and ready transport are afforded by the Central Argentine Railway, even Buenos Ayres itself may be supplied with this article of extensive and necessary consumption.

The lime produced from the burned stone is of superior quality and strength, one part being equal to $2\frac{1}{2}$ parts of that obtained from shells on the Paraná, one of the present and former principal sources of lime for building purposes at Buenos Ayres. These calcareous deposits are also certain to become a source of considerable wealth, as excellent marble, which may be cut into flags for court-yards, foot-paths, and the embellishment of buildings, can be easily obtained from them.

Almost everywhere throughout the Sierra excellent

refractory material is found, suitable for the construction of furnaces. Steatite (soapstone) exists in great quantity, and, when properly prepared, lasts as well in the furnace as English fire-bricks.

COPPER MINING DISTRICT OF CALAMUCHITA.

This mineral district is situate 16 leagues southwards from the capital, at the base of the lower ranges or eastern slopes of the Sierra de Cordoba. The mines in this district, discovered many years ago, were in the beginning rather enthusiastically worked, but are now being merely kept open, awaiting the completion of the railway. The principal are the following :—

The mine *El Tio* belongs to Mr. Samuel F. Lafone, of Monte Video, and was closed from the year 1859 to 1868; the workings were paralyzed owing to an illegal embargo (in consequence of a lawsuit) having been placed upon the establishment to which the ores raised were previously sent for reduction. Operations have been resumed of late and at the period of my visit about 90 tons of ore were on the surface, holding 15 per cent. of copper, consisting of yellow sulphides of copper, highly ferrugineous. At seven fathoms the carbonates and silicates, which abounded above that depth, entirely disappeared, but the vein continues in the above ore a yard in width. The workings have been followed to the lowest levels, which are $22\frac{1}{2}$ fathoms in vertical depth, and the vein had widened at this point to about $1\frac{1}{2}$ yards. There is a vertical shaft in five fathoms of water. In the same claim there are two other lodes, which run parallel and are well formed, but divided by a wall of gneiss and mica-schist, thirty yards thick, in the centre of which is a very narrow though rich vein of grey copper. The direction of the veins is from north-west to south-east; their visible longitudinal extent is not very great. They may, however, be buried under surface, as the vegetation and soil are thick about the spot.

Not more than 40 to 50 yards are worked longitudinally, and water already interferes with the lower workings; but an adit might be easily driven from the foot of the ravine, which would drain to a vertical depth of 35 fathoms. This mine is at present solely worked to keep it open and to prevent its being denounced.

The same may be said of the *Tauro* mine, which is five leagues further north, and also belongs to Mr. Lafone. This vein is a yard in width and consists of iron and copper pyrites—yellow and purple sulphides. The vertical depth of the workings is 24 fathoms, nearly all of which are invaded by water. The ores of this mine are purer than those of the preceding, and the dressed first class hold 18 per cent. of copper. There are 100 to 120 tons of dressed ore on the surface. Only two men were employed. The situation of this mine is not so favourable for the driving of an adit as that of *El Tio*, and good pumping machinery will be necessary to free it of water.

The *Tacurú* mine, which belonged to Mr. Daniel Gowland, of Buenos Ayres, is now full of water, and some of the workings choked up with debris. It has been abandoned for many years. Its ores are very similar to those of the *Tio* mine, but owing to the water I was not able to inspect the levels, which are 40 fathoms in depth.

Within a radius of a league round the *Tio* mine there are many veins—some of them of importance—consisting of silicates, and carbonates with oxides of copper. The Central Argentine Railway will immensely facilitate and cheapen transport, and under this stimulus these lodes (30 in number) are certain to be eventually worked to a good profit; meantime they are commercially worthless.

The smelting works for reduction of copper ores are located close to the shaft of the *Tauro* mine, and at a distance of 12 leagues from the capital. They consist of a reverberatory furnace, which is well constructed with English fire-bricks. The establishment belongs to to Mr. Samuel Lafone; but smelting operations were suspended in 1859, owing to the lawsuit and embargo above referred to; and, though the questions at issue have been settled, operations have not since been resumed.

The situation is very favourable, with plenty of water, pasture, and firewood in the neighbourhood. There are also good dwelling houses. Mr. Lafone has expended on these reduction works, and on the *Tio* and *Tauro* mines, about £25,000.

COAL DEPOSITS.

I cannot assert that, up to the present, coal has been found in Cordoba, but, from the data in my possession, I have no hesitation whatever in expressing the conviction that it will be discovered in the northern and western districts of the province. I believe that the same sandstone schistose formation, encountered in Los Llanos (Rioja), extends to the points indicated, and from specimens I have seen obtained in the neighbourhood of the city of Cordoba itself, I am disposed to conclude that the existence of coal is less doubtful than has hitherto been supposed.

In any case a matter of such importance merits the serious attention of the National Government, and an appropriation of £4,000 or £5,000 for thoroughly exploring and examining the parts pointed out in my report on the provinces of San Juan and Rioja would be a most useful expenditure and likely eventually to prove exceedingly advantageous to the revenues of the country.

Thirty leagues north of the city, I have found the sandstone formation identical almost with that of San Juan, and from this and other appearances and data I am of opinion that, at a depth of 300 to 400 feet, beds of excellent coal will be discovered.

The province of Cordoba is by nature fairly provided with carriage roads, owing to its physical advantages and the even character of its plains. It is only in the Sierra that these are needed, and the one now being made, passing through Soto, in the direction of San Juan, will materially aid in developing the mining industry of the province. A good carriage road is, however, necessary from Soto to the mineral districts, and will, I believe, be made by the local Government. The greater part is already constructed, and for about £400 to £500 it might be carried to Taninga and Pocho.

With respect to mule tracks, it would be very advantageous to improve that crossing the Sierra from San Roque to Ojo de Agua, and afterwards that descending from the Cuesta de Piná to the plains of Los Llanos. The latter is much frequented, and passes through some rather important centres of population. An excellent road for pack mules might be constructed for about £850.

GENERAL OBSERVATIONS.

IT will be seen by the preceding table, or general summary, that mining industry in the Argentine Republic is by no means so insignificant as has been hitherto believed.   It is now an indisputable fact that mineral riches exist in the country, and whose extent cannot be excelled by those of any other in South America.   Up to the present the Republic has been thought to possess no other wealth than that represented by its cattle, its sheep, its wools, and its hides.   This is a great mistake, for those products, however valuable and abundant they may be, can never form the sole basis of permanent and enduring prosperity.   They cannot advantageously pass certain limits of production; because, when this takes place, the foreign buyers, and even consumers in the country itself, will decline to pay such prices as would leave a profitable result to the producer. On the other hand, wages and other necessary expenses are greatly increased, causing a still further reduction in the profits of producers.   This has actually happened as respects wool-growing, and at this very moment we are experiencing the natural results of costly overproduction and diminished value of the article produced. A continuance of this must soon bring about a crisis, and ruin an industry on whose prosperity the country is, under existing circumstances, almost wholly dependent.

Economists have always pointed out the danger of allowing the resources of a nation to depend upon a single article of production, or a single branch of industry, however lucrative or profitable. It is therefore our duty to seek other occupations, other articles of production, and to have in view other resources for the future, whose value exported may at least equal that of our imports, which, during the past year (1867), alarmingly exceeded the value of our principal exports.

I now refer solely to the products of the Littoral, or riverine provinces, which alone are *exportable*, or realizable in foreign markets. The immense agricultural capabilities of the interior provinces, it must be understood, are as yet compulsorily limited to the supply of local wants, whilst the abundant produce of the soil is almost valueless for export, owing to the onerous charges at present incurred for its transport to the coast. But how valuable and important would that produce become if only a ready market were created and made available for its local consumption?

It is to be hoped, and I firmly believe, that the next generation will be able to give a satisfactory solution to this question. Those great civilizers—railways, roads, and schools,—are already being rapidly and energetically extended to the very confines of the Republic, whilst the wild gaucho of the pampa and the untutored savage will soon awaken to the fact that their rule is at an end, and that barbarism must succumb before the onward march of progress.

These convictions are not the offspring of momentary enthusiasm; they are based on substantial facts, and strengthened by the brilliant example which has been presented to us by our great model, the United States of North America. The Argentine Confederation to-day is precisely in the same economic position as California, Nevada, Arizona, and Colorado, the Western Pacific States, in the year 1850. These States occupy an area of 903,019 square miles of territory, with a population of 780,000 souls, or less than one to every square mile. Of this population only 52,000 are exclusively employed in mining operations, and it is their labour and energy which impart commercial vitality to the whole; for it cannot be denied that California is purely a mining country, and that its great progress and importance are due to the development of its mineral wealth.

In the year 1867 California produced gold and silver bullion to the value of £15,000,000, the very existence of which in that territory was nineteen years ago quite unknown to the civilized world. How gratifying this result must be to the people of the United States, where mining industry is protected and fostered by the General Government as a source of inexhaustible wealth, and above all as a material guarantee for the maintenance of peace and the continuance of national prosperity.

I have now before me a most valuable work,—the voluminous report presented to the Government of Washington by Mr. Ross Browne on the mineral resources of the States situate west of the Rocky Mountains, and printed by order of Congress. It is the result of many years of labour, and contains the accumulated information of numerous scientific men, thoroughly competent to furnish reliable details on the subject matter of the report, the data of which have been most carefully revised and corrected by Mr. Browne. In the United States they have an advantage which we in the Argentine Republic do not possess—a skilled and commercial mining population, accustomed to keep books and accounts showing their expenditure, receipts, and produce. It is therefore an easy matter to collect data there, whereas here not one miner in a hundred preserves any record whatever of either the disbursements or produce of their mines.

It would occupy too much space to extract for introduction in these pages even a tenth part of Mr. Browne's remarks with regard to the high importance and civilizing influences of mining industry in California; but I cannot refrain from quoting the following paragraphs, extracted from the general observations at the end of his work :—

" Within the brief space of nineteen years our people have opened up for settlement a larger area of territory, valuable as a source of supply for nearly all the necessities of man, than has ever before in the world's history been brought within the limits of civilization in so short a time. Nineteen years ago California, Arizona, Colorado, Montaña, Idaho, and Nevada, occupying more than one-third of the entire area of the United States, were regions chiefly known to trappers and traders, traversed and occupied for the most part by barbarous hordes of Indians. That this extraordinary advance, with all its concomitant results to the trade and commerce of the world, has been achieved by the discovery and development of our mineral resources, no reasonable man pretends to dispute. Every day's progress in our history speaks for itself and the facts are patent to all.

"It seems a little singular, on considering the millions of treasure thus added to our national wealth, the vast range of industry opened to our people, the wonderful impulse given to agriculture, commerce, and manufactures, that, of all our great national interests, the business of mining has had the hardest struggle to enlist the favourable consideration of our Government. Of late years, through the irresistable logic of results, something has been achieved in the way of more intelligent federal legislation.

"If we take mining only in its past condition and its present transition state we must admit that, with all its evil effects upon individuals, it has caused most important general benefits, especially in anticipating by generations the peopling of the immense territories of the west, and thus widening the field for the display of national energies, broadening the spirit and firmly bracing the national credit. But for the mining furor of the last nineteen years California would probably have remained a vast cattle range to this day, and all the great territories adjoining it, now peopling with civilized communities and nearly traversed by a railroad uniting both shores of the continent, would still be savage wastes, held and controlled by barbarians, who are fast retiring before the forces of modern progress.

"The direct effect of mining upon agriculture and commerce is strikingly shown in California. How much wheat would now be exported from San Francisco but for the mines and the population attracted by them; how many interior towns would have been built; how far would the Pacific railroad have been constructed; where would have been the overland mail, the telegraph, and the China steamship line, but for the necessities created by the development of our mineral wealth? The mines have not only led to those things, but they have built up a great manufacturing interest, which already, in San Francisco alone, estimates its annual product by a figure nearly as high as that of the gold fields."

The importance of mining as a populating and civilizing agent will be apparent from the above extract. Our country to-day is in the same position as California twenty years ago; and why may we not entertain the hope of making similar progress within the next twenty years? We have thousands of leagues of mountains, more metalliferous than those of California, as is proved by the riches of Copiapó, Potosi, and Famatina. We have immense territories, only awaiting colonization and cultivation, infinitely more fertile and productive than those of North America. We have the staples and basis of many manufactures, which might soon become of vast importance and a source of great profit to the country, but which are yet lying useless and devoid of commercial value. We have wool for the manufacture of cloths; hides for the manufacture of leather of almost every description; indigenous indigo, equal in quality to the best Guatemala, and growing in a wild state, covering large tracts of territory in the fertile province of Santiago del Estero; the sugar cane for the manufacture of sugar; as well as rice and tobacco in Tucuman and coffee in Salta and Jujuy. The fines timber exists in the country, the value of which would be incalculable had we but facile and economic mean of transport. Having all these advantages, what then is needed to secure their profitable utilization? *Peace* and tranquillity, with rulers and men possessing *skill* and energy,—railways to traverse our vast deserts, but neither so broad nor so difficult as those of California, and, above all, a foreign immigration of industrious labourers, the scions of a vigorous race, and capable of successfully contending with the difficulties and drawbacks of a comparatively new and unknown country.

In many parts of the Republic,—more especially in Rioja and Catamarca—the want of water is greatly felt in the travesias or deserts; but this evil is not without a remedy. Artesian wells should be sunk in those places. A Government engineer, I understand, has stated that such wells would be useless, since there exists no surface current of water; but this theory is quite untenable in presence of facts and in view of the geological formation of the country. In the Llanos of Rioja, as well as in Catamarca and San Juan, all the probabilities are in favour of finding good water in reaching the igneous rocks. These works would serve a double purpose: they would solve the problem of the existence of coal in those places where its presence is so strikingly indicated, while giving water to a large extent of territory at present desert and intransitable for want of this essential element. The Central Argentine Railway will soon be prolonged towards the north, and it is necessary that the Government should adopt such measures as will promote and advance its civilizing influence.

I am glad now to be in a position to state that a numerous immigration is being daily attracted to the shores of the River Plate, and that men of powerful position and influence in Europe are using their best efforts to promote a continuance of this beneficial and enriching current.

I have not referred at any length in the foregoing pages to the great advantages offered by the province of Santa Fé as a field for immigration, and I cannot close this work without calling special attention to that rich and important agricultural province.

As stated in the introductory remarks, the well-known house of Messrs. Thomson, Bonar and Co., of London, have acquired a large tract of land in that province, and I cannot do better than insert here my official reply to their questions concerning the Argentine Republic, and especially the province of Santa Fé, in reference to the intended colonization of their lands. In this note will be found important details, which will serve as a guide to intending emigrants, and others who may be desirous of going to the River Plate :—

PROVINCE OF SANTA FE AS A FIELD FOR IMMIGRATION AND COLONIZATION.

Consulate General of the Argentine Republic,
London, *February* 28*th*, 1870.

To Messrs. J. Thomson, T. Bonar and Co.,
Old Broad Street, E.C.

GENTLEMEN,

In reference to our conversation on colonization in the Argentine Republic, I have much pleasure in giving you all the information in my possession concerning that country. In doing this officially, I shall be only complying with the instructions received from his Excellency the President, who has honoured me with a special mission from his Government to Europe, with the view, amongst others, of making known more generally the advantages which the Argentine Republic possesses for a foreign immigration, and the vast field for enterprise open there for development.

A residence of over twelve years in South America, eight of which I have spent in the Argentine Republic, holding a high official position, enables me to speak with authority on all matters connected with that country.

Without further preface, I will proceed to reply to the various questions and points which you were good enough to submit for my consideration and reply, bearing in mind, however, that my observations will only apply to that part of the territory proposed to be colonized by your house, adding a few general remarks on the country, its Government, and its people.

Climate.—There is probably no country on the face of the earth so favoured by nature. It is so entirely situated in the south temperate zone, which enjoys, perhaps, the healthiest climate on the globe, and the soil is so varied and fertile, that it produces, with ordinary care, nearly all the great staple commodities of home consumption and foreign commerce. Meteoro logical observations taken at Buenos Ayres, the capital, gave the following average temperature for the year :—

20 days	(very cold)	45	to 55	degrees Fah.	
182 „	(moderate)	55	„ 75	„	„
60 „	(warm)	75	„ 88	„	„
45 „	(hot)	80	„ 85	„	„
58 „	(intensely hot)	85	„ 105	„	„

———

365

The temperature in that part of the province of Santa Fé where your land is situate, being about four degrees further north, is of course somewhat warmer; that is to say, the proportion of hot weather is greater, and the thermometer rarely falls below freezing point. In point of salubrity I consider the site of the proposed colony to be superior to Buenos Ayres.

Soil.—The general character of the surface soil is that of a rich black vegetable earth, averaging in some places from three to five feet in depth, resting on a sub-stratum of yellowish clay, forming the great alluvial deposit of the pampas, whose depth in some parts is over one hundred feet; this is excellent for making bricks. The surface soil is so rich that any crop can be produced without the aid of manure, and this I have no doubt will continue to be the case for many years.

Products.—*Cereals.*—One crop of maize or Indian corn and one of wheat can be raised annually; the sowing time for wheat is April to September, for maize from September to January. Wheat is reaped in December and January, and maize in April and May; in bad seasons wheat yields about thirteen bushels to the acre, in good seasons about thirty; maize averages all round about one hundred bushels to the acre, and requires about one bushel of seed to seven acres; these remarks apply generally to barley. Besides the above, rice, mandioca, sugar, cotton, tobacco, coffee, and flax of every kind may be easily cultivated of a superior quality. Vegetables will grow with scarcely any exception, with ordinary care and skill; potatoes especially are very fine and in great abundance.

Fruits.—Pears, apricots, peaches, nectarines, oranges, and lemons grow in great abundance; likewise melons, water melons, pumpkins, and grapes.

Grazing.—Various classes of grass abound admirably suited for horned cattle, horses, and sheep. It is said that one acre will maintain at the rate of two to four sheep annually with every success. In addition to the natural pasture, alfalfa, or lucerne, will grow most abundantly, requiring no further labour when once sown than irrigation by water from the rivers adjoining, and a field of this fattening pasture will last for many years, if eaten down regularly and allowed to flourish afresh by irrigation.

Timber.—Abundance of excellent timber for building purposes and fuel exists on the lands and adjoining territories, where colonists exercise the right of feeding so long as it remains Fiscal or Government property. The principal and most durable of the timber is the " algarrobo," which is almost imperishable in the ground or under water; this is a species of mahogany and makes excellent furniture. The " ñandubay " is of a similar class as regards durability and usefulness.

Game.—Game is in abundance, and fish in almost fabulous quantities; the former consists of large and small deer, "carpinchos," or species of water pig, armadillos, ducks, snipe, geese, wild swans, wild turkeys, partridges, large and small moor-fowl, besides a sprinkling of foxes and wild hogs, and vast numbers of the American ostrich. In the woods and away from the inhabited parts the jaguar is occasionally met with. Reptiles and vermin are no more numerous or obnoxious than in many parts of Europe.

Cattle.—Bullocks and cows can be bought for fattening on waste lands at from 13s. 6d. to 25s. each, the latter in good condition and fit for slaughter; sheep, 3s. 4d. to 6s. each; horses from £1 to £3 each; milch cows, from £2 each; team of bullocks broken for the plough, £10. The class of animals here quoted are obtainable in large numbers all through the inhabited districts of the province.

Water.—In addition to the unlimited supply obtainable from the rivers, by using Norton's Abyssinian pump on almost any part of the lands, a sufficient supply may be obtained for domestic uses. If larger quantities be required proportionately powerful pumping apparatus can be used.

Communication and Roads.—Although the country offers every facility for road traffic, I would recommend the adoption of small steamers and boats, or launches, to ply between the capital, Santa Fé, and the colony. The San Javier river is navigable for steamers far above the colony. The Saladillo "Dulce" and " Armargo" are, I believe, navigable for small craft. This being the case, uninterrupted communication can be had with nearly all the farms in the colony. From Buenos Ayres to Santa Fé there is a by-weekly communication, and from Santa Fé to San Javier (close to the colony) a weekly communication by regular steamer subsidised recently by the National Government   Communication between Europe and Buenos Ayres is now almost weekly.

Markets for Produce and Prices.—According to the data in my possession the following may be set down as the average prices obtainable for produce at Santa Fé, Parana, Goya, La Paz, &c. :---On the river Parana, wheat from 6s. to 8s. per bushel; in the colony perhaps 5s. may be realised. Maize 3s. to 4s. per bushel; 2s. may be realised in the colony. Potatoes about 10s. per cwt. It is quite possible that at harvest time purchasers of produce will wait upon the colonists and buy on the spot, thereby saving them the trouble and expense of sending to market.

Provisions.—Flour, placed in the colony, imported from Rosario, will cost from 25s. to 30s. per 100 lbs.; tea, 4s. to 6s. per lb.; sugar, 2d. to 4d. per lb.; rice, 4d. per lb.; beef, 1d. to 2d. per lb.

Capital required by Emigrants.—For the first families who might be sent to the colony as pioneers, I would not recommend them to be provided with less capital than, say, £300 to £500 each family of four persons, which would be ample for all disbursements (including purchase of farm of 100 acres) until returns through produce would be obtained. The following tabular statement will not, I think, be far out, and may be a better guide to intending emigrants :—

	£	s.	d.
Passage per steamer, with rations, &c., for a family of four persons, say	55	0	0
Outfit, say	40	0	0
Tools, say	10	0	0
On arrival at the colony the following disbursements may be calculated upon :—			
Temporary house, say	25	0	0
Two horses, at £3 each	6	0	0
Four bullocks and cows at £2 5s. each	9	0	0
Two milch cows at £2 2s.	4	4	0
Twenty-five sheep at 5s. each	6	5	0
Two teams bullocks for ploughing, at £10	20	0	0
Pigs, poultry, &c.	7	0	0
Implements, carts, &c.	75	0	0
Living and clothing expenses	100	0	0
Purchase money for farm	25	0	0
Total	£382	9	0

Produce.—I consider that a family of four persons should get under cultivation about 50 acres of wheat

land in the first year, and this, as near as I can judge,
ought to produce as follows :—

<pre>
For first year, at the rate of 15 bushels per
    acre, at 5/- per bushel £187 10 0
Indian corn, to be sown after wheat in second
    six months, will produce, say, 75 bushels
    to acre, at 2/- .....⁎....................... 375   0 0
                                                 ____
            Total £562 10 0
</pre>

From the foregoing it will be seen that the outlay for
the first year, allowing an ample margin, is £382 9s.
and the produce, estimated at a very low figure, will
realise £562 10s., leaving a balance profit of £180 1s.,
or at the rate of about 47 per cent. per annum on
capital.

Class of people who should go out.—It will be necessary
to exercise much care in the selection of the first emigrants to be sent out. I would strongly recommend
that the first 150 should be of the agricultural class, of
steady, sober, and industrious habits, possessing testi-
monials from the clergyman of their district, and having
at their disposal sufficient means to enable them to get
through the first year in the colony. Married men, with
a family of two or three grown up children would be
the most desirable; but I would also recommend that
four young men should be considered as a family, and,
working together, receive the same privileges as the
married men. A fair proportion of artizans, such as
carpenters, blacksmiths, bricklayers, shoemakers, and
tailors, in the ratio of 5 to 7 per cent., should accompany
each batch of the agricultural class. These artizans
should possess similar recommendations, and may not
necessarily be of the higher branches of their trade.
In the appendix to this note you will find a tariff of

wages for these, as set down by the Immigration Committee appointed by the National Government at Buenos Ayres, which is more or less correct.   Later on—when the colony becomes more populated, and if the proprietors of the farms should require it,—I would recommend to be sent out a batch of agricultural labourers, to be distributed amongst them, they reimbursing to you the cost of their passage, which might be deducted by instalments from their wages.

Agricultural Implements.—Although these may be had at Buenos Ayres and Rosario, it might be well for the emigrants to take out a supply of ploughs, harrows, cultivators, hoes, chains, cordage, and a box of rough carpenter's tools.   I will, however, defer entering into details on this subject until my arrival out, and a careful inspection of the Californian colony adjoining your land, where, up to the present, the greatest success has been achieved.   From their practical experience we shall be enabled to determine more safely and definitely the requirements of emigrants under this head.   I am, however, of opinion that the sums set down under the head of " Capital required" will be ample for the outlay in this respect.

Outfit, arms, &c.—I would recommend each emigrant to take a fair supply of woollen clothing, as all such articles are much more costly out there and less suited to rough work.   These should be of two classes—light for summer wear, and rather heavier for winter; say, one dozen coloured flannel shirts, fine; half-dozen heavy blue woollen serge, or Guernseys, as worn by sailors; two monkey jackets, light and heavy ; four pairs trousers, two light Tweed or Indian flannel, and two of strong Bedford cord; two soft felt hats; two straw ditto, with a roll of strong muslin or light calico wound around to keep off the sun; two pairs of strong jack boots, to come to the knees; two of light laced boots (elastic sides should be avoided, as the climate soon renders them useless); one dozen pairs of merino or light woollen socks; a strong waterproof Mackintosh, with cap and leggings. These being the only necessary articles of clothing, I do not mention others of a finer description which may be taken by the emigrants according to their means, position, and requirements. Bedding:—Two pairs of ordinary heavy blankets; two waterproof canvas sheets (lined with India-rubber), and two pairs of cotton sheets; a curled hair mattress, to fold in three, with pillows to suit; light iron bedstead, with hoop-iron slips. Knives, forks, and spoons to suit the requirements of each; a strong waist belt, with pockets, sheath knife, and revolver. A saddle, bridle, and horse gear complete will be very essential. I would recommend a plain, strong, military saddle, with expanding holsters, and small valise to strap on behind, with bridle and head-stall in one. A set of culinary utensils, consisting of two pots, two saucepans, a frying pan, gridiron, two kettles, teapot, cups, saucers, plates, and dishes of delf-lined ironware. A supply of stationery to suit each person's wants would be advisable; thin foreign note paper is the best for correspondence. Strong boxes of light pine, with the corners bound by iron hoops and a secure lock. A supply of good American axes for felling timber would be essential; these I indicate specially as forming *extras* in the tool chest already recommended. An assorted supply of fish hooks and lines, with nets, for fishing in the numerous streams and rivers close by; an eight-day American clock, and, amongst every four or five families, a serviceable Aneroid barometer, very useful in indicating sudden changes of the weather. A small medicine chest, with a few of the principal remedies for household use, such as citrate of magnesia, cream of tartar, carbonate of soda, tartaric acid, epsom salts, senna, castor oil, calomel, tartar emetic, jalap, ipecacuana, Rubini's tincture of camphor, sulphate of quinine, and such others as each emigrant may desire to take. These should be accompanied by a few appliances for external injuries, such as lint, oiled silk, adhesive plaister, tincture of arnica, friar's balsam, and simple cerate. For those who prefer the homœpathic remedies, I would recommend them, as being more portable and efficacious for the climate and requirements of the country. My own experience of this extends over a period of seven years, in the roughest campaigning and explorations, and I have found them fully adequate to all the requirements of such an eventful life. The strongest *tinctures* should be taken.

Houses or Dwellings.—These may be erected in a temporary manner of timber, consisting of two rooms, each 15 feet square, for the sum estimated in outlay—say £25. Of " adobes," or sun-dried bricks, it may cost a little more. For a permanent house, built of brick and lime, same size, say, £250 to £300, but this latter I cannot estimate correctly just at present, and, having our own masons and carpenters sent out from Europe, I have no doubt it will come out less. I shall be able to inform you more fully on this on my arrival out.

Indians.—In a correspondence lately published in the *Field* newspaper, it was stated that one of the greatest objections to emigration to the Argentine Republic was the exposed state of the frontier lands, and consequent insecurity for life and property owing to

Indian raids. Those statements applied generally to the frontiers of Cordoba and Santa Fé, distant more than three hundred miles from your colony; but, however true they may have been in reference to a period of the past, and I admit they were so, happily for the interests of the landed proprietors in those districts, and thanks to the advanced and energetic system of government initiated by President Sarmiento and his Administration, that terrible bugbear to progress and civilisation has now almost totally disappeared. The conclusion of the Paraguayan war has fortunately enabled the Government to direct all its energies in the War Department towards securing immunity to settlers on the frontiers, effectually keeping back the previously too frequent raids of the savages by a judicious distribution of Line troops and National Guards all over the country. More than 2,000 men, with an able general and efficient officers, have within the last year extended the southern frontier to a distance of 100 miles and established a line of forts protected by natural barriers of rivers and lagoons. The effect of this energetic action has been to bring the Indian chiefs to the feet of their conquerors, suing for peace and a cessation of hostilities, and giving hostages to the Government for a due fulfilment of their treaty. I must here state that those Indians of the south are a hardy and warlike race, well mounted and armed, having the advantage of an almost woodless, uninterrupted, level country, favourable either for their raids or escape, whilst those on the northern frontiers, or contiguous to your colony, are a miserable, degenerated tribe, without horses, armed only with spears and arrows, and with an almost impenetrable forest in their rear and about them. They are, on the other hand, semi-civilised, and the only fear to be entertained regarding them is their propensity to theft. As to fighting, I have no hesitation in asserting that, with fifty breach-loaders in the hands of good marksmen, the colony would be effectually protected from any marauding visit on their part. In addition to this, there are other colonies, or inhabited places, between their territory and your colony, and I have little fear, should it prove necessary or desirable, of obtaining from the Minister of War the extension of the actual frontier and its reinforcement by troops of the Line, in sight of the important colony about being established in that district.

System of Government.—I now come to the last of your questions, and, in addition to various extracts from authentic works bearing upon the country, its resources, and government, I will give you, in as few words as possible, a general sketch of its actual state and prospects.

In the first place, the Government is Republican, consisting of a President, elected for six years, and a Federal Congress of Senators and Deputies for three and six years—as nearly as possible identical with that of the United States of North America. These form what is called the National Government, which represents the country in its relations with foreign Powers, collects the customs dues on imports and exports, administers the postal service, attends to the national debt, has complete control over the army and navy, and undisputed jurisdiction on the rivers and sea coasts. In addition to this, which is the general or head Government, the Republic is divided into fourteen distinct and independent provinces, each of which has its legislative, executive, and judicial authorities, who, within their respective territories, are independent of the National Government, and inviolable in their sovereignty so long as they maintain and govern in accordance with the original constitution of the Republic. And it is only in cases where, by violence or other unconstitutional means, the duly constituted authorities of the provinces are deposed, that the National Government can interfere by force of arms or otherwise to reinstate them, and then only at their specific and official request. It is a remarkable fact that the Argentine Republic, which was the first to declare itself independent by throwing off the Spanish yoke, and the medium through which nearly all the other South American Republics followed its example, is the only one which, from its foundation, declared by its constitution absolute freedom of religious worship. We find now flourishing, at Buenos Ayres and other parts of the country, religious institutions and churches of nearly all persuasions. This in itself must be a great inducement to foreigners to settle in the country, where they can have clergymen of their own denomination without interference on the part of the natives. These, though Roman Catholics, are as a rule most tolerant and free from bigotry. Their general behaviour and conduct towards foreigners is most corteous and polite, and, after a residence of many years amongst them, it is only just to state that I know of no country out of England more agreeable to live in.

For the first time almost since the independence of the country—now nearly half a century back—it enjoys the blessings of peace, with a progressive and enlightened Government, selected by the will of the people; for his Excellency, President Sarmiento, was selected to fill this high post during his absence as Minister at Washington, without having used any personal influence to procure his return to the Presidential chair. He has still almost five years of office before him, and should he employ them as he has done his past one by the initiation of railways, telegraphs, steam navigation, mining enterprise, colonization, and other industrial projects, brilliant hopes may be indeed entertained of a prosperous future and a peaceful administration. He has travelled so much in Europe and the United States, studying our institutions and acquiring our language, that his appreciation of foreigners, especially American and English, is the surest safeguard and guarantee we can have for the lives and properties of colonists, who of themselves tend to increase the prosperity of the country by populating and cultivating its almost boundless territory.

Taxation.—To foreigners, especially colonists, this is an item of expenditure so trifling and unimportant that it scarcely deserves more than a passing remark. Foreigners, not colonists, in the rural districts pay only what may be literally translated a " property tax" (*contribucion directa*) of 4 per 1,000 on the capital invested therein. Colonists, as per concession from the Government, are exempted from taxes for a period of ten years, after which they will of course be obliged to contribute in the same ratio as other foreigners not of their class. In the cities and towns, where municipal authorities are established, the usual lighting, police, and paving taxes are payable in addition to those already mentioned.

In conclusion, I have only to remark that I consider the Argentine Republic, as a field for immigration, inferior to none of our British colonies, and fully equal, if not superior, to the United States or California. To this latter country it may be more truthfully compared, from its physical conditions and geographical position, the salubrity of its climate, and natural productions. It has, however, the great advantage of being so much nearer to Europe, and consequently more accessible to the agricultural classes, or others with small means. The territory is so extensive and so sparsely populated that for many years to come no fear need be entertained of over-crowding and consequent depreciation in the value of produce. According to the last census, taken in the year 1869, I find, from official data before me, that the entire population of the Republic amounts only to 1,852,110, including 50,000 Indians, which the Minister of War sets down as being distributed as follows:—In the Gran Chaco, or territory to the north of your colony, 15,000; on the Pampas south and west of Buenos Ayres, 20,000; Patagonia, south of Pampas, 15,000. When we recollect that only this million and three quarters of souls are distributed over a superficial area of 1,281,000 geographical miles (more than four times the size of France) it may be easily conceived what a great want and necessity it must become to populate it, and how long a time must elapse before a sufficient number of inhabitants will be there to develop its varied and almost unlimited resources. In the province of Buenos Ayres alone, more than 150,000 foreigners reside now, nearly all of whom are well to do, or at least make a far better living than they could possibly expect to do in the too densely populated districts of the Old World. For us it is a consolation and a guarantee to know that more than 40,000 British subjects are already settled in the country, many of whom have already achieved, whilst others have laid the foundation of considerable fortunes.

On my arrival out at the colony, and after a careful exploration, I shall have much pleasure in supplying you with more detailed and local information concerning the lands and prospects for emigrants.   Meanwhile,

I have the honour to remain, Gentlemen,

Your very obedient Servant,

F. IGNACIO RICKARD, F.G.S., &c.,

Government Inspector of Mines,

(In Commission.)

APPENDIX.

The following information, relating to the country, is published for the use of emigrants, by the Argentine Government, and largely distributed by their agents throughout Europe.   It is therefore given here as official and authentic merely in confirmation of the foregoing statements prepared from personal experience and knowledge of the country :—

"The recommendations of the Argentine Republic to Europeans are :—

" 1. That the climate is as healthy and as favourable to vigour and longevity as that of England, or any other country of Europe.

" 2. That its cultivable lands are practically of unlimited extent, and require no outlay for clearing.

" 3. That it contains already, and especially at Buenos Ayres, the capital, a large and prosperous European population, composed of Italians, French, English, Scotch, and Irish, Germans, Portuguese, and others.

" 4. That the Government is solidly established and perfectly liberal, the aim of all parties being to maintain the financial honour of the country, to preserve peace, and to promote the development of industry and commerce.

" 5. That, while the State religion is Roman Catholic, complete toleration is upheld, churches of all denominations being established at Buenos Ayres and other places, where a considerable portion of the settlers are English or German Protestants or Scotch Presbyterians.

" 6. That there is weekly postal communications with England and the Continent by powerful mail steamers from Southampton, London, Liverpool, Falmouth and Bordeaux.

" 7. That the commercial policy of the country is in the direction of free trade.

" 8. That there is a treaty of amity, commerce, and navigation between Great Britain and the Republic, and that foreigners are exempted from compulsory military service or forced loans.

" 9. That there are a sufficient number of British subjects in the Republic to render a knowledge of the Spanish language non-essential for immigrants, and that this language is capable, during a short residence, of being more easily acquired than any other; likewise, that an English daily newspaper is published at Buenos Ayres, and that there is an influential English bank and other institutions.

" 10. That the staple productions of the country are such as at all times command the markets of the world, the principal exports being tallow, hides, and wool; while, during the past year, a trade in preserved meat has been opened up, which seems to promise, if sufficient attention be given to establish a scientific process of curing, to assume proportions as sudden and profitable as those of the newly-developed petroleum trade of North America; that there is also a mining district in the interior provinces on the slope of the Andes, which appears from the operations thus far conducted, to be one of the richest silver, lead, and gold regions yet discovered.

" 11. That the country is being opened up in all directions by English Railway enterprises, one of which, the Rosario and Cordoba line, will be 247 miles in length, and is considered to be ultimately destined to cross the entire country to Chili, and thus to form a highway for the traffic between the Atlantic and the Pacific.

" 12. That the acquisition of land is easy and its tenure secure, and that additional and extraordinary facilities for settlement are being daily offered by the Government and private individuals and companies.

"Finally, it is to be observed that the debt of the country, foreign and internal, the interest on which is paid with unfailing punctuality, is comparatively small; that it is gradually in course of extinction by a large redeeming fund, and that the Six per Cent. Buenos Ayrian Bonds in the London market range from 95 to 100, and those of the Republic between 85 and 90; that there are no direct taxes, and that the commerce of the country is increasing with such rapidity that in the Board of Trade returns of British exports it figures higher on the list than Chili or Peru, and as regards

European countries, higher than Prussia, Sweden, Norway, Denmark, and many others with which we have an important traffic.

" The present population of the Argentine Republic is but about 2,000,000, and immigration may be said to be its only want. This is felt and acknowledged by all classes, and every arrival is therefore warmly welcomed. The tide thither is gradually increasing, and persons best acquainted with the country express a conviction that the growth of Buenos Ayres, which at present is a fine city, with about 200,000 inhabitants, will, during the next twenty years, rival that which has been witnessed at New York during the like period in the past. In several cases persons of moderate capital have emigrated from Australia and New Zealand to the Argentine Republic, owing to the advantages of its greater proximity to England and its superior facilities for the acquisition of land.

By far the greater portion of the country consists of rich alluvial plains, constituting what are called the Pampas. The climate is subject to a great difference of temperature in winter and summer, but the changes are gradual and regular. The winter is about as cold as the English November, with white frosts, and ice at sunrise. Taken as a whole, the Pampas may be said to enjoy as beautiful and as salubrious an atmosphere as the most healthy parts of Greece and Italy, and without being subject to malaria.

"The country is universally celebrated for the abundance of its cattle, horses, sheep, goats, asses, mules, and swine. The number of cattle fifteen years ago was estimated at 12,000,000, and the horses, mules, and asses at more than 4,000,000, and they are supposed since that period to have largely increased.

" The salubrity of the climate seems especially beneficial to immigrants from this country, its influence being singularly restorative wherever there is a tendency to bronchial or pulmonary affections. In some districts, such as that of the beautiful city and province of Cordoba, these disorders appear to be almost unknown, and as on the completion of the Central Argentine Railway it will be possible to reach the city of Cordoba from London in little more than a month, that place may probably become a sanitarium for Europeans in a majority of the most important cases where change of climate is desirable.

" The following is a list of classes of immigrants most required in Buenos Ayres:—

MONTHLY WAGES WITH BOARD.

Gardeners	£3	15	0	to £4	10	0
Farm Servants	2	5	0	to 3	0	0
Home Servants, Men					2	5	0
„ „ Women	2	0	0	to 3	0	0
Cooks, Men	3	0	0	to 3	15	0
„ Women	2	5	0	to 3	0	0
Boys, from 10 to 15 years	0	15	0	to 1	5	0
Sempstresses					2	15	0
Milliners					2	15	0
Dressmakers					2	15	0
Laundresses					2	16	0

DAILY WAGES WITHOUT BOARD.

Bricklayers	6/-
Joiners	6/6
Blacksmiths	6/6
Shoemakers	7/6
Tailors	6/- to 9/-
Labourers	4/6
Railway, ditto	6/-
Miners	—

NOTE.—Higher wages may be calculated upon in the interior provinces, and artizans of superior merit will always obtain more than is quoted.

" In the rural establishments, merely situated in the suburbs of the capital, thousands of families may engage themselves immediately.

" With respect to those immigrants who may come to establish themselves in the flourishing colonies of Santa Fé, Baradero, San José, or others actually forming in various parts of the Republic, we do not hesitate to say that, owing to the fertility of the land, they will rapidly acquire a modest fortune.

" In summer, farm labourers get 6s. to 7s. 6d. per day.

" The scarcity of domestic servants is notorious—a preference being given to women.

" Sempstresses, milliners, dressmakers, and laundresses, however numerous the arrivals, are certain of employment.

" Artizans of all descriptions, and immigrants, even though of no fixed calling, will get employment to their satisfaction immediately on landing.

" The railways now employ a large staff, but some thousands of labourers are required for the earthworks that are being pushed forward with the greatest activity.

" Immigrants—above all those with a knowledge of minerals—will find very lucrative employment in the rich and numerous mines of San Juan, Mendoza, La Rioja, Catamarca, and Cordoba, which are now being worked with the most satisfactory results.

" A fortnightly journal, called *The Brazil and River Plate Mail*, is published in London by Messrs. Bates, Hendy and Co., 4, Old Jewry, E.C.

MINES

	VALUE.			OBSERVATIONS.
	A			
	£	s.	d.	
CATAMA	...			Capital and Produce included in Reduction Works.
	8,311	5	0	Animals Employed—Oxen 220
				„ Mules 3,000
	8,311	5	0	„ Asses 290
				3,510
SAN JU	7,934	15	10	
	8,549	1	3	
	6,483	17	1	
LA RIO	5,625	0	0	
	1,968	15	0	
	7,693	15	0	
MENDO	4,989	4	6	There was Silver Regulus on surface to the value of
	4,248	8	8	about £1,000.
	9,237	13	0	
CORDOB	...			Value included in Reduction Works.
	8,917	16	4	Animals Employed — Oxen 302
				„ Mules 297
	8,917	16	4	599
SAN LU	1,750	0	0	
	50	0	0	The Gold is included in the Mines, valued at the
	3,637	1	8	rate of £2 18s. 4d. per ounce.
	5,437	1	8	
TOTAL.	0,299	0	2	
	2,045	6	3	
	3,647	1	8	
	5,991	8	1	

Propo|relation to the inhabitants of the Argentine Republic
, 6.666 per cent., or 66 2-3rd per 1,000.

GENERAL SUMMARY.

TABLE SHOWING THE MINES AND REDUCTION WORKS IN ACTIVE OPERATION IN THE ARGENTINE REPUBLIC, THEIR PRODUCE, CAPITAL INVESTED, NUMBER OF PERSONS EMPLOYED, &c.

1868.

Mines and Reduction Works in Active Operation.	Whether Gold, Silver, or Copper — Gold.	Silver.	Copper.	Number of Persons Occupied.	Capital Invested. (£ s. d.)	Produce — Gold Ounces.	Silver Ounces.	Copper Cwt.	Value. (£ s. d.)	Observations.
Catamarca. — Mines	5	5	0	138						Capital and Produce included in Reduction Works. Animals Employed—Oxen ... ; Mules ... 2,000 ; Asses ... 750
Reduction Works	2	2	2	846	61,718 15 0	1,002	84,759	14,842	58,311 5 0	
Totals			...	1,044	61,718 15 0	1,002	84,759	14,842	58,311 5 0	
San Juan. — Mines	14	22 (and 11 lead)		430	73,046 17 6		101,979		17,934 15 10	
Reduction Works	2	5	1	133	112,500 0 0		79,838		18,540 1 3	
Totals		...		563	185,546 17 6		181,817		36,483 17 1	
La Rioja. — Mines	2	7	2	125	2,696 5 0		59,200		13,625 0 0	
Reduction Works	5	5	1	24	8,417 10 0	96	22,570	200	1,068 15 0	
Totals				149	11,093 15 0	96	81,770	200	14,693 15 0	
Mendoza. — Mines	3	4		96	6,250 0 0		33,855		4,089 4 6	There was Silver Bagulas on surface to the value of about £2,000.
Reduction Works			1	48	4,061 10 0				4,748 8 8	
Totals				144	10,311 10 0		33,855		8,837 13 2	
Cordoba. — Mines		8 (and lead)		247	12,515 12 6					Value included in Reduction Works. Animals Employed—Oxen ... ; Mules ...
Reduction Works	3	3 (and lead)		316	10,625 0 0		36,000		8,917 16 4	
Totals				583	23,140 12 6		36,000		8,917 16 4	
San Luis. — Mines	4		2	50	3,437 10 0	600			1,750 0 0	The Gold is included in the Mines, valued at the rate of £3 17s. 6d. per ounce.
Reduction Works	1		1	491	2,015 12 6			20	50 0 11	
Placer Washings	28			95	703 2 6	1,266			3,637 1 8	
Totals				244	6,156 5 0	1,866		20	5,437 1 8	
Total. — Mines	28	40	11	1,086	97,026 5 0	600	195,034		40,299 0 2	
Reduction Works	13	15	6	1,906	199,359 7 6	1,788	223,167	15,032	97,045 6 3	
Placer Washings	28			95	703 2 6	1,266	...	...	3,647 1 8	
Totals				2,087	297,068 15 0	3,654	418,201	15,032	135,991 8 1	

Proportion of the produce in relation to the capital invested, 45.60 per cent. Proportion of persons employed in relation to the inhabitants of the Argentine Republic (population 1,500,000), .179 per cent., or 17 9-10th per 1,000; Ditto, California (population 780,000), 6.666 per cent., or 66 2-3rd per 1,000.

39 Paternoster Row, E.C.
London: *January* 1870.

GENERAL LIST OF WORKS

PUBLISHED BY

Messrs. LONGMANS, GREEN, READER, and DYER.

History and Politics.

Lord Macaulay's Works. Complete and uniform Library Edition. Edited by his Sister, Lady TREVELYAN. 8 vols. 8vo. with Portrait, price £5 5s. cloth, or £8 8s. bound in tree-calf by Rivière.

The History of England from the fall of Wolsey to the Defeat of the Spanish Armada. By JAMES ANTHONY FROUDE, M.A. late Fellow of Exeter College, Oxford. 12 vols. 8vo. price £8 18s. cloth.

The History of England from the Accession of James II. By Lord MACAULAY.

LIBRARY EDITION, 5 vols. 8vo. £4.
CABINET EDITION, 8 vols. post 8vo. 48s.
PEOPLE'S EDITION, 4 vols. crown 8vo. 16s.

An Essay on the History of the English Government and Constitution, from the Reign of Henry VII. to the Present Time. By JOHN EARL RUSSELL. Fourth Edition, revised. Crown 8vo. 6s.

Speeches of Earl Russell, 1817– 1841. Also Despatches selected from Correspondence presented to Parliament 1859–1865. With Introductions to the Speeches and Despatches, by Earl Russell. 2 vols. 8vo. [*Nearly ready.*

Varieties of Vice-Regal Life. By Major-General Sir WILLIAM DENISON, K.C.B. 2 vols. 8vo. [*Nearly ready.*

On Parliamentary Government in England: its Origin, Development, and Practical Operation. By ALPHEUS TODD, Librarian of the Legislative Assembly of Canada. 2 vols. 8vo. price £1 17s.

The History of England during the Reign of George the Third. By the Right Hon. W. N. MASSEY. Cabinet Edition. 4 vols. post 8vo. 24s.

The Constitutional History of England since the Accession of George III. 1760—1860. By Sir THOMAS ERSKINE MAY, K.C.B. Second Edit. 2 vols. 8vo. 33s.

History of the Reform Bills of 1866 and 1867. By HOMERSHAM COX, M.A. Barrister-at-Law. 8vo. 7s. 6d.

Ancient Parliamentary Elections: a History shewing how Parliaments were Constituted, and Representatives of the People Elected in Ancient Times. By the same Author. 8vo. 8s. 6d.

Whig and Tory Administrations during the Last Thirteen Years. By the same Author. 8vo. 5s.

A

Historical Studies. I. On Precursors of the French Revolution; II. Studies from the History of the Seventeenth Century; III. Leisure Hours of a Tourist. By HERMAN MERIVALE, M.A. 8vo. 12s. 6d.

Revolutions in English History. By ROBERT VAUGHAN, D.D. 3 vols. 8vo. price 30s.

A History of Wales, derived from Authentic Sources. By JANE WILLIAMS, Ysgafell, Author of a Memoir of the Rev. Thomas Price, and Editor of his Literary Remains. 8vo. 14s.

Lectures on the History of England, from the Earliest Times to the Death of King Edward II. By WILLIAM LONGMAN. With Maps and Illustrations. 8vo. 15s.

The History of the Life and Times of Edward the Third. By WILLIAM LONGMAN. With 9 Maps, 8 Plates, and 16 Woodcuts. 2 vols. 8vo. 28s.

History of Civilization in England and France, Spain and Scotland. By HENRY THOMAS BUCKLE. New Edition of the entire work, with a complete INDEX. 3 vols. crown 8vo. 24s.

Realities of Irish Life. By W. STEUART TRENCH Land Agent in Ireland to the Marques of Lansdowne, the Marquess of Bath, and Lord Digby. With Illustrations from Drawings by the Author's Son, J. TOWNSEND TRENCH. Fourth Edition, with 30 Plates. 8vo. 21s.

An Illustrated History of Ireland, from the Earliest Period to the Year of Catholic Emancipation. By MARY F. CUSACK. Second Edition, revised and enlarged. 8vo. 18s. 6d.

The History of India, from the Earliest Period to the close of Lord Dalhousie's Administration. By JOHN CLARK MARSHMAN. 3 vols. crown 8vo. 22s. 6d.

Indian Polity: a View of the System of Administration in India. By Major GEORGE CHESNEY, Fellow of the University of Calcutta. 8vo. with Map, 21s.

Home Politics: being a Consideration of the Causes of the Growth of Trade in relation to Labour, Pauperism, and Emigration. By DANIEL GRANT. 8vo.
[*Nearly ready.*

Democracy in America. By ALEXIS DE TOCQUEVILLE. Translated by HENRY REEVE. 2 vols. 8vo. 21s.

Waterloo Lectures: a Study of the Campaign of 1815. By Colonel CHARLES C. CHESNEY, R.E. late Professor of Military Art and History in the Staff College. Second Edition. 8vo. with map, 10s. 6d.

The Oxford Reformers—John Colet, Erasmus, and Thomas More; being a History of their Fellow-Work. By FREDERIC SEEBOHM. Second Edition. 8vo. 14s.

History of the Reformation in Europe in the Time of Calvin. By J. H. MERLE D'AUBIGNÉ, D.D. VOLS. I. and II. 8vo. 28s. VOL. III. 12s. VOL. IV. price 16s. and VOL. V. price 16s.

England and France in the 15th Century. The Contemporary French Tract intituled *The Debate between the Heralds of France and England,* presumed to have been written by CHARLES, DUKE of ORLEANS: translated for the first time into English, with an Introduction, Notes, and an Inquiry into the Authorship, by HENRY PYNE. 8vo. 7s. 6d.

The History of France, from Clovis and Charlemagne to the Accession of Napoleon III. By EYRE EVANS CROWE. 5 vols. 8vo. £4 13s.

Chapters from French History; St. Louis, Joan of Arc, Henri IV. with Sketches of the Intermediate Periods. By J. H. GURNEY, M.A. late Rector of St. Mary's, Marylebone. New Edition. Fcp. 8vo. 6s. 6d.

The History of Greece. By C. THIRLWALL, D.D. Lord Bishop of St. David's. 8 vols. fcp. 28s.

The Tale of the Great Persian War, from the Histories of Herodotus. By GEORGE W. COX, M.A. late Scholar of Trin. Coll. Oxon. Fcp. 3s. 6d.

Greek History from Themistocles to Alexander, in a Series of Lives from Plutarch. Revised and arranged by A. H. CLOUGH. Fcp. with 44 Woodcuts. 6s.

Critical History of the Language and Literature of Ancient Greece. By WILLIAM MURE, of Caldwell. 5 vols. 8vo. £3 9s.

History of the Literature of Ancient Greece. By Professor K. L. MÜLLER. Translated by LEWIS and DONALDSON. 3 vols. 8vo. 21s.

Roman History. By WILHELM IHNE. Translated and revised by the Author. VOLS. I. and II. 8vo. The First and Second Volumes of this work will be published together early in 1870; and the whole work will be completed in Three or at most Four Volumes

History of the City of Rome from its Foundation to the Sixteenth Century of the Christian Era. By THOMAS H. DYER, LL.D. 8vo. with 2 Maps, 15s.

History of the Romans under the Empire. By Very Rev. C. MERIVALE, D.C.L. Dean of Ely. 8 vols. post 8vo. price 48s.

The Fall of the Roman Republic; a Short History of the Last Century of the Commonwealth. By the same Author. 12mo. 7s. 6d.

The Conversion of the Roman Empire; the Boyle Lectures for the year 1864, delivered at the Chapel Royal, Whitehall. By the same Author. Second Edition. 8vo. 8s. 6d.

The Conversion of the Northern Nations; the Boyle Lectures for 1865. By the same Author. 8vo. 8s. 6d.

History of the Norman Kings of England, from a New Collation of the Contemporary Chronicles. By THOMAS COBBE, Barrister, of the Inner Temple. 8vo. 16s.

History of European Morals from Augustus to Charlemagne. By W. E. H. LECKY, M.A. 2 vols. 8vo. price 28s.

History of the Rise and Influence of the Spirit of Rationalism in Europe. By the same Author. Cabinet Edition (the Fourth). 2 vols. crown 8vo. price 16s.

God in History; or, the Progress of Man's Faith in the Moral Order of the World. By the late Baron BUNSEN. Translated from the German by SUSANNA WINKWORTH; with a Preface by the Dean of Westminster. VOLS. I. and II. 8vo. 30s. VOL. III. nearly ready.

Socrates and the Socratic Schools. Translated from the German of Dr. E. ZELLER, with the Author's approval, by the Rev. OSWALD J. REICHEL, B.C.L. and M.A. Crown 8vo. 8s. 6d.

The Stoics, Epicureans, and Sceptics. Translated from the German of Dr. E. ZELLER, with the Author's approval, by OSWALD J. REICHEL, B.C.L. and M.A. Crown 8vo. [*Nearly ready.*

The History of Philosophy, from Thales to Comte. By GEORGE HENRY LEWES. Third Edition, rewritten and enlarged. 2 vols. 8vo. 30s.

The Mythology of the Aryan Nations. By GEORGE W. COX, M.A. late Scholar of Trinity College, Oxford, Joint-Editor, with the late Professor Brande, of the Fourth Edition of 'The Dictionary of Science, Literature, and Art,' Author of 'Tales of Ancient Greece,' &c.
[*In the press.*

The English Reformation. By F. C. MASSINGBERD, M.A. Chancellor of Lincoln. 4th Edition, revised. Fcp. 7s. 6d.

Egypt's Place in Universal History; an Historical Investigation. By BARON BUNSEN, D.C.L. Translated by C. H. COTTRELL, M.A. with Additions by S. BIRCH, LL.D. 5 vols. 8vo. £8 14s. 6d.

Maunder's Historical Treasury; comprising a General Introductory Outline of Universal History, and a Series of Separate Histories. Fcp. 10s. 6d.

Critical and Historical Essays contributed to the *Edinburgh Review* by the Right Hon. Lord MACAULAY:—
CABINET EDITION, 4 vols. 24s.
LIBRARY EDITION, 3 vols. 8vo. 36s.
PEOPLE'S EDITION, 2 vols. crown 8vo. 8s.
STUDENT'S EDITION, crown 8vo. 6s.

History of the Early Church, from the First Preaching of the Gospel to the Council of Nicæa, A.D. 325. By the Author of 'Amy Herbert.' Fcp. 4s. 6d.

Sketch of the History of the Church of England to the Revolution of 1688. By the Right Rev. T. V. SHORT, D.D. Lord Bishop of St. Asaph. Seventh Edition. Crown 8vo. 10s. 6d.

History of the Christian Church, from the Ascension of Christ to the Conversion of Constantine. By E. BURTON, D.D. late Regius Prof. of Divinity in the University of Oxford. Fcp. 3s. 6d.

Biography and *Memoirs.*

The Life and Letters of Faraday. By Dr. BENCE JONES, Secretary of the Royal Institution. 2 vols. 8vo. with Portrait, 28s.

The Life of Oliver Cromwell, to the Death of Charles I. By J. R. ANDREWS, Barrister-at-Law. 8vo. 14s.

A Life of the Third Earl of Shaftesbury, compiled from Unpublished Documents; with a Review of the Philosophy of the Period. By the Rev. W. M. HATCH, M.A. Fellow of New College, Oxford. 8vo. [*In preparation.*

Dictionary of General Biography;
containing Concise Memoirs and Notices of
the most Eminent Persons of all Countries,
from the Earliest Ages to the Present Time.
Edited by WILLIAM L. R. CATES. 8vo.
price 21s.

Memoirs of Baron Bunsen, drawn
chiefly from Family Papers by his Widow,
FRANCES Baroness BUNSEN. Second Edition, abridged; with 2 Portraits and 4
Woodcuts. 2 vols. post 8vo. 21s.

The Letters of the late Right
Hon. Sir George Cornewall Lewis. Edited
by his Brother, the Rev. Sir G. F. LEWIS,
Bart. 8vo. [*Nearly ready.*

Life of the Duke of Wellington.
By the Rev. G. R. GLEIG, M.A. Popular
Edition, carefully revised; with copious
Additions. Crown 8vo. with Portrait, 5s.

Father Mathew: a Biography.
By JOHN FRANCIS MAGUIRE, M.P. Popular
Edition, with Portrait. Crown 8vo. 3s. 6d.

History of my Religious Opinions.
By J. H. NEWMAN, D.D. Being the Substance of Apologia pro Vitâ Suâ. Post 8vo.
price 6s.

Letters and Life of Francis
Bacon, including all his Occasional Works.
Collected and edited, with a Commentary,
by J. SPEDDING, Triu. Coll. Cantab. VOLS.
I. & II. 8vo. 24s. VOLS. III. & IV. 24s.

Felix Mendelssohn's Letters from
Italy and Switzerland, and *Letters* from
1833 to 1847, translated by Lady WALLACE.
With Portrait. 2 vols. crown 8vo. 5s. each.

Captain Cook's Life, Voyages,
and Discoveries. 18mo. Woodcuts. 2s. 6d.

Memoirs of Sir Henry Havelock,
K.C.B. By JOHN CLARK MARSHMAN.
Cabinet Edition, with Portrait. Crown 8vo.
price 5s.

Essays in Ecclesiastical Biogra-
phy. By the Right Hon. Sir J. STEPHEN,
LL.D. Cabinet Edition. Crown 8vo. 7s. 6d.

The Earls of Granard: a Memoir of
the Noble Family of Forbes. Written by
Admiral the Hon. JOHN FORBES, and Edited
by GEORGE ARTHUR HASTINGS, present
Earl of Granard, K.P. 8vo. 10s.

Vicissitudes of Families. By Sir
J. BERNARD BURKE, C.B. Ulster King of
Arms. New Edition, remodelled and en-
larged. 2 vols. crown 8vo. 21s.

Lives of the Tudor Princesses,
including Lady Jane Grey and her Sisters.
By AGNES STRICKLAND. Post 8vo. with
Portrait, &c. 12s. 6d.

Lives of the Queens of England.
By AGNES STRICKLAND. Library Edition,
newly revised; with Portraits of every
Queen, Autographs, and Vignettes. 8 vols.
post 8vo. 7s. 6d. each.

Maunder's Biographical Trea-
sury. Thirteenth Edition, reconstructed and
partly re-written, with above 1,000 additional
Memoirs, by W. L. R. CATES. Fcp. 10s. 6d.

Criticism, Philosophy, Polity, &c.

England and Ireland. By JOHN
STUART MILL. Fifth Edition. 8vo. 1s.

The Subjection of Women. By
JOHN STUART MILL. New Edition. Post
8vo. 5s.

On Representative Government.
By JOHN STUART MILL. Third Edition.
8vo. 9s. crown 8vo. 2s.

On Liberty. By the same Author. Fourth
Edition. Post 8vo. 7s. 6d. Crown 8vo.
1s. 4d.

Principles of Political Economy. By the
same. Sixth Edition. 2 vols. 8vo. 30s. or
in 1 vol. crown 8vo. 5s.

Utilitarianism. By the same. 3d Edit. 8vo. 5s.

Dissertations and Discussions. By the
same Author. Second Edition. 3 vols. 8vo.
36s.

Examination of Sir W. Hamilton's
Philosophy, and of the principal Philoso-
phical Questions discussed in his Writings.
By the same. Third Edition. 8vo. 16s.

A System of Logic, Ratiocinative
and Inductive. By JOHN STUART MILL.
Seventh Edition. 2 vols. 8vo. 25s.

Inaugural Address delivered to the
University of St. Andrews. By JOHN
STUART MILL. 8vo. 5s. Crown 8vo. 1s.

Analysis of the Phenomena of
the Human Mind. By JAMES MILL. A
New Edition, with Notes, Illustrative and
Critical, by ALEXANDER BAIN, ANDREW
FINDLATER, and GEORGE GROTE. Edited,
with additional Notes, by JOHN STUART
MILL. 2 vols. 8vo. price 28s.

The Elements of Political Eco-
nomy. By HENRY DUNNING MACLEOD,
M.A. Barrister-at-Law. 8vo. 16s.

A Dictionary of Political Economy;
Biographical, Bibliographical, Historical,
and Practical. By the same Author. VOL.
I. royal 8vo. 30s.

Lord Bacon's Works, collected and edited by R. L. ELLIS, M.A. J. SPEDDING, M.A. and D. D. HEATH. VOLS. I. to V. *Philosophical Works*, 5 vols. 8vo. £4 6s. VOLS. VI. and VII. *Literary and Professional Works*, 2 vols. £1 16s.

Analysis of Mr. Mill's System of Logic. By W. STEBBING, M.A. New Edition. 12mo. 3s. 6d.

The Institutes of Justinian; with English Introduction, Translation, and Notes. By T. C. SANDARS, M.A. Barrister-at-Law. New Edition. 8vo. 15s.

The Ethics of Aristotle; with Essays and Notes. By Sir A. GRANT, Bart. M.A. LL.D. Second Edition, revised and completed. 2 vols. 8vo. price 28s.

The Nicomachean Ethics of Aristotle. Newly translated into English. By R. WILLIAMS, B.A. Fellow and late Lecturer of Merton College, and sometime Student of Christ Church, Oxford. 8vo. 12s.

Bacon's Essays, with Annotations. By R. WHATELY, D.D. late Archbishop of Dublin. Sixth Edition. 8vo. 10s. 6d.

Elements of Logic. By R. WHATELY, D.D. late Archbishop of Dublin. New Edition. 8vo. 10s. 6d. crown 8vo. 4s. 6d.

Elements of Rhetoric. By the same Author. New Edition. 8vo. 10s. 6d. Crown 8vo. 4s. 6d.

English Synonymes. By E. JANE WHATELY. Edited by Archbishop WHATELY. 5th Edition. Fcp. 3s.

An Outline of the Necessary Laws of Thought: a Treatise on Pure and Applied Logic. By the Most Rev. W. THOMSON, D.D. Archbishop of York. Ninth Thousand. Crown 8vo. 5s. 6d.

The Election of Representatives, Parliamentary and Municipal; a Treatise. By THOMAS HARE, Barrister-at-Law. Third Edition, with Additions. Crown 8vo. 6s.

Speeches of the Right Hon. Lord MACAULAY, corrected by Himself. Library Edition, 8vo. 12s. People's Edition, crown 8vo. 3s. 6d.

Lord Macaulay's Speeches on Parliamentary Reform in 1831 and 1832. 16mo. price ONE SHILLING.

Walker's Pronouncing Dictionary of the English Language. Thoroughly revised Editions, by B. H. SMART. 8vo. 12s. 16mo. 6s.

A Dictionary of the English Language. By R. G. LATHAM, M.A. M.D. F.R.S. Founded on the Dictionary of Dr. S. JOHNSON, as edited by the Rev. H. J. TODD with numerous Emendations and Additions. 4 vols. 4to. price £7.

Thesaurus of English Words and Phrases, classified and arranged so as to facilitate the expression of Ideas, and assist in Literary Composition. By P. M. ROGET, M.D. New Edition. Crown 8vo. 10s. 6d.

The Debater; a Series of Complete Debates, Outlines of Debates, and Questions for Discussion. By F. ROWTON. Fcp. 6s.

Lectures on the Science of Language, delivered at the Royal Institution. By MAX MÜLLER, M.A. Fellow of All Souls College, Oxford. 2 vols. 8vo. FIRST SERIES. Fifth Edition, 12s. SECOND SERIES, Second Edition, 18s.

Chapters on Language. By F. W. FARRAR, M.A. F.R.S. late Fellow of Trin. Coll. Cambridge. Crown 8vo. 8s. 6d.

A Book about Words. By G. F. GRAHAM. Fcp. 8vo. 3s. 6d.

Manual of English Literature, Historical and Critical: with a Chapter on English Metres. By THOMAS ARNOLD, M.A. Second Edition. Crown 8vo. 7s. 6d.

Southey's Doctor, complete in One Volume, edited by the Rev. J. W. WARTER, B.D. Square crown 8vo. 12s. 6d.

Historical and Critical Commentary on the Old Testament; with a New Translation. By M. M. KALISCH, Ph.D. Vol. I. *Genesis*, 8vo. 18s. or adapted for the General Reader, 12s. Vol. II. *Exodus*, 15s. or adapted for the General Reader, 12s. Vol III. *Leviticus*, Part I. 15s. or adapted for the General Reader, 8s.

A Hebrew Grammar, with Exercises. By the same. Part I. *Outlines with Exercises*, 8vo. 12s. 6d. KEY, 5s. Part II. *Exceptional Forms and Constructions*, 12s. 6d.

A Latin-English Dictionary. By J. T. WHITE, D.D. of Corpus Christi College, and J. E. RIDDLE, M.A. of St. Edmund Hall, Oxford. Third Edition, revised. 2 vols. 4to. pp. 2,128, price 42s.

White's College Latin-English Dictionary (Intermediate Size), abridged from the Parent Work for the use of University Students. Medium 8vo. pp. 1,048, price 18s.

White's Junior Student's Complete Latin-English and English-Latin Dictionary. Revised Edition. Square 12mo. pp. 1,058, price 12s.

Separately { ENGLISH-LATIN, 5s. 6d.
 { LATIN-ENGLISH, 7s. 6d.

An English-Greek Lexicon, containing all the Greek Words used by Writers of good authority. By C. D. YONGE, B.A. New Edition. 4to. 21s.

Mr. Yonge's New Lexicon, English and Greek, abridged from his larger work (as above). Square 12mo. 8s. 6d.

A Greek-English Lexicon. Compiled by H. G. LIDDELL, D.D. Dean of Christ Church, and R. SCOTT, D.D. Master of Balliol. Fifth Edition. Crown 4to. 31s. 6d.

A Lexicon, Greek and English, abridged for Schools from LIDDELL and SCOTT's *Greek-English Lexicon.* Twelfth Edition. Square 12mo. 7s. 6d.

A Practical Dictionary of the French and English Languages. By Professor LÉON CONTANSEAU, many years French Examiner for Military and Civil Appointments, &c. New Edition, carefully revised. Post 8vo. 10s. 6d.

Contanseau's Pocket Dictionary, French and English, abridged from the Practical Dictionary, by the Author. New Edition. 18mo. price 3s. 6d.

A Sanskrit-English Dictionary. The Sanskrit words printed both in the original Devanagari and in Roman letters; with References to the Best Editions of Sanskrit Authors, and with Etymologies and comparisons of Cognate Words chiefly in Greek, Latin, Gothic, and Anglo-Saxon. Compiled by T. BENFEY. 8vo. 52s. 6d.

New Practical Dictionary of the German Language; German-English, and English-German. By the Rev. W. L. BLACKLEY, M.A. and Dr. CARL MARTIN FRIEDLÄNDER. Post 8vo. 7s. 6d.

The Mastery of Languages; or, the Art of Speaking Foreign Tongues Idiomatically. By THOMAS PRENDERGAST, late of the Civil Service at Madras. Second Edition. 8vo. 6s.

Miscellaneous Works and *Popular Metaphysics.*

The Essays and Contributions of A. K. H. B. Author of 'The Recreations of a Country Parson.' Uniform Editions:—

Recreations of a Country Parson. FIRST and SECOND SERIES, 3s. 6d. each.

The Commonplace Philosopher in Town and Country. Crown 8vo. 3s. 6d.

Leisure Hours in Town; Essays Consolatory, Æsthetical, Moral, Social, and Domestic. Crown 8vo. 3s. 6d.

The Autumn Holidays of a Country Parson. Crown 8vo. 3s. 6d.

The Graver Thoughts of a Country Parson. FIRST and SECOND SERIES, crown 8vo. 3s. 6d. each.

Critical Essays of a Country Parson, selected from Essays contributed to *Fraser's Magazine.* Crown 8vo. 3s. 6d.

Sunday Afternoons at the Parish Church of a Scottish University City. Crown 8vo. 3s. 6d.

Lessons of Middle Age, with some Account of various Cities and Men. Crown 8vo. 3s. 6d.

Counsel and Comfort Spoken from a City Pulpit. Crown 8vo. 3s. 6d.

Changed Aspects of Unchanged Truths; Memorials of St. Andrews Sundays. Crown 8vo. 3s. 6d.

Short Studies on Great Subjects. By JAMES ANTHONY FROUDE, M.A. late Fellow of Exeter College, Oxford. Third Edition. 8vo. 12s.

Lord Macaulay's Miscellaneous Writings:—
LIBRARY EDITION, 2 vols. 8vo. Portrait, 21s.
PEOPLE'S EDITION, 1 vol. crown 8vo. 4s. 6d.

The Rev. Sydney Smith's Mis- cellaneous Works; including his Contributions to the *Edinburgh Review.* 1 vol. crown 8vo. 6s.

The Wit and Wisdom of the Rev. SYDNEY SMITH: a Selection of the most memorable Passages in his Writings and Conversation. 16mo. 3s. 6d.

The Silver Store. Collected from Mediæval Christian and Jewish Mines. By the Rev. S. BARING-GOULD, M.A. Crown 8vo. 3s. 6d.

Traces of History in the Names of Places; with a Vocabulary of the Roots out of which Names of Places in England and Wales are formed. By FLAVELL EDMUNDS. Crown 8vo. 7s. 6d.

Essays selected from Contribu- tions to the *Edinburgh Review.* By HENRY ROGERS. Second Edition. 3 vols. fcp. 21s.

Reason and Faith, their Claims and Conflicts. By the same Author. New Edition, revised. Crown 8vo. price 6s. 6d.

The Eclipse of Faith; or, a Visit to a Religious Sceptic. By HENRY ROGERS. Eleventh Edition. Fcp. 5s.

Defence of the Eclipse of Faith, by its Author. Third Edition. Fcp. 3s. 6d.

Selections from the Correspondence of R. E. H. Greyson. By the same Author. Third Edition. Crown 8vo. 7s. 6d.

Families of Speech, Four Lectures delivered at the Royal Institution of Great Britain; with Tables and a Map. By the Rev. F. W. FARRAR, M.A. F.R.S. Post 8vo. [*Nearly ready.*

Chips from a German Workshop; being Essays on the Science of Religion, and on Mythology, Traditions, and Customs. By MAX MÜLLER, M.A. Fellow of All Souls College, Oxford. Second Edition, revised, with an INDEX. 2 vols. 8vo. 21s.

Word Gossip; a Series of Familiar Essays on Words and their Peculiarities. By the Rev. W. L. BLACKLEY, M.A. Fcp. 8vo. 5s.

Menes and Cheops identified in History under Different Names; with other Cosas. By CARL VON RIKART. 8vo. with 5 Illustrations, price 10s. 6d.

An Introduction to Mental Philosophy, on the Inductive Method. By J. D. MORELL, M.A. LL.D. 8vo. 12s.

Elements of Psychology, containing the Analysis of the Intellectual Powers. By the same Author. Post 8vo. 7s. 6d.

The Secret of Hegel: being the Hegelian System in Origin, Principle, Form, and Matter. By JAMES HUTCHISON STIRLING. 2 vols. 8vo. 28s.

The Senses and the Intellect. By ALEXANDER BAIN, LL.D. Prof. of Logic in the Univ. of Aberdeen. Third Edition. 8vo. 15s.

The Emotions and the Will, by the same Author. Second Edition. 8vo. 15s.

On the Study of Character, including an Estimate of Phrenology. By the same Author. 8vo. 9s.

Mental and Moral Science: a Compendium of Psychology and Ethics. By the same Author. Second Edition. Crown 8vo. 10s. 6d.

Strong and Free; or, First Steps towards Social Science. By the Author of 'My Life and What shall I do with it?' 8vo. 10s. 6d.

The Philosophy of Necessity; or, Natural Law as applicable to Mental, Moral. and Social Science. By CHARLES BRAY. Second Edition. 8vo. 9s.

The Education of the Feelings and Affections. By the same Author. Third Edition. 8vo. 3s. 6d.

On Force, its Mental and Moral Correlates. By the same Author. 8vo. 5s.

Mind and Manner, or Diversities of Life. By JAMES FLAMANK. Post 8vo. 7s. 6d.

Characteristics of Men, Manners, Opinions, Times. By ANTHONY, Third Earl of SHAFTESBURY. Published from the Edition of 1713, with Engravings designed by the Author; and Edited, with Marginal Analysis, Notes, and Illustrations, by the Rev. W. M. HATCH, M.A. Fellow of New College, Oxford. 3 vols. 8vo. VOL. I. price 14s.

A Treatise on Human Nature; being an Attempt to Introduce the Experimental Method of Reasoning into Moral Subjects. By DAVID HUME. Edited, with a Preliminary Dissertation and Notes, by T. H. GREEN, Fellow, and T. H. GROSE, late Scholar, of Balliol College, Oxford. [*In the press.*

Essays Moral, Political, and Literary. By DAVID HUME. By the same Editors. [*In the press.*

*** The above will form a new edition of DAVID HUME's *Philosophical Works*, complete in Four Volumes, to be had in Two separate Sections as announced.

Astronomy, Meteorology, Popular Geography, &c.

Outlines of Astronomy. By Sir J. F. W. HERSCHEL, Bart. M.A. New Edition, revised; with Plates and Woodcuts. 8vo. 18s.

Saturn and its System. By RICHARD A. PROCTOR, B.A. late Scholar of St. John's Coll. Camb. and King's Coll. London. 8vo. with 14 Plates, 14s.

The Handbook of the Stars. By the same Author. Square fcp. 8vo. with 3 Maps, price 5s.

Celestial Objects for Common Telescopes. By T. W. WEBB, M.A. F.R.A.S. Second Edition, revised and enlarged, with Map of the Moon and Woodcuts. 16mo. price 7s. 6d.

Navigation and Nautical Astronomy (Practical, Theoretical, Scientific) for the use of Students and Practical Men. By J. MERRIFIELD, F.R.A.S. and H. EVERS. 8vo. 14s.

A General Dictionary of Geography, Descriptive, Physical, Statistical, and Historical ; forming a complete Gazetteer of the World. By A. KEITH JOHNSTON, F.R.S.E. New Edition. 8vo. price 31s. 6d.

M'Culloch's Dictionary, Geographical, Statistical, and Historical, of the various Countries, Places, and principal Natural Objects in the World. Revised Edition, with the Statistical Information throughout brought up to the latest returns. By FREDERICK MARTIN. 4 vols. 8vo. with coloured Maps, £4 4s.

A Manual of Geography, Physical, Industrial, and Political. By W. HUGHES, F.R.G.S. Prof. of Geog. in King's Coll. and in Queen's Coll. Lond. With 6 Maps. Fcp. 7s. 6d.

The States of the River Plate : their Industries and Commerce, Sheep Farming, Sheep Breeding, Cattle Feeding, and Meat Preserving ; the Employment of Capital, Land and Stock and their Values, Labour and its Remuneration. By WILFRID LATHAM, Buenos Ayres. Second Edition. 8vo. 12s.

Maunder's Treasury of Geography, Physical, Historical, Descriptive, and Political. Edited by W. HUGHES, F.R.G.S. With 7 Maps and 16 Plates. Fcp. 10s. 6d.

Physical Geography for Schools and General Readers. By M. F. MAURY, LL.D. Fcp. with 2 Charts, 2s. 6d.

Natural History and *Popular Science.*

Ganot's Elementary Treatise on Physics, Experimental and Applied, for the use of Colleges and Schools. Translated and Edited with the Author's sanction by E. ATKINSON, Ph.D. F.C.S. New Edition, revised and enlarged ; with a Coloured Plate and 620 Woodcuts. Post 8vo. 15s.

The Elements of Physics or Natural Philosophy. By NEIL ARNOTT, M.D. F.R.S. Physician-Extraordinary to the Queen. Sixth Edition, re-written and completed. 2 Parts, 8vo. 21s.

Dove's Law of Storms, considered in connexion with the ordinary Movements of the Atmosphere. Translated by R. H. SCOTT, M.A. T.C.D. 8vo. 10s. 6d.

Sound : a Course of Eight Lectures delivered at the Royal Institution of Great Britain. By Professor JOHN TYNDALL, LL.D. F.R.S. Crown 8vo. with Portrait and Woodcuts, 9s.

Heat Considered as a Mode of Motion. By Professor JOHN TYNDALL, LL.D. F.R.S. Third Edition. Crown 8vo. with Woodcuts, 10s. 6d.

Light : its Influence on Life and Health. By FORBES WINSLOW, M.D. D.C.L. Oxon. (Hon.) Fcp. 8vo. 6s.

A Treatise on Electricity, in Theory and Practice. By A. DE LA RIVE, Prof. in the Academy of Geneva. Translated by C. V. WALKER, F.R.S. 3 vols. 8vo. with Woodcuts, £3 13s.

The Correlation of Physical Forces. By W. R. GROVE, Q.C. V.P.R.S. Fifth Edition, revised, and Augmented by a Discourse on Continuity. 8vo. 10s. 6d. The *Discourse on Continuity*, separately, price 2s. 6d.

Manual of Geology. By S. HAUGHTON, M.D. F.R.S. Fellow of Trin. Coll. and Prof. of Geol. in the Univ. of Dublin. Second Edition, with 66 Woodcuts. Fcp. 7s. 6d.

A Guide to Geology. By J. PHILLIPS, M.A. Prof. of Geol. in the Univ. of Oxford. Fifth Edition. Fcp. 4s.

The Scenery of England and Wales, its Character and Origin ; being an Attempt to trace the Nature of the Geological Causes, especially Denudation, by which the Physical Features of the Country have been Produced. By D. MACKINTOSH, F.G.S. Post 8vo. with 89 Woodcuts, 12s.

The Student's Manual of Zoology and Comparative Physiology. By J. BURNEY YEO, M.B. Resident Medical Tutor and Lecturer on Animal Physiology in King's College, London. [*Nearly ready.*

Van Der Hoeven's Handbook of ZOOLOGY. Translated from the Second Dutch Edition by the Rev. W. CLARK, M.D. F.R.S. 2 vols. 8vo. with 24 Plates of Figures, 60s.

Professor Owen's Lectures on the Comparative Anatomy and Physiology of the Invertebrate Animals. Second Edition, with 235 Woodcuts. 8vo. 21s.

The Comparative Anatomy and Physiology of the Vertebrate Animals. By RICHARD OWEN, F.R.S. D.C.L. With 1,472 Woodcuts. 3 vols. 8vo. £3 13s. 6d.

The Primitive Inhabitants of Scandinavia. Containing a Description of the Implements, Dwellings, Tombs, and Mode of Living of the Savages in the North of Europe during the Stone Age. By SVEN NILSSON. With an Introduction by Sir JOHN LUBBOCK, 16 Plates of Figures and 3 Woodcuts. 8vo. 18s.

Homes without Hands: a Description of the Habitations of Animals, classed according to their Principle of Construction. By Rev. J. G. WOOD, M.A. F.L.S. With about 140 Vignettes on Wood (20 full size of page). New Edition. 8vo. 21s.

Bible Animals; being a Description of Every Living Creature mentioned in the Scriptures, from the Ape to the Coral. By the Rev. J. G. WOOD, M.A. F.L.S. With about 100 Vignettes on Wood (20 full size of page). 8vo. 21s.

The Harmonies of Nature and Unity of Creation. By Dr. G. HARTWIG. 8vo. with numerous Illustrations, 18s.

The Sea and its Living Wonders. By the same Author. Third Edition, enlarged. 8vo. with many Illustrations, 21s.

The Tropical World. By the same Author. With 8 Chromoxylographs and 172 Woodcuts. 8vo. 21s.

The Polar World: a Popular Description of Man and Nature in the Arctic and Antarctic Regions of the Globe. By the same Author. With 8 Chromoxylographs, 3 Maps, and 85 Woodcuts. 8vo. 21s.

A Familiar History of Birds. By E. STANLEY, D.D. late Lord Bishop of Norwich. Fcp. with Woodcuts, 3s. 6d.

Kirby and Spence's Introduction to Entomology, or Elements of the Natural History of Insects. Crown 8vo. 5s.

Maunder's Treasury of Natural History, or Popular Dictionary of Zoology. Revised and corrected by T. S. COBBOLD, M.D. Fcp. with 900 Woodcuts, 10s. 6d.

The Elements of Botany for Families and Schools. Tenth Edition, revised by THOMAS MOORE, F.L.S. Fcp. with 154 Woodcuts, 2s. 6d.

The Treasury of Botany, or Popular Dictionary of the Vegetable Kingdom; with which is incorporated a Glossary of Botanical Terms. Edited by J. LINDLEY, F.R.S. and T. MOORE, F.L.S. assisted by eminent Contributors. Pp. 1,274, with 274 Woodcuts and 20 Steel Plates. Two PARTS, fcp. 8vo. 20s.

The British Flora; comprising the Phænogamous or Flowering Plants and the Ferns. By Sir W. J. HOOKER, K.H. and G. A. WALKER-ARNOTT, LL.D. 12mo. with 12 Plates, 14s. or coloured, 21s.

The Rose Amateur's Guide. By THOMAS RIVERS. New Edition. Fcp. 4s.

London's Encyclopædia of Plants; comprising the Specific Character, Description, Culture, History, &c. of all the Plants found in Great Britain. With upwards of 12,000 Woodcuts. 8vo. 12s.

Maunder's Scientific and Literary Treasury; a Popular Encyclopædia of Science, Literature, and Art. New Edition, thoroughly revised and in great part rewritten, with above 1,000 new articles, by J. Y. JOHNSON, Corr. M.Z.S. Fcp. 10s. 6d.

A Dictionary of Science, Literature, and Art. Fourth Edition, re-edited by the late W. T. BRANDE (the Author) and GEORGE W. COX, M.A. 3 vols. medium 8vo. price 63s. cloth.

The Quarterly Journal of Science. Edited by JAMES SAMUELSON and WILLIAM CROOKES, F.R.S. Published quarterly in January, April, July, and October. 8vo. with Illustrations, price 5s. each Number.

Chemistry, Medicine, Surgery, and the Allied Sciences.

A Dictionary of Chemistry and the Allied Branches of other Sciences. By HENRY WATTS, F.C.S. assisted by eminent Scientific and Practical Chemists. 5 vols. medium 8vo. price £7 3s.

Handbook of Chemical Analysis, adapted to the *Unitary System* of Notation. By F. T. CONINGTON, M.A. F.C.S. Post 8vo. 7s. 6d.

Conington's Tables of Qualitative *Analysis,* to accompany the above, 2s. 6d.

Elements of Chemistry, Theore- tical and Practical. By WILLIAM A. MILLER, M.D. LL.D. Professor of Chemistry, King's College, London. Fourth Edition. 3 vols. 8vo. £3.

PART I. CHEMICAL PHYSICS, 15s.
PART II. INORGANIC CHEMISTRY, 21s.
PART III. ORGANIC CHEMISTRY, 24s.

A Manual of Chemistry, De- scriptive and Theoretical. By WILLIAM ODLING, M.B. F.R.S. PART I. 8vo. 9s. PART II. nearly ready.

A Course of Practical Chemistry,
for the use of Medical Students. By
W. Odling, M.B. F.R.S. New Edition, with
70 new Woodcuts. Crown 8vo. 7s. 6d.

Outlines of Chemistry; or, Brief
Notes of Chemical Facts. By the same
Author. Crown 8vo. 7s. 6d.

Lectures on Animal Chemistry Delivered
at the Royal College of Physicians in 1865.
By the same Author. Crown 8vo. 4s. 6d.

Lectures on the Chemical
Changes of Carbon, delivered at the Royal
Institution of Great Britain. By W.
Odling, M.B. F.R.S. Reprinted from the
Chemical News, with Notes, by W. Crookes,
F.R.S. Crown 8vo. 4s. 6d.

Chemical Notes for the Lecture
Room. By Thomas Wood, F.C.S. 2 vols.
crown 8vo. I. on Heat, &c. price 3s. 6d.
II. on the Metals, price 5s.

A Treatise on Medical Elec-
tricity, Theoretical and Practical; and its
Use in the Treatment of Paralysis, Neu-
ralgia, and other Diseases. By Julius
Althaus, M.D. M.R.C.P. &c.; Senior Physician to the Infirmary for Epilepsy and
Paralysis. Second Edition, revised and
enlarged and for the most part re-written;
with Plate and 62 Woodcuts. Post 8vo.
price 12s. 6d.

The Diagnosis, Pathology, and
Treatment of Diseases of Women; including
the Diagnosis of Pregnancy. By Graily
Hewitt, M.D. &c. President of the Obste-
trical Society of London. Second Edition,
enlarged; with 116 Woodcuts. 8vo. 24s.

Lectures on the Diseases of In-
fancy and Childhood. By Charles West,
M.D. &c. Fifth Edition. 8vo. 16s.

On the Surgical Treatment of
Children's Diseases. By T. Holmes, M.A.
&c. late Surgeon to the Hospital for Sick
Children. Second Edition, with 9 Plates
and 112 Woodcuts. 8vo. 21s.

A System of Surgery, Theoretical
and Practical, in Treatises by Various
Authors. Edited by T. Holmes, M.A. &c.
Surgeon and Lecturer on Surgery at St.
George's Hospital, and Surgeon-in-Chief to
the Metropolitan Police. Second Edition,
thoroughly revised, with numerous Illustrations. 5 vols. 8vo. £5 5s.

Lectures on the Principles and
Practice of Physic. By Sir Thomas Watson, Bart. M.D. Physician-Extraordinary
to the Queen. New Edition in preparation.

Lectures on Surgical Pathology.
By J. Paget, F.R.S. Surgeon-Extraordinary
to the Queen. Edited by W. Turner, M.B.
New Edition in preparation.

Cooper's Dictionary of Practical
Surgery and Encyclopædia of Surgical
Science. New Edition, brought down to
the present time. By S. A. Lane, Surgeon to
St. Mary's, and Consulting Surgeon to the
Lock Hospitals; Lecturer on Surgery at
St. Mary's Hospital; assisted by various
Eminent Surgeons. Vol. II. 8vo. com-
pleting the work.   [*Early in* 1870.

On Chronic Bronchitis, especially
as connected with Gout, Emphysema, and
Diseases of the Heart. By E. Headlam
Greenhow, M.D. F.R.C.P. &c. 8vo. 7s. 6d.

The Climate of the South of
France as Suited to Invalids; with Notices
of Mediterranean and other Winter Sta-
tions. By C. T. Williams, M.A. M.D.
Oxon. Assistant-Physician to the Hospital
for Consumption at Brompton. Second
Edition, with Frontispiece and Map. Cr.
8vo. 6s.

Pulmonary Consumption; its
Nature, Treatment, and Duration exem-
plified by an Analysis of One Thousand
Cases selected from upwards of Twenty
Thousand. By C. J. B. Williams, M.D.
F.R.S. Consulting Physician to the Hos-
pital for Consumption at Brompton; and
C. T. Williams, M.A. M.D. Oxon.
        [*Nearly ready.*

A Treatise on the Continued
Fevers of Great Britain. By C. Murchison.
M.D. Physician and Lecturer on the Practice
of Medicine, Middlesex Hospital. New
Edition in preparation.

Clinical Lectures on Diseases of the
Liver, Jaundice, and Abdominal Dropsy.
By the same Author. Post 8vo. with 25
Woodcuts, 10s. 6d.

Anatomy, Descriptive and Sur-
gical. By Henry Gray, F.R.S. With
about 410 Woodcuts from Dissections. Fifth
Edition, by T. Holmes, M.A. Cantab. With
a New Introduction by the Editor. Royal
8vo. 28s.

Clinical Notes on Diseases of
the Larynx, investigated and treated with
the assistance of the Laryngoscope. By
W. Marcet, M.D. F.R.S. Assistant-Physician to the Hospital for Consumption and
Diseases of the Chest, Brompton. Crown
8vo. with 5 Lithographs, 6s.

The House I Live in ; or, Popular Illustrations of the Structure and Functions of the Human Body. Edited by T. G. Girtin. New Edition, with 25 Woodcuts. 16mo. price 2s. 6d.

Outlines of Physiology, Human and Comparative. By John Marshall, F.R.C.S. Professor of Surgery in University College, London, and Surgeon to the University College Hospital. 2 vols. crown 8vo. with 122 Woodcuts, 32s.

Physiological Anatomy and Physiology of Man. By the late R. B. Todd, M.D. F.R.S. and W. Bowman, F.R.S. of King's College. With numerous Illustrations. Vol. II. 8vo. 25s.

Vol. I. New Edition by Dr. Lionel S. Beale, F.R.S. in course of publication ; Part I. with 8 Plates, 7s. 6d.

A Dictionary of Practical Medicine. By J. Copland, M.D. F.R.S. Abridged from the larger work by the Author, assisted by J. C. Copland, M.R.C.S. Pp. 1,560, in 8vo. price 36s.

The Theory of Ocular Defects and of Spectacles. Translated from the German of Dr. H. Scheffler by R. B. Carter, F.R.C.S. Post 8vo. 7s. 6d.

A Manual of Materia Medica and Therapeutics, abridged from Dr. Pereira's *Elements* by F. J. Farre, M.D. assisted by R. Bentley, M.R.C.S. and by R. Warington, F.R.S. 1 vol. 8vo. with 90 Woodcuts, 21s.

Thomson's Conspectus of the British Pharmacopœia. Twenty-fifth Edition, corrected by E. Lloyd Birkett, M.D. 18mo. 6s.

Manual of the Domestic Practice of Medicine. By W. B. Kesteven, F.R.C.S.E. Third Edition, thoroughly revised, with Additions. Fcp. 5s.

Essays on Physiological Subjects. By Gilbert W. Child, M.A. F.L.S. F.C.S. Second Edition. Crown 8vo. with Woodcuts, 7s. 6d.

Gymnasts and Gymnastics. By John H. Howard, late Professor of Gymnastics, Comm. Coll. Ripponden. Second Edition, with 135 Woodcuts. Crown 8vo. 10s. 6d.

The Fine Arts, and *Illustrated Editions.*

In Fairyland ; Pictures from the Elf-World. By Richard Doyle. With a Poem by W. Allingham. With Sixteen Plates, containing Thirty-six Designs printed in Colours. Folio, 31s. 6d.

Life of John Gibson, R.A. Sculptor. Edited by Lady Eastlake. 8vo. 10s. 6d.

Materials for a History of Oil Painting. By Sir Charles Locke Eastlake, sometime President of the Royal Academy. Vol. II. 8vo. 14s.

Albert Durer, his Life and Works ; including Autobiographical Papers and Complete Catalogues. By William B. Scott. With Six Etchings by the Author and other Illustrations. 8vo. 16s.

Half-Hour Lectures on the History and Practice of the Fine and Ornamental Arts. By W. B. Scott. Second Edition. Crown 8vo. with 50 Woodcut Illustrations, 8s. 6d.

The Lord's Prayer Illustrated by F. R. Pickersgill, R.A. and Henry Alford, D.D. Dean of Canterbury. Imp. 4to. 21s.

The Chorale Book for England ; a complete Hymn-Book in accordance with the Services and Festivals of the Church of England: the Hymns Translated by Miss C. Winkworth; the Tunes arranged by Prof. W. S. Bennett and Otto Goldschmidt. Fcp. 4to. 12s. 6d.

Six Lectures on Harmony. Delivered at the Royal Institution of Great Britain. By G. A. Macfarren. 8vo. 10s. 6d.

Lyra Germanica, the Christian Year. Translated by Catherine Winkworth; with 125 Illustrations on Wood drawn by J. Leighton, F.S.A. Quarto, 21s.

Lyra Germanica. the Christian Life. Translated by Catherine Winkworth; with about 200 Woodcut Illustrations by J. Leighton, F.S.A. and other Artists. Quarto, 21s.

The New Testament, illustrated with Wood Engravings after the Early Masters, chiefly of the Italian School. Crown 4to. 63s. cloth, gilt top ; or £5 5s. morocco.

The Life of Man Symbolised by the Months of the Year in their Seasons and Phases. Text selected by Richard Pigot. 25 Illustrations on Wood from Original Designs by John Leighton, F.S.A. Quarto, 42s.

Cats' and Farlie's Moral Em-
blems; with Aphorisms, Adages, and Pro-
verbs of all Nations: comprising 121 Illustrations on Wood by J. LEIGHTON, F.S.A.
with an appropriate Text by R. PIGOT.
Imperial 8vo. 31s. 6d.

Shakspeare's Midsummer Night's
Dream, illustrated with 24 Silhouettes or
Shadow Pictures by P. KONEWKA, engraved
on Wood by A. VOGEL. Folio, 31s. 6d.

Shakspeare's Sentiments and
Similes Printed in Black and Gold, and illu-
minated in the Missal style by HENRY NOEL
HUMPHREYS. In massive covers, containing
the Medallion and Cypher of Shakspeare.
Square post 8vo. 21s.

Goldsmith's Poetical Works, Il-
lustrated with Wood Engravings, from
Designs by Members of the ETCHING CLUB.
Imp. 16mo. 7s. 6d.

Sacred and Legendary Art. By
Mrs. JAMESON. With numerous Etchings
and Woodcut Illustrations. 6 vols. square
crown 8vo. price £5 15s. 6d. cloth, or
£12 12s. bound in morocco by Rivière. To
be had also in cloth only, in FOUR SERIES,
as follows :—

Legends of the Saints and Martyrs.
Fifth Edition, with 19 Etchings and 187
Woodcuts. 2 vols. square crown 8vo.
31s. 6d.

Legends of the Monastic Orders. Third
Edition, with 11 Etchings and 88 Woodcuts.
1 vol. square crown 8vo. 21s.

Legends of the Madonna. Third Edition,
with 27 Etchings and 165 Woodcuts. 1
vol. square crown 8vo. 21s.

The History of Our Lord, as exemplified
in Works of Art. Completed by Lady
EASTLAKE. Revised Edition, with 13
Etchings and 281 Woodcuts. 2 vols.
square crown 8vo. 42s.

The Useful Arts, Manufactures, &c.

Drawing from Nature. By GEORGE
BARNARD, Professor of Drawing at Rugby
School. With 18 Lithographic Plates and
108 Wood Engravings. Imp. 8vo. 25s. or
in Three Parts, royal 8vo. 7s. 6d. each.

Gwilt's Encyclopædia of Archi-
tecture. Fifth Edition, with Alterations
and considerable Additions, by WYATT
PAPWORTH. Additionally illustrated with
nearly 400 Wood Engravings by O. JEWITT,
and upwards of 100 other new Woodcuts.
8vo. 52s. 6d.

Italian Sculptors: being a History of
Sculpture in Northern, Southern, and Eastern Italy. By C. C. PERKINS. With 30
Etchings and 13 Wood Engravings. Imperial 8vo. 42s.

Tuscan Sculptors, their Lives,
Works, and Times. By the same Author.
With 45 Etchings and 28 Woodcuts from
Original Drawings and Photographs. 2
vols. imperial 8vo. 63s.

Hints on Household Taste in
Furniture, Upholstery, and other Details.
By CHARLES L. EASTLAKE, Architect.
Second Edition, with about 90 Illustrations.
Square crown 8vo. 18s.

The Engineer's Handbook; ex-
plaining the principles which should guide
the young Engineer in the Construction of
Machinery. By C. S. LOWNDES. Post 8vo. 5s.

Lathes and Turning, Simple, Me-
chanical, and Ornamental. By W. HENRY
NORTHCOTT. With about 240 Illustrations
on Steel and Wood. 8vo. 18s.

Principles of Mechanism, designed
for the use of Students in the Universities,
and for Engineering Students generally.
By R. WILLIS, M.A. F.R.S. &c. Jacksonian
Professor of Natural and Experimental
Philosophy in the University of Cambridge.
A new and enlarged Edition. 8vo.
[Nearly ready.

Handbook of Practical Tele-
graphy, published with the sanction of the
Chairman and Directors of the Electric
and International Telegraph Company, and
adopted by the Department of Telegraphs
for India. By R. S. CULLEY. Third Edition. 8vo. 12s. 6d.

Ure's Dictionary of Arts, Manu-
factures, and Mines. Sixth Edition, chiefly
re-written and greatly enlarged by ROBERT
HUNT, F.R.S. assisted by numerous Contributors eminent in Science and the Arts,
and familiar with Manufactures. With
2,000 Woodcuts. 3 vols. medium 8vo.
£4 14s. 6d.

Treatise on Mills and Millwork.
By Sir W. FAIRBAIRN, F.R.S. With 18
Plates and 322 Woodcuts. 2 vols. 8vo. 32s.

Useful Information for Engineers. By
the same Author. FIRST, SECOND, and
THIRD SERIES, with many Plates and
Woodcuts. 3 vols. crown 8vo. 10s. 6d. each.

The Application of Cast and Wrought
Iron to Building Purposes. By the same
Author. New Edition, preparing for pub-
lication.

Iron Ship Building, its History and Progress, as comprised in a Series of Experimental Researches on the Laws of Strain; the Strengths, Forms, and other conditions of the Material; and an Inquiry into the Present and Prospective State of the Navy, including the Experimental Results on the Resisting Powers of Armour Plates and Shot at High Velocities. By Sir W. FAIRBAIRN, F.R.S. With 4 Plates and 130 Woodcuts, 8vo. 18s.

Encyclopædia of Civil Engineer- ing, Historical, Theoretical, and Practical. By E. CRESY, C.E. With above 3,000 Woodcuts. 8vo. 42s.

The Artisan Club's Treatise on the Steam Engine, in its various Applications to Mines, Mills, Steam Navigation, Railways, and Agriculture. By J. BOURNE, C.E. New Edition; with Portrait, 37 Plates, and 546 Woodcuts. 4to. 42s.

A Treatise on the Screw Pro- peller, Screw Vessels, and Screw Engines, as adapted for purposes of Peace and War; with notices of other Methods of Propulsion, Tables of the Dimensions and Performance of Screw Steamers, and Detailed Specifications of Ships and Engines. By JOHN BOURNE, C.E. Third Edition, with 54 Plates and 287 Woodcuts. Quarto, 63s.

Catechism of the Steam Engine, in its various Applications to Mines, Mills, Steam Navigation, Railways, and Agriculture. By JOHN BOURNE, C.E. New Edition, with 89 Woodcuts. Fcp. 6s.

Recent Improvements in the Steam-Engine in its various applications to Mines, Mills, Steam Navigation, Railways, and Agriculture. By JOHN BOURNE, C.E. being a SUPPLEMENT to his 'Catechism of the Steam-Engine.' New Edition, including many New Examples, among which are several of the most remarkable ENGINES exhibited in Paris in 1867; with 124 Woodcuts. Fcp. 8vo. 6s.

Bourne's Examples of Modern Steam, Air, and Gas Engines of the most Approved Types, as employed for Pumping, for Driving Machinery, for Locomotion, and for Agriculture, minutely and practically described. Illustrated by Working Drawings, and embodying a Critical Account of all Projects of Recent Improvement in Furnaces, Boilers, and Engines. In course of publication, to be completed in Twenty-four Parts, price 2s. 6d. each, forming One Volume, with about 50 Plates and 400 Woodcuts.

Handbook of the Steam Engine. By JOHN BOURNE, C.E. forming a KEY to the Author's Catechism of the Steam Engine. With 67 Woodcuts. Fcp. 9s.

A History of the Machine- Wrought Hosiery and Lace Manufactures. By WILLIAM FELKIN, F.L.S. F.S.S. With 3 Steel Plates, 10 Lithographic Plates of Machinery, and 10 Coloured Impressions of Patterns of Lace. Royal 8vo. 21s.

Mitchell's Manual of Practical Assaying. Third Edition, for the most part re-written, with all the recent Discoveries incorporated. By W. CROOKES, F.R.S. With 188 Woodcuts. 8vo. 28s.

Reimann's Handbook of Aniline and its Derivatives; a Treatise on the Manufacture of Aniline and Aniline Colours. Revised and edited by WILLIAM CROOKES, F.R.S. 8vo. with 5 Woodcuts, 10s. 6d.

Practical Treatise on Metallurgy, adapted from the last German Edition of Professor KERL'S *Metallurgy* by W. CROOKES, F.R.S. &c. and E. RÖHRIG, Ph.D. M.E. In Three Volumes, 8vo. with 625 Woodcuts. VOL. I. price 31s. 6d. VOL. II. price 36s. VOL. III. price 31s. 6d.

The Art of Perfumery; the History and Theory of Odours, and the Methods of Extracting the Aromas of Plants. By Dr. PIESSE, F.C.S. Third Edition, with 53 Woodcuts. Crown 8vo. 10s. 6d.

Chemical, Natural, and Physical Magic, for Juveniles during the Holidays. By the same Author. Third Edition, enlarged with 38 Woodcuts. Fcp. 6s.

Loudon's Encyclopædia of Agri- culture: comprising the Laying-out, Improvement, and Management of Landed Property, and the Cultivation and Economy of the Productions of Agriculture. With 1,100 Woodcuts. 8vo. 21s.

Loudon's Encyclopædia of Gardening: comprising the Theory and Practice of Horticulture, Floriculture, Arboriculture, and Landscape Gardening. With 1,000 Woodcuts. 8vo. 21s.

Bayldon's Art of Valuing Rents and Tillages, and Claims of Tenants upon Quitting Farms, both at Michaelmas and Lady-Day. Eighth Edition, revised by J. C. MORTON. 8vo. 10s. 6d.

Religious and *Moral Works.*

An Exposition of the 39 Articles,
Historical and Doctrinal. By E. HAROLD
BROWNE, D.D. Lord Bishop of Ely. Eighth
Edition. 8vo. 16s.

Examination-Questions on 'Bishop
Browne's Exposition of the Articles. By
the Rev. J. GORLE, M.A. Fcp. 3s. 6d.

Archbishop Leighton's Sermons
and Charges. With Additions and Corrections from MSS. and with Historical and
other Illustrative Notes by WILLIAM WEST,
Incumbent of S. Columba's, Nairn. 8vo.
price 15s.

Bishop Cotton's Instructions in
the Principles and Practice of Christianity,
intended chiefly as an Introduction to Confirmation. Sixth Edition. 18mo. 2s. 6d.

The Acts of the Apostles; with a
Commentary, and Practical and Devotional
Suggestions for Readers and Students of the
English Bible. By the Rev. F. C. COOK,
M.A. Canon of Exeter, &c. New Edition,
8vo. 12s. 6d.

The Life and Epistles of St.
Paul. By the Rev. W. J. CONYBEARE,
M.A. and the Very Rev. J. S. HOWSON,
D.D. Dean of Chester:—

LIBRARY EDITION, with all the Original
Illustrations, Maps, Landscapes on Steel,
Woodcuts, &c. 2 vols. 4to. 48s.

INTERMEDIATE EDITION, with a Selection
of Maps, Plates, and Woodcuts. 2 vols.
square crown 8vo. 31s. 6d.

PEOPLE'S EDITION, revised and condensed, with 46 Illustrations and Maps. 2
vols. crown 8vo. 12s.

The Voyage and Shipwreck of
St. Paul; with Dissertations on the Ships
and Navigation of the Ancients. By JAMES
SMITH, F.R.S. Crown 8vo. Charts, 10s. 6d.

Evidence of the Truth of the
Christian Religion derived from the Literal
Fulfilment of Prophecy. By ALEXANDER
KEITH, D.D. 37th Edition, with numerous
Plates, in square 8vo. 12s. 6d.; also the
39th Edition, in post 8vo. with 5 Plates, 6s.

The History and Destiny of the World
and of the Church, according to Scripture.
By the same Author. Square 8vo. with 40
Illustrations, 10s.

Ewald's History of Israel to the
Death of Moses. Translated from the German. Edited, with a Preface and an Appendix, by RUSSELL MARTINEAU, M.A.
Professor of Hebrew in Manchester New
College, London. Second Edition, continued
to the Commencement of the Monarchy. 2
vols. 8vo. 24s.

Five Years in a Protestant Sis-
terhood and Ten Years in a Catholic Convent; an Autobiography. Post 8vo. 7s. 6d.

The Life of Margaret Mary
Hallahan, better known in the religious world by the name of Mother Margaret. By her RELIGIOUS CHILDREN.
With a Preface by the Bishop of Birming-
ham. 8vo. with Portrait, 10s.

The See of Rome in the Middle
Ages. By the Rev. OSWALD J. REICHEL,
B.C.L. and M.A. Vice-Principal of Cuddes-
don College. 8vo. [*Nearly ready.*

The Evidence for the Papacy
as derived from the Holy Scriptures and
from Primitive Antiquity; with an Introductory Epistle. By the Hon. COLIN
LINDSAY. 8vo. [*Nearly ready.*

A Critical and Grammatical Com-
mentary on St. Paul's Epistles. By C. J.
ELLICOTT, D.D. Lord Bishop of Gloucester
and Bristol. 8vo.
Galatians, Fourth Edition, 8s. 6d.
Ephesians, Fourth Edition, 8s. 6d.
Pastoral Epistles, Fourth Edition, 10s. 6d.
Philippians, Colossians, and Philemon,
Third Edition, 10s. 6d.
Thessalonians, Third Edition, 7s. 6d.

Historical Lectures on the Life of
Our Lord Jesus Christ: being the Hulsean
Lectures for 1859. By C. J. ELLICOTT, D.D.
Lord Bishop of Gloucester and Bristol.
Fifth Edition. 8vo. 12s.

The Destiny of the Creature; and other
Sermons preached before the University of
Cambridge. By the same. Post 8vo. 5s.

An Introduction to the Study of
the New Testament, Critical, Exegetical,
and Theological. By the Rev. S. DAVIDSON,
D.D. LL.D. 2 vols. 8vo. 30s.

The Greek Testament; with Notes,
Grammatical and Exegetical. By the Rev.
W. WEBSTER, M.A. and the Rev. W. F.
WILKINSON, M.A. 2 vols. 8vo. £2 4s.
VOL. I. the Gospels and Acts, 20s.
VOL. II. the Epistles and Apocalypse, 24s.

Rev. T. H. Horne's Introduction to the Critical Study and Knowledge of the Holy Scriptures. Twelfth Edition, as last revised throughout. With 4 Maps and 22 Woodcuts and Facsimiles. 4 vols. 8vo. 42s.

Rev. T. H. Horne's Compendious Introduction to the Study of the Bible, being an Analysis of the larger work by the same Author. Re-edited by the Rev. JOHN AYRE, M.A. With Maps, &c. Post 8vo. 6s.

The Treasury of Bible Knowledge; being a Dictionary of the Books, Persons, Places, Events, and other Matters of which mention is made in Holy Scripture; Intended to establish its Authority and illustrate its Contents. By Rev. J. AYRE, M.A. With Maps, 15 Plates, and numerous Woodcuts. Fcp. 10s. 6d.

Every-day Scripture Difficulties explained and illustrated. By J. E. PRESCOTT, M.A. VOL. I. *Matthew* and *Mark*; VOL. II. *Luke* and *John*. 2 vols. 8vo. price 9s. each.

The Pentateuch and Book of Joshua Critically Examined. By the Right Rev. J. W. COLENSO, D.D. Lord Bishop of Natal. Crown 8vo. price 6s.

The Church and the World; Three Series of Essays on Questions of the Day, by various Writers. Edited by the Rev. ORBY SHIPLEY, M.A. 3 vols. 8vo. 15s. each.

The Formation of Christendom. By T. W. ALLIES. PARTS I. and II. 8vo. price 12s. each.

Christendom's Divisions; a Philosophical Sketch of the Divisions of the Christian Family in East and West. By EDMUND S. FFOULKES, formerly Fellow and Tutor of Jesus Coll. Oxford. Post 8vo. 7s. 6d.

Christendom's Divisions, PART II. *Greeks and Latins,* being a History of their Dissensions and Overtures for Peace down to the Reformation. By the same Author. Post 8vo. 15s.

The Hidden Wisdom of Christ and the Key of Knowledge; or, History of the Apocrypha. By ERNEST DE BUNSEN. 2 vols. 8vo. 28s.

The Keys of St. Peter; or, the House of Rechab, connected with the History of Symbolism and Idolatry. By the same Author. 8vo. 14s.

The Power of the Soul over the Body. By GEO. MOORE, M.D. M.R.C.P.L. &c. Sixth Edition. Crown 8vo. 8s. 6d.

The Types of Genesis briefly considered as Revealing the Development of Human Nature. By ANDREW JUKES. Second Edition. Crown 8vo. 7s. 6d.

The Second Death and the Restitution of All Things, with some Preliminary Remarks on the Nature and Inspiration of Holy Scripture. By the same Author. Second Edition. Crown 8vo. 3s. 6d.

Essays and Reviews. By the Rev. W. TEMPLE, D.D. the Rev. R. WILLIAMS, B.D. the Rev. B. POWELL, M.A. the Rev. H. B. WILSON, B.D. C. W. GOODWIN, M.A. the Rev. M. PATTISON, B.D. and the Rev. B. JOWETT, M.A. 12th Edition. Fcp. 5s.

Religious Republics; Six Essays on Congregationalism. By W. M. FAWCETT, T.M. HERBERT, M.A. E. G. HERBERT, LL.B. T. H. PATTISON, P. H. PYE-SMITH, M.D. B.A. and J. ANSTIE, B.A. 8vo. price 8s. 6d.

Passing Thoughts on Religion. By the Author of 'Amy Herbert.' New Edition. Fcp. 5s.

Self-examination before Confirmation. By the same Author. 32mo. 1s. 6d.

Readings for a Month Preparatory to Confirmation from Writers of the Early and English Church. By the same. Fcp. 4s.

Readings for Every Day in Lent, compiled from the Writings of Bishop JEREMY TAYLOR. By the same. Fcp. 5s.

Preparation for the Holy Communion; the Devotions chiefly from the works of JEREMY TAYLOR. By the same. 32mo. 3s.

Thoughts for the Holy Week, for Young Persons. By the same Author. New Edition. Fcp. 8vo. 2s.

Principles of Education drawn from Nature and Revelation, and Applied to Female Education in the Upper Classes. By the same Author. 2 vols. fcp. 12s. 6d.

Bishop Jeremy Taylor's Entire Works: with Life by BISHOP HEBER. Revised and corrected by the Rev. C. P. EDEN. 10 vols. £5 5s.

England and Christendom. By ARCHBISHOP MANNING, D.D. Post 8vo. price 10s. 6d.

The Wife's Manual; or, Prayers, Thoughts, and Songs on Several Occasions of a Matron's Life. By the Rev. W. CALVERT, M.A. Crown 8vo. 10s. 6d.

Singers and Songs of the Church: being Biographical Sketches of the Hymn-Writers in all the principal Collections; with Notes on their Psalms and Hymns. By JOSIAH MILLER, M.A. Second Edition, enlarged. Post 8vo. 10s. 6d.

'Spiritual Songs' for the Sundays and Holidays throughout the Year. By J. S. B. MONSELL, LL.D. Vicar of Egham and Rural Dean. Fourth Edition, Sixth Thousand. Fcp. price 4s. 6d.

The Beatitudes: Abasement before God; Sorrow for Sin; Meekness of Spirit; Desire for Holiness; Gentleness; Purity of Heart; the Peace-makers; Sufferings for Christ. By the same Author. Third Edition, revised. Fcp. 3s. 6d.

His Presence not his Memory, 1855. By the same Author, in memory of his SON. Sixth Edition. 16mo. 1s.

Lyra Germanica; Two Selections of Household Hymns, translated from the German by Miss CATHERINE WINKWORTH. FIRST SERIES, the *Christian Year*, Hymns for the Sundays and Chief Festivals of the Church; SECOND SERIES, the *Christian Life*. Fcp. 8vo. price 3s. 6d. each SERIES.

Lyra Eucharistica; Hymns and Verses on the Holy Communion, Ancient and Modern: with other Poems. Edited by the Rev. ORBY SHIPLEY, M.A. Second Edition. Fcp. 5s.

Shipley's Lyra Messianica. Fcp. 5s.

Shipley's Lyra Mystica. Fcp. 5s.

Endeavours after the Christian Life: Discourses. By JAMES MARTINEAU. Fourth and Cheaper Edition, carefully revised; the Two Series complete in One Volume. Post 8vo. 7s. 6d.

Invocation of Saints and Angels; for the use of Members of the English Church. Edited by the Rev. ORBY SHIPLEY, M.A. 24mo. 3s. 6d.

Introductory Lessons on the History of Religious Worship; being a Sequel to the same Author's 'Lessons on Christian Evidences.' By RICHARD WHATELY, D.D. New Edition. 18mo. 2s. 6d

---

Travels, Voyages, &c.

England to Delhi; a Narrative of Indian Travel. By JOHN MATHESON, Glasgow. Imperial 8vo. with very numerous Illustrations.

Letters from Australia. By JOHN MARTINEAU. Post 8vo. price 7s. 6d.

Travels in the Central Caucasus and Bashan, including Visits to Ararat and Tabreez and Ascents of Kazbek and Elbruz. By DOUGLAS W. FRESHFIELD. With 3 Maps, 2 Panoramas of Summits, 4 full-page Wood Engravings, and 16 Woodcuts. Square crown 8vo. 18s.

Cadore or Titian's Country. By JOSIAH GILBERT, one of the Authors of the 'Dolomite Mountains.' With Map, Facsimile, and 40 Illustrations. Imp. 8vo. 31s. 6d.

The Dolomite Mountains. Excursions through Tyrol, Carinthia, Carniola, and Friuli. By J. GILBERT and G. C. CHURCHILL, F.R.G.S. With numerous Illustrations. Square crown 8vo. 21s.

Pilgrimages in the Pyrenees and Landes: Their Sanctuaries and Shrines. By DENYS SHYNE LAWLOR. Post 8vo.

Pictures in Tyrol and Elsewhere. From a Family Sketch-Book. By the Author of 'A Voyage en Zigzag,' &c. Second Edition. 4to. with many Illustrations, 21s.

How we Spent the Summer; or, a Voyage en Zigzag in Switzerland and Tyrol with some Members of the ALPINE CLUB. Third Edition, re-drawn. In oblong 4to. with about 300 Illustrations, 15s.

Beaten Tracks; or, Pen and Pencil Sketches in Italy. By the Authoress of 'A Voyage en Zigzag.' With 42 Plates, containing about 200 Sketches from Drawings made on the Spot. 8vo. 16s.

The Alpine Club Map of the Chain of Mont Blanc, from an actual Survey in 1863—1864. By A. ADAMS-REILLY. F.R.G.S. M.A.C. In Chromolithography on extra stout drawing paper 28in. × 17in. price 10s. or mounted on canvas in a folding case, 12s. 6d.

Pioneering in the Pampas; or, the First Four Years of a Settler's Experience in the La Plata Camps. By R. A. SEYMOUR. Second Edition. Post 8vo. with Map, 6s.

The Paraguayan War: with Sketches of the History of Paraguay, and of the Manners and Customs of the People: and Notes on the Military Engineering of the War. By GEORGE THOMPSON, C.E. With 8 Maps and Plans and a Portrait of Lopez. Post 8vo. 12s. 6d.

Notes on Burgundy. By CHARLES RICHARD WELD. Edited by his Widow: with Portrait and Memoir. Post 8vo. price 8s. 6d.

History of Discovery in our Australasian Colonies, Australia, Tasmania, and New Zealand, from the Earliest Date to the Present Day. By WILLIAM HOWITT. With 3 Maps of the Recent Explorations from Official Sources. 2 vols. 8vo. 20s.

The Capital of the Tycoon; a Narrative of a 3 Years' Residence in Japan. By Sir RUTHERFORD ALCOCK, K.C.B. 2 vols. 8vo. with numerous Illustrations, 42s.

Guide to the Pyrenees, for the use of Mountaineers. By CHARLES PACKE. Second Edition, with Maps, &c. and Appendix. Crown 8vo. 7s. 6d.

The Alpine Guide. By JOHN BALL, M.R.I.A. late President of the Alpine Club. Post 8vo. with Maps and other Illustrations.

Guide to the Eastern Alps, price 10s. 6d.

Guide to the Western Alps, including Mont Blanc, Monte Rosa, Zermatt, &c. price 6s. 6d.

Guide to the Central Alps, including all the Oberland District, price 7s. 6d.

Introduction on Alpine Travelling in general, and on the Geology of the Alps, price 1s. Either of the Three Volumes or Parts of the *Alpine Guide* may be had with this INTRODUCTION prefixed, price 1s. extra.

Roma Sotterranea; or, an Account of the Roman Catacombs, especially of the Cemetery of San Callisto. Compiled from the Works of Commendatore G. B. De Rossi, by the Rev. J. S. NORTHCOTE, D.D. and the Rev. W. B. BROWNLOW. With Plans and numerous other Illustrations. 8vo. 31s. 6d.

Memorials of London and Lon- don Life in the 13th, 14th, and 15th Centuries; being a Series of Extracts, Local, Social, and Political, from the Archives of the City of London, A.D. 1276–1419. Selected, translated, and edited by H. T. RILEY, M.A. Royal 8vo. 21s.

Commentaries on the History, Constitution, and Chartered Franchises of the City of London. By GEORGE NORTON, formerly one of the Common Pleaders of the City of London. Third Edition. 8vo. 14s.

Curiosities of London; exhibiting the most Rare and Remarkable Objects o Interest in the Metropolis; with nearly Sixty Years' Personal Recollections. By JOHN TIMBS, F.S.A. New Edition, corrected and enlarged. 8vo. Portrait, 21s.

The Northern Heights of Lon- don; or, Historical Associations of Hampstead, Highgate, Muswell Hill, Hornsey, and Islington. By WILLIAM HOWITT. With about 40 Woodcuts. Square crown 8vo. 21s.

The Rural Life of England. By the same Author. With Woodcuts by Bewick and Williams. Medium, 8vo. 12s. 6d.

Visits to Remarkable Places: Old Halls, Battle-Fields, and Scenes illustrative of striking Passages in English History and Poetry. By the same Author. 2 vols. square crown 8vo. with Wood Engravings, 25s.

Narrative of the Euphrates Ex- pedition carried on by Order of the British Government during the years 1835, 1836, and 1837. By General F. R. CHESNEY. F.R.S. With 2 Maps, 45 Plates, and 16 Woodcuts. 8vo. 24s.

The German Working Man; being an Account of the Daily Life, Amusements, and Unions for Culture and Material Progress of the Artisans of North and South Germany and Switzerland. By JAMES SAMUELSON. Crown 8vo. with Frontispiece, 3s. 6d.

Works of *Fiction.*

Vikram and the Vampire; or, Tales of Hindu Devilry. Adapted by RICHARD F. BURTON, F.R.G.S. &c. With Illustrations by Ernest Griset. Crown 8vo. 9s.

Maboldean, or Christianity Re- versed; being the History of a Noble Family: a Social, Political, and Theological Novel. By OWEN GOWER, of Gaybrook. 3 vols. post 8vo. 31s. 6d.

Through the Night; a Tale of the Times. To which is added ONWARD, or a SUMMER SKETCH. By WALTER SWEETMAN, B.A. 2 vols. post 8vo. 21s.

Stories and Tales by the Author of 'Amy Herbert,' uniform Edition, each Tale or Story a single volume:—

AMY HERBERT, 2s. 6d.	KATHARINE ASHTON, 3s. 6d.
GERTRUDE, 2s. 6d.	
EARL'S DAUGHTER, 2s. 6d.	MARGARET PERCIVAL, 5s.
EXPERIENCE OF LIFE, 2s. 6d.	LANETON PARSONAGE, 4s. 6d.
CLEVE HALL, 3s. 6d.	URSULA, 4s. 6d.
IVORS, 3s. 6d.	

A Glimpse of the World. Fcp. 7s. 6d.

Journal of a Home Life. Post 8vo. 9s. 6d.

After Life; a Sequel to the 'Journal of a Home Life.' Post 8vo. 10s. 6d.

The Warden; a Novel. By ANTHONY TROLLOPE. Crown 8vo. 1s. 6d.

Barchester Towers; a Sequel to 'The Warden.' Crown 8vo. 2s.

Uncle Peter's Fairy Tale for the XIXth Century. Edited by ELIZABETH M. SEWELL, Author of 'Amy Herbert,' &c. Fcp. 8vo. 7s. 6d.

Becker's Gallus; or, Roman Scenes of the Time of Augustus. Post 8vo. 7s. 6d.

Becker's Charicles: Illustrative of Private Life of the Ancient Greeks. Post 8vo. 7s. 6d.

Tales of Ancient Greece. By GEORGE W. COX, M.A. late Scholar of Trin. Coll. Oxford. Being a collective Edition of the Author's Classical Series and Tales, complete in One Volume. Crown 8vo. 6s. 6d.

A Manual of Mythology, in the form of Question and Answer. By the Rev. GEORGE W. COX, M.A. late Scholar of Trinity College, Oxford. Fcp. 3s.

Cabinet Edition of Novels and Tales by J. G. WHYTE MELVILLE:—

THE GLADIATORS, 5s. | HOLMBY HOUSE, 5s.
DIGBY GRAND, 5s. | GOOD FOR NOTHING, 6s.
KATE COVENTRY, 5s. | QUEEN'S MARIES, 6s.
GENERAL BOUNCE, 5s. | THE INTERPRETER, 5s.

Doctor Harold's Note-Book. By Mrs. GASCOIGNE, Author of 'The Next Door Neighbour.' Fcp. 8vo. 6s.

Our Children's Story. By One of their Gossips. By the Author of 'Voyage en Zigzag,' 'Pictures in Tyrol,' &c. Small 4to. with Sixty Illustrations by the Author, price 10s. 6d.

Poetry and *The Drama.*

Thomas Moore's Poetical Works, the only Editions containing the Author's last Copyright Additions:—
Shamrock Edition, price 3s. 6d.
Ruby Edition, with Portrait, 6s.
Cabinet Edition, 10 vols. fcp. 8vo. 35s.
People's Edition, Portrait, &c. 10s. 6d.
Library Edition, Portrait & Vignette, 14s.

Moore's Lalla Rookh, Tenniel's Edition, with 68 Wood Engravings from Original Drawings and other Illustrations. Fcp. 4to. 21s.

Moore's Irish Melodies, Maclise's Edition, with 161 Steel Plates from Original Drawings. Super-royal 8vo. 31s. 6d.

Miniature Edition of Moore's Irish *Melodies*, with Maclise's Illustrations (as above), reduced in Lithography. Imp. 16mo. 10s. 6d.

Southey's Poetical Works, with the Author's last Corrections and copyright Additions. Library Edition. Medium 8vo. with Portrait and Vignette, 14s.

Lays of Ancient Rome; with *Ivry* and the *Armada*. By the Right Hon. LORD MACAULAY. 16mo. 4s. 6d.

Lord Macaulay's Lays of Ancient Rome. With 90 Illustrations on Wood, Original and from the Antique, from Drawings by G. SCHARF. Fcp. 4to. 21s.

Miniature Edition of Lord Macaulay's Lays of Ancient Rome, with Scharf's Illustrations (as above) reduced in Lithography. Imp. 16mo. 10s. 6d.

Goldsmith's Poetical Works, Illustrated with Wood Engravings from Designs by Members of the ETCHING CLUB. Imp. 16mo. 7s. 6d.

Poems. By JEAN INGELOW. Fifteenth Edition. Fcp. 8vo. 5s.

Poems by Jean Ingelow. A New Edition, with nearly 100 Illustrations by Eminent Artists, engraved on Wood by the Brothers DALZIEL. Fcp. 4to. 21s.

Mopsa the Fairy. By JEAN INGELOW. With Eight Illustrations engraved on Wood. Fcp. 8vo. 6s.

A Story of Doom, and other Poems. By JEAN INGELOW. Third Edition. Fcp. 5s.

Poetical Works of Letitia Eliza- beth Landon (L.E.L.) 2 vols. 16mo. 10s.

Bowdler's Family Shakspeare, cheaper Genuine Edition, complete in 1 vol. large type, with 36 Woodcut Illustrations, price 14s. or in 6 pocket vols. 3s. 6d. each.

Arundines Cami. Collegit atque edidit H. DRURY, M.A. Editio Sexta, curavit H. J. HODGSON, M.A. Crown 8vo. price 7s. 6d.

Horatii Opera, Pocket Edition, with carefully corrected Text, Marginal References, and Introduction. Edited by the Rev. J. E. YONGE, M.A. Square 18mo. 4s. 6d.

Horatii Opera, Library Edition, with Copious English Notes, Marginal References and Various Readings. Edited by the Rev. J. E. YONGE, M.A. 8vo. 21s.

The Æneid of Virgil Translated into English Verse. By John Conington, M.A. Corpus Professor of Latin in the University of Oxford. Crown 8vo. 9s.

The Iliad of Homer in English Hexameter Verse. By J. Henry Dart, M.A. of Exeter College, Oxford. Square crown 8vo. 21s.

The Iliad of Homer Translated into Blank Verse. By Ichabod Charles Wright, M.A. 2 vols. crown 8vo. 21s.

Dante's Divine Comedy, translated in English Terza Rima by John Dayman, M.A. With the Italian Text. 8vo. 21s.

Hunting Songs and Miscellaneous Verses. By R. E. Egerton Warburton. Second Edition. Fcp. 8vo. 5s.

Rural Sports, &c.

Encyclopædia of Rural Sports; a Complete Account, Historical, Practical, and Descriptive, of Hunting, Shooting, Fishing, Racing, &c. By D. P. Blaine. With above 600 Woodcuts (20 from Designs by John Leech). 8vo. 42s.

Col. Hawker's Instructions to Young Sportsmen in all that relates to Guns and Shooting. Revised by the Author's Son. Square crown 8vo. with Illustrations, 18s.

The Dead Shot, or Sportsman's Complete Guide; a Treatise on the Use of the Gun, Dog-breaking, Pigeon-shooting, &c. By Marksman. Fcp. with Plates, 5s.

A Book on Angling: being a Complete Treatise on the Art of Angling in every branch, including full Illustrated Lists of Salmon Flies. By Francis Francis. Second Edition, with Portrait and 15 other Plates, plain and coloured. Post 8vo. 15s.

Wilcocks's Sea-Fisherman: comprising the Chief Methods of Hook and Line Fishing in the British and other Seas, a glance at Nets, and remarks on Boats and Boating. Second Edition, enlarged, with 80 Woodcuts. Post 8vo. 12s. 6d.

The Fly-Fisher's Entomology. By Alfred Ronalds. With coloured Representations of the Natural and Artificial Insect. Sixth Edition, with 20 coloured Plates. 8vo. 14s.

Blaine's Veterinary Art: a Treatise on the Anatomy, Physiology, and Curative Treatment of the Diseases of the Horse, Neat Cattle, and Sheep. Seventh Edition, revised and enlarged by C. Steel. 8vo. with Plates and Woodcuts, 18s.

Horses and Stables. By Colonel F. Fitzwygram, XV. the King's Hussars. Pp. 624; with 24 Plates of Illustrations, containing very numerous Figures engraved on Wood. 8vo. 15s.

Youatt on the Horse. Revised and enlarged by W. Watson, M.R.C.V.S. 8vo. with numerous Woodcuts, 12s. 6d.

Youatt on the Dog. (By the same Author.) 8vo. with numerous Woodcuts, 6s.

The Horse's Foot, and how to keep it Sound. By W. Miles, Esq. Ninth Edition, with Illustrations. Imp. 8vo. 12s. 6d.

A Plain Treatise on Horse-shoeing. By the same Author. Sixth Edition, post 8vo. with Illustrations, 2s. 6d.

Stables and Stable Fittings. By the same. Imp. 8vo. with 13 Plates, 15s.

Remarks on Horses' Teeth, addressed to Purchasers. By the same. Post 8vo. 1s. 6d.

Robbins's Cavalry Catechism; or, Instructions on Cavalry Exercise and Field Movements, Brigade Movements, Out-post Duty, Cavalry supporting Artillery, Artillery attached to Cavalry. 12mo. 5s.

The Dog in Health and Disease. By Stonehenge. With 70 Wood Engravings. New Edition. Square crown 8vo. 10s. 6d.

The Greyhound. By the same Author. Revised Edition, with 24 Portraits of Greyhounds. Square crown 8vo. 10s. 6d.

The Ox, his Diseases and their Treatment; with an Essay on Parturition in the Cow. By J. R. Dobson, M.R.C.V.S. Crown 8vo. with Illustrations, 7s. 6d.

Commerce, Navigation, and Mercantile Affairs.

The Theory and Practice of Banking. By Henry Dunning Macleod, M.A. Barrister-at-Law. Second Edition. entirely remodelled. 2 vols. 8vo. 30s.

The Elements of Banking. By Henry Dunning Macleod, M.A. of Trinity College, Cambridge, and of the Inner Temple, Barrister-at-Law. Post 8vo.
[*Nearly ready.*

The Law of Nations Considered as Independent Political Communities. By Sir Travers Twiss, D.C.L. 2 vols. 8vo. 30s. or separately, Part I *Peace*, 12s. Part II. *War*, 18s.

Practical Guide for British Shipmasters to United States Ports. By Pierrepont Edwards. Post 8vo. 8s. 6d.

M'Culloch's Dictionary, Practical, Theoretical, and Historical, of Commerce and Commercial Navigation. New Edition, revised throughout and corrected to the Present Time; with a Biographical Notice of the Author. Edited by H. G. Reid, Secretary to Mr. M'Culloch for many years. 8vo. price 63s. cloth.

Works of Utility and General Information.

Modern Cookery for Private Families, reduced to a System of Easy Practice in a Series of carefully-tested Receipts. By Eliza Acton. Newly revised and enlarged; with 8 Plates, Figures, and 150 Woodcuts. Fcp. 6s.

On Food, its Varieties, Chemical Composition, Nutritive Value, Comparative Digestibility, Physiological Functions and Uses, Preparation, Culinary Treatment, Preservation, Adulteration, &c. Being the Substance of Four Cantor Lectures delivered before the Society for the Encouragement of Arts, Manufactures, and Commerce. By H. Letheby, M.B. M.A. Ph.D. &c. Crown 8vo.

A Practical Treatise on Brewing; with Formulæ for Public Brewers, and Instructions for Private Families. By W. Black. Fifth Edition. 8vo. 10s. 6d.

Chess Openings. By F. W. Longman, Balliol College, Oxford. Fcp. 8vo. 2s. 6d.

Whist, What to Lead. By Cam. Third Edition. 32mo. 1s.

The Cabinet Lawyer; a Popular Digest of the Laws of England, Civil, Criminal, and Constitutional. 25th Edition; with Supplements of the Acts of the Parliamentary Sessions of 1867, 1868, and 1869. Fcp. 10s. 6d.

The Philosophy of Health; or, an Exposition of the Physiological and Sanitary Conditions conducive to Human Longevity and Happiness. By Southwood Smith, M.D. Eleventh Edition, revised and enlarged; with 113 Woodcuts. 8vo. 7s. 6d.

A Handbook for Readers at the British Museum. By Thomas Nichols. Post 8vo. 6s.

Maunder's Treasury of Knowledge and Library of Reference: comprising an English Dictionary and Grammar, Universal Gazetteer, Classical Dictionary, Chronology, Law Dictionary, Synopsis of the Peerage, Useful Tables, &c. Fcp. 10s. 6d.

Hints to Mothers on the Management of their Health during the Period of Pregnancy and in the Lying-in Room. By T. Bull, M.D. Fcp. 5s.

The Maternal Management of Children in Health and Disease. By Thomas Bull, M.D. Fcp. 5s.

How to Nurse Sick Children; containing Directions which may be found of service to all who have charge of the Young. By Charles West, M.D. Second Edition. Fcp. 8vo. 1s. 6d.

Notes on Hospitals. By Florence Nightingale. Third Edition, enlarged; with 13 Plans. Post 4to. 18s.

Instructions in Household Matters. Written by a Lady for the use of Girls intended for Service on leaving School. Seventh Edition. Fcp. 1s. 6d.

Mary's Every-Day Book of useful and Miscellaneous Knowledge; illustrated with Stories, and intended for the use of Children. By F. E. Burbury. 18mo. 3s. 6d.

Tidd Pratt's Law relating to Benefit Building Societies; with Practical Observations on the Act and all the Cases decided thereon, also a Form of Rules and Forms of Mortgages. Fcp. 3s. 6d.

Collieries and Colliers: a Handbook of the Law and Leading Cases relating thereto. By J. C. Fowler, of the Inner Temple, Barrister, Stipendiary Magistrate. Second Edition. Fcp. 8vo. 7s. 6d.

Willich's Popular Tables for Ascertaining the Value of Lifehold, Leasehold, and Church Property, Renewal Fines, &c.; the Public Funds; Annual Average Price and Interest on Consols from 1731 to 1867; Chemical, Geographical, Astronomical, Trigonometrical Tables, &c. Post 8vo. 10s.

Coulthart's Decimal Interest Tables at Twenty-four Different Rates not exceeding Five per Cent. Calculated for the use of Bankers. To which are added Commission Tables at One-eighth and One-fourth per Cent. 8vo. 15s.

INDEX.

SPOTTISWOODE AND CO., PRINTERS, NEW-STREET SQUARE AND PARLIAMENT STREET.